Praise for the Dune Saga

"This vital link between the first two books of the Dune saga begins immediately after the close of *Dune*. . . . This is good reading. . . . Standing well enough on its own for Dune novices, it goes without saying that it's must reading for established fans."

—*Booklist* on *Paul of Dune*

"Drawing on Frank Herbert's massive body of notes, the coauthors of the new Dune series continue their expansion and illumination of the unexplored pieces of one of the genre's most significant and powerful stories. A priority purchase for libraries of all sizes. Highly recommended."

—*Library Journal* (starred review) on *Paul of Dune*

"Dune addicts will happily devour Herbert and Anderson's spicy conclusion to their second prequel trilogy."

—*Publishers Weekly* on *Dune: The Battle of Corrin*

"Sit back and enjoy."

—*Booklist* on *Dune: The Machine Crusade*

"The kind of intricate plotting and philosophical musings that would make the elder Herbert proud."

—*Publishers Weekly* (starred review) on
Dune: T̶_____n Jihad

THE DUNE SERIES

PAUL OF
DUNE

•

Brian Herbert
and
Kevin J. Anderson

•

TOR®

Tor Publishing Group
New York

This is a work of fiction. All of the characters, organizations, and events portrayed in this novel are either products of the authors' imaginations or are used fictitiously.

PAUL OF DUNE

A Tor Book
Published by Tom Doherty Associates/Tor Publishing Group
120 Broadway
New York, NY 10271

www.tor-forge.com

Tor® is a registered trademark of Macmillan Publishing Group, LLC.

ISBN: 978-0-7653-5150-0

Our books may be purchased in bulk for promotional, educational, or business use. Please contact your local bookseller or the Macmillan Corporate and Premium Sales Department at 1-800-221-7945, extension 5442, or by email at MacmillanSpecialMarkets @macmillan.com.

First Edition: September 2008
First International Mass Market Edition: April 2009

Printed in the United States of America

15   14   13   12   11   10   9   8   7   6

*TO JANET HERBERT AND
REBECCA MOESTA ANDERSON*

*Thank you for your patience, your wisdom, and your love,
and for so much more than we can possibly list here.
If we were to describe everything you've contributed,
it would require a book much longer than this novel.*

ACKNOWLEDGMENTS

While we are busy writing new novels in the incredible Dune universe, many other people contribute to what the reader sees on the printed page, and are important to the series. We would like to thank Tor Books, Hodder & Stoughton, WordFire Inc., the Frank Herbert family, Trident Media Group, New Amsterdam Entertainment, and Misher Films for their contributions and support. As always, we are especially grateful to Frank Herbert, who left the most remarkable literary legacy in all of science fiction, and to Beverly Herbert, who devoted so much of her own talents and energy to the success of the series.

History is a moving target that changes as fresh details are discovered, as errors are corrected, as popular attitudes shift. Historians carve the sculpture that is Truth not out of granite, but out of wet clay.

—from the preface to *The Life of Muad'Dib, Volume 1,* by the PRINCESS IRULAN

Forgive my impertinence, Mother Superior, but you misunderstand my purpose. In writing about the life of Paul Atreides, the Emperor Muad'Dib, my intent is not simply to chronicle historical events. Have we not learned lessons from our own Missionaria Protectiva? Deftly handled, myths and legends can become tools or weapons, while mere facts are just . . . facts.

—the PRINCESS IRULAN, letter to the Mother School on Wallach IX

PART I

Emperor Muad'Dib

10,194 AG
One Year After the Fall of Shaddam IV

*Much more remains of my father than these few
fragments. His bloodline, his character, and his
teachings have made me who I am. As long as the
universe remembers me as Paul-Muad'Dib, so too
will Duke Leto Atreides be remembered. The son
is always shaped by the father.*

—inscription on the Harg Pass Shrine

A serene ocean of sand stretched as far as the eye
could see, silent and still, carrying the potential for
terrible storms. Arrakis—the sacred world Dune—was
becoming the eye of a galactic hurricane, a bloody Jihad
that would rage across the planets of the crumbling Imperium. Paul Atreides had foreseen this, and now he had
set it in motion.

Since the overthrow of Shaddam IV a year ago, millions of converts had joined Paul's armies in addition to
his own Fremen warriors, all of whom had pledged their
lives to him. Led by his fanatical Fedaykin and other
trusted officers, his holy warriors had already begun to
fan out from staging areas, bound for specific star systems
and targets. Just that morning, Paul had sent Stilgar and
his legion off with a rousing speech that included the
words, " 'I bestow strength on you, my warriors. Go now
and perform my holy bidding.' " It was one of his favorite
passages from the Orange Catholic Bible.

Afterward, in the heat of the afternoon, he had taken
himself far from the bedlam of the city of Arrakeen, from
the agitated troops and the fawning clamor of worship-
pers. Here in the isolated mountains, Paul required no

Fremen guide. The high desert was silent and pure, giving him an illusion of peace. His beloved Chani accompanied him, along with his mother, Jessica, and his little sister. Not quite four years old, Alia was vastly more than a child, pre-born with all the memories and knowledge of a Reverend Mother.

As Paul and his companions ascended the stark brown mountains to Harg Pass, he tried to cling to a feeling of serene inevitability. The desert made him feel small and humble, in sharp contrast to being cheered as a messiah. He prized each quiet moment away from the devoted followers who chanted, "Muad'Dib! Muad'Dib!" whenever they glimpsed him. Before long, when news of the military victories started streaming in, it would get even worse. But that could not be avoided. Eventually, he would be swept along by the Jihad. He had already charted its course, like a great navigator of humanity.

War was one of the tools at his disposal. Now that he had exiled the Padishah Emperor to Salusa Secundus, Paul had to consolidate his power among the members of the Landsraad. He had sent his diplomats to negotiate with some of the noble Houses, while dispatching his most fanatical fighters against the defiant families. A number of lords would not lay down their arms and vowed to put up fierce resistance, claiming either that they would not follow a rebel or that they'd had enough of emperors altogether. Regardless, the armies of Muad'Dib would sweep over them and continue onward. Though Paul sought to reduce and even eliminate the violence, he suspected that the bloody reality would prove far worse than any prescient vision.

And his visions had been frightening.

Centuries of decadence and mismanagement had filled the Imperium with deadwood—tinder that would allow his firestorm to spread with startling speed. In a more civilized time, problems between Houses had been settled with an old-fashioned War of Assassins, but that solution seemed quaint and gentlemanly now, no longer plausible. Faced with the tide of religious fervor approaching their worlds, some leaders would simply surrender, rather than try to stand against the invincible onslaught.

But not all of them would be that sensible. . . .

On their trek, Paul and his three companions wore new stillsuits covered by mottled cloaks to camouflage them in the desert. Though the garments looked well worn, they were actually finer than any Paul had used when he'd lived as a fugitive among the Fremen. Their makers claimed that these durable offworld imports were superior to the simpler versions that had traditionally been made in hidden sietches.

The manufacturers mean well, he thought. *They do it to show their support for me, without realizing the implied criticism in their "improvements."*

After selecting the perfect position high on the ridge, a small natural amphitheater guarded by tall rocks, Paul set down his pack. He uncinched the straps and pulled aside the cushioning folds of velvatin cloth with a reverence comparable to what he saw in the faces of his most devout followers.

In respectful silence he removed the clean, ivory-colored skull and several broken bone fragments—two ribs, an ulna, and a femur that had been brutally snapped in two, all of which the Fremen had preserved for years after the fall of Arrakeen to the Harkonnens. These were the remains of Duke Leto Atreides.

He saw nothing of his warm and wise father in the bones, yet they constituted an important symbol. Paul understood the value and necessity of symbols. "This shrine is long overdue."

"I have already built a shrine to Leto in my mind," Jessica said, "but it will be good to lay him to rest."

Kneeling beside Paul, Chani helped him clear a spot among the large boulders, some of which had just begun to show a mottling of lichen. "We should keep this place a secret, Usul. Leave no marker, give no directions. We must protect your father's resting place."

"The mobs will not be kept at a distance," Jessica said in a resentful tone. She shook her head. "No matter what we do, tourists will find their way here. It will be a circus, with guides wearing false Fremen clothing. Souvenir vendors will chip off flakes of rock, and countless charlatans will sell splinters of bone fragments, claiming that the objects come from Leto's body."

Chani looked both disturbed and awed. "Usul, have you foreseen this?" Here, away from the crowds, she used his private sietch name.

"History has foretold it," Jessica answered for him, "time and time again."

"And it must be done, to build the appropriate legend." Alia spoke sternly to her mother. "The Bene Gesserit planned to use my brother in this way for their own purposes. Now he creates the legends himself, for *his* own purposes."

Paul had already weighed the options. Some pilgrims would come here out of sincere devotion, while others would make the journey simply to boast that they had done it. Either way, they would come. He knew it would be folly to stop them, so he had to find another solution. "I will have my Fedaykin mount a round-the-clock vigil. No one will desecrate this shrine."

He arranged the bones and carefully set the skull atop them, tilting it upward a little so that the hollow, empty sockets could look toward the cloudless blue sky.

"Alia is right, Mother," Paul said, not looking at either his sister or Jessica. "While we manage the business of war, we are also in the business of creating a myth. It is the only way we can accomplish what is necessary. Mere appeals to logic and common sense are not enough to sway the vast population of humankind. Irulan is uniquely talented in that area, as she has already demonstrated by the popularity of her history of my ascension to power."

"You are cynical, Usul." Chani sounded disturbed at the reminder that Paul's wife, in name only, served any useful function at all.

"My brother is pragmatic," Alia countered.

Paul stared for a long moment at the skull, imagining the face of his father: the aquiline nose, gray eyes, and an expression that could shift from anger toward his enemies to unmatched love for his son or Jessica. *I learned so much from you, Father. You taught me honor and leadership. I only hope you taught me enough.* What he knew he must face in the coming years would go far beyond the greatest crises Duke Leto had ever confronted. Would the lessons apply on such a grand scale?

Paul picked up a large rock and placed it in front of the skull, beginning the cairn. Then he gestured for his mother to set the second stone, which she did. In turn, Alia contributed to the pile, sounding wistful. "I miss my father. He loved us enough to die for us."

"It's too bad you never actually knew him," Chani said quietly, placing her first rock on the cairn.

"Oh, but I did," Alia said. "My pre-born memories encompass a trip my mother and father took to the Caladan wilderness after little Victor was killed. That was where Paul was conceived." Alia often made eerie, unsettling comments. The lives crammed into her mind stretched far. She looked up at her mother. "You even caught a glimpse of the Caladan primitives then."

"I remember," Jessica said.

Paul continued piling stones. As soon as the cairn completely covered his father's bones, he stepped back to share a poignant, solitary moment with those who had loved Leto best.

Finally, Paul touched the communicator stud on the collar of his stillsuit. "Korba, we are ready for you now."

Almost immediately, loud engines shattered the searing calm of the desert. Two 'thopters bearing the green-and-white Imperial crest of Emperor Muad'Dib rose from behind the sheer ridge and dipped their wings. The lead 'thopter was flown by the leader of Paul's Fedaykin, Korba, a man who displayed his allegiance with religious fervor. Yet he was more than a mere sycophant—Korba was much too smart for that. All of his actions had carefully calculated consequences.

Behind the small fliers came a train of heavy-lift vehicles, with polished stone blocks dangling by suspensors beneath their bellies. The stone blocks, carved by artisans in Arrakeen, were embellished with intricate images that, when assembled, would make a continuous frieze of great events in the life of Duke Leto Atreides.

Now that the respectful communication silence had been broken, squad commanders barked orders to their teams of laborers, calling them to begin their work at the new sacred site.

Silent and stoic, Jessica stared at the small cairn of rocks as if burning Leto's shrine into her memory, rather than the monstrosity that was about to take shape.

The echoing noise of machinery reflected back upon the amphitheater of rocks. Korba landed his 'thopter and emerged, reveling in the grandiose production and proud of what he had arranged. He looked at the handmade pile of rocks and seemed to think it quaint. "Muad'Dib, we will create a proper monument here, worthy of your father. All must stand in awe of our Emperor and everyone who has been close to you."

"Yes, they must," Paul said, doubting that his Fedaykin commander would notice the wryness in his tone. Korba had become quite a student of what he called "religious momentum."

The work teams threw themselves into the job like gaze hounds attacking prey. Since the haulers had no room to land in the small natural bowl at the top of the pass, the pilots disengaged their suspensor tethers and deposited the carved blocks on a flat, stony area, then retreated into the air. Paul's advisers had designed the shrine memorial by committee and distributed the blueprints to all crew chiefs. The substantial pyramid would symbolize the foundation that Duke Leto had been in the life of Muad'Dib.

At the moment, though, as Paul considered this ostentatious memorial, he could think only of the dichotomy between his private feelings and his public image. Although he could not abdicate his role in the ever-growing machinery of government and religion around him, only a very few loved ones saw the real Paul. And even with this select group, he could not share everything.

Jessica stepped back and looked at him. Clearly, she had made up her mind about something. "I feel I am done here on Arrakis, Paul. It is time for me to depart."

"Where will you go?" Chani asked, as if she could not imagine a more preferable place to be.

"Caladan. I have been too long away from home."

Paul felt a yearning in his own heart. Caladan had already accepted his rule, but he had not returned there since House Atreides had come to Arrakis. He looked at his mother, the stately, green-eyed beauty who had so captivated his gallant father. Though Paul was Emperor of the Known Universe, he should have realized the simple fact himself. "You are right, Mother. Caladan is part of my empire as well. I shall accompany you."

> *Among Muad'Dib's staunchest friends was Gurney Halleck—troubadour-warrior, smuggler, and planetary governor. More than all his triumphs, Halleck's greatest joy was to play the baliset and sing songs. His heroic exploits provided his fellow troubadours with material for many songs.*
>
> —A Child's History of Muad'Dib by the
> PRINCESS IRULAN

These Fremen recruits from the deep desert had never seen such a large tank of water in their lives, and rarely one so sloppily open to the air. Back on Caladan, this would have served as no more than a village pool, and a lackluster one at that. But here, as Gurney's fledgling commandos stared at the rippling surface and smelled the raw moisture evaporating wastefully, they viewed it with superstitious awe.

"You will jump in, one by one," he said in his loud, gruff voice. "Submerge yourselves. Get your heads wet. Before you're finished here today, I want you to swim to the other side."

Swim. The very idea was foreign to them. Several muttered uneasily.

"Muad'Dib has commanded it," said one rail-thin young soldier named Enno. "Therefore, we shall do it."

Yes, Gurney thought. Paul had merely to suggest a thing, and it happened. In other circumstances it might have seemed gratifying, even amusing. These Fremen soldiers would throw themselves out of a spaceship airlock or walk barefoot into a Coriolis storm, if Muad'Dib commanded them to do so.

With his blue, glass-splinter eyes, he surveyed the lines of fresh fighters. More volunteers arrived from the desert every day; it seemed the sietches were manufacturing recruits out in the bled. Many planets in the galaxy still did not know what they would be facing.

These unruly young men were far different from the disciplined Atreides soldiers he remembered so well. Their wild fighting style was a far cry from the military precision of a Great House, but they were still damned good warriors. This "desert rabble" had overthrown Beast Rabban and ended the rule of House Harkonnen here on Dune, along with the defeat of Emperor Shaddam Corrino and his powerful Sardaukar troops.

"That water is only three meters deep, and ten across." Gurney paced along the edge of the pool. "But on other planets, you may encounter oceans or lakes that are hundreds of meters deep. You must be ready for anything."

"Hundreds of meters! How could we survive that?" asked a dusty young recruit.

"The trick is to swim *on top* of the water."

The hard-eyed Fremen recruits did not respond to his humor.

"Does Muad'Dib not say that 'God created Arrakis to train the faithful'?" Gurney quoted. "So, prepare yourselves."

"Muad'Dib," the men said in a reverent tone. "Muad'Dib!"

Paul had ordered the pool constructed so that his desert fighters could train for inevitable water battles on distant worlds. Not every watery planet would be as accepting of his rule as Caladan had been. Some in Arrakeen saw the training pool as a display of Muad'Dib's largesse, while others considered it an extravagant waste of moisture. Gurney understood it as a military necessity.

"We studied the information Muad'Dib provided,"

said Enno. "We took every word to heart. The words showed us how to swim."

Gurney was sure that each of these men had pored over the instruction manual with the intensity of a priest studying a religious text. "And does reading a filmbook manual on sandworms make one a wormrider?"

The absurdity of the question finally made the intense Fremen chuckle. Both eager and hesitant, the group reached the edge of the deep pool. The very thought of being immersed in water was enough to terrify them more than facing any enemy on the battlefield.

Gurney reached into the pocket of his stillsuit and withdrew a gold coin, one of the old Imperial solaris that featured the haughty face of Shaddam IV. He held it up so that its golden hue glinted in the light. "The first one of you to retrieve this coin from the bottom of that pool will receive a special blessing from Muad'Dib."

Any other army would have competed to win an increase in pay, a promotion in rank, or an extra bit of furlough. The Fremen didn't care about such things. But they would push themselves to the limit for a blessing from Paul.

Gurney tossed the solari coin. It twinkled in the sunlight and dropped into the water near the center of the pool, where it continued to flash like a little fish as it sank to the bottom. A depth of three meters would not challenge a good swimmer, but he doubted any of these dry-desert Fremen would be able to retrieve it. He was interested in testing the mettle of the men, however; he wanted to see which ones would try the hardest.

"And God said, 'They shall show their faith by their actions,'" Gurney intoned. "'The first in my eyes shall be first in my heart.'" He looked at them and finally barked, "What are you waiting for? This isn't a buffet line!"

He nudged the first man on the edge, and the Fremen

toppled into the water with a splash, coughed, and thrashed his arms repeatedly, going under and rising to the surface again.

"Swim, man! You look like you're having a grand mal seizure."

The fighter splashed, stroked, and struggled until he pulled away from the edge.

Gurney pushed two more Fremen in. "Your comrade is in trouble. He may be drowning—why aren't you helping him?"

Another pair plunged into the water; finally, Enno jumped in of his own volition. Having watched the others, he panicked less and stroked more. Gurney was pleased to see that he was the first to make it to the opposite side of the pool. Within an hour, most of the desert recruits were swimming, or at least floating. A few clung shivering to the side, refusing to let go. He would have to reassign or dismiss them. The Fremen, bred for desert warfare, had achieved incomparable victories on Dune, but as soldiers in Paul's widening conflict, they would have to fight in many environments. He could not rely on men who would become paralyzed in an unexpected situation. Swimming might be the least of the ordeals they would have to face.

Several of the trainees bobbed underwater, trying to get to the coin that glinted tantalizingly at the bottom, three meters below, like a patch of spice out in the open sand. But no one came close to reaching it. Gurney supposed he would have to swim down there and retrieve it himself.

Then Enno stroked back across the pool, dove down, and swam deep, but not quite deep enough.

Still not there, but not bad, Gurney thought.

The man came back up, gasping, then dunked under again, refusing to give up.

Amid the din of splashing and shouting, Gurney

heard the hum of ships landing in the Arrakeen space-port: hundreds of military-grade gliders, expanded troop transports, and bumblebee-like cargo ships loaded with military supplies to feed Paul's armies. If they wanted spice for their navigators, the Spacing Guild had no choice but to supply Muad'Dib with the vessels he needed. Gurney had to crew them with fighters, and the best men came from Arrakis. Everyone in the Imperium would soon know that.

Suddenly he noted a change in the cries and splashing sounds from the pool. The Fremen were calling for help. Gurney saw a body floating face-down, bobbing in the water. *Enno.* "Bring him here, lads, now!"

But the Fremen could barely keep themselves afloat. One man grabbed Enno's body; another tugged at his arm, but succeeded only in ducking his head under deeper.

"Roll him over, you fools, so he can breathe!"

Seeing how clumsy they were, Gurney dove in. The warm water was a shock to his parched skin. He stroked quickly out to the knot of men and shoved them aside. Grabbing Enno by the back of his collar, he pulled the young man up, flipped him over, and paddled with him back to the edge of the pool.

"Call for a medic. Now!" Gurney shouted, spitting water out of his mouth.

Enno was completely limp, not breathing. His lips were pale blue, his skin clammy, his eyes closed. With a surge of adrenaline strength, Gurney hauled the drip-ping man up over the edge of the pool and onto the sun-warmed paving tiles. Water streamed away from him, drying quickly.

Gurney knew what to do and did not wait for help to arrive. He pumped Enno's legs and used standard resus-citation procedures as familiar to anyone from Caladan as a stillsuit was to a Fremen. Seeing their comrade's mishap, the remaining recruits scrambled pell-mell out of the water.

By the time a puffy-eyed military medic arrived with his kit, Gurney's emergency measures had already brought the young man around. Enno coughed, then rolled over to vomit some of the water he had swallowed. The doctor, after nodding respectfully to Gurney, gave Enno a stimulant and wrapped him with a blanket to keep him from going into shock.

Enno eventually pushed the blanket away and forced himself to sit up. He looked around with glazed eyes. Grinning weakly, he raised a hand and opened his tightly clenched fist to reveal the water-slick gold coin in his palm. "As you ordered, Commander." He touched his dripping hair with wonder. "Am I alive?"

"You are *now*," Gurney said. "You've been revived."

"I died . . . from too much water. Truly, I am blessed with abundance!"

The Fremen recruits began to mutter and whisper with a clear undertone of awe. A *drowned* Fremen!

Their reaction made Gurney uneasy. These spiritual people were as incomprehensible as they were admirable. Many splinter groups followed Muad'Dib's religion by borrowing tenets from Fremen mysticism; others participated in water-worshipping cults. Upon learning of this drowning incident, Paul's bureaucratic priesthood, the Qizarate, could very well choose to make Enno into an inspirational figure.

The trainees stood around the pool, dripping, as though they had all been baptized. They seemed more determined than ever. Gurney knew he'd have no trouble loading the Guild ship with eager, inspired fighters like the best of these men.

The Fremen were ready to set forth and shed blood in the name of Muad'Dib.

The universe is an ancient desert, a vast waste-
land with only occasional habitable planets as
oases. We Fremen, comfortable with deserts, shall
now venture into another.

—STILGAR, *From the Sietch to the Stars*

Shortly after the overthrow of the Padishah Emperor, the armies of Muad'Dib had begun to spread out from Dune like echoes of thunder. Heavily armed legions traveled from one rebellious system to the next, spreading the Truth, consolidating the Imperium for Muad'Dib.

As part of the initial surrender terms, Muad'Dib had appointed Stilgar governor of Arrakis and promised him an additional title as Minister of State, but the Fremen naib had no use for such designations or for the duties associated with them. He was a man of the desert—a leader of brave Fremen warriors, not a soft functionary who sat at a desk.

Aboard a heavily loaded military frigate, Stilgar and the legion under his command were headed for the most important battlefield on his list of assignments. He'd been ordered to take over Kaitain, once the long-standing capital of the Corrino Imperium. Excitement and antici-pation flowed through him. This would be the greatest razzia raid in Fremen history.

The tall, rugged man sat at a wide windowport, star-ing into the Heighliner's cavernous bay, where row after row of armored frigates hung in separate cradles waiting to be deployed. The immensity of the ship made Stilgar feel small, yet it reinforced his belief in the greatness of Muad'Dib.

Until recently, he had never been off-planet, and he felt both the thrill and fear of exploring the unknown. The great distances he had traveled by sandworm across Dune's Tanzerouft wasteland were as nothing compared to the sheer vastness separating the stars.

He had seen so many new things since helping assemble the fighters for the Jihad that unusual and astonishing sights seemed almost commonplace. He had learned that most inhabited worlds possessed far more water than Dune, and that their populations were much softer than the Fremen. Stilgar had delivered speeches, inspired men, recruited them for the holy war. Now his best Fremen fighters would seize Kaitain, the jewel in the crown of the fallen Corrino Imperium.

He took a sip of water . . . not because he was thirsty, but because it was there. *How long have I taken water for granted? When did I start drinking water because it is a thing to do, rather than a thing for survival?*

For days now, military frigates had been shuttling up to orbital space from the surface of Dune, locking into cradles within the Heighliner's hold, preparing for departure. Such a battle could not be commenced without thorough, time-consuming preparations. Once the Guild ship was fully loaded, though, the actual foldspace journey would be brief.

Stilgar descended to the open cargo deck of the frigate. Although these military ships had many individual cabins for passengers, his Fremen fighters chose to eat and sleep in the cavelike atmosphere of the large, metal-walled bay. The Fremen soldiers still considered the ship's standard amenities to be luxuries: ready food supplies, spacious quarters, plentiful water even for bathing, moist air that made stillsuits unnecessary.

Stilgar leaned against a bulkhead and surveyed his people, smelling the familiar odors of spice coffee, food, and close human bodies. Even here in a metal ship in space, he and his men tried to re-create some of the comforting familiarity of sietch life. He scratched his dark beard and looked at the Fremen commandos, who were so anxious to fight that they needed no rousing speech from him.

Many sat reading copies of Irulan's book, *The Life of Muad'Dib*, Volume 1, a record of how Paul Atreides had left Caladan to go to Dune, how the evil Harkonnens had killed his father and destroyed his home, how he and his mother had run into the desert to the Fremen, and how he had eventually emerged to become the living legend, Paul-Muad'Dib. Printed on cheap but durable spice paper, copies of the book were given freely to any citizen who asked, and were included as part of any new soldier's kit. Irulan had started writing the chronicle even before her father had gone into exile on Salusa Secundus.

Stilgar could not quite fathom the woman's motives in writing such a story, since he could see she had gotten some of the details wrong, but neither could he deny the effectiveness of the book. Whether propaganda or inspirational religious text, the story of the most powerful man in the galaxy was spreading throughout the planets of the Imperium.

Two young men saw Stilgar and ran up, calling his name. "Will we be departing soon?" asked the younger, who had cowlicks of thick, dark hair that stuck out in all directions.

"Is it true we are going to Kaitain?" The older boy had recently undergone a growth spurt and stood taller than his half brother. These were the sons of Jamis— Orlop and Kaleff—young men who had become the responsibility of Paul Atreides when he killed their father in a knife duel. The two of them held no grudge, and they idolized Paul.

"We fight for Muad'Dib wherever the Jihad takes us." Stilgar had checked the schedule and knew the Heighliner was due to depart within the hour.

The siblings could barely contain themselves. Around Stilgar, the chatter of gathered fighters on the cargo deck took on a different tone, as he felt a vibration through the hull of the immense Heighliner. The foldspace engines were powering up. Remembering so many raids against the Harkonnens, followed by the adrenaline glow of victory over Shaddam IV, was better than any dose of spice.

In a rush of excitement, Stilgar raised his bearded chin and shouted, "On to Kaitain!"

The fighters cheered resoundingly and stomped their feet on the deck plates, causing so much ruckus that he almost didn't feel the shifting as space folded around him.

⟨❦⟩

THE GUILD VESSEL disgorged thousands of military frigates onto the pampered world that had been the Imperium's capital for thousands of years. Kaitain could not possibly withstand the onslaught.

The warriors of Muad'Dib knew little about Imperial history, and did not revere the museums and monuments to legendary figures: Faykan Butler, Crown Prince Raphael Corrino, Hassik Corrino III. Kaitain had remained in flux since Shaddam's defeat and exile; noble families of the Landsraad either flooded in to fill the local power vacuum or packed up their embassies and escaped to safer worlds. Those who remained behind tried to claim neutrality, but the Fremen soldiers did not follow the same rules.

Filled with passion and determination, Stilgar led his men into battle on the streets of the former capital. With his sword in one hand and crysknife in the other, Stilgar ran ahead of the troops in the opening encounter, shouting, "Long live Emperor Paul-Muad'Dib!"

Although this world should have been the most fortified and well-defended of all that now faced the storm of the Jihad, Imperial security was predicated upon family ties and alliances, marriages, treaties, taxes, and penalties. The Rule of Law. All of that meant nothing to the Fremen armies. Kaitain's security troops—a mere handful of Sardaukar no longer duty bound to protect a defeated Emperor—lacked cohesiveness. The Landsraad nobles were too shocked and astonished to put up a real fight.

Commandos raced through the streets, screaming the name of their young Emperor. At their head, Stilgar watched the grinning sons of Jamis rush forward to demonstrate their prowess and spatter themselves with blood. This planet would be a highly significant conquest, an important piece in the high-stakes political game of the Imperium. Yes, Muad'Dib would be pleased.

Leading his men farther into the carnage, Stilgar shouted in the Fremen tongue, *"Ya hya chouhada! Muad'Dib! Muad'Dib! Muad'Dib! Ya hya chouhada!"*

Yet Stilgar drew little satisfaction from the actual battle as he and his Fremen swept so easily over their opponents. These civilized people of the Landsraad were not, after all, very good fighters.

*When Duke Leto Atreides accepted the fief of Ar-
rakis, Count Hasimir Fenring ceased being the
planet's Imperial Regent and was instead given
provisional control of the Atreides homeworld,
Caladan. Though he served as siridar-absentia
there (at the behest of Shaddam IV), Fenring took
scant interest in his new backwater fief, and the
people of Caladan matched his disinterest with
their own. They had always been a proud and
independent people, more concerned with ocean
harvests than galactic politics. Caladanians were
slow to understand the importance of the heroes
they had created in their midst. After Shaddam's
fall and the ascension of Muad'Dib, Gurney Halleck in turn became involved in the governance of
this world, though the obligations of the Jihad often kept him far away.*

—excerpt from biographical sketch of Gurney Halleck

Leaving behind the violent Jihad he had spawned,
Paul looked forward to returning to Caladan, a place
bright with memories. Knowing the battles that were even
now being launched across the Imperium, and aware
through prescience of how much worse they would become, Paul decided that this short visit would renew him.

Caladan . . . the seas, the windswept coast, the fishing
villages, the stone towers of the ancient family castle.
He paused halfway down the frigate's ramp in the Cala
City spaceport, closed his eyes, and drew a long, slow
breath. He could smell the salt air, the iodine of drying
kelp, the ripening sourness of fish, and the moisture of
sea spray and rain. All so familiar. This had once been

home. How could he have forgotten so quickly? A smile touched his face.

As he recalled the shrine he had commissioned for his father's skull, he now wondered if Duke Leto might have preferred to be interred here instead, on the planet that had been home to House Atreides for twenty-six generations.

But I wanted him close to me. On Dune.

On the surface this world seemed completely unchanged since his family's departure, but as he stepped away from the ship Paul realized that *he* himself had changed. He had left as a boy of fifteen, the son of a beloved Duke. Now he returned, only a few years later, as the Holy Emperor Muad'Dib, with millions of fighters ready to kill—and die—for him.

Jessica placed her hand on his shoulder. "Yes, Paul. We're home."

He shook his head, kept his voice low. "Much as I love this place, Dune is my home now." Paul could not go back to the past, no matter how comfortable it might be. "Caladan is no longer my entire universe, but a speck in a vast empire that I have to rule. Thousands of planets are depending on me."

Jessica rebuked him, using an edge of Voice. "Your father was Duke Leto Atreides, and these were his people. You may control an Imperium, but Caladan is still your homeworld, and its people are still your family as surely as I am."

He knew she was right. Paul found a smile, a real one this time. "Thank you for reminding me when I needed it." He feared that his preoccupation might grow worse as he faced further crises. Shaddam IV had treated many of his planets with disdain, seeing them only as names in a catalogue or numbers on star charts. Paul could not let himself fall into the same trap. "Every fishing boat on Caladan needs its anchor."

The crowds of locals at the edge of the spaceport cheered when they saw the pair step forward. Paul scanned the hundreds of faces: men in dungarees and striped shirts, fishwives, net-weavers, boat-builders. They had not burdened themselves with ridiculous court finery, nor were they attempting to put on haughty airs.

"Paul Atreides has returned!"

"It's our Duke!"

"Welcome, Lady Jessica!"

His personal Fedaykin guards accompanied him, led by a man named Chatt the Leaper. They stood close by Paul, ever alert for assassins in the crowd. His fighters were uneasy in this strange place that smelled of fish and kelp, with its cottony clouds, fog clinging to the headlands, and crashing surf.

Absorbing the resounding welcome of the people, Paul couldn't help feeling excitement, as well as pangs for the halcyon life he might have led if he'd remained here, comfortably accepting the duties of Duke when the time came. Memories from his childhood came rushing back—peaceful days spent fishing with his father, trips to the back country the two of them had made, and hiding with Duncan in the jungles during the terrible War of Assassins that had embroiled Atreides and Ecaz against House Moritani. But even the violence of that conflict paled in comparison with Paul's Jihad, where the scope and scale of carnage would be exponentially greater, and the stakes infinitely higher.

"We should have brought Gurney with us," Jessica said, interrupting his thoughts. "It would do him good to come back to Caladan. He belongs here."

Paul knew she was right, but he could not afford to surrender the services of such an unquestionably loyal and skilled officer. "He is doing vital work for me, Mother."

Officially, Gurney had been granted an earldom on

Caladan as part of Shaddam's surrender terms, but Paul
had given Gurney no chance to settle here. Not yet. In
the interim, Gurney had assigned planetary management to the representative of a minor noble family from
Ecaz, Prince Xidd Orleaq. Until the Jihad was over, Paul
would have to keep Gurney, Stilgar, and the best Fremen
out on the front lines.

The pudgy, red-faced Prince Orleaq greeted Paul and
Jessica, shaking hands vigorously with each of them. To
Paul he seemed energetic and dedicated, and reports
on the nobleman were good, though the people of Caladan had been slow to warm to him. He might be efficient enough, but he would always be an outsider to them.
"We have made the castle ready for you both—your old
quarters restored to the way they were, as best we could
manage. My own family is living there, since we're the
provisional government, but we know we're only stew-
ards. Would you like us to vacate the castle for you while
you are here?"

"Not necessary. The rooms you arranged will be
sufficient—I cannot remain here long. My mother . . . has
not entirely decided what she will do."

"I may stay a bit longer," Jessica said.

Orleaq looked from one to the other. "We'll be ready
for you either way." He raised his voice to the crowd,
who took his teasing good-naturedly. "Make sure you've
tidied everything up! On the morrow, Duke Paul Atreides
will tour the village. Perhaps we could talk him into
spending an afternoon in his great chair, listening to your
concerns as his father used to do. Maybe we can even
stage a bullfight in the arena? It has been empty for too
long." As if just remembering that the Old Duke had
been killed by a Salusan bull in the arena, Orleaq flushed
scarlet. "We can find plenty to keep him occupied here."

The crowd whistled and applauded, while Paul raised

his hand to them, feeling somewhat ill at ease. "Please, please—my schedule has not yet been set." Already feeling the call of his responsibilities, he wondered what difficulties Alia and Chani might be facing as they managed the government in Arrakeen in his absence. Even though the people of Caladan were right here in front of him, his thoughts raced to distant star systems, where worlds would eventually—sometimes painfully—fall under his banner. "I will stay here as long as I am able."

The people cheered again, as if he'd said something important, and Orleaq hurried them toward a luxurious groundcar that would take the noble visitors and their entourage up to the ancestral castle on the cliffs above the sea. Sitting across from Paul in the rear passenger compartment of the vehicle, Chatt the Leaper looked extremely suspicious of the Caladanians, until Paul signaled for him to relax slightly. The young ruler remembered learning that Old Duke Paulus had insisted that he need not fear his people because they loved him, but many conspirators already wanted to kill Muad'Dib. Even this planet wasn't necessarily safe for him. And assassins had come after Paul in Castle Caladan before, a long time ago. . . .

"You are everything to the citizens of Caladan, Sire," Orleaq said. "They loved Duke Leto, and they remember you as a boy. You are one of their own, and now you have become the Emperor and married Shaddam's daughter." He grinned. "Just like a fairy tale. Sire, is it true that you're going to make Caladan your new capital world instead of Arrakis or Kaitain? The people would be so honored."

Paul knew he could have no capital other than Dune, but his mother broke in before he could say anything. "Rumors are just rumors. Paul has made no . . . firm decision."

"I now serve in a capacity that goes beyond the Duke of Caladan," Paul said in a somewhat apologetic tone, looking out the window at the crowd as the long vehicle passed them. "The first battles for the Jihad are raging on at least thirty planets. I could be called away at any time."

"Of course, Sire. We all understand that you are the Emperor Paul-Muad'Dib, a man with much greater responsibilities than one world." But Orleaq didn't sound as if he understood at all. "Still, they know you have fond memories of them. If you establish your Imperial capital here, think of what it can do for Caladan."

"Muad'Dib has visited your world," Chatt the Leaper said in a gruff voice. "You have already been touched by greatness."

THAT EVENING IN the familiar old castle, Paul did enjoy sleeping in his boyhood room again. On the wall hung a magnificent quilt, hand-stitched in squares by representatives of local villages; Paul remembered that it had been a gift to Duke Leto, but he could not recall the occasion it commemorated.

"I should have brought Chani with me," he murmured to himself. But she had not wanted to leave Dune. Perhaps one day, though . . .

In an unguarded moment when he allowed himself to forget about the Jihad, he imagined what it would be like to retire on Caladan and walk with Chani along the ocean cliffs, seeing the spray like tiny diamonds on her brown cheeks and forehead. The two of them could dress in ordinary clothing and spend their time in uncomplicated happiness, strolling through the gardens and fishing villages. As he drifted off to sleep thinking of that unlikely dream, his fatigued mind convinced him it might be possible. But not for many years. His erratic prescience did not tend to show him peaceful, noncritical moments.

When he arose the next day, Paul found the castle's main reception hall bedecked with flowers and ribbons, the stone-block walls papered with notes, letters, and drawings. To welcome him, the joyful people had brought presents—colored shells, large reefpearls floating in oil, dried flowers, and baskets of fresh fish. The simple locals meant well, lining up outside in the courtyard, through the gates, and partway down the hill just for a chance to see him.

But already, he felt restless.

His mother was up and watching the activities, having greeted the throngs outside the main gates. "They have been waiting a long time to have their Duke back. They want Paul Atreides. When you return to being the Emperor Muad'Dib, who will fill that role? Do not just abandon these people, Paul. They are worth a great deal to you."

Paul picked up one of the handwritten letters, perused a message from a young woman who remembered having met him in the village years ago, when he'd been walking with Duke Leto. She said that at the time she'd been carrying a banner of silver and blue ribbons. Hearing this, the Emperor looked up at his mother. "I'm sorry, but I don't remember her."

"She certainly remembers *you*, Paul. Even the smallest things you do have an effect on these people."

"On all people." Paul could never completely escape his violent visions of the Jihad's horrific fallout, how difficult it would be to control the monster that would have been unleashed with or without him. The only true path to survival of the human species lay as narrow as a razor, and slippery with blood.

"So now you are too important for Caladan?" Her remark stung him. Could she not see that was exactly the case? The more excitement he witnessed among these people, the more uncomfortable he felt here.

Prince Orleaq rushed them through an extravagant breakfast, eager to take Paul on a procession through the village. The nominal leader of Caladan finished his meal, then wiped his mouth with a lace napkin. "You must be anxious to revisit the places you miss so much, Sire. Everything has been prepared specially for your visit."

Paul walked outside with his mother and the others. As he made his way through the harbor town, he could not brush aside the odd and overwhelming sensation that he no longer belonged here. The air was damp and clammy, every breath sodden with moisture. As much as he cherished his boyhood home, it now seemed, in its own way, as alien as Fremen civilization had ever been.

He felt simultaneously connected to, and entirely separate from, these people—*his* people. He was no longer a man of one world—or even two. He was Emperor of thousands. The conversations around him about fishing, Duke Leto, the upcoming storm season, Old Duke Paulus and his spectacular bullfights . . . all seemed small and lacking in perspective. He found his thoughts drawn to the initial military campaigns he knew were taking place across the Imperium. What was Gurney doing now? And Stilgar? What if Alia and Chani needed him for pressing matters of state? What business did he have leaving Dune at such an early stage of this war?

In one of his first acts as Emperor, he had increased taxes and levies on any world that did not immediately accept his rule, and many had swiftly pledged themselves to him, if only for economic reasons. Paul was convinced that this bit of monetary coercion would save many lives by preventing unnecessary battles. But much of the fighting could not be avoided, and he could not escape his responsibilities, even here on his boyhood world.

That evening, watching from a viewing platform where he stood with his mother, along with Prince Orleaq and other local dignitaries, Paul could hardly focus on the Caladanian dancers who performed for him in their colorful costumes. He felt detached from his roots, like a tree that had been moved across the galaxy and replanted somewhere else. Plants did not grow as easily on Dune as on Caladan, but the desert world was where he needed to be, where he thrived. He had not expected to feel like this.

Abruptly, a messenger arrived from the Cala City spaceport on a fast groundcycle. Seeing the flushed courier and the armband she wore, Paul motioned for Chatt the Leaper to let her pass.

The villagers were slow to react to the interruption. The dancers faltered, then stood to the side of the stage, waiting to resume their performance. Orleaq looked concerned. Paul was intent only on the courier's message. Urgent news was rarely good news.

The courier spoke in a breathless voice. "Emperor Muad'Dib, I bear a battlefield message from Stilgar. We felt the news important enough to divert a Heighliner in order to inform you as soon as possible."

Orleaq spluttered. "You diverted a whole Heighliner just to bring a *message*?"

A thousand scenarios thundered through Paul's mind. Had something terrible happened to Stilgar? "Speak your words." His prescience had not warned him of any immediate disaster.

"Stilgar bade me to say this to you, 'Usul, I did as you requested. Your armies have captured Kaitain, and I shall await you in the palace of the fallen Emperor.'"

Unable to contain his joy, Paul stood and shouted to the crowd. "Kaitain is ours!"

In response to his excitement, an uncertain wave of applause passed through the crowd. Jessica stepped closer to him. "I take it you will be leaving then?"

"I have to." He couldn't stop smiling. "Mother—it is Kaitain!"

Unsettled, Orleaq raised his hands, gesturing toward the dancers. "But, Sire, all the fishing boats are festooned for tomorrow's regatta, and we thought you'd want to place a wreath at the statues of Old Duke Paulus and young Victor."

"Please forgive me. I cannot stay." When he saw the crestfallen expression on the man's face, he added, "I'm sorry." He raised his voice so the whole crowd could hear. "People of Caladan—I know you wanted your Duke back, but I'm afraid I can't fill that role for you now. Instead, as your Emperor as well as your Duke, I give you my mother to watch over Caladan, to guide this world in my name." He smiled at his solution. "She will be your new Duchess. I formally install her in that role."

Jessica kept her voice much lower than his. "Thank you, Paul." The people applauded, somewhat uncertainly at first and then with growing enthusiasm as she stepped forward to deliver an impromptu speech.

While his mother occupied the spectators, Paul quickly turned to the courier, whispering, "Is the Heighliner ready to depart?"

"The Navigator awaits your command, Muad'Dib."

"I shall leave within the hour. First, send word to Arrakeen instructing Irulan to meet me on Kaitain. Her presence is required." The courier rushed off to make the arrangements, and Paul turned toward a crestfallen Orleaq.

"Have we displeased you, Sire?" the nobleman asked, his voice cracking. "We expected you to stay a little while longer."

"I cannot." Paul knew that the Atreides part of him would always cling to Caladan, while his heart resided on Dune, and the part of him that was *Muad'Dib* would sweep across the entire galaxy.

The Guild delegation had arrived, and the three
men were making their way through the fanmetal
hutment that had been designated the temporary Imperial Audience Chamber. The haughty Guildsmen seemed
irritated after being detained at each of the guard
checkpoints, but they would have to follow protocol
and security if they wanted an audience with Emperor
Muad'Dib.

Standing beside the throne with all the erectness and
poise befitting her position, a cool, blonde-haired Princess
Irulan watched the trio enter the great metal-walled chamber. The men looked dignified in their gray uniforms, the
sleeves of which displayed the Spacing Guild's analemma
sigil of infinity. In single file from shortest to tallest, each
of the men had slightly odd features, offset from the norm
of humanity.

The short one at the front had an oversized head, the
left side of which was covered with a barbed metal plate,
and half a head of ragged orange hair flowed back as he
walked. The second man was exceedingly thin with a narrow face that bore the scars of reconstruction, while the
tallest one at the rear turned his metal eyes nervously in

all directions. Irulan noted the abrupt change when the Guildsmen simultaneously saw little Alia waiting on the impressive throne itself.

Wrapped in a cloak of his own importance, Korba stood at the foot of Paul's throne like a guardian. He had embellished his traditional stillsuit and robes with marks of rank, and mysterious religious symbols drawn from archaic Muadru designs. Irulan doubted that Korba expected anyone to spot the influence, but with her Bene Gesserit training she had easily noticed what he was doing. The logical part of her mind saw the purpose of Korba's obvious plan.

There is more power in religion than in being a glorified bodyguard, she thought.

Perhaps she should have created a similar role for herself.

As the eldest daughter of Shaddam Corrino IV, Irulan had always known that one day she would marry for political and economic reasons. The Emperor and the Bene Gesserit had groomed her for that duty, and she had willingly accepted it, even offering herself as a solution when Paul had faced her father after the Battle of Arrakeen.

While she had never expected Paul Atreides to fall in love with her, she had counted on conceiving his child. The Bene Gesserit Sisterhood demanded it for their breeding program. But Paul would not touch her, and by placing Irulan in a position clearly subordinate to Alia and Chani, he sent a message to everyone at court.

Now Irulan performed a barely perceptible Bene Gesserit breathing exercise, to ease her tension. She had stopped feeling the irony that Muad'Dib had made his initial audience chamber out of the massive hutment that her father had transported to Arrakis for his disastrous military strike. The days of Corrino glory were gone, and she had been relegated to this comparatively minor role, her own form of exile.

I am but a pawn on the Imperial chessboard.

Many people crowded the chamber—CHOAM functionaries, minor nobles hoping to increase their standing
through public support of Muad'Dib, rich water sellers,
former smugglers who now considered themselves re-
spectable, as well as other visitors seeking an audience
with Muad'Dib. Today, though, with Paul away on Caladan, they would see his sister Alia instead. The deceptively small girl in a four-year-old body perched like a
bird on the translucent green throne that had once held
Shaddam IV.

In a high royal chair beside Alia sat the red-haired
Chani, opposite from where Irulan stood, with no throne
of her own. Though Irulan was the Emperor's wife, Paul
had never consummated their marriage, and said he never
would, because his Fremen concubine held all of his af-
fections. With the avenue of mate and potential mother
cut off from her, Irulan struggled to define her own role.

"We have an audience to see Emperor Muad'Dib,"
said the shortest Guildsman. "We have journeyed from
Junction."

"Today, Alia speaks for Muad'Dib," Chani said, then
waited.

Discomfited, the second Guildsman said, "This is Ertun and I am Loyxo. We have come on behalf of the Spacing Guild to request an increased allotment of spice."

"And who is the tall one?" Alia looked past the others.

"Crozeed," he said, bowing slightly.

"Very well, I shall speak to Crozeed, since he at least
has the good sense not to speak out of turn."

Crozeed's eyes glittered. "As my companion said, if
the Guild is to function properly in support of Muad'Dib's
conquests, we will require more spice."

"Interesting that the Guild never requests *less* spice,"
Chani said.

Alia added, "My brother has already been generous

with you. We all must make sacrifices in support of the greater good."

"He has commandeered many of our Heighliners and Navigators for his war effort," interjected Ertun. "The Guild needs those ships to conduct business throughout the worlds of the Imperium. CHOAM has already reported drastically reduced profits."

"We are in the midst of a war," Irulan pointed out, even though the little girl could well have said it herself. "What is your business worth if you have no spice to fuel the prescience of your Navigators?"

"We do not wish to displease Muad'Dib." Loyxo brushed orange hair out of one of his eyes. "We merely state our needs."

"Pray, then, that his Jihad is swiftly completed," Alia said.

"Tell us how we might please the Emperor," Ertun said.

Alia pondered the question as if receiving a telepathic message from her brother. "The divine Muad'Dib will increase the Guild's spice allotment by three percent per annum if you contribute another two hundred ships to his Jihad."

"Two hundred Heighliners!" Crozeed said. "So many?"

"The sooner my brother consolidates his rule, the sooner you can have your precious monopoly back."

"How do we know he will not be defeated?" Loyxo asked.

Alia glared at him. "Ask your Navigators to look into their prescience to see if Muad'Dib rules the future."

"They have looked," Ertun said, "but there is too much chaos around him."

"Then help him reduce the chaos. Help him put everything in order, and he will be eternally grateful. Muad'Dib's generosity—like his rage against his enemies—knows no bounds. Do you wish to be in the same category as the foolish houses who dare oppose us?"

"We are not the Emperor's enemies," Ertun insisted. "The Spacing Guild's constant neutrality is our safety net."

"There is no safety for you in such a position," Alia said. The words were terse, weighted. "Understand this, and understand it well. All those who do not openly support Muad'Dib may be considered his enemies." The girl made a gesture of dismissal. "This audience is concluded. Others have waited long to speak with me. The Spacing Guild shall have its increased spice only after the ships are delivered."

After the three dissatisfied representatives marched awkwardly out of the chamber, an aged bald man with a high forehead entered, accompanied by a female attendant. The man's steps were halting, and he used his sonic staff as a walking stick instead of an instrument of state.

Surprised, Irulan caught her breath. Though she had not seen him in years, she recognized her father's Court Chamberlain, Beely Ridondo. At one time Ridondo had been a person of considerable influence, managing Landsraad and palace schedules for the Padishah Emperor. Ridondo had gone into exile on Salusa Secundus with Shaddam IV, but now he had come here.

Maybe she should give Ridondo an inscribed copy of her book . . . or would that only enrage her father?

As the chamberlain neared the throne, clicking his ornate cane on the blood-red marble floor, Irulan noticed that the years had not been kind to him. His white-and-gold suit was dusty and slightly wrinkled on the sleeves; at one time he would never have gone to an Imperial function looking anything other than immaculate. Leaving his attendant behind, the man stopped in front of the throne. After a long and awkward silence, Ridondo spoke, "I am waiting to be announced."

"You may announce yourself." Alia's voice was high-pitched. "As Shaddam's chamberlain, you have sufficient experience."

Irulan could see his indignation. "I bring an important message from his Excellency Shaddam Corrino, and I demand to be treated with respect."

Taking a half step forward, Korba put a hand to the crysknife at his waist, acting the good Fedaykin again, but at a gesture from Alia he relaxed.

The girl looked bored. "I shall announce you. Comes now Beely Ridondo, personal chamberlain to the exiled Emperor." She gazed at him with Fremen-blue eyes out of an oval face that was just beginning to lose its baby fat.

Ridondo turned to Irulan, as if hoping for a better reception from her. "Your father will be pleased to know you are well, Princess. Is that still your proper title?"

"Princess will do." *Empress* Irulan would have been more fitting, but she did not expect that. "Please state your business."

Gathering himself to his full height, Ridondo stood free of the sonic staff. "I speak the words of the Padishah Emperor, and he—"

Chani cut him off. "The *former* Padishah Emperor."

Alia said, "Very well, what does Shaddam have to say?"

Pausing only a moment to recover, he said, "With respect, my . . . Lady . . . when Emperor Paul-Muad'Dib exiled the Padishah Emperor to Salusa Secundus, he promised that the world would be improved. Shaddam IV inquires when such measures will begin. We live in squalor, at the mercy of a harsh environment."

Irulan knew that the very severity of Salusa's landscape had been a fine catalyst for toughening the pool of men from which her father drew his Sardaukar. By softening that training ground through terraforming, Paul meant to soften the former Emperor's potential soldiers as well. Apparently Shaddam did not see the virtues of such extreme hardships now that he, his remaining family, his retainers, and a small police force of Sardaukar had been exiled there.

"We've been preoccupied with our Jihad," Alia said. "Shaddam will need to be patient. A bit of discomfort will not harm him."

The chamberlain did not back away. "The Emperor promised us! Here are Muad'Dib's exact words, spoken when he sentenced Shaddam Corrino to exile: 'I will ease the harshness of the place with all the powers at my disposal. It shall become a garden world, full of gentle things.' He does not appear to be using all the powers at his disposal. Does Paul-Muad'Dib break his word?"

Just then Korba leaped forward, sliding his crysknife from its sheath. Irulan shouted, trying to stop him, but the Fremen leader did not listen to her. Neither Alia nor Chani spoke a word as Korba slit the chamberlain's throat before the old man could raise his sonic staff to defend himself.

The crowd blocked the female aide from escaping, and Korba stalked forward, clearly intending to dispatch her as well, but Alia stopped him. "Enough, Korba." Alia stood from the throne and gazed down at the chamberlain's fallen body. A widening pool of blood spilled out onto the impermeable polished stones, where it could be collected and reclaimed.

The Fedaykin commander lifted his chin. "Forgive me, Lady Alia. My enthusiasm to defend the honor of Muad'Dib knows no bounds." He uttered a quick prayer, and some members of the audience echoed his words.

Irulan stared in horror at the dead chamberlain, then slowly turned to glare at Alia and Chani. "He came here as an ambassador, bearing a message from the former

Emperor. He had diplomatic immunity and should not have been harmed!"

"This is not the old Imperium, Irulan," Alia said, then raised her voice. "Send the aide safely back to Salusa Secundus. She can tell Shaddam and his family that Emperor Muad'Dib will send terraforming experts and machinery as soon as they become available."

The crowd chanted, "Muad'Dib! Muad'Dib!"

With a feral gaze, obviously in a mood for more killing, Korba glanced at Irulan, but only for a moment before wiping his knife and resheathing it. Unafraid, but sickened by the bloodshed, the Princess stared at him defiantly. Given her Bene Gesserit training, he would not have had such an easy time dispatching her.

Servants hurried forward to whisk away Ridondo's body and mop up the blood. Alia sat back on her throne. "Now, who wishes to be announced next?"

No one stepped forward.

I leave my footprints in history, even where I do not tread.

—*The Sayings of Muad'Dib* by
the PRINCESS IRULAN

T he shuttle from the Heighliner set down on Kaitain. From the viewing lounge of the craft, Paul watched the hordes of victorious Fedaykin commandos presenting themselves on the landing field. He could hear the din even over the engines. In a perverse dichotomy, the screaming crowds and cheering soldiers at the spaceport only reinforced the feeling that he was alone.

On Caladan he had briefly hoped to feel like one of the common people again—as his father had always insisted a Duke should be—only to be reminded that he was irrevocably different. As it must be. He was no longer simply Paul Atreides. He was *Muad'Dib,* a role he had assumed so easily and perfectly that he was not always entirely certain which was the mask and which was his real personality.

Wearing an implacable expression, he took a deep breath and flung his long faux-stillsuit cape behind his shoulder. He moved with Imperial grace down the ramp to stand before the cheering mob. The Fedaykin closed ranks around him to form an extravagant escort. A conquering hero.

The resounding wave of shouts and cheers nearly

pushed him backward. He understood how tyrants could allow themselves to feel infallible, buoyed by a swell of overconfidence. He was acutely aware that with a word, he could command all of these fighters to slaughter every man, woman, and child on Kaitain. That troubled him.

In his childhood studies, he had seen countless images of the glorious capital, but now he noticed a dark stain of smoke across the sky. The towering white buildings had been gutted by fire, majestic monuments toppled, government halls and lavish private residences ransacked. From ancient history, Paul was reminded of barbarians sacking Rome, ending one of humanity's first titanic empires and bringing about the start of centuries of Dark Ages. His detractors were saying that about his own regime, but he was doing only what was necessary.

Stilgar presented himself to his commander in a stained and battle-scuffed uniform. Marks that must have been dried blood showed prominently on his sleeves and chest. A wound on the naib's left arm had been bound and dressed with a colorful, expensive scarf that might have been torn from a rich noble, but Stilgar used it as a gaudy rag. "Kaitain has fallen, Usul. Your Jihad is an unstoppable storm."

Paul gazed out across the war-torn former capital. "Who can stop a storm from the desert?"

Even before launching his Jihad, Paul had known there would be far too many battlefields for a single commander to oversee. How he wished Duncan were still alive to participate in a succession of precise military strikes with Stilgar, Gurney Halleck, and even several flinty-eyed Sardaukar commanders, who had shifted their loyalty to the man who had conquered them. In the wake of their astonishing defeat on the plain of Arrakeen, Shaddam's elite soldiers had been shaken to the core, and many had transferred their loyalty to the only military commander who had ever bested them. Though Sardaukar fervor did not spring from religious passion, it was fanaticism nevertheless. And useful. Wisely, though, Paul had not asked any of the Sardaukar to participate in the sacking of Kaitain.

"When will Irulan arrive?" Paul asked Stilgar. "Did she receive my summons?"

"The Guild informs me that another Heighliner is bringing her within the day." His voice carried an unmistakable note of distaste. "Although why you want *her* I cannot imagine. Chani is bound to be incensed."

"I do not *want* Irulan, Stil, but she is necessary, especially here. You'll see."

Stilgar was joined by Orlop and Kaleff, the sons of Jamis. "Let us show you, Usul!" said Orlop, who had always been the more talkative brother. "This planet is full of miracles and treasure. Have you ever seen the like?"

Paul didn't want to dampen the boys' enthusiasm by telling them he had seen so many things, both wondrous and horrible, that his eyes were weary. "All right, show me what has gotten you so excited."

In the center of the once-magnificent city, Fremen warriors had torn down Landsraad banners and smashed the stained-glass crests of noble houses. As conquerors, the soldiers had chased the terrified citizens, taking some prisoner, killing others. It had been a wild blood orgy, and though violent, was reminiscent of the spice orgy a Sayyadina would host when Fremen felt the need to celebrate in their sietches. Looking around, Paul knew that trying to control these victory celebrations would only make matters worse in the long run. It was a price he had to accept, and the worst was already over. . . .

He had his own advisers, though he longed for the wise counsel of Duke Leto, Thufir Hawat, or Duncan Idaho . . . all long dead. He was sure Duke Leto would have disapproved of what had happened here. Nevertheless, Paul had learned to make his own decisions. *I have created a universe in which the old rules do not apply. A new paradigm. I am sorry, Father.*

Paul saw the damage done to the Landsraad Hall, the museums, and the off-planet embassies. The old domed rock garden erected by House Thorvald as a wedding gift to Emperor Shaddam had been blown up, and now lay in a pile of wreckage. Paul couldn't conceive what his fighters had been trying to accomplish. It was destruction for its own sake.

In the public square seven garroted men with cords still tied around their purple throats had been strung upside down to dangle like macabre trophies in an arbor. Judging by their fine clothes, they were noble leaders who had not surrendered with sufficient promptness. Paul felt a dark twinge of anger; such lynchings would make his job of forging alliances, or at least a peace, with the Landsraad even more difficult.

A group of yelling, laughing Fremen came running out of the Landsraad Hall, carrying long pennants. He recognized the varied colors of House Ecaz, House Richese, and House Tonkin. The Fremen didn't know any of the historically great families, nor did they care. As far as they were concerned, the Landsraad itself had teetered, fallen, and splintered into disarray.

"Not even Shaddam would want this place back now," Paul muttered to himself.

Fremen carried makeshift baskets and satchels full of booty. In the melee, they'd discarded priceless historical artifacts. Four muscular warriors had thrown themselves into a wide, shallow fountain adorned with statuary and dancing jets of water. They drank water until they were sick and splashed in the pool as if they had finally found paradise.

Kaleff came running up, his face sticky with juice.

Cradled in his arm, he held half a dozen perfectly round portyguls, an orange fruit with a hard rind and sweet flesh. "Usul, we found an orchard out in the open—trees just standing there, lush and green and full of fruit . . . fruit for the taking! Here, would you like one?" He extended the oranges.

Paul accepted one, bit through its bitter rind, and squeezed the crisp citrus juice into his throat. He supposed these were Emperor Shaddam's portyguls, and that made the fruit taste even sweeter.

~

WHEN THE SECOND Heighliner arrived, bringing an icily reticent Irulan, Paul asked for her to be brought to him at the steps of the old Imperial Palace. He had guessed she would be very shaken to come here and see this. But he needed her.

Shaddam's daughter wore a gown of rich blue in a style that had once been the height of Imperial fashion. Her golden hair was done up in ringlets that draped down her long neck. She had performed her duties with considerable grace after her father's defeat; she was not hungry for power herself, but she was intelligent enough to see and acknowledge the new realities.

At first, Irulan seemed to think that her Bene Gesserit seduction techniques would let her slip easily into Paul's bed and produce an heir binding the Corrino and Atreides bloodlines—almost certainly at the orders of the Bene Gesserit Sisterhood. But thus far in his reign he had been immune to her tricks. Chani possessed all of his heart and all of his love.

Thwarted in her primary goal, Irulan followed instead the basic tenet of the Sisterhood: adapt or die. Thus she had worked to find a new function for herself in the government, and quickly achieved her own fame by publishing *The Life of Muad'Dib*, Volume 1. It was rapidly written, swiftly published and distributed, and wildly popular. Most of Paul's Fremen warriors carried well-read copies of her book.

Here, at the downfall of Kaitain, however, the Princess could play a more traditional role.

Crowds followed him everywhere, expecting him to issue some profound announcement at any moment. They had already gathered in front of the Palace.

Perfectly regal and requiring no escort, Irulan came up the polished steps from the plaza level to where Paul stood at the first landing. Stilgar remained at the base of the waterfall of stairs, looking up toward the royal pair. With all the Imperial pride she could manage, Irulan took her place at Paul's side, dutifully slipping her arm through his. "You summoned me, my Husband?" She seemed exceedingly wary, angry at the destruction she saw around her.

"I needed you here. This is likely to be the last time you will see Kaitain."

"This is no longer my Kaitain." She looked around the Palace, clearly unable to reconcile what she saw with what she remembered. "This is a raped and pillaged corpse of what was once the grandest of cities. It will never be the same."

Paul could not deny her statement. "Wherever Muad'Dib goes, nothing is the same again. Didn't you write that in your book?"

"I wrote the story you told me. As I interpreted it, of course."

He gestured toward the crowd. "And here is more of the tale."

As a special honor, Paul had already given instructions to Kaleff and Orlop, and at his signal they trotted up the stairs, streaming the long banners of his fighting forces: green-and-white, green-and-black. Paul stared out at the sea of faces as the shouts rose to a deafening tumult, then diminished to an anticipatory silence.

"This is Kaitain, and I *am* the Emperor." He clasped Irulan's hand, and she stared stonily ahead. They both knew the reason she had to be there. "But I am much more than the successor to the Padishah Emperor, Shaddam Corrino IV. I am Muad'Dib, and I am unlike any force the galaxy has ever seen."

Behind them, fire began to catch hold inside the Imperial Palace. Pursuant to his orders, loyal fighters had set blazes at dozens of flashpoints inside the great structure. He had seen this in his visions, and had fought against it, but he had also seen the obligation, the powerful tool of the symbolism here. These fires, at least, would burn out quickly.

Most of the noble Houses had no love for Shaddam and his excesses. Now they would be terrified of Paul-Muad'Dib. The sacking of Kaitain should be enough to shock the rest of the Landsraad into submission, to stop the need for the Jihad before it spread further. He sighed, because his terrifying visions had told him that nothing could stop the full multi-planet iteration of the fanatical war that he had set in motion. He could only make a limited number of choices that would prove most beneficial in the long, long run.

Oh, the immensity of the burden on his shoulders! Only he could see through the curtains of bloodshed, pain, and sorrow. How humanity would hate him . . . but at least they would *survive* to hate him.

The crowds watched in awe as flames began to consume the giant Palace. The conflagration grew in force and brilliance, so that Paul stood looking on from the edge of an inferno.

Beside him, Irulan trembled. "I shall never forgive you

PAUL OF DUNE   47

for this, Paul *Atreides*. The Corrinos will never forgive you." She said more, but her words were drowned out by the background roar of the crowd and the crackling of the growing fire.

He leaned close and said with great sorrow, "I did not ask for anyone's forgiveness." Then Muad'Dib turned to the crowd again and shouted as the fire grew more intense. "This Palace was a symbol of the old regime. Like everything else about the decadent old Imperium, it must be swept aside. Kaitain is no longer the capital. *Dune* is our capital now. And in Arrakeen I command that a new Palace be built, one to dwarf the grandest works of all previous rulers."

Glancing over his shoulder, he saw the legacy of Shaddam IV going up in fire and smoke. The construction of his own new palace would require great sacrifices, an unparalleled workforce, and unimaginable wealth.

Even so, he had no doubt whatsoever that his grand vision would be accomplished.

There are rules, but people invariably find ways of getting around them. So it is with laws. A true leader must understand such things and be prepared to take advantage of each situation.

—EMPEROR ELROOD IX, *Ruminations on Success*

Shaddam Corrino glared at the face that looked back at him from the gold-framed mirror, noting the clear signs of age beyond his actual years. His father, the vulturish Elrood IX, had been 157 years old when Shaddam and Fenring had finally poisoned him.

I am less than half that old!

Age implied weakness. Only a few years ago, there might have been some gray hairs mixed with the red, though not enough for him to notice. But since his exile to this dismal world, the gray had become much more prominent. Perhaps it was caused by some taint in the air or water. He had considered coloring his hair, but could not decide whether that would make him appear stronger, or merely vain.

Back when he was the Padishah Emperor, Shaddam had prided himself on his youthful appearance and energy; he'd had many court concubines and several disappointing wives since the death of Anirul. But, sadly, all of that was gone, and he felt as if most of the life had been sucked out of him. Now, simply seeing the lines on his face made him feel tired. Even melange could not prolong his life forever, perhaps not even long enough for him to regain the Lion Throne. Nevertheless, four of his daughters had accompanied him into exile, and they would bear grandchildren for him, even if Irulan did not. One way or another, the Corrino line would endure.

An Atreides upstart dares to call himself Emperor!

He feared that Irulan had become one of them, though he could not be certain of her role. Was she an insider who could help him, or a willing participant who had betrayed her father? Was she a hostage? Why would she not improve the lot of her own family? And that damnable book she had written, glorifying the "heroic" life of Paul-Muad'Dib Atreides! Even the witches were in an uproar over that.

No matter. He could not imagine that the usurper's government would endure, based as it was on religious nonsense and primitive fanaticism. The Landsraad wouldn't stand for it, and though many noblemen already cowered, the rest would stand together. Soon enough, they would call him back to the throne to restore order. More than ten thousand years of history and eighty-one Corrino emperors since the end of the Butlerian Jihad, a galactic Imperium spanning uncounted star systems . . . now being overrun by unsophisticated desert people who still called themselves *tribes*! It sickened him. From Golden Age to Dark Age in a single reign.

And here am I, ruling a world nobody wants.

Shaddam left the mirror and its disappointing image, going instead to a large faux window, with a view transmitted from external imagers. The Salusan sky was sickly orange, dotted with the dark shapes of carrion birds that were constantly on the alert for scant prey.

Weather-control satellites should have improved the conditions in this particular region of the planet, but weather control was not consistent. At the beginning of the brief growing season, when plants and trees started to offer a splash of greenery, the satellites had gone offline. By the time they were repaired, horrible storms had wiped out the plantings and made ongoing construction work nearly impossible.

During his former reign, Shaddam had kept this planet harsh for his own reasons. Salusa Secundus had been the Corrino prison world, a desolate place where malcontents and convicts were sorted by the rigors of survival. In those days, more than 60 percent of them had died, while the stronger ones had become candidates for his elite terror troops, the supposedly invincible Sardaukar. Unlike the unprepared prisoners dumped here, though, Shaddam had amenities, supplies, servants, family, and even a contingent of loyal soldiers. But Salusa was still his prison.

Far from expediting the reclamation of this world, as he had promised, Paul Atreides seemed to be shutting down the systems. Did he hope to leave Shaddam with a dwindling pool of potential soldiers from the hard-bitten survivors of the prison population . . . or did he only want the shamed Emperor to suffer for a few years?

Shaddam had just learned that his long-devoted chamberlain Beely Ridondo had been executed at Muad'Dib's court simply for asking that the fanatical new Emperor keep his word. Shaddam had not expected the gambit to succeed, since he no longer believed the usurper had any honor. Even when the Fremen rabble had stormed his hutment on the Arrakeen plain, forcing the Padishah Emperor to entertain terms of surrender, the upstart had asserted that "Muad'Dib" was not bound by the same promises made by "Paul Atreides"—as if they were two different men!

How convenient.

And now his reports also said that Fremen fanatics had conquered Kaitain. Barbarians were sacking his beautiful capital world!

Am I really expected to be content here while the whole galaxy goes mad?

Worse, edicts constantly arrived, words couched in terms from the mockery of a religion that had formed around Muad'Dib, all signed by a self-important functionary named Korba.

A Fremen commander gives me orders!

It was an outrage. After a taste of Muad'Dib's appalling bloodshed, the people would welcome Shaddam's return with songs and roses. Utilizing intrigue, kanly, or outright assassination, he vowed to dispatch his enemies, one by one. But so far he had seen no opportunities.

In the past year, Shaddam had taken steps to outsmart his distant captors. Among the hardened prison population, his Sardaukar commanders had located men with mechanical and inventive skills. He had put those men to work constructing a new city that could withstand the vagaries of the hostile weather. Some were hardened criminals—murderers, smugglers, thieves—but others had been put on the planet for political reasons, some by House Corrino, many more by Muad'Dib. The men, caring only that they were being offered better living conditions, were happy to work for Shaddam now.

Ringing the site of his new capital city were three huge piles of refuse and construction debris, each higher than his tallest makeshift buildings. He had ordered scavenging teams to reclaim materials from all over the planet, to seize them from other prison camps and a few ancient but sturdy ruins that had survived the long-ago atomic attack. But the recovery operation had produced pitiful results.

The city's great dome was not sealed yet, but eventually plants would grow inside a controlled environment. With the hodgepodge of construction activities, he felt like the manager of a large junkyard, salvaging parts to build a shantytown. Even his best efforts had resulted in nothing more than a pale imitation of the great Imperial Palace on Kaitain.

His private residence was a fortified structure inside a domed city that was continuously under construction. Through the supposed generosity of Muad'Dib, the residence was opulently furnished with Corrino antiques, handmade Kaitain rugs, and other articles moved from his Imperial Palace. Precious family heirlooms—a mocking reminder of the things he had lost. He had all of his royal clothing, even his personal weapons. Oddly, and perhaps as a slap in the face, his "benefactors" had even sent him a container full of his childhood toys, including a stuffed Salusan bull.

Several separate but connectable keeps housed his family members and the top advisers who had accompanied him into exile. Shaddam's private keep was substantially different from the others. By far the largest, it had its own suspensor system that actually enabled the structure to fly out over the barren landscape of Salusa, where he could observe conditions firsthand. At least it gave him the illusion of mobility.

An Emperor should not have to scrounge for survival. He touched a fingerpad on the wall to replace the false window with shifting images of Kaitain—electronic artwork that he had been permitted to keep. *They are so kind to me.*

He turned to see an officer in the doorway dressed in Sardaukar gray with silver and gold trim. An elderly but powerfully built man, the colonel-bashar held his black helmet in one hand and saluted with the other. His face was craggy and weathered, as if sculpted on Salusa, where he had trained and served for so many years. "You summoned me, Sire?"

Shaddam was glad to see one of his steadfastly loyal commanders. "Yes, Bashar Garon. I have an important task for you."

Zum Garon had once led all of Shaddam's Sardaukar legions, but now only a portion of the once-glorious fighting force remained—the few thousand Sardaukar that Paul Atreides had allowed him to keep. Garon's mouth twitched as he waited for his master to continue.

Shaddam went to a bureau from which he retrieved an ornate knife with a gold handle inset with jewels. "The tyrant Muad'Dib and his fanatics ignore the rules of diplomacy and decency. Those of us who stand for civilization and stability must put aside our differences. I cannot do this all by myself." He tapped the flat of the blade against his palm, then handed the weapon to the bashar, hilt first. "Find my dear friend Hasimir Fenring and tell him how sorely I need his help now. He left us only months ago, so he cannot have entrenched himself elsewhere. Give him this blade as a gift from me. He will understand the significance."

Garon took the knife. Behind his stony façade, the Sardaukar commander often seemed to be holding back a flood of emotions.

Shaddam added, "I have not spoken with him since he departed from his exile here—unlike me, he was here on a voluntary basis. I want you to ask about his dear wife and their child. Why, the baby would be almost three years old by now! And be sure to remind him that my daughter Wensicia just married his cousin, Dalak Zor-Fenring. My friend might not know that yet."

He forced a smile, tried to swallow the bitterness in his throat. So many little defeats! With no other betrothal prospects in exile, Shaddam had arranged for his own middle daughter Wensicia to marry Hasimir Fenring's cousin after the Count had left. He secretly hoped that his boyhood companion would look upon this favorably and return to his side. How he missed Fenring! Despite their falling-out, Shaddam was sure that their long friendship would outweigh the wounds. Corrino and

Fenring had been inextricably twined for most of their lives. Soon enough, he hoped, a grandchild would be on the way, to strengthen the ties.

Garon cleared his throat. "Count Fenring may not be easy to locate, Sire."

"Since when does a Sardaukar commander flinch from a difficult task?"

"Never, Sire. I will do my best."

It is easier to judge an alien culture than to understand it. We tend to look at things through the filters of our own racial and cultural biases. Are we capable of reaching out? And if we do, are we capable of comprehension?

—excerpt from a Bene Gesserit report
on galactic settlements

Count Hasimir Fenring had encountered many unusual races in his work for Shaddam IV, but the Bene Tleilax pushed the very definition of humanity. Through genetic manipulation, the ruling caste of Tleilaxu Masters had intentionally adopted strange physical characteristics—probative little eyes, sharp teeth, and a furtive way of moving about, as if constantly on the alert for predators. Other members of their race were taller and looked like ordinary people, but in their topsy-turvy society, the rodent-men were the highest of the Tleilaxu castes.

And now he and his family had made a home among them.

Feeling out of place and trying to ignore it, the Count and his wife, Margot, strolled along a lakeshore walk in the city of Thalidei, where the Tleilaxu Masters had allowed them to stay. Beyond rooftops, he saw the high, fortified wall that encircled the industrial complex that had been built at the edge of a dead and noisome lake, almost an inland sea. For these people, the pollution, the mix of chemicals, the unusual organic reactions were all seen as *possibilities*, an experimental brew that yielded interesting compounds to be harvested and tested.

Unlike the sacred city of Bandalong, outsiders were permitted here, though the Tleilaxu still took considerable measures to isolate the Fenrings. Security scanning devices were visible in front of many smooth-walled structures, bathing entryways in pearlescent light and blocking the passage of infidels. Some of the most important Tleilaxu programs were carried on in Thalidei, including the sophisticated and mysterious process of Twisting certain Mentat candidates. Sooner or later, Fenring had vowed to see the details for himself.

Only a month after Paul Atreides sent the deposed Emperor to Salusa Secundus, Fenring realized that he could not bear to share exile with Shaddam and his dismal, complaining moods. The two had quarreled constantly, and so the Count had made arrangements to leave. If forced to stay longer, he feared he might have killed his long-time friend, and that was one murder he did not particularly want to commit.

Since Muad'Dib's exile order did not directly relate to him, Fenring had easily slipped away from Salusa. He had been able to move from planet to planet in disguise as he wished, though he had openly admitted his identity to the Tleilaxu, with whom he had previously worked. Margot had a precious little daughter, and Salusa Secundus was not a good place to raise her. Instead, the Count had chosen Tleilax as an unexpected location to go to ground—a comparatively safe, unobtrusive place to train and school their daughter, out of view. The Tleilaxu were annoying enough, but they did know how to keep secrets. They certainly had plenty of their own.

Fenring had called in many favors, hinted at dangerous knowledge he had acquired in his previous dealings with the Tleilaxu—which would be widely released if any harm came to him. With only a little grumbling, the Tleilaxu had allowed the Fenrings to stay, and the family planned to remain for several years. But they did not really fit in. They were *powindah*.

"Look at those men standing on street corners doing nothing," Margot said in a low tone. "Where are the women?"

"Those are upper-caste men," Fenring said. "They consider themselves, hmmm, *entitled* to do nothing, although I would find that rather dull."

"I've never seen even lower-caste women or female children here." Lady Margot looked around with her piercing gaze. They both had their suspicions that the Tleilaxu held their females as slaves or experiments.

"Without question, my dear, you are, hmmm, the most beautiful woman in Thalidei."

"You embarrass me, my love." She gave him a quick kiss on the cheek and moved on, ever alert. Margot always kept herself well armed with hidden weapons and in prime fighting condition; they never allowed their young daughter to be unguarded even for a moment.

In their relationship, the couple depended on each other greatly, but did not trespass into each other's private territory. Fenring had even accepted the necessity of Margot conceiving a child by Feyd-Rautha Harkonnen. Just business. When he'd chosen to marry a Reverend Mother decades ago, he had acknowledged certain things as a matter of course.

Little Marie was back in their flat now, several blocks away, looked after by a talented woman Margot had acquired from the Sisterhood—an acolyte named Tonia Obregah-Xo who served as nanny, tutor, and devoted bodyguard to the child. Though Fenring was sure the Bene Gesserit nanny was also a spy, sending reports on little Marie's progress back to Wallach IX, he was also

certain that the watchful Obregah-Xo would defend the
girl with her life. The Sisterhood wanted her bloodline
for their own uses.

The breeze turned, driving some of the polluted lake's
stench back out onto the rank water. Fishing trawlers
dredged the sediment, hauling up interesting mutations
of the few species of marine life that had survived in
such a contaminated environment. Every once in a while,
large tentacles could be seen rising out of the water, far
from shore, but none of the Tleilaxu boats ventured into
such deep waters, and the mysterious creature had never
been caught or catalogued.

Factory lines delivered fresh slime from the lake bottom
into holding pools and separation tanks, in which body-
suited lower-caste Tleilaxu waded, sampling the chemical
compositions. Black gulls circled around, screaming at the
mess. Cranes hoisted algae-covered screens from growth
solutions steeped in the shallows.

He and Lady Margot came within view of a white
building eight stories tall—eight, a sacred number to this
superstitious race. "Hmmm, at first, Master Ereboam refused to let me bring you here, my dear, but he finally as-
sented. He even decided to show us something special."

"Perhaps I should have worn an opera dress for the
occasion," she said with clear sarcasm.

"Be sweet, Margot. I know you can do it. Don't insult
our host."

"I haven't yet." She manufactured a smile. "But there's
a first time for everything." She took him by the arm and
they walked toward the building.

The Tleilaxu doctor waited for them by the security
field of the arched main doorway of the facility. The
pockets of his traditional white laboratory smock bulged,
as if filled with secrets. With milky white skin and hair
and a pointed white goatee, Master Ereboam was a startling albino in a race that was commonly gray-skinned

and black-haired—an unsettling hereditary accident among genetic experts.

Ereboam called out in a cheerful voice. "My spotters say you took the long way here. An alleyway connector would have reduced your walk by at least five minutes."

"I don't like alleys," Fenring said. *Too many shadows and places for an ambush.*

"Very well, I accept your apology." He patted Fenring on the back in a manner uncharacteristic of the normally reserved Tleilaxu. Ignoring Margot entirely, as he invariably did, Dr. Ereboam led the two of them through the security field, down a hallway, and into a windowless room where thirty tall, slender men stood with their backs turned. All wore body filmsuits, in accordance with the typical Tleilaxu prudishness; Fenring doubted if the Masters ever looked at *themselves* naked.

In unison, the men all faced forward, and Fenring chuckled, as did Margot. Though of varying ages, every one of them looked identical—all duplicates of the Baron Harkonnen's Twisted Mentat Piter de Vries, staring ahead with eyes set in narrow-featured faces.

The original de Vries had been killed on Kaitain by the witch Mohiam. Afterward, the Baron had been served by a ghola of the Mentat, who had purportedly died on Arrakis along with the captive Duke Leto Atreides in a mysterious release of poison gas.

"Gholas?" Fenring asked. "Why are there so many of them?"

"Baron Vladimir Harkonnen had a standing order for us to keep several ready for delivery. The growth and Twisting process takes a good deal of time."

"The Baron has been dead for a year," Margot pointed out.

Ereboam frowned at her, then deigned to answer. "Yes, and they are therefore no longer commercially viable. We contacted other noble houses to try to market them elsewhere, but the Baron managed to taint the reputation of this one. Such a waste of time and resources, and now this line has been discontinued. At least they can serve as experimental subjects for a new nerve poison. Observe. That is why I've brought you here."

In unison, the de Vries gholas took on identical expressions of agony and clutched at their heads. As if choreographed, they fell writhing to the floor one by one, with the degree of their reactions depending on the strength of the poison to which they'd been exposed. They all began babbling long strings of prime numbers and tables of useless facts. Fenring exchanged a quizzical glance with his wife.

"The new poison is a marketable assassination tool," Ereboam said. "How delightful; their thoughts are detonating inside their brains. Soon they will all go insane, but that is a mere side effect, however interesting it may be. Death is our primary goal with this substance."

Thick blood and mucous began running out of the mouths, ears, and nostrils. Some of the victims screamed, while others whimpered.

"Because they are all virtually identical," Ereboam continued, "these discontinued gholas provide an opportunity for us to test various potencies of the neurotoxin. A controlled experiment."

"This is barbaric," Margot said, not bothering to keep her voice down.

"Barbaric?" Ereboam said. "Compared to what Muad'Dib has set loose on the universe, this is nothing."

Count Fenring nodded, realizing that the Tleilaxu man was making some sense—in his own twisted way.

It is far better to win a battle through skilled leadership and wise decisions than violence and bloodshed. It may not seem as glorious to the uninitiated, but in the end it results in fewer wounds—of any kind.

—THUFIR HAWAT, House Atreides Master of Assassins

It was a matter of simple mathematics, and the numbers did not add up.

For years before it happened, Paul had experienced visions of his Jihad, a storm of armed and fanatical Fremen sweeping across star systems, planting the banners of Muad'Dib and slaughtering any populations that resisted. Though history would paint a dark picture of his rule, Paul could see beyond the next sand dune in the wasteland of time, to the next, and the next. He knew that his Jihad would be but a flurry compared with the titanic upheavals that lay ahead in the path of human destiny, upheavals that would be far more deadly if he failed now.

While still on Kaitain, having dispatched the Fremen warriors to other battlefields and summoned cleanup and reconstruction crews to cement the occupation of the former Imperial capital, he considered his next move. Although he missed Chani greatly, he had vital work to do here.

To win this Jihad he would have to lay down a new, enduring rule. He had to derail humanity and its politics from the rut into which it had allowed itself to fall. No, not a rut, he decided. A death spiral.

But the numbers . . .

On the entire planet of Arrakis, Paul knew there were perhaps ten million Fremen scattered among numerous sietches. Ten million, half of whom were men, of which perhaps a third could be called upon to act as warriors in his Jihad. Less than two million fighters . . . and he knew from his dreams, his calculations, and cold logic that he would have to conquer—maybe even slaughter— countless populations before this war was over.

Even with all the faithful, though, he simply did not have enough fighters to make this a strictly military conquest. His soldiers, no matter how dedicated, couldn't possibly kill everyone who disagreed with him. Besides, he had no desire to be the emperor of a galaxywide charnel house.

Though Paul's prescience told him he had to win many victories, he hoped to prevail on most leaders of the Imperium with subtlety and intelligence, using sophisticated means of persuasion. His mother had already begun to make overtures for him. He had to demonstrate that surrender to and alliance with Muad'Dib was a smart decision, the best alternative. The *only* alternative. But in order to accomplish that, he needed to employ the *Paul Atreides* side of his brain, rather than the raw Fremen side of Muad'Dib. Through all available means, he needed to control what remained of the Landsraad. He needed to gather allies.

While his initial instinct was to return to Arrakeen and summon the members of the most important noble Houses, Paul decided that could send the wrong signal, because seeing him there the noblemen might consider him a piratical leader of desert bandits. On Dune, Paul was surrounded by a groundswell of fanaticism, the resolute loyalty that was simply not understandable to anyone who did not grasp the power of blind religious devotion. After years of complacency under the secular

Corrino Imperium, many Landsraad members had paid little attention to religion, viewing the Orange Catholic Bible as nothing more than a document of deep historical interest but without true passion.

Even if Paul called in old family alliances and recruited the political friends of his father, it was not likely to be enough. Paul's jihadis might even kill some of the recalcitrant nobles, showing them a different kind of passion that even Paul might not be able to stop. There were potential second- and third-level consequences that he did not like, and he knew his prescience would not show him every possible pitfall.

So, the Emperor Paul-Muad'Dib made plans to summon them to Kaitain. A familiar place, and a symbol of how much he had already conquered in so short a time.

With the Imperial Palace torched and the marvelous city ransacked, he dispatched urgent protocol teams to prepare for the event. They cleaned the gutted Landsraad Hall of Oratory and rehung the banners of all the Houses who had agreed to attend.

Paul selected the invited representatives carefully. Duke Leto had been quite popular among important families, so much that he had unwittingly sparked Shaddam's jealousy—a resentment that had led to the Duke's political entrapment and murder on Arrakis. But even all of his father's friends would not be enough. He would also need to rely on the numerous planetary rulers who bore their own enmity toward Shaddam IV—and there were many of those from which to choose. When the guest list was set, his subordinates arranged Guild passage to bring the invited Landsraad representatives to Kaitain. For the event, Muad'Dib had personally guaranteed their safety and offered them incentives.

While Paul waited for the delegates to arrive, Fedaykin guards swept the former Imperial city. They rooted out any "suspicious" people and locked them up, all in the name of ensuring the safety of the Emperor. Paul had an unsettling realization that his own people were resorting to tactics quite similar to those the Harkonnens had used, but he also understood the very real threat posed by assassins and conspirators. He had to allow some excesses for the greater good, though he doubted his explanations would comfort the families of those innocents who fell victim to Fremen zeal. . . .

On the day of the first official Landsraad meeting in his new reign, Paul stepped onto the central speaking podium and looked out at the anxious and angry faces of the gathered nobles. Brilliant Atreides banners hung on either side of him. Instead of his stillsuit and Fremen robe, he chose to wear an old-design black House Atreides uniform with a red hawk crest prominent on the right breast. His hair had been trimmed, and he had been washed and groomed so that he looked like the proud and dignified son of a noble Duke.

But he could not bleach the blue from his eyes or mask the dark tan of his skin, the weathered creases from windblown dust, the leanness of a face that had adjusted to a much lower water content.

More than sixty noble Houses had sent representatives, and he spotted familiar faces. He noted the old one-armed Archduke Armand Ecaz, who had no legal heir, and whose holdings were primarily managed by his Swordmaster. Also a lead administrator of the technocrats of Ix (Paul was not surprised that the son of House Vernius had not come in person, considering their past). In addition, he picked out O'Garee of Hagal, Sor of IV Anbus, Thorvald of Ipyr, Kalar of Ilthamont, Olin of Risp VII, and others.

Even though his loyal Fremen guards were in evidence in the Hall of Oratory, Paul faced the Landsraad members alone. When he spoke, he raised his voice, pitching his tone to use not only the powers his mother had taught him, but also his intimate knowledge of the nuances of command from his experience in leading Fremen tribes and Atreides soldiers. He owed much to Gurney Halleck, Duncan Idaho, Thufir Hawat, and, most of all, to his father. Paul had to remind these men that he was Duke Leto's son.

"The Padishah Emperor was defeated," he said, pausing for a moment to let them wonder what he would say next. "Defeated by his own arrogance, by the overconfidence of his Sardaukar, and by the spider web of political machinations that trapped him in much the same way he intended to trap House Atreides." Another pause, scanning the faces in the assemblage to look for emotion, for anger. He saw some of that, but more fear. "Most of you knew my father, Duke Leto. He instilled in me the principles of honor and leadership, which I intend to maintain on the Imperial throne—if you will let me."

Paul let his gaze rest on a diminished-looking Armand Ecaz sitting stonily in his chair. Several noblemen and dignitaries were taking notes, and still more leaned forward curiously, waiting to see how they could benefit from the situation.

"As Shaddam had no legal sons, and I have taken his eldest daughter Irulan as my wife, I am the legitimate heir to the Lion Throne. But my rule is not a mere continuation of Corrino rule. We have all learned our lesson from that! Some have seen this transition of power as a time of turmoil, but you can help me establish stability again."

"Stability?" shouted a man from a high tier. "Not much stability left, thanks to you!" Paul saw that the outspoken man had long gray-blond hair tied back behind his shoulders, a leonine frosty beard, and piercing pale blue eyes. He recognized Earl Memnon Thorvald, the bitter brother of one of Shaddam's later wives. Paul had invited him, thinking that Thorvald might hold enough of a grudge against the Corrinos to make him an ally.

Now though, the Earl's palpable anger made it clear that he was in another category. Paul might have to isolate him.

"You may speak freely, Earl Thorvald!" Paul shouted to the upper tier. "Though few noble leaders will agree with you."

Showing surprise at the invitation, Thorvald nonetheless obliged. "Your Fremen armies are like packs of wild wolves. We can all see what they've done to Kaitain. They burned the *Imperial Palace*—and you allowed it!" He gestured. "You call this establishing a rule of stability?"

"Call it the price of war—a war I never sought." Paul spread his hands across the podium. "We can stop the bloodshed immediately. Your holdings will be safe and protected if you sign an alliance with me. You know the law is on my side, as is the power base. And," he added, bringing out his most powerful card, "I control the spice. The Spacing Guild and CHOAM are behind me."

Thorvald's anger only intensified. "So, our choice is between bloody instability and bowing to religious tyranny?"

Bolig Avati, the lead administrator of the Ixian technocrats, rose to his feet and spoke in a firm voice. "If we agree to your proposed alliance, Paul Atreides, must we worship you as a god? Some of us have outgrown the need for false and convenient deities."

The Hall filled with angry muttering, some of it directed at the dissenters, some disturbingly in agreement with them. More leaders agreed with Thorvald than Paul anticipated.

Raising his voice over the mounting commotion, Paul said, "My best fighters were bred in the harsh deserts of Arrakis. They fought the ruthless Harkonnens and the Emperor's Sardaukar. What they have seen of Imperial justice has not benefited them. But if you join me, my Jihad armies will not touch your worlds. One day when there is no enemy left to fight, there will be no more need for a powerful central army."

He drew a breath, let his expression become sterner. "If my words do not convince you, then I have the option of applying additional incentives—embargoes, monetary levies, even blockades. I have already declared a heavy tariff on any Guild flights servicing worlds that refuse to acknowledge my rule." As the muttering increased, he made his voice even louder. "I have not yet imposed a complete moratorium on transportation to those planets, but I retain that as an option. I much prefer cooperation to coercion, but I mean to put a speedy end to this wasteful conflict, regardless."

"From the beginning you planned to become a tyrant, didn't you?" Thorvald shouted, resting his large hands on the balcony rail of the high tier. "I have had my fill of emperors. The galaxy has had its fill of them. My planet will do just fine without your raving fanatics or benevolent boot heel. The Landsraad made a mistake by allowing House Corrino to rule much too long! And we still haven't learned our lesson." He called over his shoulder as he stormed out. "I only hope the rest of you awaken from your semuta trance soon enough."

Fedaykin guards moved to intercept Thorvald, but Paul signaled them to stop. This was a delicate time. He realized now that he could not, by any means, change the mind of Memnon Thorvald, and if he applied force inappropriately and acted as a bully, he would lose many of these others as well.

"I am glad this occurred," Paul said, intending to surprise his audience. "I cannot pretend not to be disappointed that Earl Thorvald spurned my offer, but I am glad the rest of you have heard me out, and have decided to be rational." He glanced from one Atreides banner to the other hanging beside his podium, before turning again to the audience. "You understand my terms."

Those who care nothing for their own lives find it easy to become heroes.

—ST. ALIA OF THE KNIFE

A month after returning from the conquest of Kaitain and his meeting with the Landsraad representatives, Paul stood at the edge of the plains of Arrakeen, looking out on the site of his most important military victory. Stilgar had joined him for the upcoming victory ceremony here, after which they would meet with other military advisers to discuss the most effective uses for the elite Fremen warriors. Gurney Halleck had already taken an enthusiastic regiment of fighters to Galacia, but there were many more conquests to plan.

And Paul knew the Jihad was just beginning.

He had demanded and obtained records from the Spacing Guild, notations of thousands of planetary systems, so many worlds that only a Mentat could remember them all. He also had full CHOAM company records, since he controlled the majority share, with his Directorship overshadowing all the others combined.

He doubted if Shaddam IV had ever truly grasped the size of his own Imperium, the wealth and territory over which he supposedly ruled. Paul was certain that the Guild and CHOAM kept some profits hidden; whole planets not marked on any charts, their locations known only to the best Steersmen, were used as hiding places for weapons caches, perhaps even stockpiles of confiscated family atomics. All of these planets had to be encompassed in the government of Muad'Dib.

The Battle of Arrakeen now seemed minuscule in comparison with the subsequent clashes that were being fought in Paul's name. Many thousands had died here, yes, but that was the merest fraction of the numbers that were perishing in ongoing fights across the galaxy.

Even so, the significance of the victory on this battlefield had been tremendous, and pivotal. Here, the notorious Baron Harkonnen had perished. Here, the Sardaukar had suffered their first defeat in history. Here, a proud Corrino Emperor had surrendered.

Now the unrelenting sun hung directly overhead, heating the sandy and rocky slopes below, where another crowd had gathered to see Muad'Dib. The observers wore stillsuits, most of which were fitted in the traditional Fremen style, unlike the replicas sold to pilgrims. Water and souvenir vendors worked the noisy crowd, calling out as they hawked their wares. Colorful banners fluttered in a hot breeze. Everyone waited for him to address the multitudes.

Paul said quietly to Stilgar, who stood like a weathered rock, "The lines of good and evil were clearly drawn when we fought on the plains of Arrakeen, Stil. We knew where we stood against the allied Houses, and used the moral high ground to rally and inspire our fighters. But so many are already dead in my Jihad, many of them innocents. In time, they will say I was worse than the Corrinos and Harkonnens ever were."

Stilgar looked scandalized, his convictions unshaken even after what he had seen in the sacking of Kaitain. "Usul! We use violence only to cleanse, to wash away evil and save lives. Many more would die if not for your Jihad. You know this. Your prescience has told you so."

"It is as you say, but I worry that there is something I have not considered, another path I should have chosen instead. I cannot merely accept anything. I must keep searching."

"In dreams?"

"With conscious prescience, too, and Mentat logic. But everything guides me back to the same path."

"Then there is no other path, Usul."

Paul smiled at the statement. If only he could be as utterly certain as Stilgar was; the naib had always been a man of absolutes.

When it was time to speak to the crowd, Paul mounted the steps of the immense monument that had been erected in his honor, a life-size replica of a sandworm sculpted by a renowned—and enthusiastically converted—sculptor from Chusuk. Plaques around its base carried the names of every world that had surrendered to Muad'Dib so far. There were many more blank plaques in anticipation of more victories.

Right now, a performance was required. Carrying a maker hook, though only as a prop, Paul mounted steps on the side of the gray plastone beast whose eyeless head turned toward the basin below and the sprawling city of Arrakeen. With his own symbolic maker hook, Stilgar followed.

When the two stood side by side atop the head of the replica worm, they secured their hooks into sculpted rings and posed as if they were again riding the behemoth to victory. Behind them on the back of the statue, real Fremen soldiers stood in similar postures. The soldiers' cheers were echoed by the crowd in a growing sonic tumult that could be heard all the way to the city.

Years ago, when preparing his son for dangers on Arrakis, Duke Leto had advised him to capitalize on the local superstition that Paul might be the long-awaited Mahdi, the Lisan-al-Gaib. But only if he had to. Now, he had done that to an extent that went far beyond anything his father had ever anticipated.

Paul's voice boomed out, transmitted by speakers on the worm. "I come here today in all humility to honor those Fremen and Atreides soldiers who died on the Shield Wall and in the basin below, fighting to free us from tyranny." The crowd let out a huge roar of approval, but he raised his hands to quiet them. "Know this from the lips of Muad'Dib. We have won the opening battles of the Jihad, but there are many more to be fought."

The holy war was becoming a living organism with its own momentum, and he had been its catalyst. Paul knew there were also moral battles to be won, challenges that promised no clear victors and losers, only murky results. One day when this phase of the Jihad was complete, there would be time for reflection, a time for the people to recognize his failings and weaknesses as a ruler, that he was not a god. That would be the beginning of understanding . . . but it would take a very long time.

Finished with the ceremonial requirements, Paul and Stilgar climbed back down the steps. The bearded Fremen reported good news. "Muad'Dib, as you expected and hoped, Ecaz surrendered to us immediately without any bloodshed. Your address to the Landsraad reminded the old Archduke of his loyalties and obligations to House Atreides. He has sent his representative to deliver his fealty in person. The delegate claims he knew you when you were but a boy."

Curious, Paul looked to where a rangy man stood at the base of the statue, dressed in the fashion of a Swordmaster, with embellished decorations, epaulets, and billowing lavender pantaloons that made him appear to be a dandy. The man seemed familiar, especially when he removed his feathered, broad-brimmed hat and bowed with a flourish. "Muad'Dib may not remember me . . . but Paul Atreides should."

Now he recognized the balding Whitmore Bludd, a
man with a purple birthmark on his forehead. He was one
of the most capable fighters in the history of Ginaz. Duncan Idaho had studied under him, and Bludd had served
as a ronin for House Ecaz for many years. "Swordmaster
Bludd! How could I forget you from my father's War of
Assassins against Grumman?"

"Ah, those were magnificent, heroic days." The foppish man unrolled a signed surrender parchment. "Ecaz
has always supported the Atreides. We owe you a debt
of honor, and blood. Of course, we accept you as the
new Emperor."

Forsaking formalities, Paul threw his arms around the
Swordmaster (much to the horror of the guards), and
said, "You helped *us*. You defended us."

Blushing, Bludd stepped back and said, "I insist it
was the other way around, my Lord. Sadly, I am all that
remains of a once-great House, just an old warrior with
my glory days confined to memory. The recent trip to
Kaitain proved a bit too much for the Archduke, and he
has retired to his home." Next, Bludd extended a small
ornamental box. "However, I brought a gift for you from
Ecaz, as a token of my allegiance."

"The box has already been inspected, Usul," Stilgar
said quietly.

Paul lifted the lid and saw a pinkish seashell fragment
the size of his own hand. Smiling, Bludd explained,
"The remains of a conch shell from Mother Earth. See
how light dances across the surface. Archduke Armand
owned it for years—now it is yours."

Paul ran a hand over the smooth, pearly luster. The
touch gave him an odd but pleasing sensation that he
was in contact with an article from the birthworld of humanity. He handed the box to a nearby Fedaykin guard.
"Have this delivered to my apartments."

Bludd spoke in a conversational, relaxed tone, "It's

frightfully hot on this planet. Fortunately, I'm not a man who perspires much, or I'd be drained to the last drop."

"This is Dune, Swordmaster. From now on, you would be wise to wear a stillsuit," Paul said. Undeniably, Bludd was a dandy, but Paul had always admired the man anyway, not only for his fighting skills and loyalty, but for his organizational talents. Interesting possibilities rolled through the Emperor's mind.

In the past weeks, he had begun to accumulate the manpower and resources he needed for the construction of his huge new palace. While Korba had expressed an interest in guiding the project "for the glory and legend of Muad'Dib," Paul wasn't entirely sure that the zealous Fedaykin had the large-scale management skills or construction experience to oversee such a mammoth project. But Whitmore Bludd, in spite of his extravagant tastes, was a no-nonsense man and quite talented. He had a knack for getting things done. Duncan Idaho had always spoken highly of him.

"I would like you to remain here with us, Swordmaster Bludd. I can use someone with your talents to oversee a construction project far superior to anything the Corrinos ever built." He explained briefly what he desired for his new Palace, then said, "I want your vision and your dedication."

Bludd took a step backward in comical astonishment. "You would entrust me with such a fabulous undertaking, my Lord? Of course I accept the challenge! Why, I will create a citadel so grand it will strike even God himself with awe!"

"I think that'll be just about good enough for Korba," Paul said with a wry smile.

So many worlds were once the subject of songs and poems. Now, alas, they seem better suited to inspire dirges and epitaphs.

—GURNEY HALLECK, *Battlefield Poetry*

In quieter times, Gurney had often played ballads about Galacia's beautiful and supposedly wanton women, but he had never before visited the small, cool world. Until now. Unfortunately, he saw more carnage than beauty. Part of it was his own fault, for promoting Enno too quickly to the rank of lieutenant—after the young soldier's near-drowning in the practice pool.

In his new position, Enno showed a proclivity for issuing orders, demanding that the fighters carry out what he saw as Muad'Dib's vision. Since his return from the dead, Enno believed that he had a holy purpose. His presence and charisma had visibly increased, and his Fremen comrades viewed him with awe. This proved to be a problem for Gurney.

After the battle frigates landed on Galacia, warriors ran through the streets of the village and marketplace that surrounded the colonnaded villa of Lord Colus, the planet's Landsraad representative. With the soldiers of Muad'Dib coming toward them like D-wolves, the villagers barricaded themselves inside their homes. A few foolhardy souls stood with makeshift weapons, trying to defend their families, but the Fremen dealt harshly with any perceived resistance.

Though Gurney was technically in charge, his control over these fighters became tenuous once they scented blood. The men took great glee in planting green-and-white banners while tearing down and defacing any signs of the ruling house of Galacia. He waded among the soldiers, using his best stage voice to command them to restrain themselves.

One Fremen soldier repeatedly pummeled the blood-ied mouth of a woman who wouldn't stop screaming. Her husband lay dead on the floor next to her, his throat slashed by a crysknife. Gurney grabbed the brutal sol-dier by the back of his collar and swung his head against the doorframe, cracking his skull with a sickening sound. The woman looked up at Gurney and, instead of show-ing any gratitude, screamed again, spraying blood from her broken teeth. Then she ran into the house and barri-caded the door.

Gurney's face was red, the inkvine scar pulsing dark on his jawline. This was the sort of thing Harkonnen troops had done during their slave-gathering parties, go-ing from village to village and brutalizing the people.

"Form ranks!" he bellowed. "Give the Galacians a chance to surrender, by the Seven Hells!"

"They are resisting us, Commander Halleck," Enno said with maddening calm. "We must show them they have no hope. They shall know the despair that Muad'Dib brings to all who stand against him."

The fighters had begun to set fire to any home whose inhabitants dared to bar the doors and windows against the invading army. The people inside would be roasted alive. Gurney heard the shrieks and saw the animal wild-ness of the unfettered army.

Though he had trained them himself, Gurney was

infuriated by their ferocity. It was all so unnecessary! But if he pushed too hard against their wild frenzy, he feared that they might turn against *him,* labeling him a heretic and a traitor to Muad'Dib.

This type of warfare bore no semblance of the code of morality and integrity that Duke Leto Atreides had demanded of his followers. How could Paul allow this to happen?

The jihadis had moved through the village, all the way up a central hill to the governmental villa. Lord Colus had barricaded himself inside his arched home and stationed household guards at every door. From within the villa, his private army could hold off an invading force, though not for long. Even the besieged nobleman seemed to realize that. Gurney moved to take charge of the situation before the mob could do further damage.

The nobleman's guards did not fire their weapons, but simply maintained defensive positions. Colus had taken down the pennants bearing the gold-and-red family crest of his house. When he raised the surrender flag, the Fremen howled and cheered and raced toward the barricaded entrance. But the gates would not open, no matter how hard the soldiers pounded against them.

Lord Colus stepped out onto a high balcony. It was dusk, and the fires in the village tinged the sky orange as the air filled with rising smoke. The nobleman's face was deeply lined; his thick gray hair was long enough to fall between his shoulder blades, secured in a tight braid. He looked weary and distraught. "I would offer my surrender, but never to animals! You have massacred my people and the village is on fire. For what? They were no threat to you."

"Surrender to us, and we will stop fighting," Enno called, grinning at Gurney. The young officer's uniform hung loosely on his rail-thin body.

"You, I do not trust! I will surrender only to the honorable Gurney Halleck. I see him there among you! I demand terms. The forms must be obeyed!"

Gurney pushed his way forward. "I am Halleck, and I accept your surrender." He turned to the Fremen. "The forms must be obeyed. Stop the bloodshed. This planet is ours, our victory already won. Go put out those fires!"

"Old Imperial rules mean nothing to us, Commander Halleck," Enno grumbled.

"It is the will of Muad'Dib." *Let them chew on that!* Gurney strode up to the gates, and Lord Colus's guards lifted the bars to open the doorway. The Atreides veteran stepped through the looming arch, and the proud nobleman came down to greet him.

But Fremen soldiers rushed in around Gurney, and he couldn't stop the tide. They flocked into the fortified villa, seized Galacian guards, and grabbed Lord Colus. The nobleman appeared saddened, but clung to his dignity as he was taken away.

❧

BY THE FOLLOWING day, the fires had been quelled and the villagers subdued, and the Fremen soldiers had temporarily taken over whatever dwellings they desired. These determined desert warriors knew how to fight, but they did not know how to govern or rebuild.

Gurney had spent a sleepless night staring up at the rough ceiling of one of the outbuildings of the estate, considering what to do. It would be best for the people of Galacia if he led the Fremen to another battlefield as soon as possible, rather than allowing the conquerors to remain here and make things worse. This defeated world would cause no further trouble for Paul's government. Gurney doubted they would have caused any in the first place. . . .

Gurney emerged from his borrowed bedchamber in the dawn light only to stare in disbelief at the severed head of Lord Colus, which was planted on a post in front of the mansion. The expression on the dead nobleman's face looked more like disappointment than fear. His eyes stared out on a world he no longer inhabited.

Appalled and revolted, yet strangely unsurprised, Gurney stepped forward with sad resignation. His muscles bunching, his fists clenching, the loyal Atreides retainer stared up at Lord Colus's slack face. "I am sorry—this was never what I intended." He intoned a verse from the Orange Catholic Bible, posing an age-old question: " 'Who is worse, the liar or the fool who believes him?' "

He had given his word to Lord Colus, who had trusted in the value of a promise made by Gurney Halleck. Now, Gurney's revulsion turned toward himself. *I am not a man to make excuses, certainly not for my own actions.* I *am in command of these soldiers. I serve Paul of House Atreides.*

The Atreides considered an "honor debt" as binding as any Fremen viewed a water debt to be. His lieutenant Enno had brought dishonor to his regiment and its commander; he had made Gurney into a liar. *This is* my *responsibility.*

In previous engagements, he had seen the blind and stubborn fury of the Jihad troops. Spurning accepted codes of warfare, they charged ahead with only vague goals and a hunger for destruction. Like maddened Salusan bulls, they stampeded any perceived enemy. Paul's most vehement supporters never stopped to think beyond rationalizing that their actions were in concert with Muad'Dib's wishes. Trying to stop them would be like trying to stop moving dunes in a powerful sandstorm. . . .

Gurney's brows drew together, and his expression became terrible to behold. He refused to salve his conscience with a weak explanation that he was not, after all, expected to control fanatics.

He was the commander; they were *his* soldiers.

And soldiers must follow orders. Enno and the Fremen had heard his explicit orders. They could not feign confusion or pretend to have misunderstood his promise. Enno had committed mutiny. He had defied the clear instructions of his superior officer.

Not even turning to see who might be listening, Gurney roared a command in a voice that had once filled noisy halls with song. "Bring me Enno—immediately! And put him in chains!" Though he did not stop looking at the head of Lord Colus, he heard several Fremen scurry off into the growing daylight in response to his instructions.

As a leader of Fremen regiments, Gurney Halleck kept a crysknife sheathed at his waist, but he did not reach for it. Instead, he drew a different blade, a well-worn kindjal with an Atreides hawk worked into the hilt. Because this was a matter of honor, an Atreides knife would work best.

Eventually, four Fremen soldiers escorted Enno to him. As he walked along, the young man looked aloof and proud, his eyes shining with conviction. Though two soldiers held Enno's arms, the prisoner was not shackled, as Gurney had ordered. The shades of Thufir Hawat and Duncan Idaho must be laughing at him now for letting his troops slip out of his control.

"Why is this man not in chains? Were my instructions not clear?" he shouted, and the Fremen soldiers flinched, taking offense at his tone. Two of them let their hands stray toward their own crysknives. Gurney stepped toward them, his inkvine scar darkening on his face. "I am your commanding officer! Muad'Dib gave you orders—orders *on your lives,* damn you!—to follow my instructions. *I* act in the name of Muad'Dib. Who are you to question me?"

Enno, though, was the main problem, and Gurney

would deal with the other insubordination later. Pointing at the grisly trophy atop the gatepost, he demanded, "Did I not accept this man's surrender? Did I not grant him terms?"

"You did, Commander Halleck. But—"

"There is no 'but' in a command! You are a subordinate officer, and you have defied my orders. Therefore you have defied the orders of Muad'Dib."

While the Fremen onlookers muttered at this, Enno retorted with great confidence, as if he were being tested. "Muad'Dib knows he must appear to be merciful. Muad'Dib knows he must show the people that he can be lenient and loving." His voice hardened. "But Muad'Dib's *fighters* know what is truly in his heart—that those who are unbelievers must fall under the scythe of his punishment. By promising mercy to Lord Colus, Commander Halleck, you may have spoken on the Emperor's behalf . . . but all soldiers of Muad'Dib understand what we must do to infidels. Colus resisted, and he ordered his people to resist. He was a dark force trying to eclipse the light of the Lisan-al-Gaib." He looked up at the severed head on the spike and nodded with plain satisfaction. "I did what was necessary, as you well know."

Gurney barely kept his fury in check. "What I know is that you defied me. The penalty for disobeying my orders is death. Kneel."

Enno's eyes flashed. He raised his chin in one more gesture of defiance. "I only did the will of Muad'Dib."

"Kneel!" When Enno did not immediately obey, Gurney motioned to the four escort soldiers who, after the briefest hesitation, pushed down on Enno's shoulders, forcing him to his knees. Gurney took the Atreides kindjal and assumed a fighting stance with it.

"I was doing the will of Muad'Dib," Enno intoned, like a prayer.

"He was doing the will of Muad'Dib," one of the soldiers said. But he and his companions stepped back, out of the way.

Before events could slip out of his control again, Gurney slashed sideways with the razor-edged knife. The blade bit deep, tearing across Enno's throat, severing the jugular and the carotid, sawing through the windpipe.

Normally, a red spray would have sprouted from the larynx like the tail of a flamebird, but the thick blood and the rapid coagulation in the Fremen genes slowed the flow somewhat, so that crimson merely bubbled and poured out, spilling across Enno's chest and the Galacian ground. Although the defiant man twitched and gurgled, his gaze never left Gurney's until he collapsed.

As the Fremen soldiers stared at what he had done, Gurney felt a thousandfold increase in his own personal danger. So be it. He could not permit such a lack of discipline to go unpunished. He stood, looking for a moment at the blood on the kindjal and on his hand, then turned to the surprised and angry-looking men. One muttered, "He was only doing the will of—"

"*I* am the will of Muad'Dib!" Gurney scowled down at the body, then looked up at the trophy on the post. "Take away Lord Colus's head and see that his people have it for a proper burial. As for Enno, you may carry his body and his water back to Dune, but his head remains here." He pointed. "On the spike."

From the uneasy muttering, Gurney knew that the superstitious Fremen would fear that an angry ghost might follow them. Gurney looked directly at the corpse as he spoke. "And if Enno's shade has something to say to me, then he can follow me as he wishes. You men are merely following my orders, as *every* soldier is required to do."

He stalked off, but the disgust and dismay in the pit of his stomach only increased. He suspected that the Fremen would portray Enno as a martyr, a man not only blessed because he had drowned and come back to life, but also a veritable holy man who had disobeyed his non-Fremen commander in order to do what Muad'Dib would have wanted.

Gurney knew Paul Atreides well, however, and knew the young Emperor was not nearly so bloodthirsty and vicious as his followers believed him to be. Not in his heart, anyway.

Gurney fervently prayed that he was not wrong in his own heart.

*Both the Bene Gesserit and the Tleilaxu are fix-
ated on the advancement of their own breeding
programs. The Sisterhood's records encompass
thousands of years as they seek to perfect humanity for their own purposes. The Tleilaxu have
more commercial aims in their genetic research—
producing gholas, Twisted Mentats, artificial eyes,
and other biological products that are sold around
the Imperium at great profit. We advise extreme
caution in dealing with either group.*

—excerpt from a CHOAM report

A military officer arrived unexpectedly at Tleilax, an-
nouncing that he was on the "business of the Emperor" and demanding to see Count Hasimir Fenring.

Fenring did not like surprises. Agitated, he rode in a
tubecar that sped away from the noxious expanse of the
dead lake and across the plain from Thalidei to the isolated spaceport where the visitor had been allowed to
land. What could this possibly mean? He had taken great
pains to keep his location a secret, but there seemed no
limit to the reach and influence of Muad'Dib.

He arrived at a high, one-story structure built of black
plasmeld that was fronted with an array of tinted windows. With its curved surfaces and organic shape, the
building looked like something that a worm might have
excreted.

He entered the lobby, and two lower-caste Tleilaxu
guided him across the glistening black floor. His escorts
seemed just as displeased by the unannounced visitor. In
the small and stuffy cafeteria, Fenring was surprised to
see a familiar, craggy-faced man. It had been years since

they'd seen each other, and it took him a moment to recall the correct name. "Bashar Zum Garon?"

The officer rose from a table where he had been drinking an oily-looking beverage. "You are a difficult person to locate, Count Fenring."

"Hmm-ahhh, intentionally so. But I should know not to underestimate the resourcefulness of a Sardaukar officer."

"No, you should not. I come at the request of Emperor Shaddam."

"Hmm-m-m, not the Emperor I expected. How did you find me?"

"Shaddam ordered it."

"And a loyal Sardaukar always follows orders, hmmm? You are still in charge of Shaddam's personal guard?"

"What little is left of it, barely more than a police force." Garon did not look happy. "I commanded the most powerful military force in the Imperium, until Muad'Dib and his fanatical Fedaykin defeated us. Now I am the glorified equivalent of a security guard." He regained his composure but not before Fenring saw the swift, sharp flicker of hatred there. "Sit with me. The Tleilaxu tea is palatable."

"I know the stuff well." Fenring had grown to loathe its faint licorice undertaste almost as much as he loathed the aftertaste of all his dealings with Shaddam. Time and again, the Emperor had stumbled into traps of his own making—and time and again, Fenring had used his resources and wiles to repair the damage. Even after the original Arrakis Affair, when the Harkonnens and the Sardaukar troops should have wiped out House Atreides, Fenring had spent more than a billion solaris on gifts, slave women, spice bribes, and tokens of rank. Squandered money and resources. Now, though, his former friend had fallen into a pit so deep he could never claw his way out.

Fenring slid into a hard plasmeld chair that was too low to the floor, designed for the shorter Tleilaxu Masters. He waited for the Bashar to explain his business. Only one other cafeteria table was occupied, by a Tleilaxu man who ate stew in a rapid and messy fashion.

Garon stirred his tea, but didn't drink. "I spent many years in Imperial service. Then, after the death of my son Cando defending Shaddam's amal project . . ." His voice trailed off, but he regained his composure. "After that, I voluntarily stripped off all marks of my former rank and departed from Kaitain, expecting never to return. For a time I retired to my estate on Balut, but that didn't last long before Muad'Dib ordered me back into service and assigned me to Shaddam. It seems that the former Padishah Emperor was insisting that I take charge of security in his exile. Not only did he kill my son, but he foolishly led the Sardaukar to suffer their first-ever military defeat."

The Count clearly remembered the catastrophic end of the amal project, "Your son died valiantly in the defense of Ix. He showed great courage leading a Sardaukar charge against overwhelming odds."

"My son died trying to protect an idiotic, greedy attempt to develop and monopolize artificial spice."

"Hmm-ahh, and does Shaddam know you feel this way?"

"He does not. If I had my son's courage, I would tell him so. Shaddam says he has fond memories of my flawless loyalty." Garon cleared his throat, changed the subject, but the bitter tone remained in his voice. "Regardless, he sent me to find you and deliver a message. Shaddam wishes you to know that he still holds you in the highest esteem. He reminds you that he allowed his Imperial daughter Wensicia to marry your cousin Dalak."

"Yes, I know." He thought back, trying to remember

his cousin. "I haven't seen Dalak since he was a boy. I believe I taught him some fighting techniques, even spent some time counseling him about the politics of the Imperium. A good boy. Not the brightest student, but he showed some promise."

Shaddam had allowed his third daughter to marry *him*? A true sign of desperation, obviously intended to influence Fenring. Did that mean there might soon be a Corrino heir with Fenring blood? He darkened. "I do not like to be manipulated."

"No one does. Even so, Shaddam begs you to return to him. He needs your counsel and friendship."

Fenring did not doubt what Shaddam must have in mind. The Count resented the fallen Emperor for his insistence on ill-advised plans as much as Bashar Garon did. *Shaddam has a dangerous sort of intelligence that leads him to believe he is much smarter than he actually is. This causes him to make serious mistakes.*

Garon drew an ornate, jewel-handled knife from his sleeve. Fenring's muscles tightened. *Has he been sent to assassinate me?* He placed his hand over the concealed needle launcher in his sleeve.

But the Bashar just slid the knife across the table, jeweled hilt first. "This is yours now, a gift from your boyhood friend. He said you would recognize it, know its significance."

"Yes, I am familiar with this." The Count turned it over to examine the sharp edge of the blade. "Shaddam presented it to Duke Leto at the Trial By Forfeiture, and later the Duke gave it back to him."

"More importantly, it is the knife with which Feyd Rautha-Harkonnen dueled Muad'Dib."

"Ahh, and if that Harkonnen pup had fought better, none of us would be here. Not that Shaddam would have continued to be anything but an unremarkable ruler."

"At least the Imperium would be stable and not torn

apart by Muad'Dib's growing Jihad," Garon said quietly.

And Feyd would still be alive . . . Marie's true father. But few people knew that.

"'Honor and the legion,'" Fenring said pensively. It was a Sardaukar motto.

"Precisely. A Sardaukar never dishonors himself, even though Shaddam has brought dishonor upon us. He remains oblivious to how much resentment his remaining Sardaukar feel toward him."

A smile worked its way across Fenring's narrow face. "Entire library planets could be filled with the things Shaddam doesn't know."

Garon finally took a sip of tea. "His foolishness has cost both of us. A man never gets over losing his son, or his honor."

"And now you are torn by your oath as a Sardaukar, your duty to serve the Corrinos, and your memories of your son."

"You understand me too well."

"If you and I had made the decisions, ahhh, we might have prevented the rise of Muad'Dib. But there are still things we can do, hmm? We have an opportunity here, you and I. If he were removed from the equation, being clever and resourceful, we could easily manipulate the ensuing turmoil to our own ends."

The old Bashar studied Fenring. "You suggest that we work together? You will return to Salusa Secundus, then?"

Fenring stared at the jewel-handled knife. "Tell the Emperor that while I appreciate his offer, my answer must be no, for the time being. I have other . . . opportunities here, and I intend to pursue them."

"Shaddam will be angry that I have failed in my mission."

"Hmm, then leave open the possibility that I *might*

change my mind. Keep him on nice, sharp tenterhooks. To maintain that illusion, I'll keep his gift of the knife. I know the way he thinks. He will, ahhh, believe that I owe him a favor in return. In the meantime, my darling little daughter requires a great deal of shaping and instruction."

"And what significance does this daughter hold?"

Sardaukar had such a tendency to see everything in black-and-white terms! "She has a great deal of significance, my dear Bashar. What if we were to bypass the fool on Salusa and find a way to overthrow Paul-Muad'Dib ourselves?"

Garon sat back in his chair, struggling not to show his shock. "Harsh times require harsh actions."

Fenring pressed his point. "Shaddam's failings as an Emperor left the people so eager to replace him that a violent upstart such as Muad'Dib could step into the vacuum, bolstered by his fanatics. Now, however, it's becoming clear that Muad'Dib may be worse than Shaddam ever was—and we need to stop the slaughter any way we can, and establish a new order."

Garon inhaled a long, deep breath, and nodded. "We must take the course of honor. In doing so, we can reverse a great wrong that is being committed against humanity. We are honor-bound to make the effort."

Fenring extended his hand across the table, and Garon grasped it firmly. Personally, the Count didn't care *that* much about honor, but this old soldier certainly did. It was both Bashar Zum Garon's strength, and his weakness. It only remained for Fenring to work out the details and put a plan into action.

He stood on the balcony, a lonely figure.

Late at night, the lights of Arakeen were low and a rising First Moon cast long shadows across the burgeoning city to the desert escarpments beyond. High on the ridge line, a delta of sand creased the broad expanse of the Shield Wall, where Paul had shattered the barrier with atomics to allow attacking sandworms into the basin. The Shield Wall was a natural object that had been blasted in battle by a mere man. *A mere man.*

The people did not see him as such. The young Emperor returned to bed but lay awake, restless. Countless military campaigns remained to be fought across the galaxy, and Paul-Muad'Dib was their inspiration on the path to eternal glory. Fremen would not let themselves see any frailties in their messiah.

Sometimes his prescient visions were only general impressions, other times vivid images and specific scenes. The Jihad itself had always been like a high mountain range across his life's path—unavoidable, dangerous. He had tried to deny it initially, but then he had forged ahead, facing the difficulties, the treacherous cliffs, the unexpected storms. He was the guide for the human race, wanting to lead them through safe passes, but knowing he could not avoid every avalanche, flash flood, rockfall, or lightning strike. Race consciousness demanded otherwise. His own terrible purpose demanded otherwise. No matter what choices he made, a great many would still perish before they reached the promised land beyond.

Paul envisioned an energy-force of pomp, ostentation, and bureaucracy that would grow around him. The signs were already apparent. At first, this would wear the guise of a powerful and necessary machine, but it would eventually metastasize and grow like a cancer. For a time, he knew he must accept the malignancy because it would fuel the Jihad.

Already, Dune was the hub of the new universe. Millions and millions of pilgrims would come here on hajj. Important decisions would be made on this hallowed ground, and from here Muad'Dib's legions would continue to be dispatched to the farthest reaches in order to enforce his wishes.

From Arrakeen, the newly planned Citadel of Muad'Dib would radiate light all across the galaxy. His palace would be enormous and breathtaking. The people, and history, demanded it.

Old neighborhoods and disjointed slums had already been razed to make room for the colossal structure. After dawn that day, construction was slated to begin.

~⊱~

THE OLD ARRAKEEN Residency would form the core of the huge building, but before long the new palace would swallow all external traces of the original home of House Atreides on Arrakis, once also the long-term base of Count Fenring and Lady Margot. Paul stood with an intense Korba and an exuberant Whitmore Bludd inside a vaulted chamber, watching the reactions of both Chani and Irulan.

Swordmaster Bludd proudly displayed shimmering projection models of the buildings, gardens, and avenues of the future Citadel of Muad'Dib. The plans alone were large enough to fill much of the room. Projection technicians busily put finishing touches on some of the models, monitored by the watchful eyes of assistant architects.

Bludd had done a remarkable job of balancing the wishes and ideas of so many people, while maintaining his personal vision for "humanity's greatest architectural triumph." For many years already, he had served as a de facto manager of all of Archduke Ecaz's holdings, and now he would coordinate the armies of workers, the flow of materials, and the budget (though even the poorest waifs sleeping on the dry streets of Arrakeen willingly offered their last coins to Muad'Dib).

Speaking on behalf of the Qizarate, Korba provided input on four immense temples that would be constructed on the grounds and connected to the main citadel complex blossoming around the old mansion. Even before the first great walls had been raised, he insisted on ornamenting the city-sized structure with religious statuary and various objects of a spiritual nature. "Every facet of the citadel must enlarge the persona and legend of the Emperor Muad'Dib, elevating him to his appropriate stature."

Glancing at Korba, Paul thought of his remaining Fedaykin, remembering the purity of their devotion. Back when the battles had been straightforward and the enemies clearly identified—Harkonnens, Sardaukar—they had sworn their lives to defend him. Many of those elite fighters were even now engaged in battles of the Jihad—the loyal Otheym, Tandis, Rajifiri, and Saajid. Knowing their skills and bravery, he had reserved his Fremen—a mere fraction of his fighting force—for the most diffi-cult conquests, the bloodiest engagements.

But Korba, though also a Fedaykin, had chosen a dif-ferent path to glory. Though subtle, the man's motives were transparent to Paul: While a warrior was just a war-rior, the head of a religion wielded a more sustainable power in the ever-widening circle of Muad'Dib's influ-ence and the increasing number of conquered or allied subjects. By fostering the development of the Qizarate, giving new and zealous priests teachings and rules to enforce, Korba created and held his own moral high ground—in the name of Muad'Dib.

In spite of the sour taste that development left in his mouth, Paul needed all of the energy that religion could provide. And he knew that he, too, had to keep up ap-pearances.

With Chani at his side, Paul walked from table to table and looked over the model structures, focusing on the multiple domes and soaring arches. A cutaway showed where a Celestial Audience Chamber would house his pri-mary throne. "Some of the individual chambers will be so large that kingly palaces could fit inside them. The entire complex is designed to be a vast fortified city, both to pro-tect its inhabitants and to impress outsiders."

The flamboyant Swordmaster used his own rapier as a pointer to show Irulan how her private gardens would be laid out, including "contemplation offices" where she could continue her writing. Paul noted the pride in the man's demeanor as he explained his grand dream, and the Princess seemed suitably impressed.

Chani glanced sidelong at Irulan. "Perhaps such things were expected in the old Imperium, but we do not need such a place, Usul. Fremen would consider this sort of extravagance . . . greedy, in the manner of off-worlders."

"No extravagance is too great for Muad'Dib," Korba

insisted. "The people will settle for nothing less than the greatest work of construction in human history."

Sadly, Paul knew that Korba was right.

Bludd cleared his throat loudly. "Those were my instructions, and that is what it shall be. From the central core, the rest of the construction will blossom like a beautiful flower in the desert." Though they had radically conflicting personalities, Korba and Bludd were developing a grudging respect for each other during the early stages of the construction project. A common ambition and goal served as a balancing point between the men.

Paul took Chani's hand, and said to her, "Such extravagance is necessary, Beloved. The magnificence itself is a lever that can move the most stubborn doubters and the newly converted. Through sheer size, scope, and grandeur, my new fortress must inspire awe in the hearts of everyone who experiences it—even in us, who know its inner workings and design. Especially in us, perhaps, because we have to play our parts well, and I must play mine the best of all."

He clapped a hand on the fine fabric of the Swordmaster's waistcoat. "You have my wholehearted approval, Bludd. Yes, this palace will be built according to your plans. With each stone laid and each tapestry hung, we will strengthen the Jihad—and hasten its conclusion. I will make public appearances on my throne and from my balconies overlooking throngs of the faithful. These places must be incomparable in their opulence.

"My private quarters, however, will be simple." Paul gestured dismissively at the plans for the royal suite that seemed to drip ostentation. "When Chani and I retire to our chambers, there will be only those traditional amenities one might find in a sietch, articles and furnishings that typical Fremen would use. In private we shall remember our roots."

Bludd and Korba looked at him in alarm, while Irulan

came closer. "My Husband, the people expect you to live as an Emperor, not as a tribal chieftain. The entire citadel, including your living quarters, should show all humankind how great and powerful Muad'Dib is. My father's royal wing in the old Imperial Palace could be a model for you."

"The simplicity of a sietch is enough for us, in our private quarters," Chani insisted, and Paul agreed, ending the discussion. His concubine had always been less comfortable in cities, in gigantic and ornate structures. "Even though he is the Emperor, Muad'Dib is still one of the people."

Yes, he thought. *My father would have liked the sound of that.*

I was destined for greatness, not to be a mere foot-note in history.

—MASTER WHITMORE BLUDD, *Personal Diaries and Observations, Volume VII*

The storehouse of expensive wine was part of the vast trove of spoils the armies of Muad'Dib were already bringing back to Arrakis. Whitmore Bludd found the uncatalogued cache during his work of managing the materials and overseeing the huge citadel construction project.

He perused the labels on the bottles, noting the vintages with growing admiration and amazement. He doubted the uncouth Fremen had any idea of the value of what they had found. They had piled the seized bottles without any sort of inventory list or temperature control.

These desert fanatics had no appreciation, no taste, no finesse. They would not know the difference between a crisp, delicate Caladanian white and a robust chianti from the greenhouse vineyards of IV Anbus. As he examined case after case of bottles inside the storehouse, Bludd realized he could not, in good conscience, let such a treasure go to waste.

Now, finding a rough-red table wine meant to be drunk in quantity rather than savored, he decided the Fremen might enjoy that more than anything too sophisticated.

Or perhaps one of the syrupy muscats. When he came across a bottle of genuine Kirana champagne, he set it aside with the fine vintages. He couldn't allow *that* to be wasted on a desert rat's unsophisticated palate!

For tonight, Bludd settled on an enhanced claret he had tasted years ago, when he and his fellow Swordmaster Rivvy Dinari had toasted their service to Archduke Armand Ecaz. The corpulent Dinari had considered the vintage exceptional, and Bludd had fond memories of that evening, owing more to the fellowship and the situation than to the wine's quality. Dinari, for all his girth, claimed to have quite a discriminating palate, although he did seem to prefer both quantity *and* quality.

Bludd had already changed into his evening clothes: a tailored maroon jacket, a belted black tunic with ruffled collar, tight black pants, and knee-high suede boots that matched the color of the jacket. As always, his long rapier hung at his hip, a weapon that was both decorative and deadly. He hefted the case of wine, balancing it on his other hip, and walked out of the storehouse with as much grace as he could summon. If these desert fighters were capable of enjoying good things—not at all a certainty—he would endear himself to them, and they would all have a fine time swapping tales of their exploits.

In a celebratory mood, he brought the wine and his own corkscrew, as well as a case of stemmed glasses, to the Fremen barracks. Smiling, he lifted out the bottles so that he could share the vintage, but the Fremen regarded him suspiciously. They accepted Bludd as one of Muad'Dib's special advisers and a long-time acquaintance, yet the overdressed Swordmaster did not match their notion of a warrior.

He sniffed and quickly hid his distaste for all the smells around him. As members of Paul's elite military stationed here on Arrakeen, they had access to enough water to bathe at least once in a while!

"I have brought fine wine from the stores of Emperor Paul Atreides"—he shrugged quickly—"or Muad'Dib, if that's what you prefer to call him. Does anyone wish to partake?" Bludd began to pour glasses and gestured for the dusty Fremen soldiers to take them, one by one. "It is tradition among Swordmasters to share a glass of good wine while we exchange our stories of battle. Having been a primary instructor at the Ginaz School, I later became one of the two highest ranking swordfighters in the Ecazi court."

Half a dozen Fremen picked up the glasses and looked at them. One, a Fedaykin named Elias, took a gulp and made a face.

"Not like that!" Bludd snapped, losing patience. "Examine its rich color, inhale its magnificent bouquet. Take a little sip. Allow the flavors to separate on your palate. This isn't one of your coarse spice beers." Elias seemed offended by the rebuff, though Bludd pretended not to notice. He held up a wineglass, took a sip, and let out a long sigh. "So . . . the stories. Since you are so enamored of Paul-Muad'Dib, shall I tell you of the time my fellow Swordmasters Rivvy Dinari, Duncan Idaho, and I went with young Paul Atreides—I believe he was twelve years old then—down into the jungles of Ginaz, where we were attacked by giant caterpillars—"

"We know all about Duncan Idaho," one of the Fremen interrupted. "He died saving Muad'Dib during his flight from the Harkonnens. That was how he and his mother came to be among us."

"So Paul's told you this story, then?" Bludd looked around, but could not find any answers on the faces.

"We have read the book by Princess Irulan," replied one of the men. The others murmured solemn assent.

Bludd had read the book as well and felt that Irulan had left out a great many important things, even suggesting that Paul had never been away from the planet

Caladan before coming to Arrakis, ignoring all of his exploits on Ecaz! That and other errors. Bludd had already spoken to the Princess about them.

The Fremen were drinking the wine, though obviously out of a sense of obligation rather than enjoyment. Bludd tried again, suggesting another story that Irulan had not included in her original chronicle. "Or shall I tell you how the War of Assassins began in Castle Caladan, with a heinous attack by the Grummans? Several people died, including—" He sniffed, drew a breath. "Perhaps I shall not tell that story, either."

Bludd expected some of them to brag about their own exploits and tell their tall tales. But these Fremen were a dour bunch.

"This wine tastes like unfiltered urine," growled Elias, whom Bludd had offended. "If we run it through a reclamation unit, at least we can get the water back."

"My dear sir, this is a fine and expensive vintage. I am not surprised, however, that you cannot taste—"

Elias drew his crysknife, and the others fell immediately still. "You insult me!"

Bludd looked around, made a bored sigh. "Now, what?"

"It is a matter of honor," said one of the other men.

"You really don't want to do this, my good sir," Bludd said.

"Draw your blade!" Elias held his crysknife and took up a fighting stance.

With utmost calmness, Bludd slid the rapier from his belt. "Have I not made it quite clear that I am an accomplished Swordmaster of Ginaz? Your wormtooth dagger is pretty, but I have four times the reach." He flicked the rapier in the air for good measure.

"Are you a coward, then?"

"In a word . . . *no*." Bludd straightened his jacket, plucked at his black ruffles. "En garde, if you insist."

Elias lunged with the crysknife, to shouts and catcalls from his comrades. Though Bludd was dressed in fine clothes, the well-fitting garments gave him perfect ease of movement. He melted away from the man's vicious thrust. Then in a flash, he circled around and pricked the Fremen's shoulder.

"There, first blood is mine. Do you yield?"

The Fremen spectators chuckled. "Bad Bludd brags more than he fights! Bad Bludd!"

"My, what a feeble play on words." His voice dripped sarcasm.

The angry Fremen fighter slashed and lunged again with surprising speed. Elias tossed the knife to his other hand and struck. Ah, so he could fight with either hand, a useful skill! Bludd parried, scissored his blade in the air, twirled, and pricked the man's other shoulder. "You are fortunate that I have decided to restrain myself."

Bludd toyed with him for several more minutes, showing off, making sweeping, grandiose moves of the type he had taught his students never to risk using. Showmanship was one thing, but victory was paramount. It did no good to have fine form if your opponent lopped off your head.

But this opponent did not seem to weaken or tire and continued with a relentless, though pedestrian, style of fighting. When Bludd realized he was starting to grow tired himself, he decided to put an end to the silly dance. He had heard how easily Fremen pride could be wounded, and did not want this man to hold a simmering blood vendetta against him. He had to give him a way to save face.

Driving forward with a flurry of intricate sword work, Bludd flailed his flexible blade so that it dizzied Elias. Then Bludd intentionally stepped in too close. He had observed the man's style and knew how he would react. When he gave the Fremen an opportunity, just a hint of one, the crysknife flashed and cut a shallow gouge in the meat of Bludd's upper left arm. There, now the man could be satisfied that he too had drawn blood. Elias responded with a feral grin.

"That's enough, then." Bludd drove the flat of his blade down hard on the back of the Fremen's knife hand, forcing the fingers to release the handle. The wormtooth dagger dropped to the floor of the barracks.

One of the other Fremen soldiers stepped forward and kicked the crysknife beyond Elias's reach. "He beat you fairly, Elias, but you drew blood as well."

The Fremen looked bewildered and still angry. Another soldier added in a low voice, "Muad'Dib has commanded us to have no tribal rivalries."

"This peacock is of no Fremen tribe," Elias said.

"Muad'Dib wants his soldiers to fight the enemy, not each other."

"And fine advice that is." Bludd sheathed his rapier, picked up one of the unopened bottles of wine, and took it with him as he left the barracks. "Next time, perhaps I will just bring spice beer."

Never turn your back on a Tleilaxu.

—ancient saying

Lady Margot Fenring rode beside her young daughter in the rear compartment of a groundcar as it negotiated the winding streets of Thalidei. Lady Margot had ordered the driver to take them to one of the dockside public markets. She rarely went anywhere without her husband, but little Marie needed time away from her ever-watchful Bene Gesserit nanny and tutor. Though Margot could easily have defeated scores of Tleilaxu men, she was forbidden to travel without an escort, for her own "safety."

Little Marie sat high on a thick cushion designed for a Tleilaxu Master. She drank in the details outside, her wide eyes filled with curious questions, but the girl was already wise enough to look for her own answers. The Fenrings had developed plans for the unique girl, determined to see to it that Marie was equipped with a breadth of experiences and abilities. She had to be prepared and armed for her destiny.

The worker-caste Tleilaxu driver assigned to them expertly avoided hitting diminutive Masters who haughtily walked out into the street without looking. Clearly uncomfortable around females, the driver did not speak to his passengers; he may even have received instructions to ignore them. Unlike all other vehicles around the city, the one in which Margot and her daughter rode had dark-tinted windows, as if the Tleilaxu did not want a female to be seen out in the open.

When traveling with her husband, Margot was treated quite differently, accepted grudgingly if not welcomed. When she went out without him, though, the Tleilaxu seemed *offended* by her flagrant actions. She didn't care this time. Let them be offended. She'd lost count of the pinpricks of displeasure her reluctant hosts had inflicted on her. Margot had grown to loathe the bigoted high-caste men, but as an adept Bene Gesserit, she'd also learned to hide her true feelings.

The young towhead smiled up at her, then gazed out the low tinted window on her left, oblivious to her mother's concerns. Like Margot, she wore a long black dress, but she had pale blue eyes instead of gray-green. *Feyd's color,* Margot remembered, *though her eyes are not so sullen as his.*

The Harkonnen na-Baron had been an adequate lover, though not as skilled as he should have been, considering his repertoire of pleasure women. In light of later events, it was clear that Feyd was also not as skilled a fighter as he believed himself to be. Nevertheless, Margot had collected his seed and allowed herself to conceive a daughter as the Sisterhood had instructed her to do. Such perfect genetics from generations of Bene Gesserit coaxing human genetic stock. Yes, little Marie was indeed special.

During the year that the Fenrings had spent on Tleilax, Lady Margot had remained in touch with the Sisterhood, exchanging clandestine messages by letter or embedded in objects that were transported by courier between here and Wallach IX. She had no doubt that the nanny Obregah-Xo also sent secret reports.

Despite the Mother Superior's personal interest in this daughter of Feyd-Rautha, Margot had plans of her own. She did not intend to let the girl become a mere pawn of the Bene Gesserit. Since the arrival of Muad'Dib—a Kwisatz Haderach that the Sisterhood could not control—and his Abomination sister Alia, Margot Fenring had begun to lose faith in the overly complex and insufficiently successful schemes of the Bene Gesserit.

She and Hasimir had too many other ideas.

Lady Margot smiled at her daughter. The child had a bright and inquisitive mind, and learned quickly. Thanks to her mother's teachings, as well as those of Count Fenring and Obregah-Xo, the girl had already mastered Bene Gesserit skills that were far beyond her years.

The vehicle drove past a bustling marketplace of tents and shacks that extended out onto the docks, with vendors selling foods and personal articles. "Driver, stop. We would like to explore the market."

"It is forbidden," the driver gruffly answered, which only served to make Lady Margot more determined.

"Nevertheless, we will get out here and walk."

"I am only authorized to drive you around the city."

Margot had had enough of Tleilaxu secrets and restrictions. She spoke with the full force of Voice. "You will stop the vehicle and do as I command."

The driver jerked involuntarily, then pulled the groundcar over to the nearest clustered market stalls.

"You will wait for us here as we observe the vendors and their wares."

Although the driver sat shuddering and almost immobile, he fumbled with a small compartment beside his seat. Sweating with the effort, yet persistent, he produced a tiny black ball, which he squeezed in his palm. It seemed to sprout into two black scarves, one large and one small. "You must cover yourselves. Each of you. Dress as man and boy."

Amazed that the driver had the strength for such independent thought while under the influence of Voice, Margot took the scarves and quickly wrapped one around her head in a fashion she had seen some of the middle-caste males wear. Without hesitation, Marie secured a scarf over her own face and tied it behind her neck. "I like dress up."

Margot and her daughter climbed out of the ground-car. Numerous byways extended away from the main pedestrian thoroughfares, and Margot wandered one way and another, mentally keeping track of where they were. Even with the head wrap, she knew that her height, off-world clothing, and complexion would make her stand out. Little Marie didn't seem to notice the men who stared at them.

Although the noisy market had been bustling before they entered, full of exotic smells of cooking food, spiced slig, and pickled vat-vegetables, Lady Margot noticed that she and Marie moved in a pocket of silence. Vendors and customers grew quiet when they saw the pair.

One of Lady Margot's pastimes since coming to this planet was studying the variety of exotic Tleilaxu poisons. In addition to their biological expertise, the Bene Tleilax excelled in tailoring toxic chemicals that could kill or paralyze in numerous ways. The market was a veritable buffet of these useful substances. Some of them were effective contact paralytics, while others required unique delivery techniques, since standard poison snoopers could detect deadly substances in food or drink. In displays arrayed before her, Margot admired glittering gems that were chemically impregnated with neurotoxins, to be released under specific circumstances. She saw innocuous-looking fabrics whose fibers—upon being stretched or heated—would shift their long-chain-polymer structures into lethal poison molecules. Yes, the Tleilaxu had interesting toys.

Stopping at a counter, the little girl studied an array of dolls that were on display. All of the figurines were male, but they represented a variety of human species wearing traditional costumes of different worlds. Marie pointed out one that looked like a youthful Paul Atreides, an idealized version of Muad'Dib as a boy. "I want that one," she said.

The clerk scowled but quoted a low price, apparently anxious to move them along as quickly as possible. After a few solaris exchanged hands, Lady Margot handed the doll to her daughter, but the child promptly gave it back.

"This is mȳ gift to you, Mother," she said. "I don't play with dolls."

Margot took the doll with a smile and nudged her daughter around. "We should get back to the driver." She had pressed the issue, and likely the Tleilaxu officials had already sent a scolding message to Count Fenring. She led the way back to the vehicle with an unerring sense of direction. The driver had waited for them, perspiring uneasily.

All the way home in the groundcar, little Marie was bursting with excitement and couldn't wait to describe to her father what they had done. To Lady Margot, that made the expedition worthwhile.

Under the right conditions, even the smallest ripple can create a mighty wave.

—Zensunni maxim

In Arrakeen the sounds of construction were as constant as the sighing desert wind and the whispering sand. The citadel complex had begun on the outskirts of the city, which was already populated by millions of pilgrims and those that preyed upon them. When completed, the palace would extend across the suburbs to the cliffside on the north, where many hastily erected homes had been built using raw materials from the wrecks of Shaddam's warships.

Within the partially remodeled Arrakeen Residency, Paul met with his advisers before the day's heat grew too oppressive. He selected a purportedly small conference room, a place where the stone walls were close enough to make him feel some sense of privacy. He called it "a comfortable place for uncomfortable discussions."

He chose his advisers less for their political clout or pedigrees, than because he trusted their abilities. Alia and Chani were there, and Irulan insisted on being a part of the discussions. Though Paul didn't entirely trust her loyalties, he did value her intelligence, both as a Bene Gesserit and as the fallen Emperor's eldest daughter. She could indeed contribute much.

Korba also joined them, as well as Chatt the Leaper, another Fedaykin whose resolve could never be questioned. After the Spacing Guild's delegation to Alia while he was away at Caladan and Kaitain, Paul had given Chatt the task of dealing with their frequent demands, pleas, and complaints. While some Guild representatives had hoped to wheedle concessions from a spokesman, Chatt merely delivered the wishes of Muad'Dib and refused to bend a millimeter. Paul wished he had more negotiators like that.

Servants brought small cups of bitter spice coffee. With the spoils and offerings that were continually delivered to Dune, Muad'Dib and his inner circle never lacked for water. He called the meeting to order by taking his seat.

"I have drawn up an agenda, Usul," Korba said, straightening in his seat. He often used Paul's familiar name from Sietch Tabr to emphasize his own closeness to the Emperor. He spread sheets of instroy paper on the tabletop as if they were sacred documents. He could have used common spice paper, but instead Korba had selected a medium that implied permanence and importance. Paul thought that the man would probably seal the sheets as holy relics.

A Fremen with a written meeting agenda. The very idea was absurd. "We have many matters to discuss, Korba. Agendas lock us into a foolishly rigid structure." Paul could not keep the curt tone from his voice. The inevitable bureaucracy sank its roots deeper.

"I merely attempted to organize the topics into an efficient order, Usul. Your time has infinite value."

Alia piped up. "My brother can organize as he wishes. Do you claim to be better at it than he is?"

Paul saw Korba's muscles bunch. If Alia's words had not been tempered by her child's form, his Fremen pride might have caused him to draw his crysknife—as he did too often already.

"What is the first item you wish us to discuss, Beloved?" Chani said, shifting the conversation. Chatt the Leaper sat in silence, listening to every word that Muad'Dib said and, to a lesser extent, the rest of the conversation. Irulan was obviously engaged in the meeting, waiting for a chance to participate.

"I wish to discuss the growth of Arrakeen," Paul said, "and I need candid answers. As world after world swears allegiance to me, the city's population increases much faster than our infrastructure can accommodate. Pilgrims, refugees, and all sorts of displaced people arrive on Dune every day, and the limited resources cannot support them."

"They do not bring enough of their own water," Alia said.

Korba made a grunt of agreement. "In the old days, Fremen tribes had to place thousands of windtraps, install catchbasins, and glean every drop of dew just so *we* could survive. Now too many outworlders bring their bodies and their mouths, without a way to support themselves and without knowledge of the desert, either."

Chani agreed. "They buy costume stillsuits from charlatans. They believe they can simply purchase water whenever they need it, or that it will fall from the sky as it does on their own worlds. Fremen tradition would say they deserve to die and give up their body's water to more intelligent people."

Irulan spoke up. "Many temporary settlements have been erected up on the Shield Wall, despite the residual radiation from your atomics."

"They do so without permits," Korba said.

"Nevertheless, they do it," Paul said. "A lack of permits means nothing to the desperate and determined."

"Radiation is not the only danger," Irulan went on. "I read the weekly reports. Every day bodies are dragged away. People are murdered and robbed, and who can say how many more corpses are never found? We know of gangs who steal the living and the dead for their water."

Paul, though, was not surprised to hear the news. "Under the circumstances, it is to be expected."

After glancing at his agenda, Korba presented a tally of melange export shipments. As the Empire expanded, so did Paul's need for a stronger goad to use against the Guild and CHOAM, so he had asked for increased spice production from the desert. And whatever Muad'Dib wished, Muad'Dib received.

Next, he reviewed reports from the latest battlefields of the Jihad. Many of the Landsraad nobles who had allied themselves with him helped to spread his banners to other worlds, to subdue those planets that still resisted. But he noted a surprising pattern: few of the worlds being "conquered" were genuine threats to his reign. Rather, the friendly nobles had a tendency to choose targets based on bygone feuds and family hatreds, using the violent Jihad as an excuse to settle old grudges. Paul had seen this, but knew that these unfortunate and unconscionable excesses added fuel to build the necessary flames higher.

Listening to the succession of victories, the offhanded recitation of casualty figures, Irulan warned, "Before long, the people will cry out for the days of my father's rule."

"Chaos always brings regrets," Paul said. *Including my own.* "We will have peace once the deadwood is removed from the old and decayed Imperium. I cannot say, though, how long that will take."

Irulan retorted, "I see how your own government is shaping up, Emperor Paul Atreides. Do you truly believe your methods can yield something superior to the Corrino Imperium? With only a few interruptions, my bloodline ruled humanity for ten thousand years. Do you imagine that yours will do the same?"

Korba shot to his feet, spouting a phrase his Qizarate chanted in the streets. "Muad'Dib will endure forever!"

"Oh, enough, Korba," Paul said wearily. "Use your maxims for the crowds, not here in private counsel."

The Fedaykin leader collapsed backward into his chair as if deflated by Paul's words.

Paul leaned forward, looking for cracks in the usual Bene Gesserit reserve. "Continue, Irulan. I find this interesting."

She drew her rosebud lips together, pleased and surprised to be taken seriously. "You claim the best of intentions, but in many ways you have become too Fremen to rule an interplanetary empire. Rulership requires finesse. Once established, political alliances do not remain static. You must monitor and tend to your allies among the noble families and their respective planets. That is why Earl Thorvald has been adept at gathering supporters to resist you. After he walked out of the Landsraad Hall in Kaitain, he began to build his own alliances, and many see him as their only viable alternative. You have embraced brute force, while he uses intricate bureaucratic machinery."

"His little rebellion consists mainly of making bold pronouncements and then hiding," Paul pointed out.

"So far." She shook her head. "I will be proven right on this. Fremen simplicity and crude violence will never master the Imperium."

"I am also the son of a noble Duke, Irulan. I can balance both sides and draw from each as necessary. I am Paul Atreides *and* Paul-Muad'Dib."

The Princess met him with a sharp gaze. "And how much do you use of what your father taught you? I see no advantage in what you are creating: A fanatically united populace under a charismatic leader, following dogma instead of a bill of rights. You have thrown out the complex—and yes, inefficient—bureaucracy of the

Landsraad. But you cannot replace it with anarchy! We need a safety net of laws and procedures, a uniform code by which decisions on all planets are made. And yet, you seek to do away with everything that preceded you!"

"Do you suggest that I let my administration grow into a bloated behemoth that wallows in its own self-important rules?"

"That is what a government *is*, Husband—as you well know."

Giving Irulan a dangerous look, Chani started to get up, but Paul stopped her by raising his hand. He kept his own annoyance under tight control. "After defeating so many planetary rulers, I will not lose my Empire to bureaucrats."

"Your target should not be bureaucracy, but efficiency," Irulan insisted. "Appoint good leaders and competent administrators—people who value achieving an end result over maintaining the status quo or cementing their own importance. Any man who can delay the processing of a form has power over all those who need that form."

Paul was glad that he'd seen the value of letting the Princess attend this meeting. Of all perspectives in his new Empire, hers was unique, but Irulan had to be kept on a short leash.

Though his mother had not been gone for long, perhaps he needed to bring her back from Caladan. She could fill an important position in his central government. Yet another strong woman in his inner circle.

"You can trust me to follow your wishes, Usul," Korba said.

"And me," added Chatt, the first words he had spoken in the meeting.

"And me." Bitterness edged Irulan's voice. "I know you do not value me as wife or mate, but you cannot fail to recognize my talent in the field of diplomacy."

"Oh, I recognize much in you, Irulan. Your skills, like your loyalties, are many, but I will not risk giving you too much power. As daughter of a Padishah Emperor, trained by the Bene Gesserit, you know why."

Irulan responded with cool annoyance. "Then what would you have me do with all my skills? Shall I simply be an ornament in my husband's court, like one of the newly planted date palms?"

Paul considered. "I am familiar with your interests, and your usefulness. Your initial book of my life, incomplete and somewhat inaccurate as it is, has proved immensely popular and effective. I shall make you my official biographer."

One does not need to participate in history to create history.

—the PRINCESS IRULAN, unpublished
private journals

As a Princess of the old Imperium, Irulan had been instructed in the esoterica of social protocol, how to sit prettily at court functions and perform musical pieces and recitations. She had been encouraged to write poetry about meaningless things that would amuse well-bred people with shallow interests.

In addition, she was Bene Gesserit trained, as were all her sisters. She had much more to offer, and Irulan did not intend to write lack-witted poetry. She was in a remarkable position to chronicle this increasingly chaotic period in human history. Her credentials were unimpeachable as the wife of Muad'Dib and daughter of Shaddam IV.

Expanding on *The Life of Muad'Dib,* she intended to explore tributaries to the river of his remarkable life. In the process, she would again see the need to alter a few details here and there, though few would realize it as long as she got the gist of the story right. Paul's propagandists and deluded religious followers remained blithely unaware of the blinders they wore, of the dark forms they refused to see.

They revered her initial, rushed chronicle as if it were scripture, though she herself could clearly see its limitations. Her recent conversations with Swordmaster Bludd had revealed that even Paul had left out large parts when recounting his younger years, but she did not intend to change what she'd already written. On the contrary, each of her works about Paul would stand on its own, without further editing. They were stepping stones out into the water, complete with rough edges and flaws.

Irulan smiled as she sat on a hard plaz seat next to a fountain that, though dry, nevertheless emitted the soothing sounds of rushing water. She had all the inspiration she needed for her writing. Though he often seemed to ignore Irulan's counsel, Paul now included her in many of his meetings.

In recent days, he had been consumed by an unexpected defeat of his Jihad forces. A Heighliner full of his soldiers, drunk on a succession of uncontested victories, had arrived at the planet Ipyr expecting to accept the surrender of another noble lord. But they had underestimated the resolve of Earl Memnon Thorvald.

There on his home world, Thorvald had gathered the military resources of eleven different planets that were also impending targets for the Jihad. He had unified those lords into a fierce resistance, a bastion of the old Imperium. They had thrown their allied armies against Muad'Dib's soldiers with surprising and resounding force.

The fact that Paul had not seen this with his prescient vision astonished his followers. But to Paul, the shocking military turnabout suggested that the rebellious Earl's detailed plotting with the eleven lords must have taken place in the blurring proximity of a powerful Navigator. By managing to keep their plans secret, they had scored a surprising victory.

The faithful could not bring themselves to accept that their supposedly infallible Muad'Dib had made a mistake. Instead, they regarded the defeat as a sign that their hubris and overconfidence had displeased God, and that they must now fight harder to redeem themselves.

Leaving the wreckage of the Jihad battle group on Ipyr, Earl Thorvald and his allies had vanished to some other hideout, blown on the stellar winds. Some said the rebels were hiding on a planet that was shielded by the Guild, although every representative that Paul interrogated—to extremes if necessary—denied any knowledge or complicity.

Irulan took careful notes, realizing that this unaccustomed defeat, and Paul's reaction to it, made interesting material for an exhaustive biography. She also set herself to learn more about Paul Atreides, son of Duke Leto, grandson of Old Duke Paulus. His genealogy and the traditions surrounding noble House Atreides contained important elements of his character, yet Paul had taken a radically different path from his father.

Invoking the holy name of Muad'Dib, the Corrino princess was able to gather stories from those who had known Paul in his younger years, though many of the accounts were obviously inflated. She wrote down the tall tales anyway and focused on finding kernels of truth.

She had just received numerous documents from Caladan, including a long letter from Lady Jessica herself. The few remaining technocratic functionaries that had served House Vernius on Ix submitted old records of Prince Rhombur's friendship with Duke Leto and the Ixian nobleman's memories of young Paul.

Because of Paul's part in the Kwisatz Haderach program, the Bene Gesserit Sisterhood on Wallach IX had closely monitored his youth. The old Reverend Mother Mohiam was no friend of Paul's, but she respected Irulan and turned over many documents, hoping that the Princess would use them against "that upstart Emperor."

Irulan absorbed it all and quickly realized that her project could grow into an incredible undertaking, one that would receive such scrutiny as no other book had—not even the Orange Catholic Bible during the Council of Ecumenical Translators. The thought did not intimidate her. Her initial effort had already proved the potential in what she could write.

And Paul knew precisely what she was doing.

Though he had denied her a prominent position in his government, Irulan adopted her new purpose with enthusiasm rather than disappointment. Whatever she published would literally become history, read by schoolchildren on thousands of worlds.

It seemed that was what her husband really wanted from her after all. . . .

One morning she went to Paul's Imperial office to talk with him, holding a copy of the first volume in *The Life of Muad'Dib*. She dropped the deep blue book on his desktop, a plane of polished Elaccan bloodwood. "Exactly how much is missing from this story? I've been talking with Bludd. In your accounts of your life, you left out vital details."

He raised his eyebrows. "Your publication has defined my life's story."

"You told me you had never left Caladan before your House moved to Arrakis. Whole parts of your youth have been left out."

"Painful parts." He frowned at her. "But, more importantly, *irrelevant* parts. We've streamlined the story for mass consumption, such as when you wrote that I was born on Caladan and not Kaitain. It sounds better that way, doesn't it? We eliminated unnecessary complications, cut off unnecessary questions and explanations."

She could not hide her frustration. "Sometimes the truth *is* complicated."

"Yes, it is."

"But if I tell a part of the story that directly contradicts what has been published before—"

"If you write it, they will believe it. Trust me."

PART II

YOUNG PAUL ATREIDES — AGE 12

10,187 AG

When Paul Atreides was twelve years old, he nearly died in the War of Assassins that consumed the noble Houses of Atreides, Ecaz, and Moritani.

These events set him on the path from boyhood to manhood, from noble son to true ducal heir, from mere human to the revered Muad'Dib. Through the people he met from an early age—friends and traitors, heroes and failures—he learned the fundamentals of leadership and the consequences of decisions.

On his life's journey, Paul faced the hatred of enemies he had never met. From the moment of his birth, he was ensnared in a web of politics. His eyes opened to the vast Imperium that spanned many worlds beyond Caladan.

In his youth he watched and learned from his father's changes in response to his own battles. Duke Leto Atreides was not an easy man to know or understand. There were cold aspects to him that occasionally thawed—and then only slightly—before they grew icy again. The Lady Jessica knew this better than anyone, and she, too, instructed their son.

In facing the tragedies that lay in store for House Atreides, Duke Leto tempered the steel of character for which he was most noted. He learned to act rather than wait, and he learned to survive.

Our story begins on the eve of my father's fifth marriage, at a time when the life of young Paul Atreides seemed to lie before him like a great adventure.

—from the introduction to *The Life of Muad'Dib, Volume 2,* by the PRINCESS IRULAN

Life shapes life. Every event and every person leaves its mark, both in fine detail and in broad strokes.

—Bene Gesserit axiom

Atreides household staff made frantic preparations for the departure from Caladan. At the Cala City Spaceport, Duke Leto's personal frigate was scrubbed and buffed until it gleamed in the hazy sunlight; its interior was oiled, polished, and perfumed. In two days a Heighliner would arrive for the trip across space, but no one would tell twelve-year-old Paul their destination, which only made him more curious.

"Are we going to Ix to visit House Vernius?" he pestered Thufir Hawat during one of their training sessions. Paul Atreides was fast and fit, but short for his age. According to the Mentat assassin, however (who was not prone to giving compliments), the boy still had fighting skills that would let him defeat men twice his age and twice his size.

"I do not know where we are going, young Master."

When he asked Gurney Halleck, sure that the lumpish good-humored warrior would give him a hint of their destination, Gurney had simply shrugged. "I go where my Duke commands, pup."

Afterward, he had tried to get information from Duncan

Idaho, his friend and trainer. "Are we going to Ginaz, to see the old Swordmaster school?"

"The Ginaz School hasn't been the same since the Grumman attack twelve years ago. Viscount Moritani called it a War of Assassins, but that implies following a set of rules, and he is a vile man who does as he pleases." Duncan's resentment was plain; he had been at the famous school when it had fallen.

"But are we going there anyway? You didn't answer my question."

"Honestly, I do not know."

Paul studied each man's reactions and expressions, seeking to learn if they told the truth or not. He concluded that no one knew where Duke Leto was taking them. . . .

At the appointed time his mother Jessica came gracefully down the long promenade staircase into the main foyer, from which she could look down the hill. Her household servants had finished packing her clothes and toiletries, piling packages on a suspensor-flatbed transporter that would take them to the spaceport and load them aboard the Duke's frigate.

Gurney came striding up, his clothes sweaty, his patchy blond hair smeared over his head. His grin was wide and infectious. "The Heighliner just arrived in orbit. The Guild gives us four hours to get ourselves securely nestled in a berth."

"Are you packed yet?" Jessica looked harried.

"I carry most of what I need in my body and in my mind. And as long as I have my baliset, all is right with the universe."

"Will you teach me to sing, Gurney?" Paul asked.

"I can teach you the words, young Master, but a melodious voice is a gift from God. You must develop that yourself."

"He'll do it along with his other studies," Jessica said.

"Come, Paul, it's time to go to the spaceport. Your father will already be there."

❧

WHITE CUMULUS CLOUDS thickened overhead as afternoon thunderstorms approached. In the village fish market, vendors shouted out lowered prices for the remnants of the morning's catch; anything not sold within the next hour would be sent to processing plants for off-world shipment. Caladan locals wouldn't eat anything more than a day old.

Leto was waiting for them at the spaceport. His long dark hair blew in the sea breeze, his aquiline nose lifted as though trying to catch a last sniff of the sea rather than the exhaust vapors from machinery. When he saw Gurney trudging along beside Jessica and Paul with a baliset slung over his shoulder, Leto said, "I'm sorry, Gurney, but there has been a change of plans."

Instantly alert, the loyal retainer frowned. "Has something happened, my Lord?"

"No, and I want to make sure it stays that way. You and Thufir will remain behind to watch over House Atreides while we are gone. This is a more private matter."

Gurney did not show that he was bothered. "As you wish, my Duke. Have you given Thufir any special instructions?"

"He knows what to do—as do you, Gurney."

In private sessions Paul studied politics, psychology, and personal interactions, knowing it would help make him a better ruler someday. Duke Leto Atreides had acknowledged Paul as his natural and legitimate son, even though Jessica was his bound concubine instead of his wife. Nevertheless, there were still dynastic games to be played. The young man knew he might face perils and intrigues that an average boy his age need never imagine. "Without Gurney and Thufir, will we be safe, Father?" he asked before walking up the ramp into the frigate.

"Duncan is already aboard. He'll be piloting." It was all Leto needed to say. If Duncan Idaho could not. protect Paul, no one could.

Barely able to contain his curiosity, Paul chose a seat by a porthole, through which he watched the other vessels coming and going in the spaceport. He felt a thrill when the frigate lifted off the ground. When the cottages of the coastal village were no more than tiny spots on the landscape below, the heavier thrusters activated. Flown expertly by Duncan, the small ship rose high above the white-flecked ocean, through the afternoon thunderclouds, and into the fading darkness of space.

Overhead, Paul saw the gigantic form of the Guild Heighliner in orbit, a single spaceship as large as some asteroids. The Atreides frigate was an insignificant speck inside the vessel that carried many other ships from numerous planets—more craft than the Cala City Spaceport would see in a Standard Year. Duncan received instructions to take them to their assigned berth.

Near the bow, Jessica sat primly in a seat. She had told Paul that space travel did not entirely agree with her, though she had made interplanetary trips before— first from the Bene Gesserit school on Wallach IX to join Duke Leto's household and then to Kaitain during her pregnancy, where she was watched over by the first wife of Emperor Shaddam.

He was surprised by a sudden thought that came into his mind as information clicked together, pieces snapping into place. Lady Anirul . . . Emperor Shaddam IV . . . Kaitain.

Anirul, the Emperor's first wife, had died under mysterious circumstances very near the time of Paul's birth.

Since then, Shaddam had taken other wives, though none of those marriages had been successful. In fact, his second, third, and fourth wives were also dead, which seemed rather suspicious to Paul. Now the Emperor was planning yet another wedding, this time to Firenza of House Thorvald.

And Duke Leto was taking his family on a mysterious journey.

"I know where we're going," Paul piped up. "Each House in the Landsraad is sending representatives to Kaitain. We're attending the Emperor's wedding, aren't we?" The event was bound to be spectacular, unlike anything he had ever seen.

Duke Leto's expression darkened, and he shook his head. "No, Paul. Considering what happened to Shaddam's previous marriages, we won't be attending this one." He sounded decidedly cool.

The boy frowned in disappointment. He had used his abilities, asked every question he could think of, and tried to put together the clues, but he didn't have enough information to make another guess.

His mother seemed impatient to learn their destination as well. "I, too, had assumed we were going to Kaitain, Leto."

With a heavy thump, their frigate settled into place within the designated docking clamp. Paul felt a vibration thrum through the hull. "Won't you tell us where we are going now? We're already aboard the Heighliner."

Leto finally sat back and, glancing at Jessica with what appeared to be a bit of guilt, answered Paul. "We are bound for Ecaz."

The universe is a sea of expectations, and of disappointment.

—EMPEROR PAUL-MUAD'DIB, third address
to the Landsraad

"An Imperial wedding must be very exciting, my Lord Baron."

More interested in the nude boy's lovely form than in his attempts at conversation, Vladimir Harkonnen balanced on the suspensor mechanism that held his body upright as he prepared for the week's festivities. The windowplaz tint had been adjusted to permit just the right amount of natural light into the guest suite in the Emperor's extravagant Kaitain palace.

"Ah, nuptials—how could I not be overjoyed?" the Baron answered sarcastically.

He had just sent a manservant running out of the suite to fetch another selection—an *adequate* selection this time—of garments for that evening's wedding rehearsal dinner. His tailors were continually preparing alternative outfits, but he would have to make his choice soon. So far, the options looked like nomads' tents hanging on his bulk. "I may govern Arrakis, but I can't show up looking like a *Fremen*!"

The boy blinked dark, doelike eyes. "Would you like a massage before you dress in those restrictive clothes, my Lord?"

"Why bother to ask? Just do it."

The boy dutifully kneaded fragrant ointments into the Baron's soft shoulders, then continued the intimate massage as he had been taught. When he was finished, however, the Baron was left feeling less satisfied than he had anticipated. Perhaps it was time to train a replacement.

⋘

A CARNIVAL AIR had prevailed on Kaitain for days: jubilant crowds, fireworks displays, and sporting events featuring the best athletes of great and minor Houses. From every building in the enduring Imperial city, scarlet-and-gold Corrino flags fluttered in a warm breeze beneath a cerulean sky. For Shaddam's wedding to Firenza Thorvald, perfect weather was guaranteed by backup satellites and technicians working long shifts.

Throngs had camped out on the route the royal procession would take on the way to the Grand Theater. Everyone wanted the best views of the Padishah Emperor and his bride-to-be. Any moment now, the two royal carriages would approach, each drawn by magnificent golden lions from Harmonthep.

Inside the dining hall for the reception, the Baron observed from a special seat designed to accommodate his bulk. The banquet table seemed as long as a street in Harko City, lined with representatives from practically every noble holding in the Landsraad. While the Baron couldn't care less about the elaborate spectacle, weddings in general, or Shaddam IV in particular, he was certain that the officious Chamberlain Ridondo and his swarms of functionaries would make careful note of which noble families declined to attend. The Baron was somewhat surprised, scandalized, and pleased to see empty seats under the House Atreides banner. So, Duke Leto had other priorities.

So do I . . . and yet, I am here.

An accented voice interrupted him from his left. "A waste of time, eh? This new one doesn't know what she's getting into. She'll end up dead like the previous wives."

Startled, the Baron turned to see a large, angular man settle into a reserved highback chair. He had heavy brows over intense, pale blue eyes, and a rough-edged appearance despite his fine clothes. A horsehead emblem adorned the lapel of his white-and-blue jacket, a stylized depiction that showed sharp spines projecting from the horse's majestic head. The Baron remained cool, uninterested in small talk. "I don't believe we've met."

"Nevertheless, we should know each other, Vladimir. I am the Viscount Hundro Moritani from Grumman."

The Baron did not like such casual familiarity. "I'm aware of your history, sir. You're a nasty piece of business, aren't you? The war with Ecaz, the attack on House Ginaz, the destruction of the Swordmaster school. Is the Imperial censure still in force against you, or has that been rescinded?"

Surprisingly, the Viscount let out a throaty, abrasive chuckle. "I am pleased you have taken an interest in my activities. I do what is necessary to protect my House and my holdings."

Impatient to eat, the Baron raised a ring-laden hand to signal a servant to bring a plate of hors d'oeuvres. Even with the regularly spaced poison snoopers hanging over the table, he produced his own device from a pocket and wafted it over the varied morsels before tasting anything. "It was interesting to observe how hard you could push before the Emperor stopped you," he said.

Moritani watched him intently. "And what have you concluded?"

The Baron began popping little sandwiches into his mouth, savoring the variety of flavors, the exotic seasonings. "I learned that while the Emperor made a great show of criticizing your actions, he did not inflict any lasting harm on House Moritani. Therefore, you achieved most of your aims, and paid a very small price."

The Viscount grumbled, and the Baron could sense the hair-trigger of anger seething there. "I did not accomplish enough. Archduke Ecaz remains alive and now denies me access to a rare medicine that would cure my son."

Awkwardly, the Baron ate another tiny sandwich. He had no interest in House Moritani's personal feuds or family troubles. House Harkonnen had feuds of its own.

Moritani motioned to his bodyguard, a redheaded man who stood nearby. Tall and well-proportioned, the pale-skinned retainer was younger than his master; one of his ears was half missing and scarred over. "Baron, this is my personal Swordmaster, Hiih Resser."

The Baron took greater interest now. "Few Houses have a dedicated Swordmaster these days."

Moritani's lips curled upward in a cruel smile. "Because the Ginaz School is not training any more of them."

"House Atreides still has Duncan Idaho," Resser pointed out. "I knew him on Ginaz."

"I have no interest in House Atreides!" the Viscount raised his voice, quick to anger. "It is time to fetch Wolfram. The banquet is about to begin, but he will need to retire early. See to it that he doesn't overexert himself." Resser bowed and left.

The chairs began to fill, and the noise level increased. At the head table, Shaddam Corrino and Count Hasimir Fenring took seats, followed by the Emperor's bride-to-be and Lady Margot Fenring.

"I'd say the Count got the better of those two women," Moritani said in a low tone, admiring Lady Margot.

Seeing the Princess Firenza for the first time, the Baron was struck by how plain and pear-shaped she was, with a loose chin and too much makeup, apparently to cover flaws on her skin. "She looks like a peasant."

"Good wide hips, though," the Viscount said. "Maybe she'll be the one to bear him the sons he wants."

"Even if she does, she is too ugly. He won't keep her long." The Baron was beginning to enjoy his candid conversation with this gruff man. "And yet we all come here to smile and celebrate. I, for one, find these dinners and parties to be quite tedious, with very little benefit. Doesn't anyone realize we are busy men?"

"Our attendance offers us an excuse to conduct other business, Vladimir." Then, visibly brightening, Viscount Moritani looked toward the main entrance doors, through which Hiih Resser escorted a sickly looking boy into the dining hall. Wolfram was around ten or eleven, with facial features that closely resembled those of his father. The boy appeared disoriented, drugged.

"You say he is ill? Not contagious, I hope?" The Baron had his own diseases to deal with.

"The boy is afflicted with a rare disorder that causes him to waste away. His mother suffered from it, too. Dear sweet Cilla. She lasted a year after Wolfram's birth, but the effort of delivering him took its physical toll." A wave of sorrow crossed Hundro Moritani's face; his emotions seemed as mercurial as the weather patterns on Arrakis. Resser led the groggy boy to the table and positioned him in a seat beside the Viscount. Moritani warmly patted his son's pale hand before turning back to the Baron.

"Wolfram finds solace in semuta. Only the deep trance and the music give him relief from the terrible pain. It's all I can do to help him. There is a cure, of course— esoit-poay, the Ecazis call it." His voice took on a razor sharpness. "In the embargo signed by the Archduke, he explicitly forbids any drop of that drug to leave Ecaz, although very few people in the whole Imperium require it." His fist clenched hard enough to bend silverware. "He does it only to gain vengeance on me."

Well, you did carpet bomb his government center and kill his oldest daughter and his brother, if I remember correctly. But instead of voicing his thought, the Baron said, "An unfortunate situation. Can you not purchase the drug on the black market?"

"Not a microgram. Even semuta has been restricted so that I must pay exorbitant prices. The Archduke knows what I need and attempts to thwart me at every turn! Out of sheer spite!" A wave of anger reddened his features again, but the man's volatile emotions quickly shifted to an expression of loving calm. "I'm left with no choice. Damn them, I have to give my son whatever he needs to ease the terrible pain."

The Baron sensed that the Grumman leader wanted to suggest some sort of bargain with House Harkonnen. Smelling a chance to make a profit if he was careful, the Baron said, "I have certain channels of my own to obtain black-market drugs, Viscount, but House Ecaz is no friend of mine, either. The Archduke is closely allied with House Atreides."

As Moritani helped his dazed son eat one of the small appetizers, his eyes shone brighter, as if a fire had been lit behind the pupils. "Have you noticed that neither Duke Leto Atreides nor Archduke Armand Ecaz are in attendance here? My spies tell me that Leto has gone to Ecaz for a secret meeting. They are undoubtedly plotting against both of us."

"Many nobles are not in attendance," the Baron pointed out. "I am not the only one weary of all the weddings. One Imperial nuptial is much like another."

"But this one, Baron, gives me the opportunity to invite *you* to Grumman as my honored guest. We have much in common. Perhaps we can help each other achieve our aims."

Wary but curious, the Baron studied the other man. "There may well be opportunities to explore. Yes, a visit to Grumman might be interesting and mutually beneficial. My people will make the arrangements."

＊

House Moritani of Grumman was censured after the disgraceful attack on the Ginaz Swordmaster school. As the aggressor, Viscount Moritani paid substantial reparations, but in the way of back-room politics, Emperor Shaddam dismissed the matter as a minor event. Nonetheless, the damage was done. Although structures could be rebuilt, new instructors recruited, and training centers re-opened, one thing was irreparable: The Sword-masters, those feared warriors, had been beaten. *Such a thing could never be erased.*

—CHOAM economic analysis, *The Fall of House Ginaz*

Once the Atreides frigate was released from the Guildship's hold, Duncan Idaho piloted it toward mottled Ecaz. The sky was full of clouds, the major land-masses a riot of different shades of green. Paul could see numerous oceans below, but none so vast as the seas of Caladan.

Ever since Duke Leto had explained their destination, Paul had detected an inexplicable chill between his parents. Duncan had offered no insights either. "It is not my business, young Master. And if it were yours, your father would tell you."

So, the boy had occupied himself during the brief journey by studying the frigate's limited library of filmbooks, eager to learn about Ecaz—a lush and fertile world filled with jungles, rainforests, and well-watered agricultural plains. The primary exports were hardwoods and exotic forest products, as well as unusual unguents, rare drugs, deadly poisons.

"Will we visit the fogtree forests?" Paul asked. He had seen spectacular images, and also read that a blight had wiped out most of the delicate and expensive fogtrees on the continent of Elacca, which was governed by Duke Prad Vidal.

"No," Leto answered. "Archduke Ecaz is waiting for us. Our business is with him alone."

"Does he know that I accompany you?" Paul heard the faint bitterness in Jessica's words.

"You are my bound concubine, the mother of my son. You must go with me."

In his reading, Paul had taken particular note of his father's connection to Archduke Armand and the vicious feud between House Moritani and House Ecaz. He was most surprised to learn that his father had been betrothed to the Archduke's eldest daughter, Sanyá—until she and her uncle had been murdered by Moritani soldiers.

Duncan guided the Atreides frigate toward a small, ornate city whose centerpiece was a large structure composed of graceful loops and arches, walkways that connected towers, and thick old trees that grew up beside the walls. The palace was a fairy tale synthesis of branches, vines, and ferns intertwined with pearlescent white stone. Paul doubted even Kaitain could have been more impressive than this.

Before they could land, however, two heavily armed warships raced into the air, circled the Ecazi Palace, and crossed in front of the Atreides frigate in a clear show of force. Incensed, Duncan activated the communication controls. "This is Swordmaster Duncan Idaho of House Atreides. We are here at the invitation of Archduke Ecaz. Explain your actions."

The two military ships peeled away, spun and darted playfully in the air, then streaked beneath the frigate. Paul was reminded of frolicking dolphins in the Caladan oceans. A booming voice came over the comline speakers. "You use that title with great pride, Swordmaster Idaho—you must have had excellent instructors."

A thin, nasal voice joined the communication. "Are we allowed to strip him of the title if he doesn't impress us enough, Rivvy?"

Duncan recognized the voices. "Swordmaster Whitmore Bludd? And Rivvy Dinari?"

The two men chuckled over the speaker. "We came to escort you. We weren't sure if your pilot was proficient enough to land in the proper place."

Paul knew the names; Duncan had often talked about his instructors from Ginaz. Duncan's face showed great pleasure as he explained to Paul, "They must have become ronin since the Ginaz School disbanded. I wouldn't have guessed that Archduke Ecaz needed both of them."

"House Moritani has made no recent aggressive moves," Leto said, "but that could change on a moment's notice. I do not believe the conflict was ever resolved to the satisfaction of either party."

"Feuds usually aren't, my Lord," Duncan said.

When the three ships had landed in an oval, paved clearing surrounded by tall, feathery trees, the two Swordmasters emerged to greet them. Whitmore Bludd had long wavy hair that was a mixture of silver and gold, a thin face, and rosebud lips that seemed to be pouting. Rivvy Dinari was an enormous globe of a man, who nevertheless seemed light on his feet; his skin was florid in the jungle heat.

Duncan bounded down the frigate's ramp to greet them, but kept his guard up, as though expecting the two teachers to hurl themselves upon him in a playful yet deadly practice session.

"Duke Leto is here on formal business," Dinari commented to Bludd in a deep voice which sounded like a kettledrum. "There will be time for swordplay later."

Bludd sniffed. "There is no *play* with swords. We will conduct a practice session. A *proving* session."

"And if I beat the two of you, how will you ever endure your shame?" Duncan teased.

"We'll manage," Dinari replied. "*If* it happens."

Leto emerged alone from the landed frigate, wearing a black doublet that sported the red Atreides hawk crest. Paul followed, still trying to understand what was going on.

The air smelled of flowers, wood resins, and sweet sap that leaked from the cracked bark of the enormous trees that towered over the palace. Ferns as tall as his head stood like curled sentries along the flagstone paths.

Leto put his hand on Paul's shoulder. "Come with me, we need to make our entrance."

"What about Mother?" Paul glanced back at Jessica, who showed no emotion whatsoever as she followed them at some distance.

"She will make her own entrance. Pay close attention. There are many subtleties here. In the next few days you will learn important lessons about being a Duke . . . and some of them may be hard."

There seemed to be as much lush foliage inside the Archduke's palace as out in the courtyards and gardens. Narrow aqueducts spilled silvery water down channels in the walls, filling the corridors and chambers with the peaceful sound of flowing streams. It wasn't quite as soothing as the majestic rush of the ocean on Caladan, but Paul found it comforting nevertheless.

When they entered the main audience room, Archduke Armand Ecaz was seated in a massive chair made of burlwood, at a long table polished to an incredible sheen. It was the largest piece of Elaccan bloodwood Paul had ever seen; colors and patterns flowed through the grain. The Archduke was a tall, thin man who did not appear old despite his silver hair. His face was narrow, his chin pointed.

As Leto came forward, the Archduke stood to greet him, and they clasped each other's forearms. "We are optimists, you and I, Armand," Leto said. "We will try this again. If we don't keep trying, then what is the point of life?"

"This is your natural son Paul?" The Archduke extended a hand. It was small and thin, but his grip was firm. Paul shook it.

"Also, allow me to present his mother, the Lady Jessica," Leto said, nodding in her direction. She bowed formally, but remained at the side of the room, marginalized.

"I have an introduction to make as well, Leto. You probably don't remember her." Armand gave a shout toward a doorway, and a willowy young woman entered. She seemed well-mannered, with large brown eyes and dark hair bound in a looping braid. She wore a thin gold chain around her neck, suspended from which was a perfectly clear yet irregularly shaped soostone. "Duke Leto Atreides, this is my daughter Ilesa."

She executed a polite curtsy, though she seemed shy. "I am very pleased to meet you."

Paul's father responded with a deep, formal bow. "I saw her once, long ago. You did not exaggerate her beauty, Armand." Now Duke Leto turned to Paul and his mother. "The arrangements have already been made. Ilesa will be my wife."

After they had been shown to separate quarters in the Ecazi Palace, Paul visited his mother in her room. Jessica was quiet, absorbed in her thoughts; she herself had taught him how to read subtle nuances, and he could see how troubled she was. Obviously, his father had not discussed the betrothal announcement with her beforehand.

Logically, and politically, the arrangement had its advantages. Marriage was a tool of statecraft in the Imperium, a weapon as powerful as any lasgun in the Atreides military arsenal. But apparently Duke Leto kept secrets and political realities even from his beloved concubine.

"It will be all right, Paul," Jessica said, and she did sound sincere. "I will stay in this room and continue my Bene Gesserit exercises, but you, Paul—no matter what else is happening, seize this as a learning opportunity. When it is time for us all to leave Ecaz, I want you to have a greater breadth of understanding. File away all these details and organize your thoughts using the techniques I have taught you."

The very strangeness of Ecaz proved an irresistible

distraction to Paul. He studied sunlit rooms whose walls reflected a trapezoidal architecture, without the perfection of perpendicular intersections. The palace grounds held an amazing topiary garden of lush plant sculptures—men, animals, and monsters—that moved with gentle grace, turning and weaving as the sun crossed the sky. A mesh-enclosed arena filled with large jewel-toned butterflies offered quite a spectacle during the twice-daily feeding-frenzy when workers entered the arena carrying dishes of syrupy nectar.

When he went to find his father, Duke Leto was locked in a conference room with Armand Ecaz. Guards and, worse, bureaucratic functionaries clustered at the doorway, and prevented him from entering. At midmorning, though, when servants delivered refreshments for the meeting, Paul finally slipped into the conference room and caught his father's eye. Duke Leto appeared tired, but he smiled when he saw the boy. "Paul, I am sorry we've ignored you. These negotiations are very complex."

Armand Ecaz lounged back in his chair. "Come now, Leto, they aren't as difficult as all that."

"Go find Duncan, Paul. He'll keep you occupied—and safe."

At a signal from Duke Leto, the stuffy Ecazi guard captain took the young man by the sleeve and led him out of the room, apologizing profusely to the Archduke for the interruption. Paul knew he would never have gotten past Thufir Hawat's security back in Castle Caladan.

He located Duncan, Rivvy Dinari, and Whitmore Bludd out on the training field embroiled in a melee. The three were shirtless and armed with blunt-ended pulse swords that could deliver potent, stinging shocks; all three men had angry-looking red welts on their arms, chests, and shoulders. As he watched, Paul couldn't quite tell who was fighting whom: Duncan threw himself upon Bludd, Dinari attacked Duncan, and then Bludd and

Duncan ganged up on the fat Swordmaster. Finally, the three lowered their weapons, exhausted, dripping with perspiration and wearing foolish grins.

"He hasn't forgotten much," Dinari admitted to the thin and foppish Bludd. "He must practice occasionally."

Finished and weary, the three switched off their shields and stood leaning on the pulse-swords on the trampled practice ground. Bludd tipped an imaginary hat in Paul's direction. "We gave the young man a magnificent demonstration."

"At least an entertaining one," Rivvy Dinari said. "You were clumsy as an ox today."

Bludd sniffed. "I scored five nasty welts on *you*. Then again, your body does have a great deal more surface area than the average opponent."

Duncan toweled himself off with a fluffy rectangle woven from Elaccan eiderdown. Paul had read in filmbooks how the substance was spun from the burst seedpods of a tall, purple-leafed tree.

Paul stepped up to him. "My mother told me to learn what I can about Ecaz, and my father told me that you would keep me occupied."

"Certainly, young Master, but no sword training right now. After my workout with these two, even you might be able to beat me."

"I have already bested you three times."

"Twice. I refused to concede one of them."

"Your refusal doesn't change the facts." Dinari and Bludd seemed to find the conversation amusing. Duncan led him inside for a round of tame filmbook studies.

*Which is more honorable—to follow a monster to
whom you have sworn loyalty, or to break your
oath and leave his service?*

—JOOL-NORET, the first Swordmaster

During the trip home to Grumman after the Imperial
wedding, Viscount Moritani spent much of the
time with his sickly son and a medical entourage in the
main stateroom of his family frigate.

Reporting to his master, Resser paused at the open
doorway of the stateroom. Inside, the Viscount sat as limp
as a discarded garment in a gilded armchair, from which
he stared at a paunchy Suk doctor and a male nurse as
they tended Wolfram. The pungent smell of semuta and
the eerie, trancelike music that accompanied its use had
calmed the boy. Even so, he whimpered in constant pain.

The heavyset Dr. Vando Terbali bore a diamond tattoo
on his forehead, and his long golden hair was bound in a
Suk school ring. "Though this disease is not incurable,
my Lord Viscount, treatment is long overdue. Wolfram's
deteriorating condition is not the fault of the Suk broth-
erhood."

"If I blamed you, Doctor, you would already be dead,"
Moritani said wearily.

The male nurse stiffened in alarm, and the Suk doctor's gaze sharpened. "Threatening me will not improve
the quality of my service."

The Viscount frowned. "And how can your treatment of my son be any worse? He is dying. Your ministrations have not prolonged his life nor significantly eased his pain."

"You need esoit-poay, my Lord, and the Ecazis refuse to give it to you. Ergo, we cannot help your son."

The Viscount's shoulders bunched. "Duke Prad Vidal was somewhat sympathetic, for a price, but even he could not make the Archduke change his mind. Vidal's personal entreaty on Wolfram's behalf was rejected out of hand, because of the Archduke's enmity toward me." He rose from his chair, a man-shaped pressure vessel filled with violence, and suddenly noticed that Resser was standing just outside the door. The Viscount's expression changed, and he spoke abruptly to Dr. Terbali. "Please, if you cannot treat his symptoms then just . . . ease his pain as much as you can."

Moritani joined the redheaded Swordmaster in the frigate's corridor and sealed the stateroom door behind him. Resser watched the muscles work in the nobleman's jaw as he clenched his teeth. "Ah, Resser, I cannot decide whom to despise more—Archduke Ecaz or the Corrino Emperor. Maybe I don't have to make the choice. I have enough hatred for both."

Resser was surprised. Knowing the enemies of House Moritani was a vital part of his job. "Why do you hate the Emperor, my Lord?"

"Come with me into my study. I will share with you the ancient documents I obtained from the Bene Gesserit. You'll see the real reason we came to Kaitain."

"I thought the real reason was to make contact with the Baron Harkonnen."

"There are several real reasons—none of which have anything to do with Shaddam and his damned wedding."

Resser stood at attention in the private room, looking at the man he had sworn to serve. Once, back in the smoldering ruins of Ginaz, Duncan Idaho had offered him a position with House Atreides. Although most of the Grumman students had been expelled by the Sword-master instructors for refusing to denounce the Viscount's dishonorable acts, Resser had insisted on staying to finish his training. He had believed that the only way to restore the respect of House Moritani would be to shepherd it back onto an honorable path. In the years since Resser's return to Grumman, he had become Viscount Moritani's most trusted man and had done his best to keep the volatile leader in check.

Smiling without humor, Viscount Moritani activated a palmlock and unsealed an armored drawer built into the frigate's bulkhead. He withdrew a long, curling sheet of instroy paper on which were printed countless names and dates in minuscule letters. "This is a very small segment of the Bene Gesserit breeding records. A chart of bloodlines."

Resser squinted to read the small script, but didn't know what he was supposed to make of all the names. Something about *House Tantor* and the *Salusa Incident*. "And how did you obtain private breeding records, sir?"

Moritani raised a bushy eyebrow and regarded him coldly. Resser knew not to ask further about that.

"My father once told me a rumor," the Viscount continued, "a tall tale that his father had told him, and so on. It always had a ring of truth to me, and I spent years digging." He tapped the long sheet of paper. "This proves what I long suspected—generation after generation, dating back thousands of years."

"*What* does it prove, my Lord?"

"This family was not always House Moritani. Once, we were named Tantor. After Salusa, though, every member of House Tantor was hunted down and killed. Every member the hunters could find, that is."

A shudder ran down Resser's spine. Now it began to

make sense. "The Salusa Incident? Not the atomic attack that nearly wiped out House Corrino and devastated all of Salusa Secundus?"

"One and the same. *We* are the renegade family whose name was erased from the historical record." The nobleman narrowed his eyes. "Thanks to the Bene Gesserit, I now have proof. I know what the Corrinos did to many of my ancestors . . . and what Archduke Ecaz is doing to my only son."

"And no one else is aware of this genealogy? Surely everyone has forgotten about the blood hunt."

"I have never forgotten. You are now one of only five persons, including myself, who even suspects such a connection. Five *living* persons, that is. I had to take certain necessary precautions to ensure the silence of an informant, and of the opportunist in whom he confided."

The Viscount replaced the instroy document in the armored bulkhead drawer. "If not for the systematic extermination of my ancestors, poor Wolfram would not be the last of our bloodline."

The implications rolled through Resser's mind. From what he knew, the execution edict against the nameless family that had unleashed the atomics on Salusa Secundus had never technically been lifted. "But shouldn't you just destroy that document, my Lord? It is dangerous to keep in your possession."

"On the contrary, I wish to keep it as a constant reminder of the destruction my noble House is capable of . . . no matter which name we bear." His mouth became a grim line. "One day we shall exact our final revenge. On House Corrino, and on House Ecaz."

Resser felt a chill in the reprocessed air of the sealed chamber, but his oath of duty and honor required him to serve without questioning his master. "I live only to serve you and your noble House, Lord Moritani."

～

Empires may rise and fall, and stars may burn for millennia, but nothing is quite so enduring as hatred.

—*The Ecaz Family Chronicle*

While the Archduke's business administrators presented options for the alliance between House Atreides and House Ecaz, Duke Leto was distracted by the ache in his heart. He had a difficult time concentrating on the nuances of the negotiations, though he knew that any mistake he made could have repercussions on his House for years to come. He could have used a Mentat to keep track of the details, but Thufir Hawat was serving a greater need by protecting Caladan.

Both Ecaz and Atreides desired this arrangement, but Leto's life was complicated by a concubine and a son he had named as his true heir. An alliance between houses, a marriage, and another son by Ilesa would change the situation considerably.

Fortunately, most of the negotiations were similar to those from sixteen years ago, when Leto had been betrothed to Armand Ecaz's elder daughter. The previous agreements had been brought out of the archives to use as a starting point, but much had changed in the years since the Grumman sneak attack had killed Sanyá. The last time he had tried to marry into the Ecazi sphere,

Leto had had another son, Victor, by another concubine, Kailea Vernius. Both were now dead, as was Sanyá.

"You look troubled, my friend," Armand said. "Did you not sleep well last night? Are your quarters not comfortable?"

Leto smiled. "Your hospitality is exemplary, Armand." *It was the discussion far into the night that kept me awake, and Jessica's deep hurt long afterward.*

Sitting on the edge of the bed in her quarters, a private room down the hall from his own, Leto had looked at her beautiful oval face, remembering when the Bene Gesserit first brought her to him as a young woman. His growing love for Jessica had been the wedge that drove Kailea from him. Out of jealousy, Kailea had tried to kill Leto but had instead caused the death of their innocent son, and brutally crippled Prince Rhombur Vernius. Now, Leto swore to himself that he wouldn't allow Ilesa to become a similar wedge between himself and Jessica.

"It is business and politics," he had said, wishing he didn't sound so defensive. He could have spent hours listing the advantages of such an alliance, but no such explanations would ever touch Jessica's heart. He assured her that he didn't love Ilesa—didn't even know her.

Jessica simply sat there with a cold expression. "I understand completely, my Duke, and I am confident you will make the appropriate decision. I am just your concubine, with no say in the matter."

"Dammit, Jessica, you can speak openly with me!"

"Yes, my Lord." She said nothing else.

He let the silence draw out, but he was no match for a Bene Gesserit. "I am sorry. Truly, I am." Though her stony mask was impenetrable, she looked so lovely to him.

"I expect nothing else from you, Leto. Your father raised you never to marry for love, only for political advantage. After all, the lack of love in his marriage to Lady Helena is reflected in your own lack of love toward your exiled mother. I have seen the Old Duke's portrait. I know what he said and what he taught you. How could you *not* believe as he did?"

"You must hate him."

"Does one hate the tide for washing away the sand? Does one hate a storm for bringing lightning?"

Leto wondered if Jessica wished she could have seen the Old Duke when he was alive, just to give him a piece of her mind.

"I will take care of you and Paul," Leto insisted. "You will always be part of Castle Caladan. You will always be with me."

"I trust my Duke's promises." Jessica turned away quickly.

Bidding her good night, Leto had taken his leave, but he had remained awake for a long time afterward. . . .

The servants brought trays of "light refreshments": a dripping comb of silver honey, roasted tree-crabs in butter on skewers, z-nuts that were startlingly sour. Leto ate while listening to breakdowns of the prime exports of Ecaz, the most profitable forest products. Armand spoke of spending huge amounts of time and money on pharmaceutical research, testing, and processing. Suk medical chemists and biopharmacists in Elaccan jungle camps constantly discovered new leaves, lichens, berries, roots, fungi.

Most important, the Archduke laid out his absolute trade embargo against Viscount Hundro Moritani of Grumman. He passed Leto a proclamation that stated: "There shall be no export of any useful item to House Moritani."

Armand pointed to the official document. "If you are to marry Ilesa, you must agree to this condition, Leto. I cannot bend this rule. Not so much as a leaf from a tree or a berry from a bush. That monster shall not have a gram of comfort from this world."

At one time, Leto had tried to negotiate an end to the simmering feud between Ecaz and Moritani, and the Emperor had' even stationed Sardaukar watchdogs on Grumman for two years. But as soon as the Imperial soldiers pulled out, Viscount Moritani struck again, publicly executing both Armand's brother and his daughter Sanyá, opening the floodgates of a full-scale war.

"Will there never be an end to it?" Leto asked.

"I recently had to reprimand Duke Prad Vidal because he attempted to make a black-market cargo shipment against my express orders. Once caught, Vidal simply offered to pay me half the profits, expecting to be forgiven, but I spat in his face. I literally spat in his face!" Armand blinked at Leto, as though surprised at himself. "He submitted a formal apology for his actions, and seemed to expect one from me in return. My administrators claim we are losing profits because of the embargo, but what is mere money? I hate the Moritanis."

In a quiet voice, Leto said, "I have heard that the Viscount's son suffers from a terrible disease, and that a cure is available here on Ecaz. If you showed compassion by providing medicine, would that not be a way to resolve your conflict peacefully?"

Armand said acidly, "How could I save his pathetic son, when *he murdered my daughter*? By denying Moritani the medicine, I'll make that madman feel some of the pain he has inflicted on my House. This dispute will not end without a complete extermination of one family or the other."

The Archduke lifted a small crystalline vial that stood near his place on the table. "This is the rare medicine the Viscount so desperately needs. Esoit-poay requires months to extract, refine, and process. Yes, I could provide this to Moritani. I *could* save his son."

Armand clenched the tiny bottle in his hand, then hurled it to the stone tiled floor, smashing the vial to glinting shards. "I would rather let the cure dry on the ground than have it touch the lips of that vile Grumman spawn." He lowered his voice. "Imagine if you were given a chance to provide comfort or save the Baron Harkonnen's young nephew. Would you do it?"

Leto sighed heavily. "I doubt it. The Harkonnens were involved in the death of my father, and quite probably were part of the scheme that cost the life of my firstborn son. No, I'd throttle Feyd-Rautha with my bare hands rather than save him."

"Then you understand my position better than most people."

Leto nodded. "I agree to the terms."

The rest of the negotiations went smoothly, and soon it was time for Leto to return home with Paul and Jessica and begin the preparations. The wedding would take place at Castle Caladan in two months.

Former friends make the most bloodthirsty enemies. Who is in a better position to know how to inflict the greatest pain?

—from *The Wisdom of Muad'Dib* by the
PRINCESS IRULAN

Centuries of exploitation by the Harkonnens had wrung nearly every resource out of Giedi Prime. Even the Baron recognized that. The Moritani home planet of Grumman, however, was in far worse shape.

House Moritani had abused the landscape for generations until it was little more than the husk of a once-fertile world, mined out and barely capable of sustaining even the hardiest crops. The natives could extract very little more from the planet, and House Moritani was hungry for a new fief. The Viscount had already petitioned the Emperor several times, specifically mentioning Ecaz as a possibility, but his requests had been turned down.

No wonder the man is always in a foul mood, the Baron thought as he gazed across the patchy steppes. Even the breezes through the dry remnants of vegetation sounded like a death rattle.

Dressed entirely in black, the large Baron stood impatiently outside a series of linked insulated yurts and stable-sized tents. Through the fluttering tent flaps he saw high wooden stall doors, and men in leathers. He heard specially bred horses neighing and kicking in their stalls, and handlers trying to calm them.

After his arrival from Giedi Prime, a rugged open vehicle had brought him and his Mentat, Piter de Vries, directly from the spaceport. A thick-armed driver with shaggy hair and a long mustache had said that Viscount Moritani would meet them there, but failed to say when. Now, the Harkonnen leader pulled his collar up around his neck. The air seemed laden with grit and dust, worse even than Arrakis. Vladimir Harkonnen was not accustomed to waiting.

Piter looked indignant on his behalf. "My Baron, this is a Grumman *barn!* Hardly an appropriate meeting place if the Viscount is trying to impress you."

The Baron frowned at him. "Use your deductive reasoning, Mentat. Hundro Moritani loves his specially bred stallions. He probably considers this an honor." He had heard the magnificent horses were huge and dangerous. The beasts certainly made a frightful amount of noise.

On the flight down from orbit, the pilot had pointed out the walled city of Ritka on the edge of a dry seabed that butted up against a low mountain range. Most of the people on Grumman were nomadic, wandering over the rugged land to eke out an existence from the sparse remaining resources. The inhabitants of Ritka depended almost entirely on offworld supplies.

Beneath the dry seabed and its surrounding plains, the crust had been riddled with interconnecting tunnels and mine shafts by Grumman mineral extractors that chewed like termites, scraping away every speck of worthwhile dust. The Baron had been nervous that the whole plain would collapse under the weight of the passenger ship as it landed outside of Ritka.

House Moritani was desperate, and for good reason. The Baron was eager to hear what the Viscount intended to propose. If he could use the Grumman hatred of Ecaz to inflict collateral misery on House Atreides, he would be well pleased. In the meantime, however, he was not pleased with this long wait.

Something caught his eye in the distant sky, a lumbering aircraft flying low over the hills. Soon he heard the steady, muffled drone of engines. A large, heavy creature dangled in a metallic sling from the fixed-wing flier—an animal with long legs, black hide, flailing mane and tail. One of their monster horses?

The plane hovered over a landing pad not far from the connected yurts and tents, easing the black brute down to the ground. The Baron could see vicious-looking spines protruding from the stallion's head. Men on speedcycles encircled the creature and fired bright yellow loops of energy at it, which they tightened on all sides as the beast pulled against the restraints. Shield ribbons, the Baron realized; he'd heard of them. Releasing the harness from the aircraft, the cycle wranglers sent the sling mechanism back up into the air. As they worked, the Baron recognized one of the wranglers as the Grumman Swordmaster, Hiih Resser. The redhead was multi-talented, it seemed. The fixed-wing flier landed nearby, and Moritani emerged from the craft, flushed and grinning.

"Piter, come meet our host," the Baron said. Buoyed by his suspensor belt, he strode purposefully toward the landing area, careful to stay clear of the thrashing animal and the cycle wranglers who fought to drag it toward a corral.

Viscount Moritani marched down the aircraft's exit ramp wearing a brown leather jerkin, a pointed cap, chaps, and glistening spurboots. "I trust you enjoyed the show, Vladimir! You should see what my stallions can do in a blood tournament."

"Perhaps later . . . after we discuss our business. I have been waiting here for quite some time."

"Apologies. A prized wild stallion was spotted on

the steppes. He led us on quite a chase, but we finally got him. Very valuable breeding stock, a thoroughbred Genga—our ancient breed is found nowhere else in the galaxy. One of the few truly profitable things left on Grumman."

Before the handlers could get the huge spiny horse into a stall, the creature broke free of the shield ribbons and charged back out, wild-eyed, toward the Baron and the Viscount. The two noblemen stumbled toward the dubious shelter of the plane. Boosted by his suspensors, the Baron reached the ramp first. The wild stallion slammed into the thin metal walkway as the Viscount tried to get around the Baron, causing the two men to stumble into each other.

The Baron shouted, "Piter, stop that beast!" The Mentat was not sure what to do with a spiny horse that neighed and roared.

The wranglers sped forward on their cycles, throwing out more shield ribbons, but missed their mark. Standing alone, unmoving, Swordmaster Resser fired a volley of stun darts at the horse as it charged toward him. Finally it collapsed in its tracks with a heavy thud.

The Baron brushed himself off, trying to regain his composure by venting his anger at Piter de Vries. Viscount Moritani roared with laughter. "Gengas are the most spirited horses in the Imperium! Each one is big and fast, a lethal combination that can defeat the largest Salusan bull."

After the drugged horse was safely hauled away, an aide hurried up to issue a weather report. Frowning, Moritani turned to the Baron. "I intended to put on a horse show for you, but alas our climate-control methods are rudimentary in comparison with those of other worlds." Black clouds had begun to gather over the mountains. "We will have to retire to my fortress in Ritka."

"Too bad," the Baron said, but he didn't mean it.

⤙⤚

THE ARCHITECTURE OF the Viscount's dim and dusty fortress made it seem like a tent made of stone, with angled slabs for ceilings. As the two noblemen took their seats at a private table of dark, age-stained wood, the Baron held out his hand to Piter. The Mentat handed him a bulky packet, which the Baron extended toward Hundro Moritani. "I bring a gift for your son, a supply of semuta-laced melange. It may help his condition." From what he'd seen of the boy, Wolfram had very little time left anyway.

Piter stepped forward to explain. "Apparently, the combination of drugs yields the same euphoric effects of semuta, but without that annoying music."

Nodding sadly, the Viscount said, "A kind gesture, considering how difficult it is to procure even semuta on the black market, now that Armand Ecaz has cracked down on his exports." With a darkening expression and a thickening accent as he grew more upset, the Viscount launched into his proposal without so much as serving refreshments, making the Baron think that the Ritka fortress received few noble guests. "Vladimir, we can help each other. You hate the Atreides, and I hate the Ecazis. I have a way to solve both of our problems."

"I already like the way you think. What do you suggest?"

"The news is fresh, but verified. Duke Leto Atreides intends to marry Ilesa Ecaz, sealing the two Houses together. The ceremony is scheduled to be held on Caladan in six weeks."

"My spies already informed me of this. How does it help us? After Shaddam's latest spectacle, I am weary of weddings. In any case, neither of us is likely to be invited to the nuptials."

"That doesn't mean we cannot send a special gift—

something to make the occasion memorable. We have atomics." The Viscount raised his bushy eyebrows. "I presume you do as well?"

The Baron reeled in alarm. "Atomics are forbidden by the strictest possible terms in the Great Convention. Any use of atomics by one House against another is cause for the immediate extinction of that House—"

Moritani cut him off. "As I well know, Baron. And if I have any hope of securing Ecaz as my own new fief, I wouldn't want to turn it into a charred ball, now would I? I mention the idea only in passing."

What kind of leader would mention atomics like that? In passing? the Baron thought.

Though open warfare involving great military forces and planetary-scale battles was nearly inconceivable these days, the rules of conflict among the Landsraad houses still allowed direct assassination attempts under specific circumstances. This dance of controlled violence permitted rulers to exhibit their dark sides without risking entire populations. This compromise had stood for ten thousand years, under the shield of the Great Convention.

"Ah, Vladimir—we can send an entirely different sort of message to Atreides and Ecaz, a much more personal one. I want Archduke Armand to know that *I* am his attacker."

The Baron narrowed his gaze. "I, on the other hand, would prefer to keep any Harkonnen involvement secret." He had not the time nor patience for a War of Assassins right now. "You may take all the credit, my dear Viscount."

The other man smiled. "Then we are in perfect accord."

*The weather changes, and friends come and go,
but blood ties withstand great cataclysms.*

—DUKE PAULUS ATREIDES

Back home on Caladan, young Paul felt withdrawn. After what he had seen and learned in the Archduke's palace, he had many questions, to which he could not find answers in filmbooks.

He went down to the dockside, wandered past the fishseller stalls, and made his way up the path to a coastal promontory. Looking for solace, or at least answers that made sense to him, Paul stopped at the colossal harbor statues of Duke Paulus Atreides and young Victor, Duke Leto's first son. *My brother,* he thought with a wave of sadness. Paul stared up at the statues. Having seen images of the real individuals, he knew that these representations were accurate, though slightly idealized. Leto had erected the towering sculptures at the mouth of the harbor so that all craft passing in or out of Cala City would see them.

Both deaths had left a great mark on his father's life, and it had been during Leto's time of deepest grief following Victor's death that Jessica had gotten pregnant. In a way, Paul realized, he owed his life, his very existence, to that tragedy. . . .

He saw his mother coming up the black rock steps,

and presently she stood beside him on the esplanade at the base of the statues. The salty breezes blew strands of her bronze hair about her face. "I thought you might be here, Paul. I sometimes come to this place myself to deal with my own questions."

He gazed at the stone figures, the burning braziers filled with bright flames. "Do they ever answer you?"

"No, the answers have to come from ourselves." She smiled at him. "Unless you would like to speak with me?"

He blurted a response, not thinking. "When my father marries Ilesa Ecaz, will I still be his heir? What is my place in House Atreides?"

"Leto has designated you, Paul. You are his son."

"I know, but if he has another child with Ilesa, his legal wife, won't that boy become his rightful heir instead of me?"

"Are you having dynastic dreams, Paul?" Jessica asked softly. "Do you want to be Duke?"

"Thufir says that anyone who *wants* to be Duke would not be a good one."

"That's the irony of political realities. Your father has promised that your status and mine will not change. Trust him."

"But how can he promise that? Didn't he also make promises to Archduke Ecaz?"

"Your father has made many promises. The challenge will be for him to balance and keep all of them—and you know he'll try. His sense of honor is his most prized possession."

"Do you believe my father is betraying you, or us, by marrying another woman?" Paul watched his mother's expression carefully. He could see the subtle signs of confusion and ambivalence as her Bene Gesserit–trained mind struggled to accept the necessities. Yet, no matter how much Jessica tried to convince herself, she was also a woman, a human being. She had feelings.

"I came to accept Kailea Vernius under similar circumstances," Jessica said. "I knew my place, and Leto knew his."

"But Kailea didn't accept it. I know what happened."

"Neither did your grandmother Helena. Your father knows he is treading on dangerous ground, but I will not try to talk him out of it."

Jessica turned from the statues and surprised Paul by hugging him fiercely. Tears brimmed in her eyes, but she brushed away the dampness. "Always remember one thing, Paul. Your father loves you, he truly does."

Yes, he knew that in a way that went beyond politics or logic. "I will never forget it."

⊸

A MONTH PASSED, and the wedding drew closer. Paul did his best to concentrate on his many duties and responsibilities as the son of a Duke.

Paul trained daily with Thufir Hawat. Gradually, the Weapons Master set the training mek to higher and higher skill levels, as if to express his own anger. The veteran Mentat had served House Atreides for generations; he had seen old Paulus and Helena during their legendary fights and watched Leto and Kailea as their relationship tumbled into disaster. But in his position as the Atreides Master of Assassins, he turned a blind eye to personal matters in the household, except where they might affect ducal security.

Paul fought against the mek, ducking to avoid its slashing metal arms, parrying with a short sword. Since the mindless, reactive device generated its own shield, he could practice the slow plunge of the knife through the resistance, adjusting the speed of his thrust to make the blade pass through. After each exhausting session, Thufir replayed Paul's moves via a holo-image so he could critique and assess the young man's strengths and weaknesses.

Now, Paul compartmentalized his thoughts as his mother had taught him, so that he could carry on a conversation while still fighting at the peak of his abilities. This habit had always startled his teachers, and Paul did it just to see the effect it had on the old Mentat. "Tell me how my grandfather died, Thufir."

"Bullfight. A Salusan bull killed him."

Paul slashed and ducked. One of the mek's cutting edges came very close to slicing open his left shoulder. "You would make a poor Jongleur. Your storytelling ability is greatly lacking."

Thufir continued to watch him, and finally said more. "Old Duke Paulus died because of treachery, and your grandmother was forced to take the veil with the Sisters in Isolation."

Pieces clicked together in Paul's mind. He had never bothered to compare the exact dates. According to stories and rumors around Castle Caladan, Lady Helena had withdrawn to the fortress nunnery out of grief. This was shocking new information. "Was she responsible for the plot?"

"Not for me to say . . . but in exile she remains. Duncan was but a stable hand at the time. Even he was implicated in the plot for a while."

"*Duncan?*" Paul nearly missed a thrust from the mek and stepped out of the way, letting the shield take the brunt of the blow when his artificial opponent thrust too quickly. "Duncan involved in the death of my grandfather? But he carries the Old Duke's sword."

"He was cleared of all charges." Thufir terminated the fighting exercise and shut down the mek. "That is enough, if you are going to insist on jabbering. You can pretend to do both at the same time, but I saw your mistakes, which could have been fatal if not for my presence. We will review them carefully, young Master. For now, go clean up, change your clothes, and prepare to receive our guests. The first members of the Ecazi wedding party arrive this afternoon."

*Politicians and predators operate on disturbingly
similar principles.*

—DUKE PAULUS ATREIDES, letter to his wife,
Helena

Several weeks after the Baron Harkonnen departed
from Grumman, where plans had been set in motion, the Viscount lost all reason for restraint.

Hiih Resser stood with a dozen members of the Moritani royal court, packed shoulder to shoulder in the sickroom of the dying boy. Viscount Moritani spoke to them
all in a voice like ripping paper. "The Suk doctor says
my son will soon breathe his last. It is only a matter of
days, or less. If only we had the drug to cure him." Moritani's broken whisper drove a knife of sorrow into
Resser's heart.

If only.

On his bed, reeking of melange and semuta smoke,
accompanied by wailing atonal music, whether or not
the melodic trance effects were necessary, Wolfram was
beyond hearing his distraught father.

Some of the witnesses sobbed softly, but Resser had
no way of judging if their tears were sincere. Looking
on, he was convinced that this clumsy demonstration
of support was largely an effort to gain favor with the
Grumman lord.

Preoccupied with his work, Dr. Terbali made adjustments to Wolfram's intravenous lines, while the wild-haired Viscount leaned over his son from the other side, kissed his sunken cheek, and spoke quietly. The unfortunate boy did not respond, but stared vacantly, only occasionally twitching a muscle or blinking his red-veined eyes.

The sick boy slipped so quietly into death that even Moritani did not notice for several seconds, though he held the boy's limp hand. Then, in delayed reaction, he let out a bestial sound that was half wail, half roar.

Dr. Terbali straightened from the bedside after checking vital signs. "I'm sorry, my Lord."

Hundro Moritani swept an arm across a tray of medical instruments, sending them clanging to the floor. He buried his face in his hands and sobbed.

The Viscount was a hard, cruel man with easily inflamed passions, and quick to respond with violence. Resser had seen how his master skirted morality for his own purposes, while putting forth false issues to disguise his motivations. But this was no pretended grief. The anguish over his only son's death was real.

The flames behind Moritani's eyes burned as brightly as stars. Resser was terrified, wondering if the Viscount would use the death of Wolfram as a catalyst to unleash the storm he had been holding inside for so long. The Grumman leader would step across the grave of his own son to obtain what he wanted for his House. With Wolfram gone, he would drum up support to take the planet Ecaz for himself, and somehow he would get another male heir. Or did he have an even larger plan? And was it simply revenge?

That is not a question for me to answer, Resser thought. *My role is to follow the orders of my master, to obey with my life, if necessary.*

The Viscount, his emotions changing in a flash,

turned on the Suk doctor. With tears streaming down his cheeks, Moritani stormed around the foot of the sickbed. "You knew the cure for Wolfram! I commanded you to obtain it for me."

"Not possible, my Lord! The Ecazis—"

Moritani hurled the portly doctor across the room into the clustered and clucking observers, but he was not finished yet. Drawing a slender, curved kindjal from his fur-trimmed jerkin, he stalked toward the stunned doctor, while others scrambled away, doing nothing to help or hinder the intended victim.

"I am a Suk—I have immunity!"

Face twisted in disgust, Moritani plunged the knife into the doctor's chest and withdrew it as swiftly as a serpent striking, then shoved the mortally wounded man aside as if he were no more than a distraction. "Then heal yourself."

Trying to assuage his grief with violence, he charged out of his son's death chamber with the bloody blade, reacting to this problem just as Resser had seen him react to so many problems before. "Where are the others? Bring the smugglers to me—every one of them!" He spun to Resser. "Swordmaster, you find them."

"Yes, my Lord."

Within the hour, eleven Ecazi drug smugglers were brought before the enraged, distraught Viscount. Hundro Moritani had paid these men to slip through the Ecazi restrictions and obtain doses of esoit-poay regardless of cost. After a few unsuccessful attempts to obtain the curative through illegal channels, they had tried to steal a shipment. In all instances, they had returned empty handed.

One by one, the Viscount had the Ecazi smugglers bound by ropes around their ankles to wild Grumman stallions. In a grisly exhibition, the men were dragged across the dry, rocky seabed until they were dead. Afterward, looking at the shredded red bodies, he snapped at

Resser, "I cannot stand the sight of the Ecazi race. Remove these corpses from my presence, and have them burned."

Resser did as he was told, knowing that Moritani was probably just beginning.

*One does not need Other Memory to be haunted
by the past.*

—REVEREND MOTHER GAIUS HELEN MOHIAM

Though Duke Leto's wedding could in no way compare to Shaddam's recent spectacle, Landsraad families who wished to pay their respects to House Atreides and House Ecaz would dutifully attend from across the Imperium. The most important visitors would stay in guest chambers at Castle Caladan. The innkeepers in Cala City had cleaned and expanded their rooms to prepare for the flood of visitors.

Two weeks before the scheduled ceremony, Archduke Armand Ecaz and his retinue landed three large lighters at the spaceport. Duncan Idaho went out to greet the Ecazis, and escorted them back to the castle in a crowded procession aboard slow-moving groundcars. Cargo flats followed them, bearing their luggage and supplies.

Paul waited inside the Castle, still feeling uncertain about his proper place in events. What he had thought to be a rock-solid island in a sea of galactic politics had become a shifting sandbar. His mother was nowhere to be found, having decided to occupy herself with household duties out of sight.

The initial party included the Archduke himself and his daughter Ilesa, accompanied by Swordmasters

Rivvy Dinari and Whitmore Bludd. Paul stared down at them from a tower window, particularly interested in his father's bride-to-be. Ilesa was beautiful, though in a different fashion from the Lady Jessica. He considered his automatic resentment toward the young woman, then consciously decided it was unfair to dislike her simply because of her abrupt insertion into the family. After all, Ilesa was also a pawn in the marriage game.

Duke Leto had explained about the political necessities, fully aware that Paul himself might—and probably would—find himself in a similar situation someday. "It is a nobleman's burden," his father had said, "heavy enough to break a man's back and a woman's heart."

Paul went to the main reception hall, where his father was greeting Armand Ecaz. Enormous Rivvy Dinari stood at attention, pretending to guard the proceedings, while Whitmore Bludd seemed much more interested in discussing the assignment of rooms with the Atreides housemaster.

An entire shipment of huge potted plants, rainbow-hued ferns, flowering bugle lilies, and spiky Elaccan evergreens had been sent by Duke Prad Vidal himself. The pots were large and elaborate, girdled with a mosaic design of broad hexagonal plates. There was an awkward moment as Thufir Hawat insisted on scanning the plants to prove that they were not poisonous. Some members of the Ecazi party were offended, but the Archduke told them to allow the most thorough inspection. "We will take no risks."

Paul saw Duke Leto watching Ilesa, who stood beside her father. "Those plants are an entirely appropriate wedding gift," Leto said. "Arrange them in the grand hallway, to give us a bit of Ecaz on Caladan. While Ilesa lives here, they will remind her of her home."

Swordmaster Bludd directed the arrangement of the pots, then moved on to numerous other preparations for the spectacular wedding, while Duke Leto finally took time to get to know his bride-to-be.

∽

THE SEAS OF Caladan whispered against the boat as Leto sailed out of the harbor and up the coast, always remaining within sight of the misty shore. The weathersats had promised a fine forecast for the ensuing two days, so Leto would have no problem handling the sloop himself. At his request, Ilesa accompanied him, as if this trip was some form of diplomatic foray.

"I've never been sailing before." Leaning back, she drew a deep breath of moist air. Instead of looking toward the rugged shoreline, she stared out at the waves that stretched far, far to the edge of the world.

"On Caladan, we are born and raised to be on the water," he said. "Everyone learns to swim, sail, judge the tides, and watch the weather."

"Then I'll have to learn those skills, since this is going to be my new home."

The sun broke through the low-lying fog, turning the sky an extraordinary, rich blue. The bright light bathed Ilesa's face, and she closed her dark brown eyes. Leto found himself observing her. With her brunette hair, her demure behavior, and her hesitant laugh, she was very different from Jessica, even from Kailea.

She leaned over the rail to the sloop's prow, where the name *VICTOR* had been painted. "Leto, tell me about your son."

"Paul is a fine young man. Intelligent and brave. I'm very proud of him. You've met him yourself, and you can see his potential."

"And Victor, if you don't mind talking about him? I only know that he died as a child."

Leto's voice became harder. "The innocent victim of

an assassination attempt against me. Victor . . . Rhombur . . . they suffered because of Kailea's jealous anger."

Ilesa raised her delicately arched eyebrows. "It wasn't a political matter, then?"

"That might have been easier to bear. No, this was far more personal. Kailea and a supposedly loyal guard captain planted a bomb in a processional airship, but the explosion killed our son instead of me." His voice hitched. "*Our son!* And it mangled Kailea's brother Rhombur, while I survived intact."

Ilesa was looking at him with deep emotion. The boat's deck swayed gently as they sailed onward. "And what happened to Kailea and this guard captain? I think my father would have staged a public execution— fast-growing birabu spikes to take root in his vital organs, perhaps." Ilesa did not even sound queasy at the prospect.

"Kailea threw herself from a high tower. But Goire . . . I did worse than execute him—I let him *live*. I sent him into exile so that he must face his crime for the rest of his days."

The two of them remained silent for a long moment, while Ilesa continued to stare out at the waves. "We are both scarred people, Leto," she said. "I know you have deep hurts within you, and I think you are aware of mine. Are we brave enough to use those past tragedies to make us stronger . . . or should we give up and just be damaged?"

Leto thought for a moment. "Ours isn't a silly romance, Ilesa. We both know why we are to be married. This may not be what you expected for your life."

"On the contrary, Leto—this is exactly what I expected. It's how I was raised. Once the Grummans killed Sanyá, I became the eldest Ecaz daughter. I have always been a name attached to a dowry. I never imagined that I'd fall in love with some brave man and then live happily ever after, like in a story. I am quite content with my circumstances."

Leto came to a conclusion, knowing it would be hard, but also realizing it was the best way. He hoped that eventually Ilesa might become much more—and much more tolerable—than just a political partner, which was all that Old Duke Paulus would have recommended.

"I want you to like Jessica and Paul. And I want them to like you. It is your job to make that happen, Ilesa. Can you do it?"

"As my Duke commands," she said.

⤸

*To the Emperor Shaddam: Please accept this gift
from House Harkonnen on the occasion of your
wedding to Lady Firenza Thorvald. This life-sized
melange sculpture of a Harmonthep lion symbol-
izes not only the lion of House Corrino but also
the enduring treasure of spice itself from the fief
of Arrakis, which your father so generously be-
stowed on us. We are always your humble servants.*

—BARON VLADIMIR HARKONNEN

The Emperor takes such a large share of our spice,
he bleeds us dry." The Baron sniffed, then nearly
sneezed from the damnable, ever-present dust in the air of
Arrakis. "For all the hells House Harkonnen endures on
this awful world, we should keep a larger percentage of it."

"And after today we will, my Baron." Piter de Vries
gave him a smug smile. "Right under the noses of
CHOAM inspectors."

Twelve years earlier, when House Harkonnen had
been accused of skimming melange and falsifying the
total tonnage reported to the Imperium, armies of audi-
tors and Mentat accountants had pored over the Baron's
records, but the inspectors had found no significant ir-
regularities. He had kept his nose clean for some time,
though he continued to search for ways to stockpile
spice secretly. Finally, de Vries had proposed an ingenious and viable idea to hide extra spice in plain sight,
and now he had successfully implemented the scheme.

The spice storage yard on the outskirts of Carthag was
well guarded by Harkonnen troops and by scanner technology. Ten immense silos baked in the afternoon sun-

light. Black attack 'thopters flew sorties around the area, constantly looking for Fremen thieves who might be lurking out in the sands, waiting for any opportunity to raid Harkonnen supplies.

He and de Vries rode a lift up the outside of the largest new silo. The lift came to a stop, and the Baron stepped out onto a high platform at the very top, from which he could survey the entire field. These silos held the spice stockpiles he was mandated to maintain, ready supplies to meet regular shipments to the Landsraad, the Guild, and CHOAM, as well as strategic reserves to guarantee the Emperor's share. "All of the silos are constructed of the new stuff?"

De Vries wiped a hand over his red-stained lips and spoke with clear pride in his voice. "Every last container has been reconstructed, including the railings and the platform on which we stand, out of polymer infused with melange. Ten extra long tons of spice not on any inventory, hidden within the structure of the outpost itself. And because of the legal spice within the silos, melange readings are naturally everywhere. No scanners would ever notice the difference. Even the slight cinnamon odor is to be expected. This is, after all, a spice storage yard. We are hiding the spice in plain sight."

The Baron passed a plump hand across a nearby safety rail, then licked his fingertips, but tasted nothing other than dust. "Ingenious, I am sure. But how are we to *take* this treasure with us, if it is molded into the structures themselves? CHOAM will notice if we dismantle and remove all of the silos."

Piter made a dismissive gesture. "We have a polymer separation mechanism, my Lord. At any time, we can quietly extract and exchange the extra spice with inert filler material, take the spice where we wish, and bank the profits without paying the Emperor's exorbitant taxes. We can siphon off a cup of hidden melange or tons of it, whenever we please."

In an uncharacteristically jovial mood, the Baron patted the slender Mentat hard on the back. Casually, he reached into his jacket pocket and brought out a sweet melange cake. He tossed the wrapping off the edge and watched it flutter down, then strode back onto the lift as he chewed and swallowed.

De Vries hurried to follow. "Perhaps we should discuss the upcoming Atreides wedding a bit more? Since the death of his son, Viscount Moritani has grown rather extreme."

When the lift reached the ground, the Baron marched off toward his waiting vehicle. "I confess he makes me uneasy, Piter. He is so . . . volatile. I am reluctant to be too closely tied with House Moritani. It's like having a rabid pet."

"You're quite right to be concerned about him, my Lord." De Vries smiled. "Nevertheless, I cannot deny that his urge toward violence works to our advantage now. Let me explain—"

The Baron held up a hand as he entered his cool, sealed groundcar. "I don't want to know the details, Piter. None of them. I want only your assurance that I won't be disappointed. Nor will I be implicated."

"You have my promise on both counts, Baron. As a follow-up plan, I have already dispatched our own operatives, each of them carefully doctored to look like Grummans should they be discovered. We leave nothing to chance."

The groundcar sped toward the Harkonnen keep, while the Baron ate another sweet spice cake. He wiped his sticky fingers on his dusty pant leg. "Our hands must be entirely clean. No mistakes."

"None, my Lord. The Viscount is only too happy to claim responsibility. He seems to revel in the prospect of blood."

"As do I, Piter. But I do it privately."

Good friends have a way of focusing our memories so that we can view even painful events in a positive light.

—DUKE LETO ATREIDES

The Duke's request seemed cold and unfeeling, a slap in the face. He wanted her to take Ilesa under her wing, to be the other woman's formal companion, and to work with the Castle Caladan and Ecazi planners on preparations for the wedding. Jessica needed all of her Bene Gesserit training to nod formally. "Yes, Leto. As you wish."

In spite of all her years of training, Jessica hated herself for her hurt feelings. She was a concubine sent under orders to become his companion, a business commodity, forced to give up the right to human emotions. She was happy with the love and devotion Leto had given her in the past, but she should not have expected it to last forever.

Even so, the truth of it struck her to the core.

Jessica was too smart to view this as a superficial or thoughtless slight. Leto knew exactly what he was requesting, and she forced herself to delve into his motivations in asking her to become Ilesa's chaperone.

Finally she pulled back the curtain of emotions to let in the light and see what the Duke really needed from her: He sincerely wanted Jessica and Ilesa to be friends, and his instructions were designed to force the two women to accept reality. He did not mean to cut Jessica out, or Paul, but rather to fold them in. It also sent just as clear a signal to the daughter of Ecaz, that Duke Leto considered his concubine an important part of his household. The two would have to do things together, while each played her separate role.

When Jessica realized this, she explained it to Paul in order to help him understand. He would need that knowledge for later in life. "A wife and a lover are two different things. It is best if they can be the same person, but politics and love are as separate as the mind and the heart. Learn this lesson, Paul. As a Duke's son, you may find yourself in the same situation someday."

And so Jessica and Ilesa did spend their days together, setting up the halls, guest rooms, and meeting chambers of Castle Caladan for the wedding. They established plans, looked over guest lists, discussed passages from the Orange Catholic Bible, and reviewed subtle variations of the wedding liturgies. Some ceremonies could take only a few minutes, while more traditional ones might drone on for endless hours. Jessica had even read of extreme instances where a wedding ceremony lasted longer than the marriage itself. Working together, Jessica and Ilesa crafted a beautifully complex and poetic ceremony.

The household staff whispered surprised gossip at how well the two seemed to be getting along. At first Jessica considered her own cooperation just a necessary role to play, but one day she had looked across the table at Ilesa, and realized that she had come to think of Ilesa as a *person,* one with whom she could indeed become a friend.

The young woman confided in her with a shy smile. "Once, there was a young man with curly, straw-colored hair and a grin. And oh, what a lovely body! He was a member of the forest guard. I used to watch him train out in the courtyard with Swordmaster Dinari."

"What was his name?" Jessica asked.

"Vaerod." An entire symphony of wistful emotions accompanied the spoken name. "We used to walk and talk together. We even kissed once." Her smile faltered. "Then my father transferred him away, and I spent days listening to lectures about my responsibility to House Ecaz. The deaths of my sister and uncle hardened him. I became the hope and future for our family. I couldn't be allowed to fall in love, or plan my own life."

She looked up, and Jessica thought the young woman seemed extremely innocent, but her words were insightful. "Why is it, do you suppose, that we noble daughters can't take our own *male* concubines? If we are required to marry for political reasons, why can't we choose someone else for love, as Duke Leto chose you?"

Jessica searched for different ways to answer the question. "Did Duke Leto tell you he loves me?"

Ilesa made a quick, dismissive sound. "Any fool can see that."

Jessica blinked. *Perhaps I am not enough of a fool.*

"There are political necessities as to why Duke Leto will marry me. He will get what he wants with this alliance, and he still has you. I know this and accept it, but what about me? What about my Vaerod?"

For so long, Jessica had thought only of why Leto had decided on this alliance. His blustery father had been adamant about the political nature of marriage, and Lady Helena Atreides had accepted her lot, too, although with great bitterness.

With true compassion, Jessica said, "One of the first precepts taught at the Bene Gesserit School on Wallach IX is that the universe is not fair. Almost daily, I see evidence of that."

∼≫

WHEN THE IXIAN frigate bearing the guests from House Vernius landed at the spaceport, Paul accompanied Thufir Hawat and Gurney Halleck to meet them. Thufir and Gurney had already told him much about Prince Rhombur.

The frigate's ramp extended and guards marched out, carrying purple-and-copper pennants emblazoned with a helix symbol. Then three figures appeared as though they were making a grand entrance. A young woman with a trim body, short brown hair, and large eyes held the hand of a boy with thick coppery hair, a squarish face, and a shy formal demeanor. Paul could see echoes of the mother's features in the boy.

Behind them came a hulking man whose mechanical movements somehow carried a calculated grace. Rhombur's face was scarred; his arm was obviously prosthetic. The flesh ended at his neck, fused with polymer wrappings. He raised an artificial hand in greeting. The smile that filled his ravaged expression was genuine. "Gurney Halleck! You still look uglier than I do." He took three thudding steps down the ramp. "And Thufir Hawat—still bearing the weight of the universe on your shoulders, I see."

A fast groundcar pulled up, and Duke Leto sprang out wearing an exuberant grin. "Rhombur, old friend! I'm so pleased you could come."

The Ixian nobleman chuckled. "You came to my wedding, Leto. How could I not come to yours?"

"I couldn't avoid yours, Rhombur—it was held at Castle Caladan."

With a strange delicateness to his flexing fingers, Rhombur took the woman beside him by the wrist. "You remember Tessia, of course."

Leto laughed. "I'm not quite senile yet. And this is your son?" He extended a hand to the copper-haired boy.

"Yes, Leto—meet Bronso. He has been longing to leave the caverns on Ix to see the oceans that I loved so much." The damaged man lowered his voice. "And he is anxious to meet Paul. Is this your son?"

Paul stepped forward. "Pleased to meet you, Rhombur. Or should I call you Prince?"

"You could call me your godfather, boy." Rhombur thrust his son close to Paul. "You two will be great friends, just like your father and I were when we were younger."

"Maybe we should initiate an exchange, as our fathers did," Leto said. "Send Paul to Ix and have Bronso here on Caladan. It certainly changed my life."

Prince Rhombur appeared somewhat troubled. "Ix is not quite what you remember, Leto. Under my father, it was a spectacular world, but the Tleilaxu occupation wounded our spirit and caused great damage. Even though House Vernius rules again, some things have changed forever. We have always been more of a business than a noble House, and the technocracy has grown more powerful. I have less influence over decisions than I used to."

"Spreadsheets and quotas command Ix now," Tessia added, not shy about speaking up for her husband. "Increasing production at the expense of decreasing humanity."

Another man now emerged from the frigate—smallish in stature and thin, with a sallow face and the diamond tattoo of a Suk doctor on his forehead. His long hair was bound in a single silver ring. He bowed formally. "I brought all the medical equipment that may be needed. Prince Rhombur's cyborg enhancements function quite well, though I still monitor them regularly."

"Dr. Wellington Yueh, you are always welcome here. I owe you my life, and Rhombur owes you his. If I could find a doctor as dedicated, I would keep him as my personal physician on Caladan."

Yueh seemed embarrassed, but Tessia interrupted before he could answer. "Politics, medical doctors, complaints? Is this the way House Atreides prepares for a wedding?"

"Tessia's right," Rhombur agreed. "We shouldn't stand around in the noise and heat of the spaceport. Take us back to Castle Caladan. I'm certain my wife wants to see Jessica again, and we're all anxious to meet your bride-to-be."

⌁

BACK AT THE Castle, Jessica greeted them, standing at Ilesa's side. Paul recognized and admired what his mother was doing, and thought she was remarkably composed and elegant.

The whole front foyer and reception hall had been decorated with Caladan pennants, ornate streamers, and large potted plants from Ecaz. Paul could smell the lush greenery, and the flowers that had already begun to bloom in the few days since they'd been set out.

"An auspicious beginning." Rhombur stroked the plants with his prosthetic hands. "Look at the blooms!"

"A wedding gift from Duke Prad Vidal," Leto said. "I think Ilesa is very pleased."

"She should be pleased just to be marrying you, Leto," Rhombur said. Then he glanced at Jessica and seemed embarrassed by his comment. "It'll all work out for the best. Leto, you always seem to manage that."

Is it impossible for the mighty and powerful to be as happy as common folk? Not impossible perhaps, but extremely difficult.

— CROWN PRINCE RAPHAEL CORRINO,
Meditations

O n the day of the wedding, Castle Caladan looked magical. Fabric streamers blended the colors of House Atreides and House Ecaz in a symbolic braid. A set of jeweled mirrors from Richese faced each other along the foyer hall. Fine crystal goblets from Balut graced every place setting for the grand banquet that would follow the ceremony. Ixian clocks chimed a harmonic sequence with every hour. Wrapped wedding gifts from countless Landsraad Houses filled tables in side alcoves, each package prominently displaying the giver's name. Lush potted plants from Elacca decorated the stage of the grand hall.

Duke Leto was most touched by a wall-sized, hand-stitched quilt that had been crafted by the locals, one square given by each family in the fishing village and merchant district of Cala City. The people had made this with their own sweat and devotion, not because they sought political favors or alliances, but because they loved their Duke. Leto told Paul to learn from it, and demanded that the quilt be kept forever in Castle Caladan.

For days, Paul had watched guests arrive—representatives of prominent noble families. Putting his formal training in etiquette, politics, and protocol to use, he made an effort to meet every guest, noting details about their mannerisms, moods, and other features, so that he could remember them. Paul had been raised to be the next Duke, and would continue to believe that was the case, despite this new marriage.

As a formality, Leto had invited his cousin Shaddam IV, but was not surprised when neither the Emperor nor any important representative from Kaitain bothered to attend, though the Emperor did send a courier with kind wishes and the gift of an ornate set of cutlery. At first, Paul wondered if Shaddam was being petulant that Duke Atreides had not attended his own recent wedding; then he realized that someone as powerful as the Padishah Emperor would never hold such a petty grudge.

His father was kept so busy making arrangements that Paul barely saw him in the hours leading up to the actual ceremony. The morning dawned sunny on Caladan. Town bells rang, and the fishermen flew colorful pennants on their boats to celebrate the Duke's marriage.

Inside his bedchamber Paul took care in getting dressed. The garments he donned—a black jacket with razor-edge collar and tasteful tails, a white shirt with crisp cuffs, black trousers—had been carefully fitted by the finest tailor on Caladan. The elegant old man even pinned a badge with the Atreides hawk crest on the boy's chest. When Paul regarded himself in the looking glass, he decided he looked like a child playing dress-up.

But Duke Leto thought otherwise. Paul turned to see his father standing in the doorway, a look of pride on his face. "This is supposed to be my special day, Paul, but you might well steal the show. You look as if you could become Emperor yourself."

Paul had never been particularly adept at accepting compliments, especially extravagant ones. "All eyes will be on you, Father."

"No, all eyes will be on *Ilesa*. It is the bride's job to be the center of the ceremony."

"And today, we all have our jobs to do, don't we?" Paul wasn't sure if he had intended the comment to sting. Seeing his father's expression falter, Paul stepped forward and reached up to straighten his collar. "I am ready to meet the guests. Tell me what I can do to assist you."

The guests had gathered in the grand hall. The costumes, faces, exotic features, and traditional adornments of so many noble Houses made Paul dizzy. Even this tiny representative slice of population demonstrated how widespread the Imperium was, how many different planets and ethnic groups the Emperor ruled. It amazed him that all could come together beneath a single ruler.

Archduke Ecaz was smiling and full of good cheer, his long silver hair held back by a thin circlet. His formal uniform was embellished with ruffles and jewels, so elaborate that he was upstaged only by his wiry Swordmaster Whitmore Bludd.

No matter how Ilesa might be dressed, Paul could not imagine that she would look more beautiful than his mother. He was right. In a long gold-and-black gown, Lady Jessica was breathtaking. He wondered if she had done that intentionally, to remind Duke Leto of all she had to offer.

Thufir Hawat wore an old military uniform, one that featured medals he had earned during his service with Duke Paulus and Earl Dominic Vernius in the Ecazi revolt so many years before. House Atreides had a long-standing history of supporting House Ecaz.

Hawat had once again scanned the grand hall, dispatching his security troops through all public areas. Each wedding guest had been searched in accordance with standard security protocols. None of the nobles took offense, for they would have imposed the same measures upon their own visitors. At every doorway, Atreides soldiers stood beside their Ecazi counterparts.

Duncan Idaho had also dressed for the day. As a Swordmaster, he often played the role of dashing warrior, the Duke's special fighter and bodyguard; now he wore the formal sword of Old Duke Paulus strapped to his side, a weapon he had carried many times into battle for House Atreides. Paul knew Duncan's abilities were unmatched, although the two visiting Swordmasters from House Ecaz were also there to show their mettle, if need be.

Despite his attempts to make himself presentable, Gurney Halleck was not designed for formal clothing. His body had been battered too many times, and the inkvine scar stood out on his jawline, defying any attempts at makeup. He was a man more accustomed to work clothes that let him move among the common folk. He was meant to sit with a nine-string baliset on his knee and sing songs to noblemen, rather than pretend to be one of them. But the grin on his face dismissed all awkwardness. Seeing Paul in his outfit, Gurney said, "Young pup, you look like a future director of CHOAM."

"Oh, I was trying to look like the son of a Duke."

Duke Leto had chosen his son as best man, and for the honor, Paul had been coached not only by his mother but by official planners and choreographers. Now, one of the choreographers motioned for him to take his place on the garlanded stage that had been erected just for the wedding. Paul walked past the huge potted plants on the stage toward the central podium that held an ancient oversized Orange Catholic Bible, the same book that had been used at the wedding of Paulus and Helena, as well as eighteen generations of Atreides before that. Armand Ecaz stood to one side of the podium with Swordmasters Dinari and Bludd, while Paul joined Duke Leto, Thufir, Gurney, and Duncan on the opposite side.

When he turned to face the room full of strangers, Paul's eyes fixed upon the large figure of Prince Rhombur, whose cyborg body was mostly covered with a formal suit, though his scarred and surreal face set him apart from the other attendees. Tessia and their reticent son, Bronso, sat on either side of him in the front row. Paul couldn't interpret the odd grimace on Rhombur's face for certain, but he thought the Ixian Prince might be grinning.

On cue, the fanfare began, and the audience hushed. Heads turned to look back toward the arched entrance where high fernlike flowers bracketed the doorway. Ilesa entered gracefully, her gown a lavish confection of pearlescent silk, its bodice covered by a spray of shimmering pearls. Her dark hair was done up in an intricate arrangement of small polished seashells.

Paul glanced at his father. Duke Leto wore an astonished expression, as if he had never expected his bride-to-be would look so beautiful.

While everyone watched Ilesa, the robed priest emerged unnoticed from a side alcove to take his position at the podium bearing the ancient book. Though there had been offers from other noble families, and even from important church officials including an Archbishop from Kaitain, Duke Leto had asked one of the most popular local priests to perform the ceremony. Archduke Ecaz had no particular preference in the matter. After the tragedies that had befallen him and the senseless pain the Grummans had inflicted upon his House, he had become decidedly nonreligious.

Ilesa glided forward, smiling. Flanked by the Swordmasters, Archduke Armand watched her, his smile rapturous. Duke Leto stood straight, showing his respect until Ilesa took her place beside him, facing the village priest. As quietly and discreetly as possible, the priest opened the book to the wedding liturgy and set out a crystal bell with which he would begin the ceremony. Leto took Ilesa's hand in his, and Paul saw that his father was holding his breath.

The priest struck a clear musical tone on the bell. "Friends of House Ecaz, House Atreides, and Emperor Shaddam IV, we welcome you to this moment of happiness." He struck a second tone.

As the priest began to speak again, Paul heard a *snick,* followed by a hum. He didn't want to tear his eyes from the bride and groom, while everyone in the room was listening so intently, but then he heard another sound and sensed a faint movement. He concentrated, forcing the background noise to fall away, and pinpointed the source of the sound: the huge Elaccan flowerpots.

Thufir Hawat snapped his head to one side. The old Master of Assassins had heard it as well.

The large hexagonal mosaic tiles had popped loose— extending slightly from the curved pots on some type of axle—and began to spin.

"Duncan!" Paul shouted, not caring that he would disrupt the ceremony.

But Duncan was already in motion. Gurney crouched, dagger in hand, ready to fight, looking for an attacker. Rivvy Dinari and Whitmore Bludd both drew their swords, advancing to protect Archduke Ecaz and Ilesa; Paul had never seen them move so fast.

The decorative hexagonal plates, thin sheets of metal, propelled themselves forward, spinning through the air like circular saw blades. Their edges, which had been mounted into the glazed clay of the pots, were razor sharp.

The air of the hall was filled with whirling blades, executioner discs that flashed toward their targets: everyone in the wedding party, any person who stood on the stage.

Duncan swept the Old Duke's sword in an arc to

strike one of the discs, sending it into the stone blocks of the wall, where it cut a deep gouge before clattering to the ground. Thufir grabbed Duke Leto by the tuxedo collar and pulled him sideways to the floor, diving upon him as another scythelike blade slashed a long rent across the old veteran's back.

More blades crisscrossed in the air, and the audience began to scream in panic. Like a charging bull, Gurney threw himself toward Paul. "Young Master, *down*!" Paul had already crouched to dodge the flying blades, and Gurney bowled him over, throwing himself between Paul and one of the deadly plates. At the last instant, Paul grabbed a handful of Gurney's blond hair and yanked the man's head. A sharp disc streaked past, missing Gurney's skull by millimeters, clipping a small lock of hair.

"Ilesa! Save her!" Rivvy Dinari bellowed. "I have the Archduke!" Whitmore Bludd sprang toward the bride, whipping his thin rapier before him. He struck one of the disks, and it caromed off into the ceiling.

Undeterred by the Swordmasters, another of the weapons struck like an executioner's hatchet into the Archduke's upper arm, neatly severing it above the elbow. Pushing himself free of Gurney, Paul watched in nightmarish slow motion as the detached limb dropped to the floor, sleeve and all, in a rain of blood.

Dinari roared, realizing his failure. He brandished his sword and stood as a human blockade, spreading himself in front of his grievously wounded master. The Archduke gasped, clutching at his stump.

More spinning blades flew directly at the Ecazi leader. The corpulent Swordmaster smashed one out of the air and sent it ricocheting into the floor. He struck another disk a glancing blow. Then four more blades slammed into his great body with the sound of cleavers cutting into tough meat, embedding themselves deep in

Rivvy Dinari's lungs, cutting through his sternum and slicing his heart in half. The last disc bit deep into his gut. Dinari's great hulk collapsed to the floor of the stage, but he had intercepted all of the deadly devices aimed toward his master.

With a howl of outrage, Bludd attempted to defend Ilesa. His rapier skewered and flung aside another executioner disc. He reached up with the thin blade to parry one more razor-edged tile, moving with both speed and precision.

He missed.

Though Ilesa was backing away, she couldn't bend far enough, and the spinning disc slashed her throat. Her delicate hands fluttered up, as if to catch the scarlet spray, but blood fountained from her neck, drenching her beautiful gown in red.

With a roar from his artificial lungs, Rhombur threw himself forward, knocking aside guests in the front row. "*Leto!*"

Squirming free of Gurney, Paul got to his hands and knees again, intent only on ensuring that his father was safe. Duke Leto, as expected, was shouting orders, organizing an immediate response, telling his guards to smash the deadly pots, calling for medics, showing concern for everyone but himself.

Acting on instinct, as if he could foresee what was about to happen, Paul sprang toward his father. Every instant stretched, drawn out to a long and syrupy timeline. Duke Leto turned, his gray eyes widening as he saw the sharp, whirling edge—

But Paul slammed him aside, and the cutter disk made only a harmless whirring noise as it passed and thudded into a wall. From the corner of his eye, extraordinarily aware of every detail, Paul saw his mother rushing toward the stage.

Like a mechanical ox, Rhombur used his artificial

limbs to smash the pots, destroying the targeting mechanisms, preventing the launch of any more razor-edged plates. Duncan struck the last three spinning discs out of the air.

Archduke Ecaz sat on the floor in shock, blood flowing from the stump of his arm, though the severed blood vessels had collapsed, slowing the massive bleeding. He could barely manage to sit upright next to the mangled corpse of the fat Swordmaster.

Whitmore Bludd stood entirely unscathed, though his fine clothes were speckled by droplets of crimson. He stared down in denial at Ilesa, who lay twitching, but already dead, on the stage.

A shimmering hologram arose from the wreckage of the flowerpots. Some small generator that must have been placed there played a microscopic crystal that held a recorded message and the image of Viscount Moritani, dressed in fine clothes fit for a funeral, not a wedding.

"Archduke Ecaz! Please accept this humble tribute from Grumman. I would have been there in person, you see, but I had to attend the funeral of my son. *My son!* Wolfram would have lived, but for you. You should have given me the gift of a cure. Now I give you the gift of these memories.

"I hope the slaughter is as extravagant as I have imagined. In all probability, you aren't even alive to hear this. But others are. Heed the cost of making an enemy of House Moritani. By all rights and all that is just, this War of Assassins is *mine.*"

∾

PART III

EMPEROR MUAD'DIB

10,197 AG
Four Years After the Beginning of the Jihad

*If a soldier dies on a battlefield and no one re-
members his name, was his service for naught?
Muad'Dib's faithful know better than this, for in
his heart he honors the sacrifices they make for
him.*

—from *A Child's History of Muad'Dib* by
the PRINCESS IRULAN

Fighting unnoticed beside his fellow soldiers,
Muad'Dib wore a ragged uniform that had been
cleaned and patchily repaired after being taken from the
body of a fallen warrior. Having spent hours in the fight,
his knife arm ached, and his ears rang from the explosions and screams. His nostrils burned from drinking in
the nauseating cocktail of smells that hung in the air—
the acrid discharges of slow explosives, spilled blood,
burned flesh, churned dirt.

From so many planetary battlegrounds and so many
victories in the four years of the Jihad, the disguised
Emperor did not know the name of this world where so
many of his followers were dying. During the horrific
combat and its aftermath, what did names matter? He
was sure this place was little different from the countless
others that Gurney and Stilgar had described.

But he had needed to see it for himself, fight with his
own hands, spill blood with his own weapons. *I owe it to
them.*

No detailed report from his generals, no council
meeting had ever driven home the depths of this hell.
Yes, he had escaped with his mother on the night of the

Harkonnen takeover of Arrakeen, and yes, he had fought with his Fremen on razzia raids against Beast Rabban, and yes, he had led them to victory against Emperor Shaddam and his Sardaukar. But few of his followers understood the noble goals of this war, especially the common soldiers. Only he could see the whirlwind, and the far worse fate that awaited the human race if his Jihad failed.

As he forged ahead into the future, he saw hazards in every decision, death and pain on every side. It reminded him of the ancient story of Odysseus and his voyage that required him to chart a perilous course between two dangers, the monster Scylla and the whirlpool Charybdis—a pair of water hazards that no one raised on Dune could grasp. But here, now, the path ahead seemed less clear, and clouded in a mist of uncertainty. Paul only knew that somewhere beyond this Jihad, perhaps many generations later, lay a safe harbor. He still believed he could guide humankind along the correct, narrow path. He *had* to believe it.

For those who could not see the large and subtle tapestry of fate, however, this battle was a slaughter of nearly helpless civilians on a formerly peaceful planet.

The reports would call it a victory.

But after years of growing more and more separated from the realities of the Jihad, he had decided he needed more than reports. Reports were not enough to convey what was truly happening across the Imperium . . . what *he* had set in motion.

One night inside his quiet, protected Arrakeen quarters that were newly finished by Bludd, he had dreamed of Gurney Halleck, Stilgar, and dozens of other commanders with their legions of Fremen warriors and converts. He valued (and was grateful to) every single one of those men, but *he* had remained on Dune, perfectly safe, while they fought and died.

Was that enough? He didn't think so. Duke Leto had personally led Atreides forces against Grumman during the War of Assassins. Paul knew that reading battlefield summaries could never give him the visceral level of understanding that came from experiencing the harsh conditions *with* his men, the lack of sleep, the explosions, the constant wariness, the blood. He had dispatched vast armies to crush worlds, and the fighters screamed his name as they died for him—while he remained in the comfort of his palace in Arrakeen.

Not enough.

But if he had publicly announced his intention to lead a battle, his generals would have found ways to shield him by choosing a soft planet where there was sure to be only minimal resistance. The battle would have been as false for him as the costume stillsuits that vendors sold to unwary pilgrims. Paul could not simply hide inside his ever-growing citadel and be treated as a god. His father had taught him better than that. The moment a leader forgot his people, he forgot himself.

Not enough, he had told himself again. He needed to do it on his own terms, and a plan had begun to form in his mind. . . .

He knew that if any of his Jihad fighters recognized his features from the silhouetted profile on so many banners or on newly minted coins, they would form a protective barrier around him fifty men thick. Battle commanders would refuse to engage the enemy, pull Muad'Dib to safety, and keep him in an orbiting Guild Heighliner for fear that he might come to harm.

That was why Paul cut and dyed his hair and procured a used uniform before beginning this masquerade as a common soldier. Telling no one but Chani where he was going, he signed up among the blur of recruits joining a new operation. Paul intentionally chose the unit of one of his lesser commanders, Jeurat, someone not familiar with him on a personal level. As a new soldier, he had passed a cursory inspection and demonstrated basic fighting proficiency to a Fremen soldier who could not have been more than eighteen years old. After that, Paul's unit had crowded aboard a military frigate and flown away from Dune.

Paul knew that the people he left behind would be frantic, though Chani would assure them he lived, without revealing where he had gone or what he was doing. Even so, they would bemoan the thousands of supposedly important decisions they needed him to make. But he wanted them to be weaned from their dependence on Muad'Dib. If they craved a security blanket, they could simply project a holo-image of him and be comforted.

If Paul did not do this thing, he feared he might lose all grasp of the true cost he was asking humanity—all unknowingly—to bear.

Only once had he heard the name of the planet that was their destination, Ehknot. Paul had never seen it marked on any star charts and wondered why it had been labeled such a threat. He doubted even Emperor Shaddam had been aware of this place.

On Ehknot the ground battles of the Jihad changed, and Paul's unit was forced to fight using different tactics. On two previous embattled worlds, the truly desperate rebels against Muad'Dib—prodded by Earl Memnon Thorvald—had begun to use lasguns recklessly and maliciously, firing upon *shielded* warriors. Although anyone shooting a lasgun into a shield would be killed by the feedback pulse, the pseudo-atomic detonation produced by the interaction was so devastating that it wiped out thousands of Jihad soldiers at a time. The death toll in those engagements had been appalling. Such fighting had been reviled and forbidden for millennia, antithetical to all civilized rules of warfare. But the rebels discarded civilized rules. One of the greatest taboos of conflict had been broken.

People used such tactics only when they had nothing left to lose, and Muad'Dib's soldiers learned their lesson, becoming wary. To guard against these shocking suicide tactics, they discarded personal shields, and here on Ehknot they fought on a more primal level. Fremen, who had never liked to rely upon body shields, now took up hand-to-hand fighting with crysknives for close-range work, and projectile weapons to shoot down distant targets. Remembering the old Harkonnen military assault on Arrakeen, some of the commanders even used large artillery guns to blast away physical barricades.

Paul could barely remember his own actions here during the fighting. Once the bloodshed started, he had lost all control of himself. His sight had become only a red haze, and he went into a frenzy more consuming than the most potent spice vision. He did not focus on the razor-thin path to a safe future, did not ponder the vast canvas of history or the requirements prescience had imposed upon him. He merely killed.

Paul's fighting skills were still superior to those of most of his warriors, for he had been taught by the best: Duncan Idaho, Thufir Hawat, and Gurney Halleck. His mother had shown him Bene Gesserit fighting methods, and among the Fremen he had learned yet another set of skills.

The battle was a long, difficult moment of insanity for him, though his fellow soldiers came to regard him as a Blessed One, a fanatic of fanatics. By the time the fighting ended, the survivors glanced in his direction with awe, as if they believed he was possessed by a holy spirit.

In the smoldering aftermath, he heard wailing voices call, "Muad'Dib, save me! Muad'Dib!" With a start,

Paul wondered if someone had recognized him, then realized that the wounded were merely invoking any help they could imagine.

No wonder a hardened Gurney gave no more than lukewarm responses when asked to lead more and more offensives. Planets fell, one after another, and now Paul became aware of the truly heavy toll he had placed on his friend. Affable Gurney, the troubadour warrior whose talent with a baliset was as well known as his skill with a sword. He had made the man an earl of Caladan, then denied him any time to settle there and make a real life. *Gurney, I am sorry. And you did not complain for a moment.*

As far as he knew, Stilgar still felt that he belonged with his Fremen warriors, but Paul made up his mind to find a new, planetbound assignment for Gurney, a role that might give him a sense of accomplishment, something other than . . . this. He deserved better.

Paul was covered with blood, and his borrowed uniform was torn, but he had only superficial cuts and scrapes. Suk doctors and scavengers combed the battlefield, tending the injured and harvesting the dead. He saw groups of Tleilaxu moving furtively from one fallen warrior to another, taking the most time with the greatest of the dead fighters. The Tleilaxu had always served as handlers of the dead, but these men seemed to be collecting *samples.* . . .

Simply one more horror among all the others.

Paul looked up with eyes that were blue-within-blue from spice addiction, but dry of tears. He saw a shaven-headed man, formerly a Fremen but now a priest, a member of the Qizara. The priest seemed to be experiencing a state of rapture. He raised his hands over the clouds of dust and curls of smoke, absorbing the horror of the battlefield that still throbbed in the air. He looked directly at Paul, but did not recognize him. With Paul's haunted eyes and blood-spattered face, and covered from head to foot with the filth of battle, he wondered if even Chani would know who he was.

"You are blessed by God, protected so that you can continue our holy work," the priest said to him. He swept his gaze slowly across the battlefield, and a smile appeared on his lips. "Ehknot, behold the invincibility of Muad'Dib."

Paul did behold, but did not see what the priest saw. And at the moment, no matter what the priest said, he did not feel at all invincible.

~

When negotiating the dangerous waters of the Imperium, it is wise to calculate the odds of various outcomes that might follow important decisions. This is art, not science, but at the most basic level it is a methodical process, and a matter of balance.

— *Acolyte's Manual of the Bene Gesserit*

Lady Margot Fenring had not been to the Bene Gesserit homeworld in some time, but it had not changed. Sienna tiles still covered the roofs of the sprawling Mother School complex, which surrounded the main buildings that dated back thousands of years. To the Sisterhood, Wallach IX was a ship of constancy floating in a vast and changing cosmic sea.

For all their intense study of human nature and society, the Sisterhood was an extremely conservative organization. "Adapt or die" was a primary Bene Gesserit axiom, though they seemed to have forgotten how to follow it. Margot had gradually come to realize this. As far as she was concerned, they were not her superiors. The unparalleled disaster of Paul Atreides and the almost complete loss of Bene Gesserit political power had eroded her respect for them.

She and her husband had spent years in isolation among the Tleilaxu, raising Marie, developing an overall plan. And now the Mother Superior had summoned her with orders to bring her daughter in "for inspection."

Since childhood, Lady Margot had been trained to obey the commands of her superiors—commands that had required her to bear the child in the first place—but the Sisterhood might not get the answers they anticipated. Margot came to Wallach IX on her own terms.

She hoped the Sisterhood had no additional breeding plans for her. Yes, Lady Margot looked considerably younger than her years, and her willowy beauty had been enhanced by careful and regular consumption of melange and a regimen of prana-bindu exercises. With good fortune, her seductive appearance and reproductive functions would last for several more decades . . . and Hasimir was so understanding.

But little Marie should be her culminating achievement. The Sisterhood had to be made to see that.

Margot had commanded the nanny Tonia Obregah-Xo to remain behind in Thalidei, though the woman had obviously expected to accompany them to Wallach IX. Tonia sent regular reports to the Mother School, using clandestine methods that were only too familiar to Margot herself. Once, Lady Margot had intercepted a message to the Sisterhood and had surreptitiously added her own postscript. That had caused rancor among the Bene Gesserits and a change in secret reporting procedures, but Margot had wanted to let them know that she was her own woman, and that she served at *her* pleasure, not theirs.

Nevertheless, she had agreed to make the journey and let the Reverend Mothers "inspect" five-year-old Marie all they wanted, but the Sisterhood would not control her destiny. Too much was at stake.

Now, she and Count Fenring sat on a garden bench with the girl between them. All of them waiting. Waiting. An obvious and childish game the Sisters were playing. Behind them was the stylized black quartz statue of a kneeling woman: Raquella Berto-Anirul, the founder of the ancient school. Thick rain clouds hung over the school, and the temperature was cool, though not uncomfortable. The courtyard sheltered them from the wind.

Finally, Reverend Mother Gaius Helen Mohiam approached with a group of five Sisters, her bird-bright gaze intent on little Marie.

Lady Margot stood. "I have brought my daughter as requested, Reverend Mother." *An automatic response.*

Mohiam frowned pointedly at Count Fenring. "We do not often allow males to enter the grounds of the Mother School."

"Your hospitality is, ahh, noted." He smiled, keeping a protective hand on the little girl's shoulder. The Bene Gesserits knew full well that Count Hasimir Fenring was a deadly assassin and master spy himself, so Lady Margot had no doubt that her husband's presence here caused great consternation among their order.

Hasimir was himself a failed Kwisatz Haderach, a genetic eunuch and a dead end near the finish line of the millennia-long breeding program. But the *actual* Kwisatz Haderach, Paul Atreides, had backfired on them, with consequences too disastrous to imagine. From this point on, with Marie's amazing potential, Count Fenring and Lady Margot were perfectly capable of developing and implementing their own dynastic schemes.

Both she and her husband had worked for inept superiors. The failures of Shaddam Corrino IV were not unlike those of the Sisterhood. Through a strange and cruel twist of fate, two immense and foolish courses of action had merged into one another to amplify a horrible result. The human race would be a long time recovering from Muad'Dib.

Reverend Mother Mohiam bent forward, turning her attention to the young girl. "So this is the child." Reaching out, the old woman passed a hand through the child's light blonde hair. "I see you have your mother's lovely features."

She's also noticed a similarity to Feyd-Rautha Harkonnen, Margot thought.

"And such milky smooth skin." Mohiam rubbed one of the girl's forearms. Marie endured the attention in silence. "Like your mother's."

Mohiam's hand went quickly into a pocket of her robe, surreptitiously depositing the hair and skin samples she had just taken. It was a matter of procedure, of constant observation and documentation, more information for the breeding files, data points with dates and places and names on them.

"And the child's training regimen?" Mohiam looked at Margot.

"A combination of my knowledge and my husband's, as well as instructions from her Bene Gesserit nanny. Surely Tonia has sent you detailed reports?"

Mohiam ignored the latter comment. "Good. We are glad you brought her here so that her education can continue properly. We will keep her, of course."

"I am afraid that will, ahhh, not be possible," her husband said, his voice as taut as a garrote.

Mohiam was taken aback. The Sisters with her stared at him. "That is not your decision."

Smiling prettily, Margot said, "We did not bring Marie to leave her at the Mother School. She does quite well with us."

"Ahh, quite well," Fenring added.

Margot noted the tension in the air, saw furtive shapes moving behind windows, Sisters hurrying through the porticos. While these five Sisters were watching the little girl most closely, others had been assigned to observe Count Fenring and Margot. Subtle body movements of the three subjects would be recorded and analyzed in the most minute detail. More data points. Somewhere back there lurked the Mother Superior herself.

"This sudden intractability—has Muad'Dib enlisted

you as an ally?" When Mohiam asked this, her robed companions moved closer like a small flock of black birds, as if to protect the old woman from attack.

Count Fenring laughed, but said nothing; little Marie laughed in a similar tenor.

"We do not mock you, Reverend Mother," Margot said. "My family is merely amused at your suggestion that we might be cooperating with the man who overthrew Shaddam Corrino. You all know that my Hasimir considered the former Emperor quite a close friend." After exchanging glances with the Count, she added, "Rather, we came in response to your summons, with an interesting proposal."

Little Marie piped up, "The Imperium has the head of a monster, and it must be decapitated."

The Sisters were visibly startled by such bold talk from the child. "Muad'Dib *is* a monster," Lady Margot said. "Your own Kwisatz Haderach is completely out of control, and you are at fault. Your plans failed to account for the damage he's inflicted upon the universe. We must make alternative plans to take care of him."

Fenring leaned forward on the stone bench. "Is anyone more hated than the Emperor Paul-Muad'Dib, hmmm?"

Mohiam did not answer, but Lady Margot knew that the old woman loathed Paul more than most.

"Perhaps Marie can sit on the throne instead," Margot said. "Is there anyone better bred? Better suited?"

The old Reverend Mother snapped backward. Bene Gesserits did not seize power so openly. "They will never accept a child—and a girl at that!"

"After Muad'Dib, they will be inclined to accept many things, so long as he is gone," Fenring said.

The old woman paced, ignoring the other four Sisters, ignoring Marie. The girl stood perfectly still, watching intently, listening to everything. "You are an intriguing combination of motives and methods, Margot. Intriguing, indeed. You defy our ways and jab at our mistakes, while trying to involve us in a dangerous plot."

"The Sisterhood must adapt and survive. It is a simple, rational conclusion. Through my husband's experience and unique abilities, he has worked out a scenario that benefits all of us."

Fenring bobbed his head. "There are ways we can get close to Muad'Dib, ways to make him let his guard down."

Mohiam's dark eyes regarded the Count with new interest. "True enough, there is a need to adapt. There is also a need for balance—that too, is one of our precepts. I would hear your proposal, but I insist that the girl be as prepared as possible. As part of any agreement, the girl must remain here for training in the Mother School."

"Out of the question." Margot put an arm around her daughter, and the child snuggled against her.

Fenring also put an arm around the little girl. "The old ways of the Sisterhood have failed in spectacular fashion, hmmm? Now let us try ours."

"You would risk Marie's life in this enterprise?" Mohiam asked.

Lady Margot smiled. "Hardly. Our plan is perfect, as is our method of escape afterward."

The Reverend Mother's eyes flashed. "And the details?"

"The details will be an artistic performance," Margot said. "Since you are not involved, you will learn them after the fact."

Glancing up at a shadowy shape standing in a window overlooking the courtyard, Mohiam said, "Very well. We will watch with interest."

Home is more than a mere location. Home is where, more than anyplace else, one wishes to be. Home is certainly not this horrible planet that I never wanted to see again.

—GURNEY HALLECK, dispatch to Lady Jessica
on Caladan

When he returned to Arrakis, weary and unsettled from the most recent battles against Thorvald's insurgents, Gurney just wanted to rest in his dusty quarters. But he had barely managed to remove his nose plugs and unfasten his cloak before a pompous Qizarate ambassador arrived at his doorway wearing cumbersome diplomatic garments instead of a traditional stillsuit. Frowning, Gurney took the decree from the functionary, broke the seal, and read it, not caring that the man might look on.

The announcement took his breath away. "Why in the Seven Hells would Paul do that?"

The Emperor had officially given Gurney Halleck the Barony of Giedi Prime. The lumpy, scarred man stood still, breathing quickly through flared nostrils, realizing that Paul probably intended for this to be a reward, shielding him from further horrors of the Jihad by sending him back to the planet of his childhood, just as Paul himself had visited Caladan. But though Giedi Prime had surrendered to Paul almost immediately after the fall of House Harkonnen, for Gurney the place was still a battlefield—a battlefield of the mind, a battlefield of harsh memories.

Gurney shooed the functionary away and reread the decree, reflexively crumpling the spice paper, then straightening the document again. Paul had added a quiet, more personal note. "You can heal it, my loyal friend. It will take thousands of years before anyone might consider Giedi Prime a beautiful place. At the very least, try to change it from a festering wound to a scar. Do it for me, Gurney."

Sighing, Gurney said to himself, "I serve the Atreides." And he meant it. He would face his past, and use his best abilities to free the people of Giedi Prime from many generations of Harkonnen repression and imposed darkness. It would not be a simple task.

He already had an earldom on Caladan, but Jessica had taken the title of Duchess, and the people there loved her. He didn't want to take anything away from her. But . . . Giedi Prime? Paul was doing him no favors.

Gurney had often fantasized that after a lifetime of fighting he would retire to the country on a well-earned estate with a beautiful woman and a house full of rambunctious children. Somehow, though, he did not see that in his future.

Do it for me, Gurney, Paul had said.

⮑

WHEN HE ARRIVED at Giedi Prime, Gurney Halleck received a modest hero's welcome, though the decidedly subdued population did not know what to make of him. He was the newly named Baron—another painfully unsettling honor. Paul-Muad'Dib had freed this planet from the Harkonnen boot heel, but the people did not know how to rejoice. They were not accustomed to loving their leaders. Even with the yoke of repression removed, no one raised a voice to celebrate.

Seeing them crowded in Harko City reminded Gurney

of the magnitude of the challenge he faced, and he felt hollow in his chest. Noting the wan faces, pale complexions, and washed-out demeanors, he remembered seeing the same expressions on the faces of his parents and on his poor sister Bheth, who was eventually raped and murdered, an offhand casualty of Beast Rabban's cruelty.

Gurney would try to summon the energy and compassion to inspire these people, to have them turn their world around, replant it, re-energize it. But he wasn't sure they had the heart for it. "You are free now!" Simply telling that to a broken and weary populace did not undo generations of damage. The idea was a good one, in a logical sense, but did Paul honestly believe that a gift of freedom and self-determination would change the psyche of an entire planet?

Yet that was Gurney's new mission, and he intended to accomplish it—for Paul.

With his own men, mostly drawn from Caladan, Gurney took residence in the city of Barony, the former seat of Harkonnen government. He had a lot of fixing and political housecleaning to do. The gigantic mansion had blocky walls and imposing columns, everything based on squares and angles instead of soft curves. Gurney felt *wrong*. He did not belong here. Even devastated Salusa Secundus, where he'd once lived among smugglers, was somehow a purer place. At least it did not have a Harkonnen stink about it.

The giant building made him uncomfortable, as if he might find something dangerous around every corner, and he didn't trust that the Harkonnens had not left unpleasant surprises for any new and unwelcome occupants.

He ordered the great home of Baron Harkonnen to be searched, room by room, every chamber unlocked and scanned. His teams discovered numerous rooms that had obviously been used for torture, booby-trapped chambers that held nothing of obvious value, and several sealed vaults filled with solari coins, preserved melange, and incalculably expensive gems. The fact that none of these rooms had been looted, or even opened, in the five years since the fall of House Harkonnen demonstrated just how much fear the Baron must have inspired.

Gurney had all the treasures liquidated and the profits distributed to the people in the form of public works, as a gesture of goodwill.

He called his government together and summoned the administrators who had been left in de facto control of Giedi Prime for five years since Baron Harkonnen's death. In an empire so vast and sprawling, no ruler, not even Muad'Dib, could meticulously manage every planet.

The old Harkonnen administrators had been conspicuously absent since Gurney's arrival on Giedi Prime, but they could no longer avoid him. Having learned of Gurney's past here, they tried not to meet his gaze; some of them seemed fixated on his inkvine scar; others became simpering toadies trying to ooze their way into his good graces in order to keep their positions. Gurney didn't much care for any of them; their leadership might have been effective under the old regime, but the harsh methods were ingrained. Just as the people didn't know how to be free, these administrators did not understand what it meant to be compassionate. He would have to apply all his force of will to ensure that momentum did not drag Giedi Prime back to its former dark and repressive ways.

He needed to make his new philosophy clear to this group of cautious and nervous administrators. He had put this off long enough. "I need to see familiar places. I will go to the slave pits, and to my old village of Dmitri. And you will accompany me."

Though Gurney had showed very little emotion toward the former leaders, he was sure they expected him to take out his ire on them, and Gurney did not disabuse them of that notion.

First, he made a visit of state to the slave pits where he had been sentenced because he'd dared to sing songs that mocked the Baron. Here, he had mined and processed absurdly expensive blue obsidian, and Rabban had struck him with his inkvine whip. Here, he had been tied down and forced to watch in helpless horror as Rabban and his men sexually assaulted poor Bheth, then strangled her to death. Here, Gurney had found a way to escape by stowing away aboard a cargo ship that carried a load of blue obsidian bound for Duke Leto Atreides.

Looking around the site, Gurney turned white with anger. How little had changed in all the years! He would much rather have faced rebel fanatics than confront the searing memories inspired by this sight. But if he did not heal these places, then no one would.

His voice was quiet, but it may as well have been a shout. "I order these slave pits shut down immediately. Free these people and let them make their own lives. I hereby strip the slave masters of their authority."

"My Lord Halleck, you will disrupt everything! Our entire economy—"

"I don't give a damn. Let the slave masters work among the other people as equals." His lips curled in a small smile. "Then we'll see how well *they* survive."

Deciding to get the worst over with, he traveled next to the shadow of Mount Ebony and the cluster of pleasure houses that had once serviced the Harkonnen troops. Giedi Prime had many such establishments, but he intended to go to a specific one.

Gurney felt nauseated when he arrived at the doorstep.

Memories of one night long ago howled inside his head. The administrators accompanying him were clearly frightened by his expression. "Who is the proprietor that runs these houses?" He remembered an old man who had wired himself into a chair, keeping careful business records but paying no attention to what went on behind the doors of his establishment.

"Rulien Scheck has done an efficient job of managing in the absence of other leadership, my Lord Halleck. He has worked here for years, decades probably."

"Bring him to me. Now."

The old man came out, nearly stumbling, yet trying to smile as though proud of what he had accomplished. Prosthetic lines ran down his legs, keeping him from being otherwise crippled, but at least he was free from his chair now. A paunch hung over his waist, and soft rounded buttocks showed that he ate too well and sat down too much. His gray hair was heavy and oiled, as if he considered it to be stylish. Gurney recognized him immediately, but Rulien Scheck showed no sign that he remembered one particular desperate brother from one particular night. . . .

"I am honored that Giedi Prime's new Lord would come to see my humble establishment. All of my financial records are open to you, sir. I run a clean and honest business, with the most beautiful women. I have banked the expected share of profits in a sealed account, formerly designated to the Harkonnens and now available to you. You will find no evidence of impropriety, I promise you that, my Lord." He bowed.

"This very house is evidence of impropriety." Gurney pushed his way inside, but needed to see very little. He remembered the rooms, the pallets, the stains on the walls, the endless lines of sweaty Harkonnen soldiers who had come here seeking pleasure slaves like his sister

Bheth, taking more delight in inflicting abuse on the unfortunate women than in the sex itself. By cauterizing her larynx, they had prevented Bheth even from screaming.

He closed his eyes and did not turn to face the old proprietor. "I want this man garroted."

The administrators remained silent. Scheck squawked, began to argue, and Gurney pointed a blunt finger at him. "Be thankful that I do not first command a hundred soldiers to sodomize you—some of them with spiked clubs. But even though that is what you deserve, *I* am not a Harkonnen. Your death will be swift enough."

Gurney pushed past the astonished group and rushed back outside, breathing hard, anxious to get away. "And when they are done, see that all the women are freed, given a place to live—and burn this place to the ground. Burn all the pleasure houses across Giedi Prime."

Finally, he returned to the village of Dmitri, a poor and hopeless place that had not changed at all. His mother and father were gone. Because lives meant so little, the town kept no records of its people. Gurney could find no marker in the rundown and overcrowded graveyard, no sign that his parents had ever existed.

Someday, he supposed Paul would offer to erect a monument for the victims. Gurney didn't want that. His parents had not changed this world for the better. The people in the village had not stood up against tyranny. They had not defended him when the Harkonnen raiders had taken him away. They had refused to speak out against the injustice they encountered every single day.

Gurney felt sadness, but no need to mourn. "Enough of this. Take me back to Barony. . . ."

Even there, though, every day brought a foul taste to his mouth. *I am doing this for Paul,* he reminded himself. He began to issue proclamations and sweeping orders— cities would be renamed, marks of the old Harkonnen way of life would be erased. He ordered the construction of a new government center, a seat where he could rule without being reminded of the Harkonnens.

But human pain went deep into the strata of the grimy planet. He wasn't sure how much longer he could bear to stay on Giedi Prime.

Every new year brings great hope and expectations.
Every previous year fails to live up to them.

—GURNEY HALLECK, unfinished song

According to the Imperial Calendar, recalibrated so that its primary clocks and meridian were centered on Arrakis rather than Kaitain, the year changed to 10,198 A.G. Another year of Muad'Dib's greatness, another year with more and more victories in his great Jihad. In Arrakeen, the wild and hedonistic celebrations rivaled a millennial fervor.

The Emperor Paul-Muad'Dib stood at a corner of the high open balcony outside his sietch-austere bedchamber. He watched people milling below in the streets and squares, and was unsurprised by their mania. For thousands of years, the Fremen had understood the human need for animalistic release in their tau orgies. This was similar, but on a much larger scale, and he had planned it carefully.

His holiness Muad'Dib, beloved of the people, had opened his coffers to provide spice and food for all supplicants. He emptied his cisterns so that water flowed into outstretched hands, and people reveled in it. In the months to come, he could easily refill his reservoirs, if only by using the deathstill water from all the nameless dead rounded up by his undertakers from side alleys and squalid housing.

Chani joined him outside the moisture seal, barely touching him. She still hadn't conceived another child, a much-anticipated heir. They both knew the necessity, and both wanted a baby, but the deep hurt of losing their first son, Leto—killed in a Sardaukar raid in the days before Paul won his victory against Emperor Shaddam—filled them with unconscious hesitation. The doctors said nothing was physically wrong with Chani, but Paul knew they could not measure or test for a mother's broken heart.

A second child would come, however, but that, too, carried heavy consequences— especially for Chani.

They both breathed deeply of warm night air that smelled of smoke, cooking fires, incense, and unwashed bodies. So many people pushed together, rippling and swaying in a Brownian motion that Paul thought of as a large-scale unconscious dance as difficult to interpret as many of his visions.

"They love me so easily when I demonstrate my largesse," Paul said to her. "Does that mean that when times turn hard, they will be as quick to hate me?"

"They will be quick to hate someone else, Beloved."

"And is that fair to the scapegoats?"

"One should not be concerned with fairness when dealing with scapegoats," Chani said, showing her ruthless Fremen streak.

From the expansion of Arrakeen, many new houses pressed against each other, built along tried-and-true designs to huddle in the desert heat and preserve every breath of moisture. Other buildings stood defiantly (or foolishly) against tradition—homesick architects having erected structures that reminded Paul of Fharris, Grand Hain, Zebulon, and even Culat, planets so bleak and mis-

erable that their inhabitants were happy to leave them in
favor of Dune.

As project master, Whitmore Bludd had continued to
oversee the enormous construction of the new palace, and
his blueprints became more grandiose day after day. Already, remarkably, the completed portion of Muad'Dib's
citadel was larger than the Imperial Palace they had
burned on Kaitain, and Bludd was just getting started. . . .

When Korba entered their private wing, Paul noted
how easily his guards let the man pass, even bowing respectfully, making a sign from one of the Qizara rites.
He did not suspect treachery from the former head of his
Fedaykin—the man's loyalty was as unwavering as his
fervor—but Paul did not like to be so glibly interrupted.

"Korba, did I summon you?" The sharpness of Paul's
tone brought the other man up short.

"If you had, I would have been here faster, Muad'Dib."
He apparently did not see the reason for Paul's annoyance.

"Chani and I were enjoying a private moment. Were
you not raised in a sietch? A Fremen should know to respect privacy."

"Then please excuse the interruption." Korba bowed,
and blurted out the matter that concerned him so much.
"Pardon me for saying so, but I do not like these immense public gatherings. They celebrate the Imperial
Calendar. We should no longer follow that old relic."

"It is 10,198 A.G., Korba, counted from the formation
of the Spacing Guild. That is not linked to the old Imperium, or to mine. They merely celebrate the turning of
the new year, a harmless but necessary release of their
energies."

"But there should be a new age—the Age of
Muad'Dib," Korba insisted, then laid out an idea he had
obviously been planning for some time. "I propose that
we start counting the calendar from the day you over-

threw Shaddam IV and the Harkonnens. I have already asked several priest-scientists to draw up specific plans for its implementation and to search for numerological implications."

Paul refused the idea, much to Korba's consternation.

"But we are living in the greatest moment in history. We should signify it as such!"

"One cannot see history while living it. If every Emperor were to reset the calendar just because he considered himself great, we would have a new age every century or so."

"But you are Muad'Dib!"

Paul shook his head. "I am still but a man. History will determine the measure of my greatness." *Or Irulan will,* he thought.

⤚

LATER THAT NIGHT, when they lay in bed and neither of them could sleep, Chani stroked his cheek. "You are troubled, Usul."

"I am thinking."

"Always thinking. You need to rest."

"When I rest, I dream . . . and that makes me think even more." He sat up in bed, noticing how cool and slick the expensive sheets felt. He had wanted his quarters to have nothing more than a simple Fremen-style pallet, no extravagances at all, but amenities had crept in nonetheless. Despite his best intentions, and the honor that his father had taught him, Paul feared that such ready access to so much power was likely to corrupt him eventually.

"Are you worried about the battles, Usul? Thorvald and his rebellion? All enemies will fall to your armies, sooner or later. It is inevitable—the will of God."

Paul shook his head. "Some measure of popular sup-

port for Thorvald and his eleven nobles is to be expected. Against any Empire as powerful as mine, there
will be rebels. It is as natural as the sun and the moons
that he will attract supporters, and as he gains influence,
that my own supporters unite more strongly against him.
Thorvald cannot survive long. Stilgar has just left for
Bela Tegeuse to root out one of the infestations. I have
no doubt he'll be victorious."

Chani shrugged and seemed to be stating the obvious.
"He is Stilgar, after all."

As they so often did, his followers would respond
more violently than was strictly necessary. He had seen
it firsthand on the battlefield of Ehknot. He had already
pulled Gurney Halleck from such duties and granted him
the whole Harkonnen world to heal, a different kind of
battlefield where he could truly make a difference. He
had earned it.

Stroking the side of his cheek, Chani continued, "You
feel the weight of those you rule, Beloved. You count their
dead as your own, and yet you must never forget that
you have saved them all. You are the one we have been
waiting for, the Lisan-al-Gaib. The Mahdi. They fight in
your name because they believe in the future you will
bring."

Exactly the beliefs his father had told him to use, if
necessary. And the Bene Gesserit's Missionaria Protectiva had planted superstitions and prophecies, which he
also applied to his own situation. A trick, a tool. *But now
the tool wields its own user.*

"The Jihad has a life of its own. When I experienced visions as a young man, I knew this holy war could not be
stopped, but still I tried to change the future, to prevent
the rampaging violence. One man cannot stop the moving
sands."

"You are the Coriolis wind that sets the sands moving."

"I cannot stop it, but I can guide it. I *am* guiding it.

What people see as unforgivable violence and destruction, I know is the best of many unacceptable alternatives." With a sigh, Paul turned away from her. He had deluded himself into believing that it would be easy to hold the reins and guide the course of the great, living creature that was the Jihad. The *monster*. He had made his decision believing that his choices would be clear, only to find that he was more a captive of unfolding history than any person before him. His was a terrible purpose. He rode the crest of a wave that threatened to drown him and everyone around him. Even when Muad'Dib made the best possible decisions, regardless of what his heart wanted, he could see the bloody future unfolding mercilessly for years to come.

But the alternative is worse.

He had actually considered removing himself from the equation, escaping from the warp and weft of Fate's loom. Paul could have allowed himself to tumble into the abyss of historical interpretation and the enhancement of myths.

But if he chose to die, *Muad'Dib* would still become a martyr. His very presence was too prominent in the hearts and minds of his followers, and they would continue without him if necessary, in spite of him. Time would have its due. Paul feared that in premature death he might cause more damage than in life.

On the bedside table, near the broken pink conch shell from Earth that Bludd had brought Paul from Ecaz, lay a stack of reports detailing troop movements, Guildship patterns, and another long list of planets that he could easily conquer. Impatiently, he knocked the papers aside.

Chani frowned at his reaction. "Are you not pleased to see so much progress? Is this not success?" Usually, she could understand his moods, but not now. "Surely, the Jihad is almost over."

He looked at her. "Have you ever heard of Alexander

the Great? He is from long ago, forgotten in the mists of time. He was a great warlord on Mother Earth, said to be the most powerful emperor of ancient times. His armies swept across continents, his own known universe, and when he reached the shore of the sea, he wept because there were no more lands to conquer. But history considers Alexander great only because he had the good fortune to die before his empire could collapse on its own."

Chani blinked. "How can that be?"

"Alexander was like a storm. He had many soldiers and superior weapons, but after conquering each people he moved on and never had to *govern*." Paul clasped Chani's hand. "Don't you see? Our armies have chalked up victory after victory, but beating a man is different from working with him for many years. Irulan is right: Once Muad'Dib's Jihad is past, once I have won this long war, how am I to survive the peace? Would Alexander still be considered 'great' if he'd actually needed to provide food, water, shelter, education, and protection to all the people of his empire? Doubtful. He caught a fever and died before his conquests could come back to haunt him."

"You are not some ancient forgotten leader. You must follow your destiny, Usul," Chani whispered in his ear. "Regardless of where it leads, it remains your destiny."

He kissed her. "You are my desert spring, my Sihaya. You and I must enjoy every moment we have together."

They made love slowly, discovering each other again, and for the first time.

Yes, the vast universe is filled with many wonders,
but it has too few deserts for my liking.

—*The Stilgar Commentaries*

On Bela Tegeuse, even the broad daylight was dim and damp, shrouded with fog. Stilgar did not like this place one bit. Each breath was clammy in his mouth and nose. At the end of the day, he practically had to wring out his clothing to remove the excess moisture. He felt he needed a reverse stillsuit—nose plugs and a breathing mask that would filter water *out* of the air, just so he could breathe. The sound of lapping water that surrounded the wide, heavily armed gunbarges was maddening.

Stilgar knew that Paul-Muad'Dib had grown up by the ocean on Caladan. Every night, the young man had gone to sleep listening to the roar of waves outside the castle. The idea of so much water was difficult for the naib to grasp. It was a wonder the boy had not gone insane.

And the swamps on Bela Tegeuse were more treacherous than an ocean, he was certain.

Since the beginning of the Jihad, even with so many legions dispersed throughout the worlds of the Imperium, he himself had planted the green-and-white banner of Fremen-led legions, as well as the green-and-black banner carried by other loyalists, on four planets. He had shed much blood, had witnessed the deaths of many friends and foes. People died in much the same way, no matter what world they came from.

Now, by the command of Muad'Dib, Stilgar led these forces to hunt down the rebellious nobleman Urquidi Basque, one of the remaining principal lords who supported Earl Thorvald's insurgency. When Basque went to ground on Bela Tegeuse, Stilgar had assumed he would be trapped. Muad'Dib's military frigates had deployed a fleet of gunbarges and search boats constructed by local engineers who were familiar with the terrain and ready to capture Lord Basque and his swamp rats.

Swamp rats. Stilgar did not like the sound of that.

For the past two weeks, pursuing Basque and his army had been like chasing balls of static electricity across the dune tops. Under a thick layer of clouds, the gunbarges moved slowly along, pushing against the sluggish brown water. The dim sun would set soon, and the night would bring cooling air and thickening fog. *Water squeezed out of the air.*

Off in the distance, Stilgar could see only the nearest two of the ten heavily armed ships in his group. The foghorns and signal whistles sounded like lost souls begging to be taken to dry land. Visibility was worse than in a sandstorm.

Last week, when they had pursued the renegade lord across a wide, shallow sea, one of the heavy gunbarges had run aground. Basque and his swamp rats had gotten away, jeering as Stilgar was forced to unload heavy weaponry and cargo from the stranded gunbarge so that it would float free of the mud bar. He'd had half a mind to ditch the vessel and continue the chase, leaving his men to fend for themselves in the swamps. But many of the fighters were Fremen, and Stilgar refused to abandon them to this *wet* place.

After wasting all that time, the scout boats had raced

forward in search of clues. One scout returned, having found an old camp; three others vanished entirely. Stilgar ordered 'thopters for air surveillance, but the ground-hugging fog made the aircraft worse than useless in the hunt.

Finally, as dusk settled in, adding a bruised color to the sky, they pushed into a complex river delta, where Stilgar was sure he would trap Basque. Several times now, they had seen tantalizing lights in the distance, taunting signals that likely marked their quarry.

Around him, he could see the tangled hala-cypress branches and roots, trees so different from the rare palms of Dune. The river delta was thick with them, as if they were crowded spectators gaping at an accident scene. They gave off a fetid stench, just like all the water in this swamp. The odors of fish and algae nauseated him. Every meal he'd eaten on Bela Tegeuse tasted like mud.

Stilgar stood on the mist-slick deck. Some of the gun-barges were equipped with half-shields, but the barge captains complained that the shimmering fields reduced visibility. Lookouts continued to peer into the foggy distance.

Next to Stilgar, the captain was angry at himself. "My charts are useless, a year old. The currents shift the sand and the mud, and the hala-cypress walk."

"How can trees walk?"

"They move their roots in the mud slurry, shift into channels, and fill them up. A passage perfectly clear one month will be blocked the next." In disgust, the captain cast his obsolete diagrams over the side, where the thin papers floated away on the currents. "I may as well just close my eyes and pray."

"We can all pray," Stilgar said, "but that should not be our only plan."

Six mysterious lights glistened out of the growing dimness of dusk, and Stilgar saw it as the signal he had been waiting for. The decks of the gunbarges were crowded with Fremen shouting insults at the swamp rats who hid in the skeletal forests along the labyrinth of waterways.

Stilgar shouted, "They are within reach! Time to pursue them."

"I advise caution," the captain said. "Do not underestimate Lord Basque."

"And he should not underestimate the armies of Muad'Dib."

With a chattering roar that sounded like one of the attacking dragonflies that had plagued them through the marshes, ten shallow-draught needleboats ripped out of the fog, spraying a wake of brackish brown water. Onboard, Basque's swamp rats held projectile rifles, which they fired into the press of Fremen on the decks. The needleboats turned about, firing a few more potshots, then raced back into the depths of the swamp.

Without waiting for a unified effort, two gunbarges surged forward, racing after them. Stilgar immediately saw what the rebels were doing. "A trap!"

But the pilot of the second gunbarge didn't hear. The huge vessel pressed ahead with its powerful engines, and within moments found itself mired in slick mud and shallow water.

From the high hala-cypress branches, the real ambush struck, as Basque's men fired down upon the trapped gunbarge. At such close quarters the barge's heavy artillery proved useless, but that didn't stop the Fremen from launching huge explosives from the deck guns, blowing up sections of the swamp. Fireballs ignited marsh gas and caused secondary eruptions. Yelling and howling, many of the Fremen dropped down into smaller boats and raced into the maze of trees, but the water there made Stilgar greatly uneasy.

"Shields on!" the barge captain shouted. Moments

later, renewed shimmering barriers floated across the deck, protecting the soldiers but at the same time preventing them from firing their projectile weapons. The giant gunbarge pushed forward, until it scraped its keel on the mud.

"We can't go any farther," the captain said.

Stilgar activated his body shield and told his men to do the same. "We will proceed on our own rafts, and then fight on foot."

Before they could disembark, submerged rebels in breather suits rose up from the murky water, passing slowly through the gunbarge's main shield. Eight of them worked swiftly and efficiently together. Stilgar spotted them only after they had planted explosives against the gunbarge's hull and then stroked away, passing back through the shield. He howled a warning.

Several of his men dropped overboard and bobbed in the water just as Gurney Halleck had taught them to do. They tried to pry the explosive mines loose, but the devices detonated within seconds. The swift shock wave hit against the shield, then reflected back into the gunbarge, causing even more damage. A wall of fire and hot gases bowled Stilgar over, knocking him to the deck. Coughing and blinded, he staggered to the rail, feeling the deck tilt as the scuttled gunbarge lurched and settled.

Unable to catch himself, Stilgar tumbled overboard. In the water, the cool, slimy wetness soothed his fresh burns. Dozens of bodies, and parts of bodies, floated next to him. The gunbarge was wallowing.

Stilgar swam toward the trees, anxious for something solid to hold onto. One of Basque's men surfaced beside him in a breather suit and tried to attack, but Stilgar already had his crysknife out. He severed the man's air hose, slashed his neck, and shoved him still twitching into a billowing crimson cloud in the marsh water.

More screams and explosions reverberated through

the mist-muffled air. Two more gunbarges had been ruined by explosive mines, and another had run aground. Large artillery kept booming, leveling the forest, ripping the swamp to shreds, presumably hitting Basque's camp, by accident if by no other means.

Nothing stopped the Fremen, now that their anger was piqued. "Muad'Dib! Muad'Dib!" they screamed, splashing forward. Stilgar had no doubt that many of them would drown, perhaps most, as they were still so unfamiliar with water. Others launched small boats.

Though the rebels continued to pick them off, the wave of Jihad fighters proved stronger than superior firepower or better defenses. His soldiers did not know how to lose, nor how to retreat.

As he sloshed his way to the knobby hala-cypress roots, Stilgar found the chaotic battle exceedingly confusing. Despite his skill in desert warfare, he did not comprehend naval tactics. He was a dry-land fighter, undefeated in hand-to-hand combat. He knew the names for every type of wind in the desert, for the shapes of dunes, and the meanings of distant clouds. But this place was alien to him.

By the time he reached the center of the swamp, standing in thigh-deep water and holding onto the moss-slick roots, enough of the screaming Fremen had survived to reach the swamp-rat camp that they made short and bloody work of the remaining rebels. He knew he must have lost hundreds of men in his battle group, but they had died in glorious service to Muad'Dib, and their families would claim that they had wanted nothing else.

He dragged himself out of the water and saw to his disgust that his legs, chest, and stomach were covered with dozens of fat, oily leeches that swelled and pulsed as they gorged themselves on his blood. He was glad that no one had seen him, for he instinctively yelled like a woman and slashed at the parasites with his crysknife, popping each blood-filled leech and ripping it from his skin.

The fighting was mostly over by the time he composed himself and trudged toward the fires of the destroyed camp and the few remaining tortured screams, as the Fremen fell upon any swamp rat who had been unlucky enough not to die in battle.

"We have won, Stil! We crushed them in the name of Muad'Dib," said young Kaleff, who looked as if he had aged more than ten years since their conquest of Kaitain.

"Yes, another victory." Stilgar was surprised at how hoarse his voice had become. This was not the same as a razzia against Harkonnens. This did not feel as great an accomplishment as attacking the Padishah Emperor's huge metal hutment during a sandstorm. No, annihilating a rebel infestation on this swampy, gloomy world was not at all the same kind of fight to which he had been born. Leeches, walking trees, mud, and slime . . . he could not drive away the thought of how much he longed for dry sand again—the way a world was supposed to be.

The successful leader defines his own success and does not allow lesser men to change that definition.

—EMPEROR ELROOD CORRINO IX,
shortly before he was poisoned

The birth of Shaddam Corrino's first grandson—and first male heir—should have been feted with festivities and cheering crowds on glorious Kaitain. But as the fallen Emperor stood inside the birthing chamber and watched Wensicia receive her newborn baby, he thought only about what he had lost.

All those years of grooming Irulan . . . wasted. As Wensicia often reminded him, he had pinned his hopes on the wrong daughter.

Holding the infant now, Wensicia pretended to be happy, but even she could not hide her disappointment that her son, the next in the Corrino line, would never take his rightful place as Emperor.

Unless something can be done . . .

On that fateful day after the defeat on the plains of Arrakeen, Irulan had come to her father, offering a solution. "But here's a man fit to be your son."

He'd been a fool to listen to her. Though she had wed Paul Atreides, Irulan apparently had no influence with her husband, no formal role in government (not that he'd ever granted his own wives any more power than Irulan had). She was less than a trophy wife: Irulan had become Muad'Dib's puppet, writing ridiculous stories as propaganda to make the religious fanatics see him as a messiah.

In nearly five years she had not even managed to get herself pregnant, which would have at least brought the Corrino bloodline back onto the throne. That would have been the tidiest way to end this mess. Irulan was beautiful, skilled, trained by the witches. How difficult could it be to seduce a young man at the peak of his hormonal tides? Or had Irulan made the mistake of succumbing to her own fiction, believing the myths she herself created?

Shaddam's eyes slipped briefly out of focus. Even Hasimir Fenring had apparently abandoned him. Though Bashar Garon had tracked him down years ago and dutifully delivered the jewel-handled Imperial knife as a gift, Fenring had not come running back to Salusa. *Why else does he think I allowed his insipid cousin to marry Wensicia? What could be a greater gesture of penitence than that?* Even Dalak had tried to make contact, desperate to prove his worth to Shaddam, but to no avail.

If Hasimir would only work beside him again, Shaddam was sure they could find a solution to this galactic crisis. But the Count refused to come back, which led to unsettling questions. What was Hasimir really up to? Why would he voluntarily live among the disgusting Tleilaxu for years—and raise his daughter there?

Beaming and bubbling as a new father, Dalak Zor-Fenring left Wensicia's bedside and looked up at the Emperor's troubled expression. "Are you all right, Father?" The man's voice sounded almost feminine in its timbre. He was five years younger than Wensicia.

Shaddam glared at him. "I have not granted you leave to call me that."

His son-in-law backed away quickly, flushing. "Excuse me if I have been too familiar, Sire. If you are not comfortable with my expression of affection, I will never call you Father again."

"Very little about you makes me comfortable, Dalak. I will always be *Emperor Corrino* to you." *Unless, of course, you deliver Hasimir Fenring to me.*

Fenring's cousin had pinched features and overlarge, dark eyes, but his physical resemblance to the Count went no farther than that. Hasimir's dapper dress suited him well, but similar garments made Dalak look like a dandy. He was the only person in exile on Salusa who wore silk and lace. Wensicia didn't even seem to like him (a small mercy there).

Stranded here and in disgrace, he despaired of finding any better matches for his three remaining daughters. Mercifully, even though Dalak had no formal title, at least he had some noble blood flowing in his veins, and at least he had managed to create a male child. None of Shaddam's wives had succeeded in that.

Behind him, the door of the birthing room opened without his permission—another indication of the lack of decorum here. "We came to see the baby." Chalice, heavyset and tall, was a little older than Wensicia; the two youngest daughters, Josifa and Rugi, were both adults, though they remained sheltered, despite their initial Bene Gesserit–supervised instruction. They all rushed to Wensicia's bedside to coo over the infant.

"Have you chosen a name yet?" Rugi asked, looking from Wensicia to Dalak. With her medium-brown curly hair, high cheekbones, and lavender eyes, his youngest daughter was pretty enough, but she seemed waifish and quiet, with few thoughts in her head. Rugi was just . . . *there*. Despite her lack of personality, in prior days handsome young nobles would have lined the streets of Kaitain for the chance to request her hand in marriage. Not anymore.

"We have decided to call him Farad'n," Shaddam said, using the Imperial *we*. "It is an honored name in Corrino history, the most famous of which was Crown Prince Raphael's great-grandfather Farad'n. There were other illustrious Farad'ns as well, dating back to the wars of . . ."

He let his words trail off when he noticed that no one was listening to him. Josifa had picked up the baby to rock it in her arms, talking to him in a silly fashion. Shaddam grimaced. *My first grandson has just been born in the stinking armpit of the universe, and now an idiot is talking to him.*

He stepped closer to the bed. "Give him to me, Josifa." She looked startled. "And stop babbling at him like a fool. You will pollute his mind with the nonsense contained in yours. I will place Farad'n with the best tutors I can find. He is the heir to the Imperium."

Getting his way, Shaddam held the baby awkwardly. He spoke with great portent down to the bundle, "You will be a true Corrino one day, Farad'n. Mark my words."

"A Zor-Fenring-Corrino," Dalak said, a proud smile crossing his cherubic features.

"He is Farad'n *Corrino*. And you, Dalak, are never to suggest otherwise."

The room went silent, except for Shaddam's voice, as he droned on to the child about how great he would be one day.

There are many ways to teach, and many ways to unteach. It is frequently a matter of inflicting pain in precise ways.

—MASTER EREBOAM, *Manual of Laboratory Procedures*

T he Twisting process is one of the most sacred of Tleilaxu secrets," Dr. Ereboam said, an edge of warning in his voice, "and is comprised of many subtle steps." At the entrance of his cluttered office, he looked with particular ire at Lady Margot and little Marie. "You will understand, of course, that I can show you only one small part of the lengthy routine."

"Ahh, of course." Standing with his wife and little Marie, Count Hasimir Fenring did not blink. His personality, like a loaded weapon, was intimidating in itself. "We each have secrets, hmmm? In all these years I have not told my friend Shaddam about the true plans . . . and mistakes . . . you Tleilaxu made during the amal project." He ran a finger along his upper lip. "Wouldn't the Emperor Muad'Dib be interested to learn of them? Yes, I know he would."

"Hidar Fen Ajidica was a rogue researcher! His plan was not sanctioned by the kehl!" Ereboam's excuse sounded thin. His milky skin turned even paler.

"Hmmm-ahh, yes, I am sure Muad'Dib would believe you."

Lady Margot took her husband's arm. "You have

nothing to fear from the truth, Dr. Ereboam . . . if it is the truth."

Looking cornered, the albino researcher tugged on his white goatee. "You have already used that to blackmail us, and we have given you sanctuary for years. Further threats are not necessary."

"Yes, ahh-hmmm, our destinies are intertwined." A crafty smile worked at the edges of his mouth. "We should have nothing to fear from each other . . . and few secrets. Let us witness this Twisting process. Perhaps my Lady and I can learn techniques applicable to the raising of our dear daughter."

Months ago, Fenring hadn't believed Ereboam's altruistic assertions for a moment when the researcher had proposed using the Twisting process on Marie. "It could unlock hitherto unseen potentials in the female child. Do you not want the girl to be armed against any sort of challenge?" Ereboam had asked. The very existence of free and independent women offended the Tleilaxu Masters. And the girl child seemed to be a thorn in their side as well. No, Count Fenring didn't trust their motives.

Fenring said, "Hmmm, perhaps we should observe this process of yours first." When he saw how the Tleilaxu researcher balked at the idea, he knew he had reached the right decision. "I insist."

Marie gave an angelic smile. "I am just a little girl, but I want to learn."

Given Marie's superior breeding, as well as impeccable upbringing and training, Fenring knew he and Margot could accomplish a great deal with the girl. Spy, assassin, savior, child Empress . . . So much more than the Bene Gesserits would have allowed.

Now the albino researcher's long white hair was unkempt, and he had dark circles under his eyes, as if he had not slept. Even so, he spoke in an energetic—even frenetic—voice. "Come with me, but do not expect to understand all the nuances. I find it a wildly exciting process."

Ereboam led them into a laboratory chamber that contained many tall clearplaz cylinders that extended from floor to ceiling, surrounded by pipes, brackets, and two levels of upper walkways. Around the room, sullen middle-caste technicians tended humming, pulsing machinery at identical-looking control panels. Eight men with shaved heads stood near the tubes wearing modest filmsuits that did not entirely disguise their different bodily configurations. One of them shivered and two others appeared fearful, while the rest seemed stoic. Fenring did not believe they were all gholas, like the copies of Piter de Vries that had been exterminated.

Lady Margot and Marie looked as if they were about to watch a Jongleur performance. The fidgeting albino doctor was a mass of nervous energy as he paced back and forth. "You are about to witness one of the chemical phases of indoctrination, only a small part of the preparatory process to soften the subject's psyche for proper reconfiguration."

"How much damage does it cause to the original personality?" Lady Margot asked.

The Tleilaxu man looked offended. "In some areas we are competitors of the Sisterhood. You cannot expect us to reveal everything." She continued to stare intently at him, adding to his uneasiness, and finally he added, "The Twisting process includes a chemical and pharmacological component, a physical stress component, and a psychological component. In the end, the subject is broken and re-formed, completely pliable and extraordinarily trained. This is a particularly useful technique to use on Mentats, who require severe as well as delicate maneuvers to create a superior mental format."

"So, ahh, drugs, psychological stresses, imposed conflicts that reach a crisis point."

Marie watched eagerly, almost hungrily. "I want to see closer." Fenring looked at the researcher, making sure Ereboam knew this was not a request.

The eight subjects were herded, sometimes roughly, into the tubes through side hatches, which were then sealed, trapping them within a cylindrical prison. Fenring stared at the growing expressions of alarm on the subjects' faces; one of the men began to pound uselessly on the thick, curved wall.

"This is all routine," Ereboam said dismissively. "All subjects are expected to be confused and alarmed. It is part of the process."

With a gushing noise, the tubes began to fill with brown, syrupy liquid. Marie let out a cry, either of alarm or delight, as the hairless men were completely submerged. Although the eight subjects tried to swim higher as the fluid levels rose, soon they could no longer keep their heads above the surface. The gush of liquid stopped, and shadowy forms could be seen struggling in the murk. Ereboam did not move to stop the experiment.

"You're drowning them?" Lady Margot said.

Standing at the base of the nearest tube, the doctor smiled reassuringly. "Once they inhale, they will fill their lungs with a highly oxygenated mixture. They will be able to breathe—after they fully surrender to the process. It is a lesson infused with spirituality, the need to put complete faith in something beyond their comprehension. To trust *us*. The subjects are helpless, and they must know they could die in there . . . but when they submit they will also see that we—their supreme Masters—are merciful. After facing death, they pass through the first step of submission. The first of many."

"Hmm-ahh-ahh. I see how that would be effective."

In the tubes, when all eight of the men stopped thrashing, bubbles drifted through the liquid. The subjects were inhaling the liquid and blowing air back out of their lungs.

"This also keys to the primitive programming in their brains, going back to before the species crawled out of the oceans," Ereboam continued. "We expose our Twisting subjects to primordial conditions to bypass the clutter of human experience. In a sense, Twisting is a misnomer. I prefer to think of it as *un*twisting, a cleansing process by which we create a tabula rasa, a blank canvas upon which to perform our genetic arts."

Ereboam raised his arms and pointed at the adjacent tubes, then the color of the liquid clarified to reveal the submerged subjects. "They look like fish in a tank," Marie said. "Look at their lips."

"Once they realize they are still alive, that they can breathe, we begin to change the chemical content, adding drugs that make them euphoric and therefore even more submissive. Soon, by repetition and by alternating the sensations of pain and fear, we will create a framework for their new mental template. *Our* template. The entire process requires years—which is why a true Twisted Mentat commands such a high price. More than half of the subjects fail."

"They fail? Or they die?" Lady Margot asked.

Ereboam looked at her. "Failure is death. This is neither game nor diversion. We Tleilaxu have standards to uphold."

"As do we, hmmm." Fenring placed a paternal hand on the little girl's shoulder. He himself had been training their daughter in highly sophisticated combat tricks, subtle ways of killing, and other nuanced niceties of assassination. Enhanced with Bene Gesserit mental disciplines from Lady Margot and the nanny, Marie was already as adept as an acolyte twice her age. "But we do not wish to put this dear child at such risk."

Margot added, "The Bene Gesserit breeding program has proceeded for generations, and our daughter is the culmination of centuries of careful manipulation. She is a remarkable specimen."

The Tleilaxu researcher surprised them by snorting. "We know of your Sisterhood's breeding effort, and we Tleilaxu have long shared your goal of creating a Kwisatz Haderach."

"Why would the Bene Tleilax need a Kwisatz Haderach?" Lady Margot said with a note of scorn in her voice.

"The same reason your Sisterhood wants one. Your plans may have culminated before ours, but they failed utterly. Look what the witches have set loose upon the universe."

"And your plans would do better?" Margot looked at the albino man. Her own husband was a failed Kwisatz Haderach as well, but as she saw it, his "failure" had ultimately proved more triumphant than the alleged "success" of Paul Atreides.

"The fate of our candidate remains to be seen," Ereboam said. "Our most promising specimen has not yet reached his culmination. We need a few more months, and then we will have a Kwisatz Haderach of our own."

Fenring looked at his wife, the two of them sharing the same thought. A Tleilaxu-bred Kwisatz Haderach? That was another secret project they would have to insist on seeing.

Construction teams had erected tall towers and monuments throughout Arrakeen, many of them named after Alia Atreides, the unusual—and some said holy—sister of Muad'Dib. Though she had never asked for this honor, Alia found it amusing.

In the ongoing citadel project north of the city, Whitmore Bludd had designed an entire wing supposedly with her in mind, although the foppish Swordmaster had an unrealistic view of Alia's interests and preferences. Unable to change his perception that she was not a mere child, he chose gentle pastel colors for her, elaborate and flowery archways, and rooms filled with sugar-and-spice ornamentation. Toys, playthings. As if she were a normal little girl.

Instead, Alia moved into a set of chambers that Bludd had labeled "guest quarters." Her extravagant apartments remained unoccupied, much to the Swordmaster's dismay; they could be turned into warehouses, as far as Alia was concerned.

Inside the room she had chosen, a large plaz-walled tank contained scuttling black creatures, seventeen of them. She could sit for hours watching their movements under an artificial heat panel. They loved to hide in the shadows or sun themselves on the decorative rocks. For the most part, the black scorpions rarely moved, but crouched waiting for prey, which Alia provided whenever it was feeding time. The scorpions sat motionless until some impulse triggered an instinctive reaction, a genetically programmed movement and response.

From her memories of countless lifetimes, Alia knew that children generally liked to have pets. Thus, she made a conscious decision to keep some of her own, though a part of her realized that she did it for the wrong reasons.

Alia removed the lid and leaned over the tank. She could identify all seventeen individual arachnids, although she had not taken the frivolous step of naming them. She wasn't that much of a little girl.

Two of the creatures moved, while the rest remained motionless. Sometimes she would watch them fight territorial battles over their tiny patch of encapsulated ground. They were like sandworms clashing at the edges of one another's territories . . . or like her brother's armies facing off in battles of the Jihad. It was only a difference of scale.

She reached into the plaz-walled chamber, reminded of an ornamental aquarium her mother had kept in Castle Caladan . . . a memory from long before Alia's birth. *Aquarium.* A word not often spoken here on Dune. The idea of using a transparent container of water to keep fish as pets would have seemed bizarre to a Fremen. This aquarium held only dryness, creatures of the sand and rocks.

Black scorpions such as these were common in the deserts of Dune. In the sietches, Fremen kept scorpions for their poison, which was applied to crysknife blades. Their sting contained an extravagantly potent venom superior to many poisons used by the Tleilaxu.

But poisons didn't bother Alia. She had emerged from the womb with the thoughts and capabilities of a Reverend Mother. When her mother had consumed the Water of Life, it had fundamentally changed Jessica's body chemistry, along with that of her unborn daughter. A scorpion's sting need not concern her.

Her fingers were small and stubby, still those of a child. Very little extra flesh padded her short arm. As she put her hand into the tank, the black scorpions backed away, raising their curved tails in a defensive posture. The stingers were like hooked needles. The two arachnids nearest her arm raised their pincers, ready to fight.

But Alia moved slowly, reaching her other hand into the aquarium. Grasping the backs of their segmented tails with care, she plucked out one scorpion and then another, placing it on the back of her hand. They settled down quickly; she had done this often. When they moved along her arm, their sharp legs tickled her skin. They were not afraid of her. She laughed to herself.

Within her head, she had the company of many ghostly friends, sisters, and ancestors, but they were memories of full lives, with personalities formed over uncounted years and experiences. They made poor childhood playmates, leaving Alia lonely. She had no real friends, no confidante to giggle with or whisper ideas to. The scorpions weren't actually very good pets, either.

She heard an indrawn gasp of horror. "Child, what are you doing?"

Immediately recognizing Irulan's voice, Alia flinched at the interruption but did not turn around.

"Was that an assassination attempt, dear Irulan?" Alia said, still staring into the tank. "By startling me, you could have made me jerk my hand, and the scorpions would have reacted by stinging me."

Irulan came cautiously forward. "I had no such intent, Alia, as you well know—and since you so often remind me you are a Reverend Mother, you could have saved yourself from any poison."

"Then why were you worried?"

"I could not help myself. I was frightened for you."

"Such a lack of control suggests that you have forgotten some of your Bene Gesserit training. Shouldn't you be writing your new book? My brother is anxious to read it."

"The work is coming along nicely, but I have found many contradictions. I am having a difficult time choosing which version I prefer as truth. Once I write the story, most people will accept it, so I must be cautious."

"Cautious about the facts themselves, or the politics behind them?" Alia sounded impish.

"One affects the other." Irulan came closer to the tank. "Why do you keep those creatures?"

"I like to play with them. They haven't stung me yet."

Irulan seemed dismayed, but it was nothing new. The Princess did not quite understand her role regarding Paul's sister, who was ostensibly her sister-in-law. At times, Irulan even displayed oddly maternal feelings toward her, and Alia wasn't sure whether or not they were genuine. Irulan seemed to gain nothing by them, and yet . . .

"You flaunt the fact that you are more than just a child, but a part of you is still—or wants to be—a girl. I had four younger sisters with whom I could interact and squabble and share secrets, whenever some nursemaid or guard wasn't watching over us in the Imperial Palace. I am sorry that you do not have even that much of a childhood, Alia."

With an abrupt gesture, Alia swept the scorpions off her arm and back to the sands and rock in the tank. Agitated and disoriented, not knowing what had just happened in their world, the creatures began to fight each other, clacking pincers, jabbing with stingers.

"I have many childhoods—all of them in Other Memory." She could not stop herself from adding a taunt. "You will understand it one day, Irulan, if you ever become a Reverend Mother."

The Princess did not rise to the bait. "You may say that, little Alia. I know you can learn many things from Other Memory, but not everything. You need a childhood of your own."

The desert erases all footprints.

—the PRINCESS IRULAN, *The Manual of Muad'Dib*

Sietch Tabr.

Paul and his mother had gone there after fleeing from the Harkonnens so many years ago, but before that the isolated sietch had been merely one Fremen settlement, little different from all the others. Now, it was considered a sacred place. *I change everything I touch*, Paul thought.

Fremen traditionalism had preserved Sietch Tabr intact even as his enormous new citadel and governmental complex continued to grow in Arrakeen under the masterful management of Whitmore Bludd. With Stilgar off on Bela Tegeuse, Gurney on Giedi Prime, and Alia left to watch the affairs of government, he and Chani came here to remember the taste of the desert again, the smells and flavors of what life had been like. They came to reconnect with themselves and to *disconnect* from the nonsense that continued to grow around him. The Jihad . . . the monster that was becoming part of him like a second skin. Fremen would understand the mystical nature of the call to find an inner refuge for the soul.

After he and Chani settled into their old quarters within the rock walls, complete with familiar hangings across the door opening, Paul did not need prescience to know that his momentary peace would be interrupted soon.

For practical reasons, Paul had announced that he was going to Sietch Tabr to observe the expanded spice operations in the desert, to compliment the workers and the foremen, to praise their successes and mourn their losses. Melange, the lifeblood of his Imperium, continued to flow through the veins of the universe.

Dayef, the current naib of this settlement, had expressed his eagerness to take Muad'Dib out to the spice fields. Paul and Chani changed into full desert garb, took a Fremkit, checked their stillsuits. Even though he would have an army of guards, assistants, and observers with him, old habits would not permit him to be careless when facing the raw power of Arrakis. Too many accidents could occur out there.

Dayef selected a young Fremen pilot who swore he would battle the storms of hell to protect Muad'Dib. Paul simply said, "I would prefer a flight with less turbulence today."

Dayef took the seat beside him in the 'thopter, and they left the sheltering mountains and flew out into the vast ocean of dunes. This naib was more of a business leader than a warrior; he had a crysknife, but also carried an accounting tablet.

"Our production is now five times that of House Harkonnen at its peak," Dayef said. "When we find spice, we dispatch at least four spice harvesters. New specialized carryalls are being manufactured on at least six different planets and more are placed into service every month."

"What of our losses to weather and worms?" Paul remembered how such things had constantly hindered the work of House Atreides.

"We are now able to place twice as many spotters in

the air. They range farther on scouting missions and can announce wormsign sooner. That lets us work with a greater margin of safety."

"I want no accidents." How Duke Leto had hated losing men! He felt a pang inside. His father would have been appalled by Paul's Jihad, in which billions had already died in his name. Leto would have lamented the terrible cost, but Paul had to view the larger picture and see past the blood to the future. A safe future, he hoped.

"There are always accidents, Muad'Dib. However, with regular deliveries of new machinery, we are placing substantially more equipment into service than we lose to the desert, at least seventeen percent more."

"The spice must flow," Chani said.

"So it must," Dayef agreed.

Paul observed through the scratched plaz window of the 'thopter as people moved with antlike efficiency down on the active spice field. The pilot landed the craft near the first of four enormous spice factories.

"These operations have been going for only twenty minutes, and already they are at full production levels," Dayef said.

Paul was pleased to see the clockwork cooperation that could erect a veritable city in less than half an hour, all the machinery exploiting a deep rich vein that scouts had found only that morning.

Years ago, during the introductory tour that Dr. Kynes had given Duke Leto, there had been only one factory crawler. Now Paul counted six insectile structures, lumbering machines each the size of an industrial base. The work gangs rushed about at a frenetic pace: spice operators, dunemen, depth-probe operators, riggers, even a few weather-beaten CHOAM inspectors.

In addition to skilled Fremen spice crews, offworld pilgrims volunteered for the work in droves, considering it part of their sacred hajj to touch natural melange on the dunes. The armies of laborers also consisted of prisoners and slaves captured in the Jihad. Defeated and indoctrinated, they accepted Muad'Dib's guarantee of freedom after six months in a spice factory, at which time they would be released, forgiven, and offered a chance to stay on Dune. Very few survived to reap the reward.

Paul felt a twinge inside as he realized another difference between himself and his father: Duke Leto would have abhorred using forced labor for such operations, but right now this was necessary to meet obligations to the Guild and to feed the machine that ran the new Empire of Muad'Dib. *We do what is required.* And the people silently demanded it, forcing themselves to participate in these work gangs to demonstrate their altruism and their worth. And they would keep doing it for him. "This is impressive, Dayef."

"They do it to show their faith in you, Muad'Dib."

Chani chided Paul in a low voice. "Do not forget that you are just a man, Usul."

He smiled back at her. "You will never let me forget that, my Sihaya." Nevertheless, he *did* need to be reminded, since he spent his days on Arrakeen watching the construction of his ostentatious citadel, hearing the millions chanting his name, knowing that across the galaxy his banner was being planted on more worlds than he would ever bother to count.

I am just a man. I am Paul Atreides. I am only the Terrible Muad'Dib if I allow myself to be.

Because this particular spice deposit had been found in a part of the desert sheltered by a low line of rocky outcroppings, the worms could approach from only one direction, so the spotters concentrated their attention there. This meant that the harvesting process operated under a higher than usual margin of safety and was able to continue far longer than they might otherwise have expected.

The low rock wall, however, did not shelter them from a sudden sandstorm that whipped up from the east. Thermal currents from the blistering sands converged with winds that blew along the sharp ridgeline and slammed together to create a sudden, unexpected storm cell.

Within the sheltered 'thopter, Dayef listened on his communication bands as the voices began to crackle with static. The harvesting crews alerted everyone to the change in the weather, summoning their outriders back to the carryalls, but most of the crews remained at their stations. The factory crawlers continued to churn away, harvesting until the last possible moment.

"Because they know you are here, Muad'Dib, they intend to put in an extra effort until the last instant," Dayef said.

"I do not want that. Call them in. Now! It is my command. Don't risk them." He looked at Chani beside him, then at the oncoming fringe of the storm. He would not risk her either. "And we must depart before that wind hits." He remembered his father shouting, *Damn the spice!,* and the desperate measures they had taken to rescue the few stranded men. . . .

Dayef's order caused further scrambling in the temporary camp, but some of the workers still didn't evacuate. Instead, they stood outside their spice harvesters, raising their fists and chanting. Paul could barely hear the tiny echo of their voices, "Muad'Dib, Muad'Dib . . ."

With a flash of anger and dismay, Paul realized that simply by coming here to inspect the site, he had given these workers a false sense of security. Because they so wanted his praise, they felt a foolish need to show off. He could see the razor-edged dust now, curling up over the rock wall, brown plumes swirling like the smoke of a burned village. Those winds carried abrasive sand particles with enough force to scour flesh away, and the men knew it.

Carryalls dropped down to snag the large factory crawlers, lifting them into the air and lumbering away as the weather intensified. The pilot turned to Paul and Chani. "If you do not wish me to fight with the winds of hell, Muad'Dib, we need to take off now."

"Do it." Paul strapped himself in and made sure that Chani did the same. The 'thopter's articulated wings began to shudder, giving them lift. The breezes were already pushing them. A few last ground vehicles raced aboard the harvesters, calling for pickup. It was like a gigantic airlift in a war zone. Paul looked down as their 'thopter rose from the dunes, heard the hiss of sand grains across the transparent shield.

Dayef touched the communication stud in his ear, nodded. "The spice crew managers report that all of the big equipment is getting away, Muad'Dib. A dozen small rover vehicles have been lost, along with four sand diggers, and two sledges."

"What about those men down there?" Paul saw a line of thirty figures atop the crest of a low dune. The fabric of their work garb whipped about as they braced themselves. They raised their hands into the air, defying the storm.

"Merely one of your new slave crews from Omwara, hard workers but a bit unruly. Although they didn't join the rebel Thorvald, they are shamed that some of their brothers gave him temporary refuge on their planet. They wish to prove their loyalty to you."

"They can prove their loyalty by obeying my orders. Tell them to get themselves to safety! Make sure they know it is *Muad'Dib's command* that they do so. Have them board the last carrier."

The sandstorm was getting worse, sweeping down like a curtain over the ridge and already erasing the human-made marks on the desert. Dayef frowned. "Communications are down—too much static electricity."

"Can they fit in 'thopters?" Paul asked, feeling a

greater desperation. "We could land and pick them up." He clenched his fist, feeling the danger increase with every second.

A hard knot of wind struck the 'thopter, causing it to shear sideways and lurch toward the ground. Its articulated wings flapped and struggled to keep the craft airborne. Alarms whistled on the cockpit controls as the pilot fought to keep them from crashing. The storm grew more intense each moment as the front rolled over the work site.

Paul looked at Chani, having reached a hard decision. *I will not risk her.* "We can't save those men. If we brought the transports back down to retrieve them, we would lose the ships and all those other men as well."

Chani's face was drawn. "They believe you have the power to save them, Usul. They believe you can intervene and stop the winds."

But I am just a man!

The line of workers below continued shouting at the tempest. The 'thopter shuddered, and the pilot finally lifted the aircraft, carrying Paul and Chani safely above the worst of the weather. Paul continued to gaze downward. What must those poor fools be thinking now? Did they truly believe that at any moment Muad'Dib could stop the winds? As they died, would they think he had failed them?

"And the spice?" Paul asked. "Did we receive a full load?"

"I believe so, Muad'Dib."

His father would have done anything, *risked* anything to personally rescue those men, even if it cost numerous other lives, an entire spice harvest, and all the equipment. But in some things Paul was not like his father, because he was more than a Duke and had to balance the needs of an entire Empire. And without melange to grease the wheels of that Empire . . .

Below, the doomed men still stood atop the dune, facing the knife-wind of the storm. He saw three of them stumble and fall, shoved down by the abrasive blasts. Others fought to stand upright, as if to prove something to Muad'Dib . . . but what? If he were younger, Paul Atreides might have wept for their blind zeal that they called bravery. But now his Fremen training, and his anger at their wasted gesture, cut off all tears.

Sadly, he knew that the other members of the spice crew, those who had witnessed this pointless if dramatic sacrifice, would draw another conclusion entirely. As the sands and the winds curled over the abandoned site, finally engulfing the last of the defiant men from Omwara, Paul was sure the witnesses would not see this as the fate one deserved for disobeying the direct orders of Muad'Dib. They would admire those fools as true believers, and there was nothing he could do about it.

"Take us back to Sietch Tabr," Paul said to the pilot. "I have seen enough."

> *While I often use knives, I rarely kill in the same manner twice. It is much more interesting, and safer for me, to continually devise new methods and angles of attack—a constant process that hones the blade of my mind sharper with each experience. And the delicious secret of timing and surprise! Ah, that is a subject in and of itself. It speaks to the very essence of control.*

> —COUNT HASIMIR FENRING

Even after more than forty years of marriage, Count Fenring still found his wife, Margot, incredibly attractive . . . as she reminded him every time she seduced him. For the good of his marriage and his own physical well-being, Fenring never tired of allowing himself to be ensnared.

In their private sanctuary residence in Thalidei, Fenring found excitement not only in the warm and comforting sexual act, but in the fact that he had found and deactivated four more secret Tleilaxu spying devices. How many times had the gnomish little men observed their lovemaking? Angered by the intrusion, the Count had decided to track down the primary culprit and strangle him, preferably in front of other squealing Tleilaxu. On the other hand, knowing something about that race's bizarre and prudish attitude toward sex, Fenring decided that the spies had probably witnessed his and Margot's passion with some measure of disgust, rather than titillation. That idea amused him.

Fenring did not fit an Adonis-like mold of male attractiveness. His narrow, ferretlike facial features might not be particularly handsome, but his body was muscular and well-toned. He had never preened in an attempt to make women notice him. His skills had been to remain quietly *invisible*, so that he could whisper into the appropriate ears and slip into certain rooms to eavesdrop on confidential conversations.

As soon as he was confident that the Tleilaxu spy-eyes were deactivated, he and Margot disrobed, gazing on each other in the warm light of golden glowpanels. She led him to the bed, and the two of them began to demonstrate their proficiency in an ever-increasing repertoire of pleasuring skills. Over four decades, Fenring was continually amazed at how much he had learned and how many techniques he had yet to try.

"Ah, my dear, you are always a wonder to me." As they lay on the bed, he kissed her tenderly. She worked the gentlest touch of her fingertips along his ear, creating an invisible embroidery of fired neurons in his skin. He shuddered.

"We are well suited to each other," she agreed.

They had chosen each other for political reasons, as well as mutual attraction. Nearly concurrent with Shaddam's wedding to his first wife, Anirul, their own marriage ceremony had received far less attention and almost no spectacle. Even so, their union had lasted far, far longer.

The gold-handled knife that Bashar Garon had delivered as a peace offering from the deposed Emperor still lay on a bureau. Fenring occasionally looked at it and thought about Shaddam's fervent desire to be restored to the Lion Throne. Even though Paul-Muad'Dib was causing horrific damage to human civilization, Fenring had never been able to convince himself that his Corrino friend was a better alternative. No, he and Margot had their own plans.

As he made love to her, Fenring fantasized, but not about other women. He remembered the feel of warm blood on his fingers, the careful selection of proper tools of his trade. If he had enough safe time after performing his wet work, he rather enjoyed gazing upon the rich burgundy color of his victim's life essence, the way it gushed from the body and pooled and sparkled in the smallest light, as if trying to recapture life, but then stopped and coagulated and hardened. Even Shaddam did not know how many people Fenring had killed.

The first of his murders had occurred at a much younger age than the Corrino patriarch realized, when Fenring was only four. Four! He was proud of this accomplishment, because it meant that even at a young age he was able to identify enemies. The teenage yard boy he'd stabbed had deserved it anyway, because the older boy had tried to molest him. Even as a child, Fenring had seen through the tricky words and promises and had plunged a pocket knife deep into the aggressor's abdomen. His willpower always made up for any mismatch in physical strength between himself and his opponent. Young Hasimir had inflicted a hundred wounds on his victim's body before getting his fill. Because the teenager had been furtive about his abnormal sexual activities, no one had ever suspected the four-year-old.

He sighed now, feeling the thrill of remembrance. Margot held him, adjusting her own movements to his, expertly controlling her own body so that they climaxed simultaneously and thunderously.

"You make it impossible for me to even think of other things, my dear," Fenring lied.

She smiled. "My way of repaying you for being so understanding about the breeding obligations the Sisterhood placed upon me." She stroked his cheek, scratching at the stubble there. "And you've been so loving."

"I understood the need for seducing Feyd-Rautha. It was not a particularly onerous task, I presume?"

"Oh, he was cocksure, but he was just a boy who liked women telling him how good he was in bed, instead of showing him *how* to be good in bed. Besides, he is dead now. And we have little Marie from it."

"Yes, hmmm, we have her—and the Sisterhood doesn't."

"Neither do the Tleilaxu," Margot added with conditioned annoyance. "And now they claim to have their own Kwisatz Haderach. We must learn their plans."

Fenring knew he needed a way to pry that knowledge from Dr. Ereboam. "Perhaps with their plans and your knowledge of the Sisterhood—and Marie—we can make this new Kwisatz Haderach truly successful, not a fiend like Muad'Dib or a dead end like myself."

"I want to see the Kwisatz Haderach," piped up a small voice, startling Fenring. He sprang from the bed, ready to attack. Little Marie sat calmly on a makeshift seat just inside the door. She had an innocent, yet amused look on her small face.

"How long have you been there?" Fenring demanded.

"I was watching. I was learning. You are both very interesting."

Fenring had never been particularly prudish, and Lady Margot certainly wasn't, but the idea of their daughter simply observing during their lovemaking both disoriented and embarrassed him. In a very real sense, it was much worse than the inquisitive eyes of the Tleilaxu.

"You must learn to respect the boundaries of privacy," her mother said.

"That is not what you've taught me. You trained me to be invisible, so that I could spy. Did I not do a good job?"

Lady Margot didn't quite know what to say. At last,

Fenring chuckled. For countless centuries, children had been wandering in upon their parents having sex, but it should be accidental. Not a planned thing.

"Yes, you have learned well, Marie," he said wryly. "You have certainly taught us to be more careful."

The architecture of our lives creates the land-scape of history. Some of us build great and enduring fortresses, while others merely erect facades.

—the PRINCESS IRULAN, *The Manual of Muad'Dib*

*O*stentatious. That word came to mind, along with *grandiose, extravagant,* and *awe-inspiring*—they were all appropriate. But in the final analysis, Whitmore Bludd's intention was to create something that literally defied words, a palatial fortress so incredible that historians would spend centuries debating how best to describe what he had accomplished here at the heart of Muad'Dib's empire.

Even in an enclosed inspection craft that flew slowly above the construction site, Bludd needed an hour just to circumnavigate the boundaries of the stupendous main structure and its complex of buildings and gardens.

Yes, stupendous.

The citadel zone extended to the north of Arrakeen, across the suburbs to the rugged, irregular cliffs that formed a natural boundary to the north. But the project did not stop there. Bludd's master plan took advantage of the city itself, incorporating existing temples and blocky old imperial structures throughout the various districts. When the project was complete, Muad'Dib's palace would consume the dusty city, like a great worm swallowing a spice harvester.

However, as far as Bludd was concerned, the work would never be "complete," because he could always think of something else to add: a new museum wing, a higher turret, a more imposing tower, an integral sculpture of polished blue metal whose plates looked like rippling water whenever the wind stroked it. Bludd did not intend ever to retire quietly to the countryside. No, this was the pinnacle of his life and achievements, something for which he would always be remembered.

As his craft hummed along the boundary of the site, the Swordmaster-turned-architect stared out the curved windows. Thankfully, Korba remained silent for a change. Paul Atreides's Fremen leader styled himself as a prominent priest as well as an important administrator, and too often he contributed capricious ideas to the citadel design. Bludd didn't like the interference, yet he had no choice but to listen to Korba's suggestions. *Politics!*

As the two men watched, gigantic suspensor cranes lifted huge girders into place, which were then overlaid with blocks of stone that had been lascut from the Shield Wall. The labor force summoned by Muad'Dib, and the sheer quantity of imported offworld materials, were beyond anything Bludd had ever imagined.

"The amount of taxes the Emperor will have to raise for this project is beyond my ability to calculate," he muttered. No one had ever questioned a single item in the budget.

Korba just shrugged. "If Muad'Dib wishes it, then his people will pay. If they do not reach into their own pockets, the Qizarate will do it for them."

"It was just a comment in passing," Bludd replied. The other man had no sense of humor whatsoever.

The work teams were competing with one another for speediness of construction, with monetary rewards for their accomplishments and severe penalties for deficiencies. Anyone who showed signs of laziness or produced shoddy workmanship was publicly flogged; for the most egregious cases involving fraud or theft, the individuals were beheaded in the central plaza—an activity at which Korba excelled. To Bludd, these sorts of punishments seemed particularly unlike the original Paul Atreides, but Fremen traditions were much more severe. Paul seemed to be losing some of his humanity in the process . . . or at least discovering a different, darker side of it.

Bludd had intentionally styled a section of the citadel along the lines of the old Swordmaster school on far-away Ginaz. The loathsome and dishonorable Grummans had brought down the famous school as part of their feud with House Ecaz, and then expanded their vendetta to encompass House Atreides. Poor fat Rivvy Dinari, slain on the wedding day of Duke Leto and Ilesa Ecaz. *Heroic* Dinari. If only his fellow Swordmaster could see Bludd now!

Korba said blithely, "After analyzing your blueprints, I realigned several turrets so that they fall upon numerically significant positions. I have already given new orders to the construction crews."

"You can't just move one piece of it—everything fits as part of the overall architectural pattern."

"Everything fits according to the designs of *Muad'Dib*. The modifications are required for religious reasons. You do not understand the necessities of orthodoxy, Bludd."

"And you don't know a thing about architecture." Bludd knew that Korba would not change his mind, and he was wise enough not to call the man out in a duel. Though he was sure he could defeat Korba, he did not underestimate the influence and power of the Fedaykin leader.

As the inspection craft circled a helical tower whose framework seemed to defy gravity, Korba brooded down at the tiny workers. "Do not question my decisions, Bludd. I fought beside Muad'Dib in the desert and stood with him in sietch. I was one of his students of the Weirding Way. We spilled blood side by side, killed Harkonnens together. I was among the first to call him Usul, and I watched him slay Feyd-Rautha."

Bludd couldn't believe this desert fighter would try to engage in a game of one-upmanship with him. In response, he said, "I knew Paul Atreides when he was just a stripling, and I saved his life when your mother was still scraping the stink out of your swaddling clothes. Read your history, Korba—Imperial history. Rivvy Dinari got most of the credit, but I was there with him at the wedding massacre. I know the truth, and so does Paul."

"*Imperial* history," Korba sneered. "Paul Atreides. I speak of *Muad'Dib,* not the son of a Landsraad nobleman. His life before he came to Sietch Tabr and took the name of Usul has little relevance now."

"You cannot know a man by half his life," Bludd said, annoyed. "Isn't that why Princess Irulan wrote his biography, which you all carry around like a holy textbook? If his earlier life was irrelevant, he would not have placed me in such an important position." *There,* Bludd thought.

As Korba fell silent, the Swordmaster adjusted the temperature control inside the sealed vehicle. He wore formal clothing, not a dusty jumpsuit or worker's garb. Whenever he was in public, Bludd liked to present himself with proper dress and manners. These desert ruffians could learn a great deal about style from him. Korba, on the other hand, seemed unwilling to peel off his stillsuit even for routine hygienic purposes, and here in the enclosed craft, the stench of him was like like that of an unwashed beast. Bludd contemplated borrowing a set of stillsuit nose plugs just to filter the air.

He thought about his long-dead friend Dinari, sorry for his untimely death but not sorry for the memory. Although the obese Swordmaster had been killed in the

War of Assassins, he had also been rewarded with great glory for what he had done. And if not for a fraction of a second of hesitation, *Bludd* would also be remembered as a hero during the wedding massacre, rather than an inept failure. Ilesa had died, and he should have protected her. No matter what other exploits he accomplished in subsequent years, history would never forget that he had missed his singular chance to make a legend of himself.

Instead, he would be relegated to a footnote in an entry about the early life of Muad'Dib. Irulan was writing that part of Paul's life now, and Bludd wasn't certain she would treat him kindly in her supposedly objective account. She'd been polite to him, so maybe he could convince her to insert a good word or two. . . .

He straightened inside the cockpit of the inspection craft. Well, despite his earlier shame, this magnificent fortress-palace would overshadow everything else. The citadel would be his crowning achievement, his true legacy for history. It would surpass even the accomplishments of his revered ancestor Porce Bludd, who had selflessly sacrificed his fortune to save populations during the Butlerian Jihad.

"Make your suggestions for design alterations if you must, but I still have to approve them," Bludd said. "This is my project, my design, and *my* citadel."

"You forget yourself." Korba's voice carried a clear warning. "No matter what you say, no matter how you delude yourself, this will always be the Citadel of *Muad'Dib*. The Qizarate has named it so. It belongs to him, and to God. You are a mere facilitator, as are we all. Who will remember your part?"

The words stung. Previously, Bludd's feelings toward the other man had been constrained to annoyance; now he was genuinely angry at him. "*I* still know what I accomplished. That is all that really matters."

"If no one knows your name or your accomplishments, then your life is no more memorable than sand blown on the wind." Korba chuckled, but Bludd didn't think it was at all funny.

"And you, Korba, try to make your own mark by creating a religion around Muad'Dib? It's all about power you can earn from the life and legend of the Emperor, isn't it? It's all about elevating yourself."

Placing a hand over the crysknife at his waist, the Fremen growled, "Be careful what you say, man, or—"

"If you pull that blade, prepare to die," Bludd said. He pointed a long sleeve at him, which revealed bristling needle points below the wrist, ready to launch.

With a hard smile, the Fremen relaxed his hand, and looked away, out the window. "It seems we each have a stake in Muad'Dib," he said.

Your point is valid, that many of my "allies" are using the holy war as an excuse to attack rival families and resolve or inflame old feuds. You say this extravagant bloodshed has nothing to do with my rule or my decisions, but I take full responsibility nonetheless. I am accountable for each and every death.

—from *Conversations with Muad'Dib* by the
PRINCESS IRULAN

After he returned from Sietch Tabr, Paul announced he would receive visitors in the extravagant Celestial Audience Chamber, which was still not entirely completed.

Over the past few years, the temporary throne room in Shaddam's former hutment had lost its luster for him, so Paul decided to hold audiences in the new space instead, despite the fact that Bludd was still not satisfied with all the finishing touches—moldings, fine filigree, stonework, intricate sculptures, elaborately painted ceilings and walls. The Swordmaster insisted on finishing some of the perfectionistic interior work himself, permitting no one to help him.

Countless alcoves were only partially filled with statuary, usually renditions of Paul or of his Atreides ancestors. Fremen tapestries above the throne depicted colorful scenes from battles of the Jihad. Bludd had announced that some of these scenes would be replicated as ceiling frescoes, encircling the base of the high dome, when it was complete.

The previous day, Paul had walked the scaffolds that were in place high above the throne, where the finest

artists in the realm continued to work feverishly on their
commissions. Even as he held court now, they were up
there painting, voices and movements hushed reverently
in the presence of Muad'Dib.

He had been shaken by the blind and suicidal devotion that those workers from Omwara had demonstrated,
facing a sandstorm to show their faith. For generations,
House Atreides had inspired tremendous loyalty as embodied in Gurney Halleck, Duncan Idaho, Thufir Hawat,
and many others. But that loyalty had been supportive,
not reckless. What had those workers *accomplished* by
dying out there on the dunes? How had their sacrifices
served Muad'Dib?

Although the ever-growing religion around him was
an engine that drove the necessary force of his Jihad,
it might easily slip beyond his control. Religions could
be extraordinarily effective, but they could also be irre-
sponsible . . . and he was at the heart of both possibilities. The people saw only him, and not the corona of
consequences around his every action.

Now, dressed in a flowing brown-and-gold robe instead of the comfortable, dusty stillsuit he had worn in
Sietch Tabr, Paul took his seat on the large temporary
throne placed there during the construction. Eventually,
he would bring in the oversized Hagal quartz seat, the
legendary Lion Throne from the Corrino dynasty. For
the time being, even though the throne would serve as a
reminder of what he had taken from his enemies, Paul
preferred not to inspire thoughts of Shaddam IV. He
looked around the huge chamber as the audience took
standing positions according to their rank and connections.

Wearing a loose green gown adorned with a gold-
braided collar, Chani entered through a side door, followed by three Fremen women in pale gray robes
designed to conceal weapons. Six-year-old Alia entered

briskly in her black robe and came to a stop beside Paul's throne, as if she were herself a bodyguard.

Given the violence Thorvald's rebels often inspired, and the ridiculously low price on the heads of Muad'Dib and his family, Paul had assigned powerful female guards to follow and protect Chani, Alia, and even Irulan. His mother was also due to arrive soon for a brief visit, and he would grant her the same protection. He intended to take no chances.

He thought again of the group of fanatic workers standing on the dune top, facing the deadly winds to show their devotion, proving . . . what? And those men were his *supporters*.

Hearing a commotion of shouts near the massive entrance doors, Paul saw his Fremen guards scuffling with green-robed prisoners, captive priests from a splinter sect. The guards soon gained control of the situation, though they were forced to use stun goads. Paul watched without commenting on the rough treatment. Knowing what these priests had done, he found it difficult to restrain himself from ordering their immediate execution. That would come in time, he was sure. Some things were unforgivable.

Korba marched toward the throne along a rusty-red spice-fiber carpet that had been laid down only that morning. He had chosen to wear a clean white robe emblazoned with scarlet symbols, pointedly more extravagant than the green robes of the prisoners that the guards nudged along behind him. He no longer looked like a Fedaykin.

The five prisoners had cuts and bruises, and sunken red eyes that looked more dead than alive. Only one of the priests, tall and patrician, appeared defiant. With undisguised contempt, the guards flung the priests to the hard floor. All but one of them had the good sense to remain prostrate; a guard knocked the most rebellious one back down, using a boot kick.

With an elaborate bow, Korba stopped at the foot of the throne. "Exalted Muad'Dib, pillar of the universe, I bring you these disloyal priests of the ancient sect of Dur. They were captured trying to defile the sacred shrine of your father and steal his skull!" Eyes closed as if in prayer (a performance for the rapt audience), he formally pulled his cryknife from its sheath and stood ready with it, poised like an executioner.

Paul could barely control his fury. "Priests of Dur were once well-respected in the Imperium, presiding over ceremonies to marry and crown emperors. And now you attempt to desecrate the shrine of *my father*? You have become grave robbers? Defilers of the dead?"

Korba waited for a signal from him, but Paul hesitated, uncertain how to deal with this. The priests' actions were another example of the reckless irresponsibility of uncontrolled religion. But how to control a religion, whether his own or this ancient sect? Would tolerance and mercy help? Or was a stronger grip required? What would his father have advised?

One of the cowed priests, with a paunch that gave him the shape of a pear, struggled to his knees and looked beseechingly at Paul. Sweat ran down his brow into his eyes. "Sire, the charges against me are false and unfair. I do not even know these men—I serve in a different order! They forced me to wear these robes! I was on religious sabbatical."

"He lies," Korba said. "His so-called sabbatical was a conspiracy meeting, at which he and these others plotted your overthrow. Any oath of fealty he utters now would not be worth the wind it is written upon."

Paul glowered at the kneeling man. "I have been tolerant of religions other than my own, but I shall not tolerate the spreading of lies or conspiracies that threaten me—and I tolerate no desecration of my father, the honorable Duke Leto Atreides." He felt a great weariness settle upon him. "You and your companions must die for this."

When the guards tried to haul the paunchy man back to rejoin the others, he suddenly sagged in their arms, as if he had fainted. Korba touched the man's neck, sniffed his breath. "This one is dead." With a wolfish grin, he cast a scornful look at the other green-robed priests, then faced the crowds gathered inside the Celestial Audience Chamber. "Muad'Dib struck him dead with a glance! No one escapes the gaze of our Emperor." In the chamber, Paul heard a low chanting of his name.

The defiant, patrician-looking priest got to his feet. "An autopsy would prove that a poison-tipped weapon or dart killed that poor man. Parlor tricks!" He pushed himself two steps forward, even though the guards struggled to hold him back. "There is nothing holy about you. The Priests of Dur call you Paul Atreides the Demon!"

The chamber erupted in wild howling from the insult. "Gouge out their eyes!" a woman screamed, her voice shrill. One of the other priests whimpered, but his companions silenced him immediately.

Paul recalled the War of Assassins in his childhood, the battles on Ecaz and Grumman, the bloodshed and tragedies, and he remembered the great reverence with which he and his loved ones had entombed Duke Leto's skull. *My father's greatest mistake was not being harsh enough with his enemies.*

"All of you shall die for the crimes your misguided religion has inspired," Paul said, looking at the green-robed men and knowing Korba would make sure their deaths were long and painful. "From this day forward, I hereby remove my sanction of your reckless beliefs. All across my realm, I command that every one of your places of worship be leveled. Henceforth, my Qizarate will carefully reshape your followers so that they find the proper path." He stood and turned his back to the crowds, ending the audience. "There shall be no more Priests of Dur."

⤜⤛

THE NEXT DAY, in a private room behind the throne, Paul was pleased to welcome his visitors. Lady Jessica and Gurney Halleck were, however, a somber-faced pair. Paul accepted an embrace from his mother and then clasped hands with Gurney. The pair had arrived on the same Heighliner, and he was very glad to see them.

He let down his guard, sighing as he looked at them with deep affection. "Mother, Gurney, I have missed you both. Is everything well on Caladan? On Giedi Prime?"

Gurney looked somewhat abashed, but Jessica gave a quick reply. "No, Paul. Not on either planet."

Though Gurney was surprised at her blunt answer, he added, "I have made some progress on Giedi Prime, my Lord, but the whole planet throbs with the pain of old wounds. It will be generations before the people begin to stand on their own again."

Concerned, Paul glanced from one face to the other. "What has happened on Caladan, Mother?"

Jessica looked regal and every bit as beautiful as she must have appeared to Duke Leto. "There have been demonstrations, insults, bold criticism. Defectors from the Atreides guard took charge of Castle Caladan and holed up in it, forcing me to take shelter elsewhere until we could regain control. Entire villages have been burned."

"Defectors? From the *Atreides guard*?" Paul had always assumed Caladan would remain a bastion of stability, one of many coins in his pocket. He had so many other problems, in particular the increasingly violent gadfly Memnon Thorvald. He looked at Gurney. "How could this happen?"

"They remember Duke Leto, my Lord. They expected you to be exactly like him."

Muad'Dib had to deal with practical matters first. "Has the disturbance been quelled?"

"Quelled but not resolved," Jessica said. "They are upset with you, Paul. You may have expected loyalty, but you've done nothing to earn it. I have been there to speak on your behalf for years, but they feel you have snubbed and abandoned them. Caladan is the Atreides homeworld, but you have made no visit of state since early in the Jihad."

Paul drew a deep breath, tried to suppress his anger. "During that visit my armies conquered Kaitain. *Kaitain,* Mother! I have a war to conduct. Do the people expect me to return to Caladan for dancing and parades?" He paused, then looked more intently at her. "I left you to carry on in my place."

"True, but I am no Duke Leto—and neither are you."

"I see." Paul tried not to sound stung. The radical Priests of Dur had attempted to desecrate the shrine of his father's skull, but now he wondered if he, as Muad'Dib, might also be desecrating the memory of Leto Atreides.

"I should return there as soon as possible to insure the peace," Jessica said, "and I would like to take Gurney with me. The people know him. Gurney the Valorous."

"Gurney has important work to do on Giedi Prime."

Jessica's eyes flashed, and her words cut like razors. "How could you think Gurney *wanted* Giedi Prime? Do you understand so little about human nature? Every day there is a torment for him."

Paul opened his eyes in surprise. "Is that true, Gurney?"

The other man seemed embarrassed. "You ordered me to do a job, my Lord, so I have done my best. But in truth, there is no planet in all the Imperium that I hate more. It will always be the Harkonnen world to me."

Paul felt deeply moved. "I am sorry, old friend. I did

not mean to increase your pain. You will retain your title to Giedi Prime, and I hope that your name alone will insure that some of the reforms continue. I will give you personnel and financial resources to continue the work there, but in the meantime I grant you leave to return to Caladan, to watch out for my mother's safety."

Gurney bowed formally. "My heart is on Caladan, where I served noble House Atreides."

"Very well, my friend. You have helped my family and me in more ways than I can ever hope to repay," Paul said. "To Caladan it is. Heal the damage I have inadvertently caused by my neglect."

Later, after the meeting was concluded, Paul remained by himself in the small chamber. It was quiet in there now, so infinitely quiet. . . .

In a shadowed corner of his mind, he worried that he had not correctly interpreted the hints of long-term prescience, that his own warriors might be precipitating a new Dark Age more grim than humanity had experienced in the frightened times after the end of the Butlerian Jihad. Beyond these walls, his holy war swept over planet after planet. His legions left broken populations and devastation in their wake, decapitated governments, and provided nothing to fill the vacuum. Somehow, he had to put the pieces back together.

A problem Alexander the Great never had to face.

Surprises are too often unpleasant ones.

—KORBA THE PANEGYRIST, to a delegation of
Qizarate missionaries

Alert for treachery, Hasimir and Margot Fenring followed the albino Tleilaxu doctor through narrow, metal-sheathed tunnels beneath the city of Thalidei. Black streaks and patches mottled the gray plates where water had trickled down and mold had formed. As Dr. Ereboam scurried through the intricate passageways, Count Fenring thought of a white lab rat moving through a complex maze.

Fenring's persistent "persuasion" techniques had convinced Ereboam to show him what he needed to see, but the Count remained wary. He did not trust this man— not at all. At least little Marie was as safe as possible, left under the protection of Tonia Obregah-Xo, sealed in their quarters and away from any interference or counter-blackmail; the Bene Gesserit nanny would kill anyone who attempted to intrude. After years of uneasy tolerance, Fenring doubted any of the Tleilaxu would try something so bold, especially now that they had so much to gain. Marie and their would-be Kwisatz Haderach offered interesting possibilities for cooperation and synergy.

No, the danger might be directed toward *him* instead,

or Lady Margot. Count Fenring's instincts kept him alert for a trap or ambush, but he sensed both resignation and eagerness from Ereboam. They were going to see the supposedly successful Kwisatz Haderach candidate.

Although they had entered the labyrinth through a long, security-guarded stairway near Thalidei's outer walls, which fronted the deep and stinking lake, they had made so many turns that Fenring no longer had his bearings. "Are we still beneath the city, or have we gone under the lake bed?" He wiped a drip of water from his face.

Ereboam clucked. "We are in the atmosphere distribution tunnels and ventilation systems of Thalidei. Please follow. Not much farther."

A clearplaz lift in a tube carried them up into a multistory building, ascending past floor after floor where Tleilaxu researchers bustled about, preoccupied with experimental work. When the unusual lift came to a smooth stop, its doors irised open, and Ereboam hurried them along a white-walled corridor. A pink flush of excitement enlivened his narrow white face. "This way, please. Hurry, hurry. You're going to be very impressed."

At the end of a corridor that was bathed in lemon-yellow illumination, Ereboam adjusted a security scanner, and the door slid open to reveal a gray mistiness beyond. They entered.

As his eyes adjusted, Fenring noticed that the walls were heavily padded, showing numerous rips and scrape marks. Squeezing Margot's hand, he sent an urgent finger signal to be alert. She positioned herself carefully close to him, coiled to strike if necessary. He detected a chemical odor in the room, a tinge of medicinals . . . and something rank that he could not quite identify. He felt Margot's back tense against his. She had noticed, too. An *animal* smell.

Ereboam disappeared into the fog, though Fenring

could hear him murmuring something reverential in a low tone. Prayers? "No need to worry," the doctor said. "This fog is specially tuned to the subject's metabolism, and has made him sleepy."

When the mist thinned, Fenring saw the albino researcher standing next to what at first appeared to be an amorphous shape on the floor. Then he realized it was a classically proportioned human crouched over, head down, wearing a beige filmsuit that clung to his body and showed his muscles as if they had been carved by a master sculptor. One of the Twisting subjects they had seen in the laboratories? Fenring didn't think so.

The crouched figure straightened, as if unfolding his body from a chrysalis. The filmsuit hid most of his skin except for his bare hands, feet, and head. The Count noticed his wife's gaze move over the muscular form up to the strikingly handsome face, aquiline nose, and somewhat haughty pout. But Fenring could see past the physical perfection, and he was certain that Margot did as well. The mysterious man's acorn brown eyes revealed a strange inner torment.

"Meet Thallo." Ereboam's voice was filled with pride. "Our Kwisatz Haderach."

Lady Margot's green-gray eyes took on a sudden, intense interest. "From your own genetic map?"

When speaking to a female, the researcher's tone automatically became condescending. "Using sophisticated laboratory techniques instead of the unpleasant vagaries of natural human reproduction, we have achieved in only a few accelerated generations something that you Bene Gesserits could not accomplish in thousands of years."

"Hmm, that remains to be seen." Fenring walked slowly around Thallo, looking for flaws. "He looks, ahh, younger than Paul Atreides. He is what, seventeen or eighteen years old?"

Ereboam smiled. "Chronologically, Thallo is only *nine,*

but we accelerated his physical growth. He has made a great deal of progress. In some respects he is quite polished, but in others he is somewhat raw and unrefined."

Reaching up, Ereboam smoothed the dark, wavy hair on the back of Thallo's head, a gentle, caring motion. The eyes of the strange creation grew more calm as the doctor spoke. "He is the pinnacle of Tleilaxu genetic accomplishment. Our Kwisatz Haderach possesses untapped mental and even prescient abilities that we can hardly begin to fathom."

"Can it speak?" Fenring asked.

"I can speak better than the greatest orators in history," Thallo said, in an erudite tone, with perfect diction. "I know all of the facts in every encyclopedic work in the Imperium. I am a Mentat with enhanced computational abilities. I could debate with all of you simultaneously, and defeat every argument."

Ereboam brought a rectangular biscuit out of a pocket of his smock and handed the treat to Thallo, as if he were a pet. The creature chewed, fixing a hard gaze on Count Fenring. Between bites, Thallo said, "And I wish to inform these guests that I am not an *it*. I am a human being."

"Much more than a human being," Ereboam asserted. "What better way to take down Emperor Paul-Muad'Dib than with our own superman?"

"Um-m-m-m-ah," Fenring said. "Your champion would charge into the throne room and throw cookies at him?"

Thallo smiled as he chewed.

Making a true decision requires more than cursory data. The correct choice must trigger feelings and sensations. The process is instinctive.

—the PRINCESS IRULAN, unpublished notes

In the evenings, away from public appearances and closed-door meetings, Irulan relished her quiet time—but did not relax. She sat upon the billowing softness of her immense four-post bed, surrounded by the comforts that supposedly befitted her royal station. She heard only a few voices in the corridor outside, the ever-present female guards Paul had set at her door, not the normal beehive of activity that surrounded her husband.

This was her most productive time for writing.

According to Bludd's master plan, her private apartments had been decorated with trappings stripped out of her cabin in Shaddam's captured ship from the plains of Arrakeen. The Emperor's ship and the now-defeated Sardaukar had all belonged to House Corrino—a legacy that had been mismanaged for years by her father, as she'd come to realize with great sadness. Her own lot in life, as a figurehead princess and the symbolic wife of a usurper, was a constant reminder of Shaddam's failures. However, Irulan now held a role of greater potential significance than any position her Corrino destiny had offered.

A year earlier, Paul had allowed her to reestablish

contact with the exiled Imperial family on Salusa Secundus, though Irulan did not doubt that he scanned every communiqué for evidence of conspiracies. That was to be expected. With his innate truthsense, he should realize that she had no intention of overthrowing or assassinating Emperor Muad'Dib in order to bring her father back into power. But she could not blame him for being cautious.

Even from isolated Salusa, the disgraced remnants of House Corrino controlled a network of spies, smugglers, and black-market traders who could tap into the hidden wealth that the Padishah Emperor had buried in the long years of his reign. Nevertheless, her father probably had only limited and inaccurate information about what was really happening in the rest of the ravaged Imperium. Shaddam could never comprehend the scope of the Jihad, as Irulan did.

She was sure that Earl Memnon Thorvald had been in contact with her father, but Irulan knew the rebellious lord had no great love for Shaddam either. After all, Thorvald's sister Firenza had not survived long after marrying the Emperor, so many years ago. . . .

Meanwhile, she concentrated on news from her family. Supposedly meaningless things. Wensicia had given birth to a healthy son, Shaddam's first grandchild and only male heir. This event seemed to have brought her father little joy, however, since it could not restore the Corrino bloodline to the throne, as a son from Irulan and Paul would have done.

In her role here at Arrakeen, Irulan had sent formal, though heartfelt, congratulations and gifts for baby Farad'n, but her sister's reply had been surprisingly cruel and accusatory. Wensicia insisted that the entire family considered her a traitor for staying with the usurper and writing his propaganda. "Sleeping with the enemy," she called it.

Irulan could only smile bitterly at that. *If only they knew . . .*

Even sweet and innocent Rugi felt that way. Her youngest sister had scribbled a horrid little note as a postscript: "We all hate you for doing this to us! You don't know what it's like here." That part had stung the most. Rugi had always been affectionate toward her.

Dismayed, Irulan looked past the billowing Nonian lace of her bed canopy to the handmade furnishings, the antique Balut lamps, and the priceless paintings. On the surface, Paul denied her no luxuries, no trappings of wealth or noble station. The wife of an Emperor was expected to have such things.

Despite the finery around her, Irulan felt an emptiness in her soul. She tried to imagine she was a girl again, bright-eyed and full of hope for the future, instead of a lonely, childless woman in her mid-thirties. The Sisterhood still demanded that she preserve his bloodline by conceiving a child, and she wanted the same thing for herself, as much as the Imperium needed an heir.

But Paul had sworn in public that he would never share Irulan's bed, further shaming her while demonstrating devotion to his desert concubine, though even Chani had not given him a second son.

Regardless, through the writing process Irulan had come to understand and even respect Paul's relationship with Chani. The depth of the feelings those two shared went as deep as the sands of Arrakis, beyond the reach of politics or other outside influence. Irulan noticed how they gazed into one another's eyes and exchanged wordless thoughts. They had their own communication system, a private language that genuine lovers shared. The relationship seemed to be the only mark of normalcy that Paul allowed himself to show.

Under other circumstances, Irulan and Paul might have become friends, even lovers. Theoretically, they were well matched for each other. In the beginning, when she had suggested the marriage alliance as a path to peace, she had assumed she could seduce him with her Bene Gesserit skills, if given half a chance. But he was not a normal man, and he resisted her every move to get close to him. He offered his deep love for Chani as the excuse for his fidelity, but what did love have to do with dynastic concerns?

And why had Chani not yet become pregnant? Yes, their first son, Leto II, had been slain in a Sardaukar raid. Was she afraid to try again? Had the birth caused physical damage that prevented her from conceiving? Irulan thought not, though the subject was never discussed.

The Imperium needed an heir!

On the oversized bed she had arranged documents and notes in neat piles, including shigawire spools containing interviews and heavily censored battlefield reports that Korba had permitted her to have. A stark reality hit her: Her bed had become an office instead of a place where she might conceive a child. In a sudden, angry gesture, she cast aside the journal and hurled it to the floor. It landed on the plush carpeting with a soft thud.

Using a Bene Gesserit calming exercise, Irulan forced the tears not to come. Such an emotional release would make nothing better. Ironically, though, the writing helped.

The winds of the Imperium had buffeted the tiny boat of her life, driving her onto a small island where her movements were restricted and her emotions were supposed to be confined. Paul showed little outward dislike toward her; in fact, he usually ignored Irulan, keeping the daughter of Shaddam out of any direct role in his government. Her position had improved somewhat after she'd published her first book about Muad'Dib, but she still didn't know if he would let her publish her own version of the truth in subsequent books. So far he had only read snippets of her new drafts, and had made no comment on them, despite the fact that the material did not show him in an entirely positive light.

Interesting.

Her multi-volume biographical project had become much more than she had originally imagined it to be. With every bit of information she accumulated, the more she learned, the greater the potential legend became. And what to do about that? Her writings could provide important insights into the life of Paul-Muad'Dib, or they might serve another purpose entirely.

The more she learned about his younger years and his father Duke Leto, the more she thought that Paul might have spent a fine and happy life on Caladan, if not for the same cosmic choreographer that had intervened in Irulan's life. She saw clearly that her father was not blameless in this epic. Shaddam had allowed numerous improprieties during the War of Assassins, which had caused so much pain and harm to the Atreides and the Ecazis. Later, he had played political games with House Harkonnen, setting the trap on Arrakis, turning a blind eye toward the Baron's schemes in exchange for the promise of increased spice revenues. Shaddam IV had brought much of this disaster on himself.

So, her sisters considered her a traitor to the family, and her father found her beneath contempt? *I am not the traitor,* she thought. Because of the Padishah Emperor's numerous betrayals of House Atreides, Paul had more than enough reason to loathe House Corrino—and her.

Her private journal had become a bosom companion with whom she spent uncounted solitary nights, sharing her innermost thoughts with the fine spice paper pages. And, like a good friend, the journal revealed truths to her when she reread her own words and saw them in a more reflective light. On these pages, she was coming to recognize her own frailties.

She rearranged the pillows behind her and retrieved

the journal from the floor. She stared at the words she had written today. Her heart ached to think of the sorrow and shock young Paul had endured after witnessing the wedding-day massacre in Castle Caladan and escaping the subsequent attempts on his life. He had been a pawn from such a young age. And now he was the Emperor of the Known Universe.

With a resigned sigh, the Princess began to write in her journal again. It was speaking to her, urging her to continue the story. . . .

PART IV

Young Paul Atreides

10,187 AG

Those who have seen the wrath of Muad'Dib in the fighters of his Jihad say that he became bloodthirsty because of his time among the Fremen. But the Lisan-al-gaib was set on his life's course long before that.

One cannot look at Muad'Dib the man and fail to see Paul Atreides the boy, and the events and experiences that created him. He was a human being sculpted by treachery and tragedy. As a young man of twelve, he was flung into a War of Assassins that encompassed more than three noble Houses and threatened to decapitate the Imperium itself. Although Paul had been trained for years to face the dangers that were part of the upbringing of any duke's son, when Viscount Moritani from Grumman made his initial attack, those lessons suddenly became real. *Paul found himself a target, hunted by assassins, caught in the center of a whirlpool of blood.*

These experiences, though, had an even greater effect on his father, Duke Leto Atreides, who became not broken but hardened . . . tempered rather than destroyed. Duke Leto—the Red Duke, Leto the Just—had to fight repeatedly against treachery and betrayal, in matters where my father, the Padishah Emperor Shaddam IV, was not innocent.

Through those pivotal events, Young Paul watched his father prepare and respond with an extremism that some might have called ruthlessness. The ultimate lesson he learned from this, though, was that despite all of his father's retaliations, Duke Leto Atreides ultimately failed because he did not learn to be ruthless enough.

—*Muad'Dib the Man* by the PRINCESS IRULAN

Viscount, O Viscount, what have you unleashed?
What have you done?

—GURNEY HALLECK, *The Tragedy of House Ecaz*

I n the midst of the chaos and gore, Duke Leto rushed
many of the wedding attendees from the grand hall
and had soldiers escort them back to safety inside their
waiting frigates at the spaceport, though the ships were
forbidden to leave. Other guests barricaded themselves
inside interior rooms in Castle Caladan.

The horrendous slaughter, the flying executioner
discs, the failed defense by the Swordmasters and Leto's
security men—all had transpired in less than a minute.
Even as uniformed Atreides soldiers charged in through
the hall doors, the victims already lay slashed and bleeding, some chopped to pieces, others sobbing in shock
and disbelief. Prince Rhombur looked down at himself
and saw that his formal wedding suit had been cut to ribbons, though otherwise he seemed undamaged.

Dr. Yueh moved swiftly and professionally among the
injured, using an eye for triage to sort those who could
not be helped from those who could. He worked first on
Archduke Ecaz, applying a self-constricting tourniquet
to the stump of his arm.

The severed limb on the floor had been mangled and
broken in the melee. After regarding it for a moment,

Yueh spoke quietly to Leto, "It is too damaged to reattach. The Tleilaxu may have a way to regrow this flesh, but I do not know how." He gestured to where Rhombur stood, battered and scuffed. "As I did with the Prince of House Vernius, I may be able to develop a prosthetic arm for the Archduke. I possess that sort of skill."

"We can discuss it later," Leto said, wiping blood from his forehead.

Potent painkillers made Archduke Armand groggy and distant, but anger penetrated his fog. He looked at his daughter's blood-soaked body, fixated on her chalky, pale skin. As though his head moved on poorly oiled hinges, he glared at Whitmore Bludd, who was ashen and shaking. "You were supposed to protect her." His words cut the elegant Swordmaster more deeply than any disk.

Bludd's lips drew together. "I failed," he spoke in hollow disbelief. "I am a Swordmaster . . . and I failed. I would have sacrificed myself for Ilesa. Rivvy knew his duty."

Duncan stumbled over to the sprawled corpse of Rivvy Dinari, who lay on the floor like a butchered whale. The cutter discs remained embedded deeply in his wide chest. "He died a proud death, the heroic end of a true Swordmaster."

Bludd simply stared in disbelief at his thin rapier, then cast it aside in disgust, with a clatter. "Help me carry his body away, Duncan. It seems to be all I am good for."

❧

COLD AND EFFICIENT, refusing to be paralyzed by grief, Duke Leto ordered a total lockdown of the Cala City Spaceport. He offered curt apologies as he announced that no ships would be allowed to depart until a full investigation had been completed. Thufir Hawat, with the deep gash in his back sutured and bandaged, paid special attention to anyone who seemed overly upset and angered by the delay, as well as those who showed too much maudlin sympathy. These were all subjected to additional questioning.

As a small glint of good news, all of the fourteen killed had belonged to either House Atreides or House Ecaz, servants, retainers, guests. After the first wash of fear had subsided, many of the noble wedding guests had expressed their outrage, either directed at House Moritani for involving them in a blood feud or at House Atreides for inviting them into a dangerous situation. Since the ruffled noblemen had suffered only minimal damages compared to Atreides and Ecaz, however, their bluster would fade and no further interfamily quarrels would erupt because of it.

Duke Leto, however, would not forget so quickly.

Gurney Halleck and Thufir Hawat scoured every brick of Castle Caladan, searching for secondary assassination devices. Even in such an elaborate plot, the murderous Viscount might not have put all his eggs in one basket. Such a plan, layer upon layer upon layer, could have been in the works for months.

Prince Rhombur vowed to help. He was like a juggernaut, never leaving Leto's side, though his Ixian bureaucratic advisers insisted that he, Tessia, and the boy Bronso withdraw to the safety of their private frigate and remain there behind blast shields. Much to his annoyance, the technocrats pointed out that twice now Rhombur had nearly been killed in an assassination attempt against Duke Leto Atreides. This time, his cyborg body had only been scratched and slightly damaged— but if he had been mere flesh and blood, Rhombur might not have survived.

When the Ixian advisers continued to nag him, actually threatening to disrupt his rule once they returned home, Rhombur finally whirled and, without controlling his strength, struck out at one of the yammering men, Bolig Avati, knocking him across the room. Indignant, the cyborg Prince announced in a booming voice, "Tessia, Bronso, and I will remain here in Castle Caladan, beside my friend Leto Atreides."

His fellow technocrats helped Avati up, looking at Rhombur in astonishment and fear. In a group, they scuttled back to the Vernius frigate and did not bother him further.

~

DURING THE MEMORIAL service for his daughter Ilesa, the Archduke could only stand there one-armed, his mind muddied with painkillers, tears streaming down his face. He seemed to need the release of grieving, but his fuzzy state denied him the full catharsis. Nevertheless, Armand Ecaz did understand the tragedy that had befallen him, and that was enough.

Leto stood by the other man's side out on the high cliffs, where the local priest—his hand bandaged from a slight injury in the massacre—delivered a eulogy, in sharp contrast to the more joyous sermon he had been meant to give. Ilesa's preserved body would be taken back to Ecaz, where she would lie in state for a suitable mourning period before interment in a mausoleum beside her sister Sanyá and uncle Theo.

"Moritani has done this to me too many times," Armand said to Leto, his voice cold and hollow. "I survived my grief before, but this time I do not know if I can."

Duncan and Bludd arranged a private Swordmaster's pyre for Dinari. He would not be going back to Ecaz. By tradition, a Swordmaster found his final resting place wherever he fell. Though this gathering was meant to be a private matter, Duncan did allow Paul to stand at his side; Gurney Halleck and Thufir Hawat were also there. Gurney promised to compose a sonnet to commemorate the heroic last deeds of the "fattest, nimblest man" he had ever known.

Whitmore Bludd seemed broken by his failure, ashamed (and offended) by the fact that he had walked away without a scratch.

~

FOR DAYS, THE entire planet of Caladan remained off-limits to visitors, even to locals who had been offworld at the time of the tragic affair. Leto brusquely turned away two arriving Heighliners and sent messages to CHOAM representatives, refusing to let them offload the ships in their holds or take aboard any cargo or passengers. Caladan was locked down until further notice; no travel in or out. The Duke gave no explanation, despite the persistent inquiries and demands of the Guild.

Soon, the wedding guests began to show signs of unrest. Several lords sent petitions to Castle Caladan, but Leto turned them all away, claiming that he could not be disturbed during his time of grieving.

For the first day, Jessica allowed him to wrestle with his own sorrow, anger, and dismay. He had become hardened but not heartless, and it was his way to insist on covering his hurt. Finally, though, the ache in her chest drove her to him. She could not bear to leave her beloved alone.

Jessica met him in their shared bedchamber. Before the wedding, she had moved her possessions out in preparation for Ilesa's residence. As the Duke's concubine, she would customarily keep her own private rooms in a separate section of the castle, though still a place of honor befitting her position.

Now, Jessica sat beside Leto, without words. Even

though her clothes, private keepsakes, and furniture had been moved out to make way for the new bride, she felt at home just to be near Leto. She watched him wrestle with his grief, then compose himself, trying to hide it behind a stony mask.

She finally said, "Leto, at first I was angry with you for asking me to spend so much time with Ilesa, but now I'm glad I got to know her. We developed a mutual respect, and I'm certain she would have been a worthy Lady for House Atreides."

Leto walled himself off from Jessica and pretended to be indifferent. "I barely knew her myself. Yes, she would have been my wife, but it was only a political arrangement." His coldness did not convince her. "I am angrier for my friend Armand. The loss of his arm is of little consequence compared to the loss of his daughter, and his Swordmaster."

Jessica rose to go, seeing that he still wanted to be left alone. "No matter what else happens, Leto, I will stand by you."

He finally looked at her with his gray eyes. "I know, Jessica. I've always known that."

❧

FINALLY, AFTER FOUR stark and uncomfortable days, Leto met with Duncan, Thufir, and Gurney in the Atreides war room. The atmosphere in the chamber roiled with murderous anger, with Duncan the most overtly incensed of all. "House Moritani has declared a War of Assassins before, but that form of conflict has specific rules, which the Viscount has broken—*again*. No innocents should have been killed."

Thufir replied, "Even Shaddam cannot ignore this."

"We have no connections with House Moritani," Leto argued. "How could they possibly have arranged and implemented such a plot here in our own home? Some-one must have planted spies among our household servants or down in the village."

"Prad Vidal supplied those flowerpots," Gurney said. "Archduke Armand left him in charge on Ecaz during his absence."

Duncan said, "If he is the traitor, my Lord, he could be entrenching himself well."

"Moritani is the force behind this attack," Leto said with a growl. "If Duke Vidal played a role, it's bound to be only a minor one."

"It is likely neither one of them expected the Archduke to survive," Thufir said. "By blocking all communication from Caladan, no one else knows what has really happened here."

Looking weak and tired, Armand Ecaz came to stand in the doorway with all the dignity he could manage. His stump was cleanly bandaged, and he wore a simple Ecazi robe. His face was drawn and his eyes were red, but his gaze seemed clear and angry. The medics said he'd been refusing further painkillers.

"It is time for me to go home, Leto. I must bury my daughter, strengthen my household—and make my war plans against Grumman. That Moritani animal wasn't targeting House Atreides. He saw this wedding as an easy way to get to me and my family. You were merely in the way." He stood straighter, as if a formidable de-meanor would push away the mental and physical pain. "I no longer have anything to lose, so I accept the Moritani challenge. The Viscount has opened the floodgates for a bloodbath the Imperium will never forget."

I prefer bad news to no information whatsoever. Silence is like starvation.

—BARON VLADIMIR HARKONNEN

Even though the grimy air of Harko City made the Baron cough, he still felt invigorated. For all its flaws and odors, he much preferred his own planet to hot and dusty Arrakis, gaudy Kaitain, or bleak Grumman. This was *home*.

He and Piter de Vries rode a slidewalk from the Keep, heading for a luncheon engagement with his nephews Rabban and Feyd. Both young men continued to vie for his attention, waiting for him to choose one or the other as his official successor. He was in no hurry to make his selection known. So far, neither one had proved himself to the Baron's satisfaction.

As the walkway crossed a park cluttered with imposing statues of Harkonnen leaders, de Vries pointed out, "The birds have been perching on your head again, my Lord."

The Baron noted a recently commissioned sculpture of himself as a lean and handsome young man, striking a heroic pose and holding a broadsword. He thought wistfully of the muscular body that had once been a source of so much pride for him, before that witch Mohiam inflicted him with a chronic malady. To his dismay, white streaks of bird excrement ran down the statue's forehead into the bronze eyes.

"Another park attendant shall die," the Baron said matter-of-factly.

As they approached, a worker ran desperately toward the statue with a ladder and cleaning materials, but it was too late. Seeing his vigorous attention to duty, the Baron mused, "On second thought, this maintenance problem must go higher up. Let us have the supervisor put to death as well. Arrange for a bird motif of some sort at the execution, gouge out his eyes with a beak-shaped tool or something, or use a talon device to rip his face to shreds. It's the sort of thing Rabban would enjoy. We shall mention it to him at lunch."

His oldest nephew was powerful and without a conscience, an excellent enforcer, and useful in his own way. Rabban's much younger brother Feyd, though only fourteen, showed a greater deviousness and wit. That made him a more worthy candidate to be the Baron's successor . . . and more dangerous.

"Maybe you should have your nephew kill the entire park staff and start over," de Vries suggested. "He's bound to do it anyway, unless you forbid him."

The Baron shook his head. "That would be wasteful. Better to strike fear into them, but leave enough of them alive so that the work gets done. I never want to see excrement on my statues again."

When the slidewalk reached the terrace level, the Baron and his Mentat disembarked. The pair made their way between tables of diners to a roped-off area that had been reserved for them, with a view of a smoky stone-oil refinery. Rabban and Feyd were already there.

Feyd, in fluid-fabric knickers with a tie and jacket, was feeding bits of bread to pigeons that hopped around on the pavement under the tables. Just as one bird got close to the young man, the stocky Rabban lunged off his chair, startling the bird into flight. Feyd looked at his older brother with poisonous annoyance.

The Baron adjusted his suspensor belt and eased into his seat after checking for bird droppings there, too. "It seems we have a pigeon problem that we must deal with."

After de Vries explained about the soiled statues, Rabban predictably suggested executing the entire maintenance staff. Feyd, though, offered another idea. "Perhaps, Uncle, we could eradicate the birds instead."

The Baron nodded thoughtfully. "Approaching the problem from a different perspective. Very good, Feyd. Yes, let us try that solution first."

As the meal was delivered on overladen platters, de Vries lowered his voice while grinning through sapho-stained lips. "We have received no word yet, but Duke Leto's wedding ceremony should have occurred yesterday. How lovely it must be on Caladan, with the flowers, the music and festivities . . . the blood of loved ones spilled at the altar."

"Delightful images. I await the news . . . and the confirmation." The Baron smiled as he visualized what had probably happened. "Poor Duke Leto and his bride lying dead amidst the flowers, while bumbling guards run around in circles, looking for culprits."

"They will blame House Moritani, and probably Prad Vidal, but not Harkonnen," the Mentat said. "Our second-wave operatives remain in place to clean up any mistakes there, but even they will be seen as Grumman assassins if they make a move. No Harkonnen fingerprints are on the scene. As far as anyone can see, Viscount Moritani charged in like a Salusan bull to avenge himself against Ecaz for the death of his son . . . and an Atreides Duke just happened to be in the line of fire. How sad! Such a tragic loss for the people of Caladan!"

"Nicely put." The Baron held up his thick hands,

showed the puffy palms. "We must always keep our hands clean."

"As spotless as your statue is going to be from now on."

The Baron scowled at the mocking reminder, causing de Vries to move himself out of reach.

"I can't wait to hear the news," Rabban said.

"We must not be overly anxious," the Baron cautioned. "Make no inquiries of any kind. Let the announcement arrive here through regular channels, as it spreads throughout the Imperium. There's bound to be quite an uproar."

I have studied the habits of creatures on many planets, and one constant is apparent on world after world: Predators usually come out at night.

—PLANETOLOGIST PARDOT KYNES,
Zoological Report #7649

Castle Caladan was asleep, seemingly holding its breath. Even in daytime, the people rarely spoke above whispers. Though all curtains were open and every skylight cleared, the castle was full of suspicious shadows. Security was tighter than at any other time in memory.

In happier times, Duke Leto kept a full staff of servants, cooks, cleaners, and maids; he welcomed aspiring artists to paint watercolors of the landscape as viewed from the high balconies. Not anymore. As Duncan Idaho stalked the halls carrying the Old Duke's sword, it felt to him as if the castle had been wounded. Every person, even old familiar faces, underwent a thorough security scan prior to entering the fortress. Imposing such measures made Leto extraordinarily uncomfortable, but Thufir Hawat insisted.

When Duncan was a boy, he had escaped the Harkonnens and gone to work for House Atreides as a mere stable hand. There, he had observed the fury of the caged Salusan bulls, which would attack anything that moved. Viscount Moritani reminded him of those maddened bulls. Once the vile man set his sights on a particular enemy, he would strike and strike again, trampling anyone who got in his way.

Duncan did not make the mistake of assuming that the danger was past. Now, on his security rounds, he paced the halls, sword in hand, eyes alert. He opened Paul's door to make sure that nothing threatened the Duke's son. The boy slept soundly in his room, though his bedsheets were a tangle—evidence that he had been tossing and turning, as he often did when he had one of his vivid nightmares. In an adjacent bed his guest, Bronso Vernius, snored softly. Prince Rhombur had insisted that the two boys room together and watch out for each other.

Duncan continued his rounds to the dimly lit kitchens. In a plaz case, large ambulatory crustaceans crawled over each other, their claws taped; they would be served for the following day's meal. The pantries were locked, the gate to the wine cellar shut, the ovens still warm. All the kitchen staff had been dismissed for the day, but they would be back shortly before dawn, when Gurney took his shift. The troubadour warrior liked to be there at breakfast.

From one of the high windows Duncan looked down at the surf crashing against the black rocks. The ocean was dark and restless, occasionally glowing with a wash of phosphorescent plankton. The rocks, slick with spray and algae, blended in with the stone walls of Castle Caladan.

He thought he saw shapes out there, oily moving shadows that slithered up the stone walls, but the night was moonless, the stars obscured by clouds, and he could discern little. Peering into the darkness through a diamond-shaped window pane, he caught a flicker of movement again.

The ocean side of the castle was impregnable. Still, that section of the structure contained the infirmary wing where Archduke Ecaz slept, monitored by medical instruments and regular visits by Dr. Yueh. If another group of stealthy assassins meant to kill him, this would be their last chance on Caladan. The Archduke was due to leave the following morning.

Duncan changed his rounds and headed toward the infirmary.

〜

AS SOON AS the footsteps had disappeared down the corridor, Paul opened his eyes and turned over to regard the son of Prince Rhombur Vernius. For years now, Paul had been able to feign sleep well enough to fool even his guards and closest friends.

He could see Bronso's bright eyes in the dimness as he lay on a cot beside the main sleeping pallet. Though the Ixian boy was generally quiet and reserved, Paul had quickly recognized how intelligent and adaptable Bronso was. "Now tell me more about Ix," he whispered.

Sounding homesick, Bronso described the underground caverns, where he said subterranean industries produced valuable technological items, while leaving the planet's surface a pristine, natural wilderness. Paul's father had also told him stories about staying on Ix with House Vernius. Leto and Rhombur had barely escaped with their lives during the unexpected Tleilaxu takeover of that planet—a reminder that being "home" was not the same as being safe.

Now, as Bronso continued to whisper, Paul's ears picked up a stealthy movement, so subtle it almost seemed to be a subset of the silence. The corridor should have been empty, but he heard the most delicate of whispery footsteps. He lowered his voice. "Someone's coming."

Despite years of training and preparation for the

countless threats he would face as the son of a duke, Paul had never truly felt unsafe. But since the wedding-day slaughter, wherever he walked, whomever he met, Paul was aware of his surroundings with a razor clarity, looking for the tiniest fleck of detail out of place.

Bronso immediately fell silent and strained to listen. "Duncan Idaho coming back?"

"No, it's not Duncan—I would know. Find a place to take shelter until we see what this is. We can't be too cautious."

"You want me to hide like a coward?"

"I want you to stay safe, like a guest of House Atreides."

Paul slipped from his own sleeping pallet, while Bronso plumped up his blankets and pillows in a very crude deception, then crawled under his loose cot. Paul had no time to strap on his personal shield, so he crept to the assortment of keepsakes he kept on a low shelf and selected a sharp-edged lump of coral rock that he and his father had found on the beach. It was heavy enough to be an effective weapon.

The chamber door remained slightly ajar after Duncan's cursory inspection. The hall outside, though dimly lit, was still much brighter than the bedchamber, and someone was out there. Paul would have to act swiftly. He remembered some tactical advice Thufir had given him: "Strike fast, and strike where they do not expect. If you are in a position of weakness, surprise your opponent with aggression. The entire scenario can change in a millisecond."

A millisecond . . . Paul might not have much more time than that.

He held the heavy coral and crouched at floor level, just to the side of the door where no one would expect him, since the two boys were supposed to be on their sleeping pallets. Paul tensed and waited, mentally reminding himself of the most vulnerable points in a human body.

The door swung open, and hall light flooded into the room. In a mental snapshot, Paul saw a muscular stranger who seemed to be covered in tar, a skintight oily suit. Spotting a curved scimitar-like dagger in the stranger's hand, he no longer had any doubts about what this man meant to do. The dark, slick-skinned man slipped into the room.

But Paul struck first.

⟨⟩

INSIDE THE INFIRMARY, Archduke Armand was sleeping. Yueh had suggested several effective drugs and supplements to increase the man's energy and improve his stamina, perhaps even a strong dose of melange, but Armand had refused it all. He seemed to prefer his restless sleep and nightmares. Duncan could imagine the ache and misery this nobleman endured, since he had lost his own family when he was just a boy on Giedi Prime, thanks to Rabban. But Duncan had recovered from those scars.

The room was illuminated by instrument panels and medical monitors, sensing that something wasn't right, he absorbed all the details and waited.

Duncan tightened his grip on the Old Duke's sword and, preparing for the glare, he slapped the wall controls to full illumination, firing up the room's clustered glowglobes. Ducking instinctively in the dazzle, he saw three black shapes lunging at him. Each infiltrator was covered in a skin made of black oil that rippled with rainbow iridescence. The figures carried curved daggers halfway between a knife and sickle, tipped with an extra razor-sharp barb. These assassins clearly wanted to hack and slash. They meant to leave Archduke Armand not just dead, but *in pieces*—obviously, to send a message from House Moritani.

Facing the silhouetted infiltrators, Duncan brandished the sword. The assassins threw themselves toward him, moving in almost complete silence but with speed and coordination. He noted scars on their throats and wondered if they had been rendered speechless so that they might never cry out, never reveal information. The attackers' eyes bulged, and the tendons on their necks were taut, as if they were pumped up on some type of drug.

They set upon him like a wolf pack, but Duncan was able to spin away and use his sword and shield defensively. He slammed the long blade hard against one of the curved daggers, a blow that should have been enough to snap the wrist and knock the dagger free, but the assassin retained his oily black grip. The other two men moved with a manic flurry of jittery gestures.

Duncan stabbed one man through the chest, and barely withdrew the Old Duke's sword in time to knock aside another assassin's sickle-dagger as it slid through the shield. With his free hand, Duncan grasped the wrist of its wielder, pushed it back, and then thrust his sword into the second assassin. The tip sank deep into the silent man's abdomen.

Though both assassins were mortally wounded, they continued to fight him, heedless of their own injuries. The third was still uninjured. Duncan needed to end this quickly.

∽

FROM HIS LOW position, Paul smashed with the heavy coral rock, shattering the intruder's right kneecap. He heard the crunch of the patella, the snap of cartilage, and the man's eerily quiet *whuff* of pain.

Although the oily-suited man could barely stand upright, he seemed to shrug off the injury. No words came from his throat, only a raspy sound like rustling paper. When the man swung the sickle-dagger, Paul ducked, still brandishing the sharp-edged coral rock, but it was a clumsy weapon for a nimble person. The assassin's mangled knee made him walk with a dying insect's gait, yet he lurched farther into the room, slashing with the knife again.

Seeing the cot where Bronso supposedly slept, the intruder turned back to Paul, thrusting the dagger toward him as Paul attacked again with the heavy rock. Suddenly Bronso's cot burst upward, and the Ixian boy used it as a battering ram, yelling at the top of his lungs. The unexpected appearance of the lightweight rectangular bed startled the crippled assassin. The curved dagger slammed through the bedding, through the pillow, and into the thin mattress pad, but Bronso twisted the cot, snagging the blade.

Paul smashed the man's shoulder with his coral rock, then shouted, "Guards! Duncan! We're being attacked!"

With a great burst of strength the oil-skinned killer tore his knife free from the pallet. Paul and Bronso backed together into a defensive position.

Outside the door, Paul heard a sound like a stampeding bull—footfalls crashing down the corridor. Prince Rhombur Vernius smashed into the room in a fury of prosthetics, knocking the door off its hinges. The silent assassin whirled at the new arrival, and Rhombur grabbed him by the throat.

Refusing to surrender, the intruder drove the curved dagger down, slicing into Rhombur's reinforced chest, chopping repeatedly into his shoulder, trying to stab the cyborg's spine. Rhombur's synthetic grip tightened. With a final clench of his hand, he crushed the man's throat and cast him like a limp doll to the floor.

The dead assassin's arms and legs twitched and jittered, as from a heavy pulse of electricity, and the black, oily suit burst into flame, incinerating his entire body in an astonishing self-destruct process.

"Bronso, are you all right?" Rhombur demanded. "Paul, what happened here?"

"We are safe," Paul said.

Bronso added, "Neither of us is as defenseless as that man believed."

⇔

THE COMMOTION AND lights in the infirmary had awakened Armand Ecaz, who was still in a weakened state. The Archduke saw Duncan fighting the assassins and, knowing he could not fight alongside Duncan, he did his best to help nonetheless. He yanked the medical monitors from his body, cutting off his vital signs.

Instantly, shrill medical alarms echoed from the monitors.

The sound startled the third assassin for just a moment, and with a broad sweep of the sword Duncan decapitated him, cutting through the oily black hood that extended over the man's hair. The other two men, though dying from their sword wounds, still struggled to come at him.

Duncan stood back, wondering how much information could be gleaned from them before they perished. He had no doubt that they were a second wave of Moritani killers sent to murder Archduke Ecaz. But what if a third wave of assassins was hidden on Caladan . . . or a fourth?

As the three attackers died, their black suits activated a final fail-safe measure. The headless man burst into flames first. His incendiary suit created a pyre that filled the ward with a thick greasy smoke and the stench of roasting flesh. The white-hot flames grew brighter, cremating the remains to the bone—eliminating any evidence. The mortally wounded pair fell next and were also immolated as soon as they died.

The Archduke lay back in his bed coughing, fighting for words. "Too weak to fight . . . it was the only way I could summon help."

"It made all the difference." Fuming with anger at the invasion, Duncan heard shouts from down the hall. "At least you are safe, Archduke."

"I am not safe," the one-armed man replied hoarsely. "And neither are you—nor any member of House Atreides."

Even if you lose all your riches, your home, and your family . . . so long as you retain your honor, you are still a wealthy man.

—DUKE PAULUS ATREIDES

In the War Council chamber, Leto could barely find words to express his outrage. "One massacre wasn't enough for the Viscount? Not only has he violated my home, crippled my friend, cut down a great warrior, and murdered my bride-to-be—now he has tried to kill my son!"

Archduke Armand sat wearily at the table, his arm stump still wrapped in bandages, a few scabbed cuts showing on his face and hands, like badges of honor. "You are not the reason for this, Leto. The Viscount meant to attack me. Those boys were just convenient additional targets."

"No, Armand, it was no accident. That assassin purposely sought out Paul's chamber. Now that Moritani has set his sights on killing my son, he will not stop. None of us are safe." Leto's expression remained dark. "If I ever was a mere bystander, I am not anymore. I am as involved as you."

He turned to his own Swordmaster. "Duncan, I charge you with a task more important than any other service you have performed for House Atreides. I think it likely the Grummans have other assassins in hiding. Take Paul away from Castle Caladan and keep him safe—go someplace where he will never be found."

Duncan frowned. "Does such a place exist, my Lord?"

"The Eastern Continent, the Sisters in Isolation. Their abbey is a veritable fortress. Have him stay there with his grandmother."

"My son was also a target last night," Rhombur rumbled like a steam engine about to explode. "You are not in this alone, Leto. If you join this War of Assassins, I will fight at your side—even though the technocrats would prefer that I go back and watch over the assembly lines."

"No, that is exactly what you should do, my friend," Leto said. "Thanks to House Moritani, this firestorm has already spread beyond the Ginaz School and Ecaz to involve Caladan. If you bring Ix into this as well, Emperor Shaddam will punish all of us rather than let this explode into a conflict that spreads through the whole Landsraad."

"But you can't just let him get away with this!" Rhombur exclaimed.

"No indeed—we must take the offensive." Leto looked at Archduke Ecaz. "My marriage to your daughter was not completed, but I am still bound by my word of honor. House Atreides and House Ecaz are allies—not just for politics and commerce, but in all things. I pledge the forces of House Atreides to your military. My military will accompany you to Ecaz to gather your forces, and together we will bring the bloodshed to the Viscount's doorstep. Perhaps God Himself can forgive Hundro Moritani for what he has done, but I shall not."

❧

WHEN LETO FINALLY lifted the travel embargo to and from Caladan, the wedding guests and noble visitors clamored for positions on the waiting Heighliner above, bidding for berths to hold their family frigates. But the Duke commandeered every available spot in order to carry an entire Atreides military fleet to Ecaz. He told the other travelers they would have to wait for the next Guildship.

The Spacing Guild representatives were at first offended that a nobleman from a minor planet would give them such instructions, but Leto displayed images of the massacre caused by Viscount Moritani. Slamming his palm on the hard tabletop, Leto said, "These matters extend outside the scope of normal commerce. I invoke the Rules of the Great Convention."

Thufir Hawat had offered specific legal arguments for Leto to cite, but the Guildsmen knew their own rules. When the representative from the orbiting ship saw the uncompromising expressions on the faces of Leto and the one-armed Archduke, he conceded. "So long as you pay for the passage of all your ships, we will take you where you need to go."

Gurney Halleck came with them, bringing his baliset, although Leto doubted there would be much opportunity for singing. In the meantime, Thufir was dispatched directly to Kaitain to present the horrific evidence of Viscount Moritani's crime and demand Imperial justice or, if possible, Sardaukar intervention.

For as long as Leto was gone, Jessica would remain on Caladan to act in the Duke's stead. She was torn between wanting to accompany him and remaining behind to shield their son—although Duncan had already taken the twelve-year-old and vanished before dawn. Without trying to sway the Duke, Jessica said goodbye to him at the Cala City spaceport, giving him an embrace that expressed her depths of emotion.

Leto froze for a moment, thinking of how lovely Ilesa had looked on their wedding day. But Jessica was here, and real, and warm against him. His expression nearly broke, his resolve wavered. But he could not allow that, neither in his mind nor in his heart. He was going to fight beside Armand Ecaz because of the attack on his House, the death of Ilesa, and the threat against Paul's life.

Leto hardened himself, just as he had done after Victor's death and the suicide of Kailea. He had no time for the weakness or hesitation of love. Wasn't that what the Bene Gesserits always taught? Leto finally pushed Jessica away, gave her one more kiss, and then marched into the frigate beside his waiting companions. Right now he had only one focus, as sharp and as all-consuming as a singularity.

A promised marriage was different from any other trade agreement or business arrangement. His father's mistake with Helena had been that he had viewed their marriage as nothing more than a strategic move in a large Imperial game. Paulus had never invested himself personally in it. He may have been a beloved Duke and a good father, but he'd never been much of a husband.

Leto felt a sense of relief when his ships rose from Caladan to be engulfed in the cavernous hold of the Heighliner. The giant doors closed them in, and it was done. He did not want, or need, a chance to change his mind.

He rode with the Archduke in the lead frigate of the Ecazi delegation. The man was damaged and deeply hurt, and Leto would remain at his side as friend and staunch ally against the evil they now faced.

Pale and agitated, Whitmore Bludd rode next to Gurney. The Swordmaster's fine clothes were rumpled now, with no indication of the peacock finery he usually wore. He carried the rapier at his side, though he seemed loathe to use it.

A small amount of the ashes from Rivvy Dinari's funeral pyre had been mixed into a polished plaz cube to be the keystone of a new monument. Archduke Ecaz had already promised to build a towering memorial to the beefy Swordmaster for his selfless bravery.

Bludd flinched as he looked at the transparent cube, in which the ashes were suspended like dark stars floating in a bright nebula. The Archduke spoke very little to him, pointedly ignoring his remaining Swordmaster. Whitmore Bludd's name would barely be mentioned in any historical recounting of this event.

Now that Leto had time to consider the scope of the military operation under way, as well as the Guild's transport fees, the realization of how much this full-scale war was going to cost finally began to sink in. If the mad Grumman leader had followed the rules set down for a War of Assassins, there would have been precise targets, specific victims, and no need for a gigantic armed fleet with all of its attendant support costs. "This could bankrupt me, Armand."

The Archduke turned a gaunt face toward him. "House Ecaz will pay half of your expenses." He blinked, and his eyelids seemed heavy. "What is the price of honor?"

Though there was nothing to see within the Heighliner's hold, the Archduke stared out the small porthole, looking at all of the Atreides military ships there, which would soon be joined with his own warships.

❦

WHEN THE HEIGHLINER reached Ecaz and the hold opened for the Atreides vessels to drop down as a magnificent escort for the Archduke's frigate, a great deal of confusion tangled the communication lines from the palace below.

With a dismissive gesture toward his surviving Swordmaster, Armand said, "Bludd, inform them who we are!

Tell them there is no threat." His face looked dead, rather than gloating, as he added, "I want to look Duke Vidal in the eye and watch him squirm. He will be most surprised to see me still alive. How will he make excuses, I wonder?"

"He will claim that the evidence we bring of his treachery was falsified," Leto said.

"He can claim whatever he likes . . . but I will believe only the truth."

But Duke Vidal did not give them the chance. On the main continent, a swarm of ships scrambled from the Ecazi Palace at the appearance of the overwhelming force coming down from orbit. Hundreds of vessels flew swiftly across the sea to the Elaccan continent. A mass exodus had begun as soon as the unexpectedly large military force began its descent.

Leto could understand the panicked reaction, though. "With a military force this size, they must think we're invading." But weren't the Ecazis honorable enough to defend their women and children, even if they thought they faced an overwhelming enemy force? Why were they fleeing like thieves in the night?

"I'll set them straight." Bludd eagerly spoke into the microphone. "Archduke Armand has returned, and he calls for an immediate war council. We bring grave news."

"The Archduke is alive?" blurted the spaceport manager. "We were told he was assassinated, along with his daughter and much of the Atreides household!"

Armand scowled. Leto rose halfway to his feet from his passenger seat. "Who told you this? How did this information come to Ecaz?"

"Why, Duke Prad Vidal announced it. He has assumed temporary control of the planet, as acting leader."

Armand's face darkened with anger, and Gurney growled. "There is no way a courier could have brought that information, my Lord. We allowed no ships to leave Caladan. We are the first. No one could have spread the word."

"He didn't need a courier," Leto said. "He *knew* the attack was going to happen, but I did not expect he would act precipitously. He's a fool."

"He is impatient. He could not have guessed we would cut off all communication from Caladan after the massacre, or that either of us would survive. It seems he was too anxious to steal my seat of power to wait for confirmation." Armand wrested the communication controls from Bludd and issued orders to the spaceport manager. "Have Duke Vidal arrested immediately. He has many questions to answer."

At the main palace, Leto could see the great confusion, numerous ships still lifting off and streaking away, an entire military force in disorganized retreat. Vidal's supporters? The small gang that supported the Elaccan governor's bid for power could not possibly withstand the full Atreides fleet, and they knew it.

"He wanted to take over my palace, but didn't realize he'd have to fight for it. Now he runs back to Elacca to hide behind his own fortifications—for all the good they'll do him." The Archduke's expression was a barely contained thunderstorm.

"Before we can crush the Grumman threat, we will have to deal with the cockroaches under your own door-mat, my Lord," Gurney said.

The stream of frantic ships continued to evacuate from the Ecazi Palace, racing toward the coast and the open ocean. Armand clenched and unclenched his one remaining fist. "Duke Leto, have your warships destroy those vessels. That will take care of our problem."

Leto straightened. "Armand, that would break the rules of the War of Assassins. Minimize collateral damage. Take out only the noble target. If this is not handled properly, you could begin a civil war here on Ecaz and be censured by the Landsraad."

Armand nodded slowly as his lead frigate came in for a landing. "I cannot accept that. A civil war would delay my strike against Grumman."

*The Harkonnens killed my family, and I survived,
even though Beast Rabban tried to hunt me down.
I fought many battles during my Swordmaster
training on Ginaz, then helped Duke Leto's troops
retake Ix from the Tleilaxu, and through it all I
survived. I cannot begin to count the number of
battles I have fought in the name of House Atreides. Those numbers do not count. The only thing
that matters is that I am still alive to defend House
Atreides.*

—DUNCAN IDAHO, *A Thousand Lives*

With his wiry black hair and distinctive features,
Duncan Idaho bore no resemblance to young Paul
Atreides. Since they could not pose as father and son
traveling together, they decided instead upon uncle and
ward.

They wore comfortable but ill-fitting clothes and carried patched travel sacks, all of which had been picked up
at a secondhand market in Cala City. Duncan concealed
the Old Duke's sword beneath a loose cape. Paul's hair
had been cropped short, and his recent scabs and scrapes
also altered his appearance. The Swordmaster inspected
him and said, "The job of a disguise is not to be perfect,
but to deflect attention."

They boarded a large passenger ferry that slowly
crossed the ocean, carrying cargo, farm crews, vacation-
ers who preferred the leisurely pace, and others who
were simply too poor to afford a long-distance flight.
Most of the passengers in the lower decks were pundi
rice farmers who moved from paddy to paddy along the
continental coasts, following the monsoon season. Short

in stature, they had broad faces and aboriginal features, and they spoke a dialect that Paul did not understand; many were descended from tribes that still resided in the dense jungles, isolated for hundreds of generations. In filmbooks Paul had read about the mysterious "Caladan primitives," but little was known about them, since for many generations the Atreides rulers had adhered to a policy of noninterference in the natural, self-contained societies.

Some passengers amused themselves by fishing from the main deck. The ferry's cook dragged a net from the stern and used his catch for the day's communal meal. All passengers ate at a common table, though Paul and Duncan kept to themselves. Paul was satisfied enough with the thin fish stew and dried wedges of paradan melon.

Once, a storm came close enough to make the large ferry sway back and forth, but Paul had his sea legs and stood on deck with Duncan, watching the clouds and whitecaps, seeing flashes of lightning in the distance. He thought of the stories of electrical creatures named ele-crans that preyed upon lost sailors, but this was a more mundane form of lightning, a simple thunderstorm that passed away to the north.

When the ferry finally arrived at the Eastern Continent's largest city, little more than a village with docks and wooden houses that extended out over the shoreline, they disembarked. Paul regarded the rugged mountains that rose abruptly from the coastline. "Are we going to the interior, Duncan? I don't see any roads."

"It will probably be no more than a trail. The Sisters keep themselves hidden, but there's no isolation so great that I can't find it."

When they asked villagers about the mysterious fortress abbey, they received sour, suspicious looks. Though the Sisters in Isolation were not revered, the locals viewed strangers with even less enthusiasm. Nevertheless, Duncan continued to press, insisting that his interest in the abbey was a private matter. Finally he received vague directions, which enabled the two of them to set off.

It took them days to make the journey on foot, following a wide road that degenerated into a dirt one, then a rutted trail, and ultimately dwindled to a muddy path that wound upward into the mountains. Around them the jungle grew denser, the trees taller, the rugged slopes steeper.

When they finally reached the fortress nunnery on the third afternoon, it seemed almost as if they had stumbled upon it by accident. Sheer black walls rose from the ground like artificial cliffs. Paul stared at the imposing razor-edged corners and lookout turrets on which small figures could be discerned. The communal home of the Sisters in Isolation had few windows, only small slots in the thick barricade—perhaps to minimize vulnerabilities, or to give the Sisters few opportunities to view the outside world.

Duncan and Paul strode up to the barred, unwelcoming gates. "They must receive visitors occasionally," Paul mused. "How else do they get supplies and equipment? They can't be entirely self-sufficient."

"No sense hiding our identity, now that we're here. I'm sure they've been watching us for the past several kilometers." Duncan threw back his hood and put his hand on the young man's shoulder. He shouted at the gate. "Hello!"

Other than the tiny figures stationed at the highest towers, he detected no movement, heard no sound. Duncan called again, "Open the gate! We demand entry in the name of Duke Leto Atreides of Caladan!"

After a moment, Paul saw a flurry above. One of the blocks of stone over the gate shifted aside to reveal a camouflaged window. "Duke Leto the Just? Your claim is easy enough for any man to make," came a gruff voice. A male voice, Paul decided. He wondered why a man would be guarding the door of the towering abbey.

"But it's not easy for a man to bring the Duke's own son, Paul," Duncan countered. "His grandmother Helena is with you. She won't recognize her grandson, since she's never looked upon him, but she *will* recognize me."

Paul turned his face upward, sure that hidden imagers were capturing every detail.

"And why should the Abbess wish to see her grandson? Your Duke himself told her never again to have contact with his family."

Paul absorbed this information quickly. *The Abbess?* He was not actually surprised. From what he'd read of Helena Atreides, she was a scheming, highly intelligent woman with lofty ambitions.

Duncan said, "That is a matter we will discuss in private with Lady Helena. She knows why she is there—or would she rather I shout the reasons at the top of my lungs?"

A mechanical click was followed by a heavy droning hum as the gates swung inward. The man who came down to meet them had once been handsome—Paul could see that from his features—but now his face was lined and weathered, as though psychological pressures and sadness had eaten away at his heart for years. Amazingly, he wore a faded and much-mended House Atreides uniform.

Duncan regarded the man, then suddenly stiffened. "Swain Goire! So you have kept yourself alive all these years."

The other man's scowl appeared to be a natural expression for him. "I remain alive only because my Duke commanded it as part of my punishment. Still, my penance can never atone for what I took from him."

"No, but you *can* help keep us alive for him." Duncan

nudged Paul through the gates and into the thick fortress
walls of the abbey.

≈

THEY REQUESTED SANCTUARY in the Duke's name,
and the Sisters in Isolation grudgingly provided them
with quarters, but very little welcome. The women were
dressed in uncomfortable black outfits; many wore dark
wimples, while others covered their faces with obscur-
ing mesh. They spoke little, if at all, and seemed to be
better at building barricades than bridges.

The Sisters in Isolation had almost no contact with
the outside, though they were known for their handmade
tapestries. Most of the women were said to have come
here because of mental injuries, scars they could not
bear. Paul suspected that they simply wallowed together
in combined grief, and for their own protection.

At sunset, brassy bells shattered the haunted silence
of the abbey, summoning everyone for dinner in a large
mess hall. The meal was plain—bread, fruits, vegeta-
bles, and preserved fish. They drank water that bubbled
up from jungle springs and was piped into the abbey.

Goire took a seat by himself at a small table on the far
edge of the room, avoiding even the two new guests. Apparently he was not welcome to dine with the Sisters.
Sentenced here after the death of Victor and Kailea, he
was one of the few males in the entire abbey.

The large chair at the head of the long table remained
empty, and Paul wondered if his grandmother would
bother to show up, or if she would spurn them. He was eager to meet this woman whose name was rarely spoken
around the castle. Even though he had pressed Duncan,
Gurney, and Thufir for details, they had only answered
him with brusque, dismissive words.

Finally, as though telepathically linked, all the silent

Sisters turned to face a wooden door at the far side of the banquet chamber. It opened, and a tall, hooded woman entered.

She wore a black mesh over her face, and spangles of Richesian circuit-embroidery wound about the wrapping at her throat. *Threaded speakers.* The woman glided forward to stand straight-backed at her chair. She looked ominous to Paul, like a superstitious old drawing of the Grim Reaper. When she turned her obscured face toward the two visitors, Paul noticed that, at the side of the room, Swain Goire had turned away from her.

The Abbess took her seat without uttering a word. Paul wondered if he should introduce himself, ask his questions. Duncan's fist clenched where it rested on the tabletop.

After a lengthy and unpleasant moment, the woman reached up with black-gloved hands to touch the sides of her hood, hesitated as though afraid, and then pulled back the fabric to reveal dark, wavy brown hair shot through with silver-gray. She peeled down the mesh that obscured her face, and Paul gazed for the first time upon his paternal grandmother.

Her features were lean and severe, but he recognized hints of his father's face. Lady Helena of House Richese had married Duke Paulus Atreides, and clearly she had not forgotten her regal bearing. She spoke in a voice that seemed ragged and rusty from disuse. "For now, at this meal, I will acknowledge that I am your grandmother, boy. But do not expect a loving welcome or celebratory feast."

"Nevertheless, we expect courtesy and your guarantee of safety," Duncan warned.

"Courtesy . . ." Helena seemed to consider this. "You ask for a great deal."

Goire stood, startling the gathered women. "And you

will give it to them. They have every right to make this request of us, and we have every obligation to grant it."

Helena's lips pursed in a scowl. "Very well. You are here, and I will learn why . . . but later. For now, let us eat in peace. And silence."

Politics is a tangled web, an intricate labyrinth,
an ever-shifting kaleidoscopic pattern. And it is
not pretty.

—COUNT HASIMIR FENRING

Baron Harkonnen sat in a swollen, self-adjusting chair in the back row of the Landsraad Hall of Oratory, waiting for the shouting match to begin and hoping that his name would not be mentioned. He had wearied of biding his time on Giedi Prime, hoping for any hint of news about poor Duke Leto's wedding-day tragedy and the murder of his innocent son (if the secondary assassins had completed their mission). Finally, unable to quell his impatience, he had decided on an unannounced trip to Kaitain to attend to "business matters." No one would think anything of it.

And so, he happened to be in the Imperial city when the Mentat Thufir Hawat from House Atreides and the official Ecazi ambassador stationed on Kaitain called an emergency session of the Landsraad and demanded a judgment from the Emperor himself.

They must be very upset indeed. Oh dear. Word of the massacre quickly spread, and the Baron was disappointed to learn that Duke Leto and his son Paul had survived. So far.

Viscount Hundro Moritani was also conveniently in the Imperial city, as if he had come here just waiting to be accused. That was both provocative and foolish, the Baron thought. Tactically, the smart thing would have been for the Viscount to go home and shore up his defenses against the combined Atreides and Ecazi retaliation that was sure to come. What was he doing here? The Baron had gone out of his way to avoid seeing the man, not sure what the vitriolic Grumman leader might be up to.

The gathered nobles in the Hall of Oratory took their assigned seats with an air of hushed anticipation. Many of them were clearly disturbed by what they had heard. The box reserved for House Moritani was conspicuously empty. Was the man insane enough to defy an Imperial summons? Possibly.

Far below, Shaddam IV called the session to order from an ornate podium on the central dais. "I summon Viscount Hundro Moritani of Grumman to face the charges being leveled here today." The Emperor raised his hand toward the vaulted ceiling, and a clearplaz bubble descended on suspensors.

Inside the transparent ball stood a tall, angular man who wrapped himself proudly in a fur-lined yellow robe. The Viscount's indignant, heavily accented voice was transmitted through speakers around the auditorium. "Why have I been imprisoned before I have been charged with any offense? Am I to be on display like a zoo animal before this chamber of my peers?"

The Emperor was entirely unperturbed. "The confinement is for your own protection."

"I need no protection! I demand that you release me so that I can stand before my accusers."

Shaddam brushed at something on his gilded sleeve. "Perhaps some members of the audience feel they need to be protected from you? A formal complaint has been lodged against Grumman." He tapped a sheet of ridulian crystal before him, as if perusing a news report. "The matters before us today concern alleged flaws in the declaration and prosecution of a legal War of Assassins. There are prescribed rules, and part of my job is to remind you of them—all of you." Shaddam looked around the Hall of Oratory, seemed to hear resounding agreement, then gave instructions for the transparent holding chamber to be opened.

Viscount Moritani stood large and ruffled before the crowd; his thick hair was mussed. "Very well, then let us discuss what I have done. And let all hear the crimes committed against *my* House as well." He glared around, perhaps looking for Baron Harkonnen, though he didn't appear to see the Baron yet among the hundreds of representatives. Despite his bulk, the Baron tried to withdraw unobtrusively into the shadows, sinking into the self-adjusting chair.

The female Ecazi ambassador stepped forward beside Hawat and said in an erudite voice, "Crimes were committed, indeed. We will present our evidence and let the Emperor and the Landsraad decide." Without further encouragement, she began her recital of the major events in the ongoing feud: the biological sabotage of fogtree forests, the murder of ambassadors, the carpet bombing of Ecaz; then the expulsion of all Grumman students from the Swordmaster school on Ginaz, followed by the startling attack that leveled Ginaz, and the murder of the Archduke's brother and eldest daughter.

As he listened, Viscount Moritani was at first stoic and then showed bitter amusement. The Landsraad members began an ugly grumbling; the Baron thought it did not bode well.

Thufir Hawat now took his turn, stepping forward. "But that was only the beginning, my Lords. These images speak for themselves."

The audience of nobles sat in horrified silence, and the Baron watched with eager anticipation as recordings of the mayhem during the wedding ceremony were played for all to see, culminating in the Viscount Moritani delivering his damning holographic message. To the Baron's great relief, no one mentioned the Harkonnen name.

Shaddam silenced the resulting uproar by banging his enhanced gavel. The Ecazi ambassador spoke again, so furious that her entire body shook. "Throughout this dispute, House Ecaz committed no illegal act. Even in the earlier phase, our Archduke formally declared kanly, as required. We responded only under the strict rules of a War of Assassins, as laid down in the Great Convention. We did nothing to provoke this vicious and irrational violence from House Moritani."

The Viscount slammed a fist against the secondary podium. "You let my only son die by denying him the drug needed to cure his disease! You murdered Wolfram as surely as if you had sent an assassin to plunge a dagger into his heart! My poor son—my only heir!—was an innocent bystander targeted by Ecazi hatred."

The Baron pursed his lips, but remained silent. Someone would probably point out that the killing of a son and heir was, strictly speaking, perfectly allowed under the terms of a War of Assassins.

The female ambassador remained unruffled. "All members of the Landsraad know Archduke Armand as a great humanitarian. Show us any formal request you made for such drugs. Prove to those assembled here that Ecaz ever directly denied your son medical treatment." She looked at him coldly. "Considering your past behavior, Viscount, it is more likely that you allowed your son to die so you would have an excuse for more violence."

Moritani turned purple with rage. Before the man could stalk down from the central stage, Sardaukar guards moved closer, ready to confine him within the clearplaz bubble again, should it prove necessary.

Emperor Shaddam pointed a stern finger. "Enough. This must not get out of hand."

Hawat answered in a strong voice. "Out of hand, Sire? House Moritani has struck not only against Ecaz but also House Atreides and House Vernius of Ix. In the massacre at the wedding, the representatives of many other noble families were put at risk and could have been killed. A Grumman sneak attack previously destroyed the Swordmaster school on Ginaz. How much more collateral damage will we tolerate? This dispute can quickly blow up into a conflagration that embroils many more Houses of the Landsraad."

"It will not," Shaddam said in a stern tone. "Viscount Moritani, I command that you cease your foolhardy course of action. You will pay reparations in an amount I will personally determine. And I require you to apologize to the Archduke for killing his two daughters. And his brother. There, that should settle the matter."

Viscount Moritani just laughed cruelly, startling the entire audience. Even the Baron wondered what the man was doing. "Oh, more Houses than Ecaz and Atreides are involved. You might be surprised." Now he seemed to be looking directly at the Harkonnen seats. *A dangerous game to play with me,* the Baron thought.

Moritani took a step toward the Emperor's podium, though the Sardaukar would not let him get closer. "Why not just send another legion of Sardaukar to breathe down my neck, Sire? I will ignore them as I did before." Now he actually turned his back on Shaddam and began to stride away as the outcry mounted in the chamber. He raised his voice bitterly, "Now if you all will excuse me, I have a funeral to plan—for my son."

The Emperor pounded his gavel again, but the Viscount did not turn. "Hundro Moritani, you are officially censured for inappropriate behavior. On behalf of the entire Landsraad and the member Houses, you are also placed on administrative probation." The noble members muttered at this light sentence for such extreme defiance, and Shaddam shouted, "If need be, House Moritani can be stripped. Any further violations, and you will face the loss of your fief!"

Now, the man turned slowly, looking back at the Emperor with unabashed loathing. "How much is my fief worth, Sire? Grumman is a worn-out and nearly valueless planet, but it is my home and I am its ruler. I will protect my people and my honor as I see fit. Come and see for yourself, if you like. See how a *Moritani* defends his honor!"

The Baron went cold. Was the man mad? After the wedding massacre, Atreides and Ecazi forces were almost certainly planning to attack Grumman, and now he provoked the Emperor as well? The Viscount no longer seemed to care about anything. Could he really have loved his son so much? The very idea made the Baron uneasy. How could he—or anyone else—control such a man?

❧

THAT EVENING IN his diplomatic quarters, before he could make arrangements to return to Giedi Prime, the Baron received an unwelcome, secret message. When he used an ornate stir stick in his spice coffee, his touch activated a cleverly hidden projector, which produced a holo-display of the smiling Grumman nobleman wafting above the food on his tray. Startled, the Baron pushed his meal away, but that could not stop the Viscount's recorded speech.

"I am on my way back to Grumman to prepare for our great battle. A magnificent battle. The Archduke will come with the Atreides military forces—they cannot resist the bait—and my planet must be defended." With a smug expression, he added, "As my ally, Baron, I expect you to send a Harkonnen military division to help Grumman stand against its enemies. I must insist, for the sake of our friendship . . . and our secrets."

The Baron knocked over the cup of spice coffee, hoping to disrupt the recorded spectral image, but the Viscount continued with his ominous ultimatum. "As I promised you, I will take the credit for these actions. There is no need for me to reveal Harkonnen involvement. If you provide men for our two Houses to fight side by side, I will be happy to let your troops wear Grumman uniforms to maintain our little masquerade. No one need know, besides ourselves.

"Two weeks should be enough time for you to prepare. Atreides and Ecaz will be delayed at least that long, thanks to Duke Vidal. Send the division—and your man Rabban to command them." He smiled, and the image flickered. "I have already lost my son. You can gamble a mere nephew."

In frustrated fury, the Baron slapped at the lingering, sneering image, but it hung maddeningly in the air, as if to remind him of his inability to assert even that small degree of control.

We build fortress walls around ourselves with thick mental barricades and deep moats. These places of sanctuary serve the dual purpose of keeping the unpleasant reminders out and locking our own guilt within.

—Bene Gesserit Azhar Book

The walls of the fortress nunnery were solid stone, but the true coldness in the weaving chamber seemed to emanate directly from his grandmother. Lady Helena Atreides clearly wanted Paul to feel uncomfortable and unwelcome, and so he flustered her by refusing to behave in an awkward manner. He had nothing to gain or lose from the older woman's companionship, and neither, he supposed, did the Abbess have anything to gain from his. He expected no sudden change to love and acceptance.

Helena's resentment stemmed from old memories of her husband, Paulus, and perhaps Leto as well, but when she tried to take it out on her grandson, Paul harmlessly deflected her attitude, as though he wore a personal body shield against emotions.

"Our women are hard at work," Helena had scolded when he entered the upper chamber of the tower one morning, asking to observe their activities. "You must not disturb them."

Paul did not slink away, though, as she apparently expected him to do. "They are forbidden to talk, Grandmother, and none of them has even looked at me, so obviously I'm not disturbing them." He peered curiously at all the feverish activity with looms and threads. "Will you please explain what they are doing?"

Thirty women worked at various looms to the percussive sliding and spin of fibers being whisked through grids, shuttles thrown to and fro, patterns tamped and reset. The filaments changed colors, drawn from skeins of yarn, spindles of thread.

The women gathered handfuls of strands that ranged from fine gossamer fibers to thick, slubby twists. The weavers incorporated them into patterns and continued to work in a well-practiced cooperative effort, entirely without conversation. It took Paul several moments to realize that, instead of one giant tangle, there were dozens of different tapestries in production. Some were like rainbows, hues blending into hues, while others were dramatic clashes of threads, intersecting lines, and impossible knots.

"Are they following a grand design?"

"Each Sister makes her own pattern. Since we do not converse with one another, who can say what memories and visions drive us?" Helena's face looked pinched as she frowned. "The famed abstract tapestries are our nunnery's most profitable enterprise. They do not have patterns and pictorial representations as typical tapestries do, but these show a different sort of image, one that is open to interpretation. CHOAM pays us handsomely to distribute them across the Imperium."

"So your religious order is a commercial operation." This statement also seemed to annoy his grandmother.

"There is always commerce in religion. We recognize that people want the products, and we accept money in exchange for them. Beyond that, this abbey is fairly self-sufficient. We grow most of our own food. You know this, because I have noticed you two poking around."

Since arriving, he and Duncan had been wandering

about the abbey grounds, viewing the cultivated areas on steep terraces outside the thick walls. The dense jungle also yielded fruits, edible leaves, and tubers, as well as game, though Paul couldn't imagine the Sisters in Isolation going on hunting expeditions. Swain Goire, however, might do it.

"The Caladan primitives are also fond of our tapestries."

Paul was surprised. "What do they use them for?"

Though the mysterious tribes from the deep jungles had very little contact with the rest of Caladan, Paul had been fascinated to study them in filmbooks. Since his father was the Atreides Duke, Paul wanted to learn all he could about every aspect of this world. Duke Leto, Paulus, and their predecessors had let the primitives lead their own lives on the Eastern Continent without harassment. The Old Duke had issued a statement that whenever the Caladan primitives wished to come to civilization, they would do so of their own accord. History was rife with sad examples of modern ways being forced upon an unwilling people.

Helena drew her brows together. "Who can understand the primitives, any more than they understand our abstract patterns? But they know what they see in the tapestries, and that is all our Sisters could ask for."

Knowing it would startle, even provoke her, Paul turned to her. "And do you feel isolated from civilization, Grandmother? Will you ever request forgiveness from my father so that you may return to Castle Caladan?"

Helena's laugh was like breaking glass. "Why would I wish to do that? I have everything I need here, and I am queen of my own domain. Why should I want to be a pawn in someone else's game?"

Paul looked down at the carefully spaced warp of tapestry strings. A Sister with close-cropped gray hair deftly wove a pink thread into the weft and then a blue one, tying them together to add to her hypnotic kaleido-scope pattern.

His grandmother's voice sounded sour. "Everything is running perfectly well here. My life has been smooth. I have not thought of either my son or my dead husband in years." Then, in a startling gesture, Helena reached out with her long-fingered hands, and hooked them like claws in the unwoven threads. She yanked and ripped them free from the loom hooks. "All was in perfect harmony, until you and Duncan came."

The silent, gray-haired sister working at the loom sat up and looked at the deliberate ruin the Abbess had made of her work.

Paul supposed her gesture was yet another attempt to intimidate him. Instead, he looked at the tangled mess of threads, viewing the colors and knots. "If each woman here creates her own design from her life experience"—he nodded toward the mess—"would I not be correct to interpret that as *your* life's pattern?"

The Forms must be obeyed. Our very civilization depends on this.

> —from the Rules of the Great Convention,
> as applied to a War of Assassins

With the sudden arrival of the House Atreides ships and thousands of well-trained, heavily armed soldiers, Archduke Armand had a ready-made planetary force that more than doubled his fighting power. Together, the two militaries should have been enough to crush the Grummans.

But first, they had an unanticipated battle to win here on Ecaz. They could not risk losing the planet to rebels in their absence.

In a private discussion chamber within the recaptured Ecazi Palace, the Archduke still trembled with weakness, both from grief and his severe injury. His voice sounded hollow, like a cold storm wind blowing. "I did not intend to fight a civil war."

Gurney lounged in his carved wooden chair, not to imply casualness but rather to remain loose and ready to fight. "Vidal has been planning this for some time—that much is obvious. This morning's overflights on Elacca mapped out the extent of his military buildup and his scrambled defenses. Mark my words, it did not happen overnight. You have proven him a liar simply by being alive, my Lord."

Leto shook his head, disturbed. "If he had simply bided his time, his treachery would not have been so obvious."

Armand heaved a deep sigh. "Vidal blithely assumed I would be assassinated. Now that he has already announced to everyone that I was killed, how can he explain my return?"

Gurney gave a rumbling chuckle. "That man is a poor leader if he banks on every plan coming off as expected."

"And now there will be tremendous bloodshed because of it." The Archduke hung his head, letting his unkempt silver hair fall forward. "And why do so many of my own people follow him? His deceit is painfully obvious. Does he plant ridiculous stories to cast doubt in the minds of his followers? Could he have suggested to them that I'm a Face Dancer? Or does he simply keep them ignorant?"

"Probably the latter," Leto mused. "But it is not the province of common soldiers to wrestle with the tangles of politics. They will follow his orders."

Whitmore Bludd sat on the opposite side of the table, near the Archduke, yet alone. Though pale, the Swordmaster tried to summon defiance, sounding uncharacteristically bloodthirsty. "We will crush the rebels, no matter the cost. Ecaz will soon be in your complete control again, my Lord. Then we can move on Grumman. It is only a matter of time before we place Hundro Moritani's head on a stake. I promise you that."

Without looking up, the Archduke nodded slowly, as if his head were too heavy for his neck. "Yes, but our path can take many different turns. How do I stomach a bloody campaign against my own people, who have been led astray by a traitor?"

"Maybe you won't have to. I propose that we not launch

a full-scale civil war," Leto offered. "Even though our armies can defeat the Elaccan rebels, it would be wasteful to set so many brave Ecazi fighters at each other's throats."

"What choice do we have? By now our case has been presented in the Landsraad court. Do you suggest we simply wait to hear from Kaitain while Vidal reinforces his fortifications? And every day of delay here gives Viscount Moritani more time to prepare for us on Grumman."

Leto traced the table's swirling grains of bloodwood. "We brought our armies here to join with yours and then move immediately on to Grumman. Now that Vidal has seen our overwhelming force, he will expect us to launch a full-scale attack, instead of the precision strikes required by the Great Convention. Vidal has never even declared himself in this War of Assassins, and yet he has joined it. Viscount Hundro Moritani has cast the rules to the winds in this conflict." His expression became hard and implacable as he crossed his arms over his chest. "But we do not have to. Others have flagrantly violated the rules, but that does not give us carte blanche to do the same. One crime does not justify another, particularly when it comes to the emotional pitfalls of internecine warfare."

Gurney could see where Leto was going. His voice was deep and resonant. "The Forms must be obeyed."

The exhausted and grieving Archduke was no longer so nimble, though. "What are you suggesting, my friend?"

"Merely that if they are prepared for a total civil war, ready to defend against a frontal assault from a large military force, we should demonstrate what a War of Assassins is all about. We *use* assassins. A defensive line can protect against a large army, but one or two carefully trained infiltrators might make it through."

"I'll do it," Gurney said. "The Orange Catholic Bible

states: 'For I have a righteous Lord, and the enemies of my Lord are the enemies of God.'"

"It is my place to spill the blood of my enemy," the Archduke said.

"You cannot go, Armand," Leto said, his voice filled with compassion, though he knew he was stating the obvious. "I'll go in your stead. Gurney and I will be the assassins."

"And I," said Bludd, a moment late. "For the honor of House Ecaz, my Lord Archduke, let me go and destroy our enemies."

The one-armed Armand did not want to admit his own frailty, yet he could not deny it. "No, stay with me, Swordmaster. I require your security. We have not yet completed a thorough sweep of the palace and the cities. I need you here."

Bludd seemed diminished by the comment, inferring—perhaps correctly, Leto thought—that the Archduke was not willing to overlook his failure. "But my Lord, how can you send a nobleman to do bloody work like this? The Duke should not put himself in such danger."

"I *should* not," Leto said, "but I will anyway. I am not defenseless. Ask Gurney here, or Duncan Idaho. They are my best fighters, my most loyal bodyguards, and they trained me."

Gurney nodded. "Duke Leto is a nobleman first and rarely allows himself to be seen in personal combat, but he is a formidable fighter. He can even best me one time out of ten."

"Four out of ten, Gurney."

The inkvine scar darkened with a bit of a flush. "It is not for me to argue with my Duke."

Armand pondered. "We will provide a diversion by continuing our military buildup as if we are preparing to attack Elacca. Vidal's spies will be watching to see when we intend to move against him. He won't expect a small, personal attack, even though it is exactly what the rules require."

"Gurney and I will make plans and slip away to the Elaccan continent at our earliest opportunity," Leto said.

When a man is pushed to extremes, which aspect manifests itself—his humanity or his brutality? That is the defining aspect of character.

—DUKE LETO ATREIDES

Atop the fortress nunnery's tallest tower, Duncan stood at midday with Swain Goire, surveying the steep jungle hills all around. Verdant plantings filled terraced gardens on the abrupt slope.

One silent Sister had come up to the tower with them to add food to the rookery. Grains and fruits were spread out as a banquet for the large black hawks. Duncan thought the raptors must be perfectly capable of hunting their own prey in the jungles. Were these women trying to turn them into vegetarians? Then he realized that the grains and fruit were not for the hawks, but served instead to lure smaller birds, which the raptors then devoured. Hawks circled high above the tower, no more than black specks in the clouds, while others swooped down to the thick jungle.

Goire wore his reticence like a thick cloak on a cold day. In his youth Duncan had not known the man well, having been away at the Ginaz School when Goire became captain of the Atreides guard. Duncan knew only what this man had done, and that was enough for him.

Goire finally spoke up. "Paul reminds me so much of young Victor. He has the look of his father about him."

"I barely knew Victor. His life was over by the time I returned from Ginaz."

Like a wave-battered rock on the coast, Goire showed no reaction despite the brusqueness of Duncan's words. "Well, I knew the boy well. I saw him every day, up until the end. I was supposed to keep him safe, and I failed."

"Paul has me to defend him," Duncan said.

Goire's eyes were weary and reddened. "I didn't intend for Victor to be harmed, but we all know that failure renders such intentions irrelevant. Actions and results are all that matter."

The two fell into a longer silence, watching the high-circling hawks, gazing at the jungle-covered hills that stretched to the horizon and the empty sky. In the distance, Duncan could see small flying ships that must have been part of the business of the coastal towns.

"What exactly are you defending Paul from?" Goire finally asked. "What sort of desperation drove you here? A mere squabble would not require such extreme measures."

With a sigh, Duncan explained about Viscount Moritani's blood feud with Ecaz, in which House Atreides was now embroiled. When he was done, the old guard said, "And you have reason to believe the danger isn't over? You suspect that more assassins are coming for Paul?"

"Viscount Moritani wants to kill the Duke's son, for whatever twisted reason he has in his head. Paul still lives, and I intend to keep it that way. I will not lower my guard."

"But it makes no sense for the Grummans to continue attacking. Paul is an innocent."

"It made no sense in the first place, and still the attack occurred. Ilesa was an innocent, too."

Goire nodded solemnly. Both of them regarded the

distant glints of silvery ships, which were now approaching, sleek fliers skimming over the untracked green canopy. Viewed from the high vantage point, these craft looked no larger than the hawks circling in the air. Within moments, the roar of engines could be heard.

Goire tensed. "I have not seen ships like that before. We get very little—"

Duncan could tell immediately they were not supply craft. "They're going to attack!"

"Yes—yes they are." Goire gave Duncan a push. "Go! Go get Paul!"

Duncan ran as angular attack fliers streaked in.

❧

DUNCAN BURST INTO the tapestry room, having already retrieved and drawn the Old Duke's sword. "They're coming. We've got to get to shelter!"

After years of training, Paul did not hesitate, but sprang into motion to join his companion.

Paying no heed to the Swordmaster's obvious urgency, Helena was about to scold him for the interruption, when the first great concussive explosions hit the side of the abbey. Duncan shouted to her. "Sound an evacuation. Get your Sisters out of here!"

"I will not." Helena stood icily. "This is our fortress. Our home." Her pride seemed more important to her than survival. "Are you saying the great Duncan Idaho cannot protect us all with that sword?"

Scowling, he grabbed Paul by the arm and rushed him toward the door and the stone stairs. "I am not sworn to protect *you,* my Lady. Your safety is on your own head now. Your fortress is under attack."

"This War of Assassins has nothing to do with us," Helena insisted.

"It does now!" Paul called from the doorway. "They're

trying to kill me. And even if you're no more than collateral damage, you will still be dead."

The other Sisters blithely continued their weaving, since the Abbess had not instructed them to do otherwise. A second explosion impacted the outer walls, and the entire tower room shook violently.

"Those aren't just assassins. This is a full-fledged military strike," Paul said.

"Viscount Moritani has already proven the lengths to which he'll go. It's my job to keep you safe." Duncan pulled him through the door and they bounded down the winding stairway three steps at a time. "We have to get out of here. These walls won't hold."

By the time the two raced out into the courtyard, the fliers had circled back to launch more targeted missiles toward the Abbey. The shock waves caused the entire structure to thrum. Cracks shot like lightning bolts through the reinforced walls. The main tower shuddered and collapsed into fire and stone dust.

His grandmother, and all those women, had been inside. Like the tapestry that Helena had destroyed, the whole tower now lay in jumbled ruins. Red mingled with the gray of the rock in a mosaic of rubble. He searched for a spot in his heart where he might be shocked and horrified by Lady Helena's death, but found nothing there for her.

With a deafening boom and buzzing whine, the attackers streaked back and forth, then came in to land and disgorge fighters who wore no uniforms, no insignia. Many Sisters ran about screaming. Some gathered makeshift weapons and raced to defend the Abbey, while others tried to flee, but they had no place to go.

Paul seized upon a crucial fact. "If they are attempting to kill *me,* and they blew up the tower, how can they know whether I am among the dead?"

Duncan shook his head, holding up the Old Duke's

sword to defend them both. "They can't. This must be one of the Viscount's grand schemes. He likes to cause damage more than anything else. He thrives on chaos."

Swain Goire ran up to them, breathless and covered with dust. His hair was matted with blood from a shrapnel injury. "Take Paul and escape into the jungle."

"Which direction?"

"Anywhere away from here—*that* is your only priority now." Goire had two wooden staves, one sharpened into a crude spear and the other to serve as a club. "I have a body shield, and I have these. I'll hold them off long enough for you to escape."

"Duncan, we can't just run!" Paul said, not willing to leave Goire to do all the fighting for them.

"My strategic imperative is to save you, young Master. Your father gave me my mission." Parts of the outer walls had crumbled during the succession of explosions, and jagged breaches now opened the barrier to the wilderness beyond. Duncan silenced Paul by pushing him toward the nearest gap. "If the only way I can accomplish my mission is to take advantage of a diversion or delay, I'll do it."

Goire activated his body shield, and the shimmering intangible barrier cocooned him. He had his weapons. Duncan felt certain Goire was trying to atone for his mistake in allowing Victor to be killed. Did he hope Duke Leto would forgive him if he sacrificed his life now, to let Paul escape? Possibly.

Duncan hesitated, wondering if he should hand Goire the Old Duke's sword—but that was *his* only weapon, and he could not surrender his best means of defending Paul.

Howling, Goire charged toward the attacking soldiers— one man against dozens, yet he rushed in. It was suicide.

Duncan dragged Paul through the broken wall rubble and into the thick foliage. The last glimpse he got of Swain Goire was when the man collided with the advancing armed soldiers, his body shield thrumming, his two wooden weapons thrashing from side to side. The assassins engulfed him, and their weapons were far sharper.

Paul and Duncan ran blindly into the jungle.

When a lasbeam strikes a shield, the destructive interaction is wholly disproportionate to the initiating energy. Both parties are completely annihilated. This is a perfect metaphor for politics.

—THUFIR HAWAT, *Strategy Lessons*

The small ornithopter flew low and fast over the grassy hills of Grumman. With whisper-quiet engines and movable wings, the vehicle made hardly any noise in its passage, just the slight, smooth sounds a large bird might make. Resser sat beside the Viscount, who piloted, ostensibly to test the new aircraft design for rounding up wild horses.

Resser was not fooled, though. He knew Hundro Moritani was preparing for war.

The Grumman soldiers, gruff and hardened warriors culled from villages out in the steppes, had been toiling in the salt tunnels and mineral shafts that riddled the ground under the dry lake bed outside of Ritka. Moritani had gathered hundreds of his stallions into corrals beyond the perimeter of the fortress shields, fitting them all with spiked armor, though he had ten times as many horses as riders. And Resser didn't see what a mere cavalry could do against a modern military force.

As the 'thopter flew along, the setting sun turned the windows of the fortress city orange, as if the structures were on fire. The Viscount looked intently at the illusion, paying little attention to his piloting. A downdraft caught the craft abruptly and they reeled downward, nearly scraping the ground before he regained control.

"It's not my time to die," the Viscount said in a matter-of-fact tone. "Nor yours. Not yet. We have work to do, Resser." Since returning from Kaitain, Moritani had been in uncharacteristically high spirits, even though he had received a censure from the Landsraad and sparked the wrath of Shaddam IV.

The redheaded Swordmaster said, "With all due respect, my Lord, I cannot understand your tactics. Did you intentionally provoke the Padishah Emperor?"

"Absolutely. When the upcoming battle looks most terrible, I expect that our paternal Shaddam will come running to stop us from hurting ourselves." He glared at Resser. "Never forget how my ancestors made their mark forever on Salusa Secundus, and how the damned Corrinos hunted them down for revenge."

"I will not forget, my Lord, but I fail to see what you can accomplish in this manner. Both Duke Atreides and Archduke Ecaz survived your assassination attempt. You heard their representatives file formal protests, but they will not stop there. As we speak, they are sure to be combining their planetary militaries in order to strike Grumman hard. You may have intended this to be a War of Assassins, but you are obviously preparing for far more than that. How can we possibly defeat the armed forces of *two* noble Houses?"

He also knew that Duncan Idaho, his old friend from Ginaz, would be with the Atreides forces.

Moritani chuckled. "Oh, Resser, how you misunderstand! We don't need to defeat them! We merely have to hold out long enough for the Corrino Emperor to come to the rescue—and mark my word, he will. Grumman is a powerful magnet that will draw all of our enemies at once." Still chuckling, he gripped the controls of the 'thopter and flew them on a daredevil run toward the stony hills behind Ritka, but Resser could see that the man's large, squarish hands were shaking. He continued in a whisper, "And then it will all be over. Whether our noble House is known by the name of Tantor or Moritani, we have always been underestimated. After this, no one will ever forget our family name again."

A terrible sense of foreboding came over Resser. "What do you intend to do, my Lord?"

"My son is dead, so my House will die with me."

"You can have other children, my Lord. You can remarry."

"No, no, Resser. When Cilla died, darkness consumed my soul. Wolfram was my proper heir, and the Ecazis just let him suffer and die—out of spite! We cannot defeat the plots of our enemies in any other way. My line shall end in a way that will be written in all of the historical chronicles. And you will help."

Resser drew a deep breath to focus. "I swore an oath to serve you, my Lord."

"Grumman will become a tomb for House Moritani and our three principal enemies—even for House Harkonnen, if we're lucky. I have commanded the Baron to send his heir apparent to lead a division of disguised Harkonnen troops." His eyes took on a distant look. "Resser, I want you to take all of the family atomics and install them in the passageways immediately beneath my fortress keep. Remove the safeguards and transfer the codes to my throne room."

"Atomics, my Lord?" Resser clung to his seat as the 'thopter soared over the rooftops of Ritka. Years ago Duncan had begged him to break his oath to House Moritani and abandon his service to the dishonorable Viscount, but Resser had refused. Though Duncan had disagreed with Resser's decision, he had clearly understood it, because he was an Atreides retainer—a good and loyal fighter for his noble House, just as Resser was for his. Resser had defiantly served his role, holding to his oath even when he knew that his master broke the rules and provoked his enemies.

But *atomics*!

Viscount Moritani shrugged, casually continuing to pilot the craft. "Do not think of the Great Convention as if it were a sacred text, like the Orange Catholic Bible. It's no more than an ancient agreement written by a frightened people who were still stinging from the wounds of the Butlerian Jihad. Those outdated rules no longer apply to us. Prepare the atomics, as I have commanded." He narrowed his dark eyes. "Or will you fail me? Shall I remind you of the blood oath you swore to me? A *blood oath*!"

The Viscount's words cut with a razor edge. Resser didn't doubt that the man would command him to leap from the flying craft if he did not provide a satisfactory answer. Resser was not afraid of dying—only of making the wrong choice. Perhaps he could fight for the controls and cause the 'thopter to crash into a hillside . . . which might, after all, be the best outcome for the sake of the Imperium. But he could never accept the thought of killing his own master, no matter how he tried to rationalize it.

Looking away, he replied sincerely, "My Lord Viscount, am I not the only Swordmaster who remains at your side, when all the others have vanished?"

With a deep growl of agreement, the Viscount changed course and headed toward the central fortress in Ritka. Torchpots had already been lit to mark the landing zone. The sky deepened into dusk, and Resser looked up to see the stars and imagined the many quiet worlds out there.

The blood is always on your own hands, even if you have someone else do the killing for you. Any leader who forgets that will inevitably become a tyrant.

—DUKE LETO ATREIDES

In the thick jungle, Paul watched dispassionately as Duncan strung up yet another assassin-tracker's body. The foliage was so suffocatingly dense that neither felt the need to hide their activities, though they remained constantly alert. They had been hunted for days since the surprise assault on the fortress nunnery.

Broad leaves formed a camouflage wall all around them. Wide, fleshy fungus gathered rain runoff into long-lived puddles that held colonies of tiny brine shrimp. Fern towers blocked the sunlight in an effort to choke their botanical rivals. Vines laced the forest floor and crawled up the sides of thick trees to pull them down, creating a convoluted mesh of snares.

During their wilderness flight, Paul had felt as if he were swimming through an underwater landscape of leaves and grasses. Their personal shields provided little protection here, yet the shimmering force fields at least discouraged the myriad biting insects.

Though he was dismayed to use such a magnificent weapon as a machete, Duncan hacked and slashed through the underbrush with the Old Duke's sword, dulling and notching the blade. The fecund wilderness grew swiftly enough to cover their path, yet the assassins had still managed to track them.

Duncan had killed five of them so far. The tangled foliage made it impossible for a Grumman military force to move as a unit, so the killers had no choice but to split up and come at them singly. The Moritani assassins were arrogant, well armed . . . and easily defeated.

The Old Duke's abused sword was still capable of killing—as Duncan's latest victim had recently discovered. Paul stood close, watching dark blood ooze from the dead man's gaping wound. Though the heart no longer pumped, gravity drew the fluid from the raw wet holes in the flesh. Holding out his hand, he intentionally caught one of the slow, thick droplets of blood, and cupped it in his palm like a crimson raindrop. "Does it ever bother you to kill these men, Duncan?"

"Not at all. I have no room for compassion toward people who are trying to slaughter us, Paul. I kill them so that *you* don't have to." He tugged on the vine and hauled the body up above their heads, so that it dangled upside down, helpless, defeated, and *insulted*.

Jungle scavengers would make quick work of the remains, but the rest of the assassins would still find the remains of the corpse, as they had found the other four. Paul had suggested hiding the bodies, but Duncan said the hunters would find them, no matter how dense the forest. "We need to leave a message that angers them," Duncan said. "Try and get them to make mistakes."

Paul looked at the killer's face but could not apply a mask of humanity to it. He didn't want to know why this man had chosen such a life, what had driven him to become a mindless murderer in the name of Viscount Moritani. Did he have a family? Did he love someone? The dead eyes had rolled up behind the lids, and he was just meat now.

Kill or be killed—no better place for that lesson than in Caladan's deep jungle.

Leaving the dead man hanging, the pair set off again. Paul had not yet figured out where Duncan was leading him; the Swordmaster apparently had no plan beyond concealment and keeping his charge safe. Nevertheless, Paul sensed that they were being watched. Though they did not know how many trackers were still in pursuit after the attack on the fortress nunnery, he knew that the five Duncan had dispatched were not enough.

Fighting the assassins was only one aspect of their wilderness survival. The jungle did not care that he was the son of Duke Leto, and it offered more threats than Paul could tally. Once, they startled a spiny boar that charged them before veering off and plunging into a thick bramble.

Then there was the challenge of obtaining food. Because the jungle was so lush, they could scavenge for fruits, stems, tubers, and mushrooms. Concerned, Duncan volunteered to test some of the species in case they might be poisonous. Paul, however, had studied the flora and fauna of Caladan and memorized a plethora of safe, edible species.

With some relief, they finally found a trampled patch of grasses: a clear but winding ribbon through the underbrush, probably some sort of game trail. Paul guessed it must lead to a stream or meadow. Exhausted from fighting for every step forward, the pair chose the path of least resistance.

Duncan warned, "This trail might make things easier, but it is also the route our trackers will take."

"And it's used by large animals. We have to be quiet enough to hide from the assassins, while making enough noise to warn any predators."

The sunlight broke through, shining down onto a glorious meadow filled with bright blue and red flowers. There was a buzz of pollinating insects. After the claustrophobic world of the jungle, Paul drew a deep breath, smiling.

Duncan froze. "I think it's a trap."

Paul's shield was already on, his hand poised on the dagger at his waist. Duncan brandished the sword. Everything was still; the tall trees in the glade rustled briefly.

With a series of rushing thumps, corpses fell from high branches, suspended by their feet from vines, limp arms flopping beneath them. The bodies dropped like an offering, jerked at their tethers and then swung like grisly fruit in a crude but unnerving imitation of what Duncan had done to his own victims. Six more assassin-trackers dangled from the trees.

Duncan looked about warily, searching for shadows or silhouettes. "I don't see anyone."

Paul stood perfectly motionless, forcing himself to use all of his senses, examining the tiniest details of the world around him. At last he managed to detect moving figures like leaf shadows amongst the curled fern fronds. "Caladan primitives," he whispered. "I can see them." With only a slight gesture, he indicated two muscular, mostly naked men huddled among the leaf shadows.

He had read enough about them to remember a few of the words and phrases the occasional coastal traders used when communicating with the tribesmen. Paul searched his mind and finally shouted out the native words for *friend* and *safe*. He wasn't sure if the primitives could tell the difference between them and the Grumman assassins—or if they even cared. Perhaps the primitives simply killed anyone who trespassed in their forest.

He and Duncan waited motionless at the edge of the glade. The slain assassins hung upside down from their slowly creaking vines. Some had been dead for days. Paul wondered how long the primitives had been killing them off. These people—whether purposely or inadvertently—had kept him and Duncan safe.

Finally, with a rustle of branches and heavy thuds, three graceful figures dropped from the trees immediately above them; with his heightened perceptions even Paul hadn't noticed these men hiding there. The trio of muscular, tattooed primitives faced them.

One was a rangy old woman with long peppery hair. Her eye hollows were deeply shadowed, stained with berry juice. A sapphire-shell beetle as large as Paul's hand decorated her hair like some sort of living ornament. Its legs twitched and moved.

"Friend," Paul said again.

Dozens more of the Caladan primitives dropped from the trees into the meadow. He could tell that Duncan was ready to fight them all if necessary, but Paul switched off his body shield, removed his hand from his dagger, and held both palms upward.

❦

APPARENTLY, THE CALADAN primitives did understand the difference between the Grumman assassins and their would-be prey. They led Paul and Duncan to their settlement, which was little more than a clearing filled with nestlike dwellings of woven pampas grasses, rushes, and willow branches. With the warm climate and the abundance of fruits and animals on the Eastern Continent, the primitives did not need permanent shelters.

The tall woman with the beetle in her hair was apparently the headwoman. Paul did not have the words to communicate well with her, but he and Duncan were made to feel welcome and reasonably safe nevertheless. She carried a gnarled wooden staff whose handle had been polished smooth by the sweat of many palms. A jagged line of inset sharp teeth ran along the striking edge of the wooden staff, making it a vicious-looking weapon.

An animal carcass roasted over a greenwood fire, filling the air with aromatic smoke. Paul had eaten only fruits and berries for the past several days, and the meat smelled delicious. The headwoman gestured for them to partake of chunks of meat, which they had to tear carefully from the hot, roasting animal with their bare fingers.

Paul didn't quite understand how he and Duncan fit in among these people. They understood so little. How long would their welcome last? The two of them had been running for days, and Paul doubted they could convince the tribe members to lead them back to civilization.

The primitives had cut down the assassins' bodies and dragged them through the forest. When the group reached the settlement, men and women fell upon the corpses, stripping them of valuables, as if this were any other day's chore. With nimble hands they removed clothing, boots, and equipment belts. The primitives had no experience with the night-vision scopes, communicators, or intricate weapons. They squabbled over the objects, which they saw only as incomprehensible *objects* rather than anything useful.

Some women wore the bloodstained tunics of the dead assassins. They hung stolen trousers and jackets next to intricately patterned tapestries from the Sisters in Isolation. Paul was surprised to see how well they cared for the woven fabrics.

When the bodies of the assassins—all impolitely naked—were piled in a heap, Paul wondered what the primitives intended to do next. Would they make a bonfire to dispose of the corpses? He feared the wilderness tribes might have some previously unrecorded tradition of cannibalism, eating the flesh of their fallen enemies.

Duncan studied some of the technological equipment taken from the hunters, trying to glean useful information. Most of the devices were Ixian, obviously bought on the black market. The assassins' clothes bore subtle but definite indications of Grumman manufacture.

"The Viscount has never been shy about taking credit for the harm he causes," Paul observed. "He is proud of it."

"True, but why would he be so blatant? What does he really hope to gain? Are we playing into his hands? He has to know that when he pushes the rules so far beyond their extremes, the Emperor is bound to respond."

Looking at one of the bodies tangled in the pile, Paul spotted a red scar in the meat of his left deltoid. The mark was repeated on all of the cadavers. "Duncan, what's that?"

Duncan sliced into the still-pliable shoulder, cutting with the point of his knife and twisting. He removed something that looked like a tiny metal spider with long fibrous legs that had extended into the muscle tissue. He held it up.

Even though it was covered with blood, Paul could clearly see what it was. A locator device. "They kept electronic trackers on their own assassins."

The reclusive people, particularly the gray-haired headwoman, curiously watched the activities of Duncan and Paul, not comprehending why they would cut into the shoulders of their fallen enemies. Perhaps they assumed it was some victory ritual, like their own.

Duncan rolled the corpse off the pile and bent over another one, finding the same surgical mark, and dug into the flesh with his knife. "Hurry, Paul! We have to remove these trackers before it's too late. Somebody may already be triangulating on them."

The largest army and most thorough tactical plans can be made vulnerable by the smallest misplaced detail.

—THUFIR HAWAT, *Strategy Lessons*

A dense seasonal fog rolled over the Elaccan continent, and Leto and Gurney crept in with it.

The daily mists provided moisture for the fogtree forests. Basketlike cradles of branches grew upward to form intricate nests. The fogtrees were fragile things that reacted to the smallest environmental changes. Years ago, before Paul's birth, an insidious biological blight had been unleashed upon Elacca, devastating the sensitive trees. House Moritani had been blamed, which had ignited an earlier flare-up of the feud.

The fogtrees, more than just an unusual natural growth, were considered an Elaccan art form. Artists, selected from across the Imperium for their telepathic abilities, could nurture the trees as saplings, using a focused mental vision to guide the branches into specific forms, sculpting them into fantastic shapes.

Vidal had built his palace stronghold within a prime-cluster of large fogtrees. The high branches had been groomed and shaped into a magnificent defensible residence ten meters above the ground. Seven large trunks stood in a circle, reaching up to the labyrinth of boughs that formed a warren of separated rooms, woven chambers for the Elaccan Duke and his household.

Vidal's fogtree fortress was more than a kilometer from his massed military ships, the barracks and tents of rebel soldiers, and all the defensive weapons he had gathered. In the dense morning mist the thin interwoven branches looked like skeletal claws tangled in cotton. As Leto peered up at the eerie sight, Gurney cautioned him. "Vidal's real guards would not stand around gawking like tourists."

Leto shuffled along beside his companion, drawing no attention to himself. The two men wore uniforms stripped from the bodies of Elaccan rebels that had been killed while attempting to escape from the Archduke's palace. It had taken only half a day for the palace tailors to launder and resize the enemy uniforms to fit Leto and Gurney, while document specialists altered the soldiers' IDs.

The key to their infiltration was a detailed topographical projection that allowed Leto and Gurney to traverse the supposedly impenetrable wilderness near Vidal's fogtree stronghold. Because Archduke Armand believed in natural science as much as commerce, he had long ago surveyed and mapped all the terrain on Ecaz, particularly the fertile cloud-forests and valleys of the Elaccan continent. With these high-resolution terrain maps, the two men had been able to slip through the densest groves and rocky valleys, weaving through difficult forest canyons, using byways that even Prad Vidal likely didn't know. They crossed an enormous fallen log over a narrow gorge to reach the fogtree fortress.

It was shortly before daybreak with a high moon silvering the fog. Twenty guards patrolled the outer perimeter in pairs.

When they neared the prime-cluster of trees, Leto and Gurney walked together, alert, sidearms ready, posing as another two guards on patrol. Preoccupied with their apparent importance, they walked right past other pairs of gruff guards.

They circled the ring of seven trees, going about their business. While Gurney served as lookout, Leto quickly knelt beside one trunk, reached into his small pack, and withdrew a silver hemispherical disk from the bottom of which extended a pair of sharp prongs. He slapped the disk against the fogtree and worked the prongs into the bark. The green ready light winked on.

"All right, Gurney—let's move." Leto planted one of the silver blisters on the next trunk as well, followed by the next, circling the perimeter until all seven had been rigged.

By now, Gurney had mentally tracked the patterns of the other guards. "Three more minutes, my Lord, and they should be at their widest dispersal."

The two intruders waited, and the mist seemed to thicken. Leto held the activator in his hand, and when Gurney nodded, he pressed the button.

The high-capacitance dischargers made almost no sound as they released a powerful static pulse into the tree trunks. The giant fogtree structures, sensitive enough to be guided by faint telepathy, were utterly vulnerable to such an intense burst. The willowy nested limbs twitched like the legs of a dying insect, then drew together to form the bars of a cage.

"Like shigawire bindings," Gurney chuckled. "The more you struggle, the tighter they pull."

The interlaced walls of the fogtree fortress now turned the separate rooms into prison cells. Though the Elaccan trees responded to any disturbance by coiling and clenching, they were not flimsy by any means. Fibers ran through their branches like plasteel cables. As the smaller rooms compressed, some of the sleeping people were crushed; a few could be heard gasping and crying out as they slowly suffocated.

Prad Vidal and his family, though, were very much alive. The Elaccan leader shouted from within his bedchamber, wrapping his hands around two of the bowed-over branches and pushing his face to a small opening. "This is an assassination attempt!"

Below, the guards ran about, trying to pinpoint the source of the attack.

Armand Ecaz had given Leto and Gurney specialty equipment used by Ecazi jungle workers. Strapping on needle-sharp claw gloves and sticky toepads, they climbed like beetles, slipping upward and unseen into the thickening mist. They had to be swift now, and bold.

Vidal spotted the two men climbing, saw their Elaccan uniforms, and thrust his hand through the opening in the clenched branches. "Free me from this! Do you have cutters?" Dangling from the trunk by their claws, Leto and Gurney halted. Without answering the rebellious leader, Leto removed a diamond-edged circular saw designed to slice through difficult branches. When Vidal saw it, he exclaimed, "Good, hurry!"

Gurney scrambled up, but Leto gave him a quick signal. "This is my responsibility."

When Leto started the whirling branch-cutter blade, the diamond teeth were enhanced by the glow of a hot laser field. The Elaccan Duke stretched out his grasping hand. It was clear he did not recognize either Leto or Gurney in their Elaccan uniforms. "Quickly! The imposter Archduke must be behind this."

"I know the Archduke very well," Leto intoned.

Watching Vidal desperately extending his arm, Leto could not drive away horrific images of his wedding day. He thought of his friend Armand, crippled for life, his arm severed. And dead Rivvy Dinari, the fat Swordmaster killed as he shielded his master with his own bulk. And Ilesa, sweet, innocent Ilesa, butchered during what should have been her happiest moment. The other dozen people dead, many more injured.

Any man who could order such a thing was a monster, an animal.

"Archduke Armand Ecaz was my friend," he shouted. "His daughter would have been my wife, but she is dead now." Leto had not yet loved her, but he *could* have. And that made all the difference.

Vidal gasped as he saw the blade getting closer. Suddenly realizing who faced him, he sucked in great astonished breaths and recoiled into the cramped room.

The diamond blade swept downward through the intertwined branches. Leto barely felt any resistance at all.

Despite his fury, grief, and horror, there were barriers an Atreides would not cross. Duke Leto descended from a long line of proud noblemen. He used the cutter to slice through the fogtree branches, carving an entrance for himself and Gurney. They pushed forward side by side, Leto holding the still-spinning saw.

Trapped inside his chamber, Vidal was unable to find the breath even to scream.

Leto remembered the threat to his household, to his son and heir Paul. The Grummans were behind the outrageous actions, but the Elaccan Duke had plotted the actual event and planted the hexagonal cutter discs in the terra-cotta pots. The wedding bloodbath had been this man's responsibility. He had thrust himself into this War of Assassins.

But Leto refused to follow his enemy over this particular moral precipice. Out of revenge, he could have cut off Vidal's arm, could have tortured him. But that was not the course of honor. Abiding by the rules of civilization was not a weakness. *The forms must be obeyed.* There were necessities, wars to end, lives to save.

"By the laws of the Great Convention, the established

rules of conflict among the Landsraad," Leto intoned, "I hereby execute you in the name of peace." Vidal writhed, tried to fight back, but Leto continued, "Thus, I end this feud on Ecaz."

He did what had to be done, without joy, without satisfaction. He pressed the blade release, and the flying cutter shot forward. With a meaty smack, the blade sliced through Vidal's neck, decapitating him cleanly.

Gurney said, "Let's hope those soldiers below will follow the rules of kanly, even if their master did not."

Now the two men stripped off their Elaccan uniforms to proudly display the red hawk crest of House Atreides. Leto also wore an armband given him by Archduke Armand himself.

In the turmoil below, the guards rushed about, still expecting a frontal attack. Some climbed the fogtrees, using crude knives to slash their way into the barred rooms where victims screamed the loudest.

Gurney wrestled with the headless body of Vidal and shoved it through the wall opening. As soon as it fell to the ground, several guards screamed in high-pitched, fearful voices.

"I am Duke Leto Atreides!" The mist seemed to make his shout from inside the chamber even louder. He lifted up Vidal's head by the hair like a trophy. "By the rules of the Great Convention, I have eliminated an enemy to Ecaz, a man declared a rebel and a traitor by your rightful Archduke. We have targeted only the man responsible— *by the rules*!

"If you throw down your arms and cease fighting, none of you will be held accountable. None of you will face trial. If you attempt to resist the commands of your lawful Archduke, we will annihilate you with the full military might of House Ecaz and House Atreides." As he spoke, the mist began to clear.

Leto thrust the severed head forward for all to see in

the dawn light. Down below, the pale, upturned faces of the Elaccan guards were wide-eyed, their mouths agape in astonishment. With a muttered epithet, Leto hurled Vidal's head down among them. It tumbled in the air, then struck the ground with a sickening sound. The guards jumped away.

"Duke Prad Vidal conspired against your Archduke and against House Atreides, aiding the true enemy of Ecaz—Viscount Hundro Moritani. They murdered Ilesa Ecaz at the bridal altar. Vidal was responsible."

The soldiers seemed uncertain, muttering. Gurney finally bellowed, "Are you fools? You know who your enemy is. The Archduke needs you and your sword arms to fight House Moritani. Whom would you rather kill—your brothers, or *Grummans*?"

*Once we decide to fight, we face another question:
Do we fight and* retreat, *or fight and* press forward?

—THUFIR HAWAT,
Weapons Master of House Atreides

By late afternoon, the celebrations of the Caladan primitives had died down. The smoky fire had burned low, and the roasted animal carcass was picked to the bone.

Paul could not relax, though. Hyperaware of his surroundings, he attuned his senses to the hum of normal existence in the jungle, the familiar sounds, the movement of leaves and insects. Now, as he and Duncan sat planning what to do next, Paul detected a subtle change around him, a faint alteration in the forest's rhythm. His brow furrowed.

The primitives sensed the same thing and instantly reacted. The headwoman grabbed her polished club and shouted a high-pitched command.

Duncan rose into an armed defensive position. "Paul, activate your body shield. Now!"

As the faint hum of the protective barrier dulled the subtle jungle sounds, Paul drew his own dagger. He summoned to mind the numerous close-in knife-fighting techniques in which Thufir, Gurney, and Duncan had mercilessly drilled him. He had never killed a man, but he had always known it was only a matter of time, unless someone killed him first. He prepared to fight.

He knew that more of the assassin-trackers had found them.

A projectile launched into the trees around the clearing made an unimpressive, hollow *thump*, followed by the gasp of outrushing gases and a distinct *snick*. Paul heard the two stages, separated by only a fraction of a second, and knew exactly what sort of weapon it was: The first was a kinetic dispersal unit, pushing out a thick fuel-air vapor to fill the largest possible volume; the second was a charge to ignite an incendiary cloud.

Orange flames rolled through the air like a Caladan hurricane, stripping towering ferns and leathery trees to the bare bones of branches in an instant. The fuel vapor was consumed swiftly, and Paul's body shield protected him from the brief but devastating thermal shock wave, but the flashfire was enough to mow down most of the unprotected primitives, leaving them charred and flattened. The merest breath of the focused heat was enough to burn lungs to ash. Some survivors gasped, clutching their chests and throats, trying to inhale, but only smoke came from their mouths.

Most of the beautiful tapestries woven by the Sisters in Isolation had been crisped in the thermal bombardment, smoking as they curled. One of the primitives, her skin blackened, had wrapped herself in a tapestry to smother the fire.

Three dark-uniformed men appeared riding a suspensor platform above the canopy, hunting for their quarry. No longer stealthy killers, the assassins screeched as they fired projectiles from their platform. "For House Moritani!" They shot at Paul and Duncan, whose shields deflected the projectiles. At the moment, the assassins didn't seem to care about any specific quarry.

Those primitives not killed by the incendiary bomb had begun to rally, grabbing weapons. Unshielded, they ran toward the three attackers—and were gunned down, their bodies ripped apart by projectiles.

Paul was not some pampered princeling who needed to be guarded every moment. He noted a flicker of indecision on Duncan's face, which Paul easily interpreted. The Swordmaster was torn between two methods of keeping the young man safe—fight or escape. Paul made the choice for him. Only three assassins remained. "We've got to fight, Duncan. No more running. We're safer if we stop them."

With a bitter quirk of a smile, he said, "As you command, young Master."

Shouting to each other in Atreides battle-language, the pair raced forward. Then, with a sword thrust so ferocious it went through the torso and out the back, Duncan dispatched the assassin who had called out in support of his Viscount.

Paul had no time to admire the kill because a second assassin tossed aside his depleted projectile weapon and retrieved a hooked dagger reminiscent of a fisherman's gutting knife. Facing him, Paul stood in the correct stance, holding his own dagger and turning his shield to meet the hooked blade.

The killer wore a baggy, flexible hooded suit that encased his entire body. When Paul slashed with the dagger, he easily cut through the oily gray cloth. This wasn't body armor, but a thermal suit. The three assassin-trackers must have expected to wade into an inferno. They probably had more incendiary bombs in their arsenal on the hovering platform.

Paul parried the barbed knife with his own, turned about, and thrust in, hoping to score a second slash, but the assassin fought with greater verve now that he had realized that this was no helpless boy.

With his entire focus on the combat at hand, Paul couldn't watch Duncan. The universe had collapsed to nothing more than himself and his opponent. He felt no reluctance about killing this enemy. The massacre and the subsequent assassination attempts had left no room for doubt, and he would not hesitate if the opportunity presented itself. He had trained well for this.

Seeing Paul struggling, Duncan shoved his own adversary aside by using his shield to inflict a blow that sent the foe staggering. He spun and hamstrung Paul's rival with a single slash of the notched sword. The man let out a brief gasp as he fell. Duncan flattened him with a kick and killed him with a thrust of the point, before turning to confront the remaining assassin.

These three hunters were ill prepared for a concerted resistance. Expecting the incendiary bomb to do their work for them, they had come here merely to recover bodies.

Seeing he was alone, the remaining killer produced a second dagger and leaped toward Duncan with a knife in each hand, yelling. In a blur of steel, Duncan thrust the Old Duke's blade through the man's abdomen. The assassin didn't even try to evade the sword.

Thinking the fight was over, Paul resheathed his own dagger.

But the Moritani assassin, whether pumped up on a stimulant or on adrenaline and bloodlust, looked down at the long blade piercing his stomach—and kept coming, pressing himself forward as if the sword didn't exist. He raised his two daggers as if they were lead weights and worked his way in through Duncan's shield.

Duncan struggled with his trapped weapon, twisting to withdraw it, but the man was too close. The sword was caught in the man's rib cage, and Duncan wrenched the hilt in a desperate gesture. The shield generator flickered off.

Paul drew his dagger again, bounded toward Duncan.

The impaled assassin grimaced and lurched forward along the sword blade, bending it. Paul couldn't get there fast enough.

But like an unintelligible banshee, the silver-haired headwoman rose up behind the assassin and swung her fang-inset club. The blow against the back of the man's skull sounded like the splitting of an overripe paradan melon.

⌒

DUNCAN AND PAUL used their field medical packs to help the surviving primitives, but even so, nearly three-quarters of the tribe had been wiped out by the flaming shock wave and projectile fire.

Paul looked around, sickened and unutterably exhausted. "If we were the targets, Duncan, why did they need to kill so many of these people?"

"Their attack shows desperation. I would speculate that these three were the last of those hunting us, but we can't be certain of that."

"So we just keep hiding?"

"The best alternative, I'd say."

Like the previous group, the assassins' bodies carried no obvious identification. Paul's father, as well as Gurney and Archduke Armand, would soon be taking their military forces to Grumman for a full-scale attack—while he and Duncan were skulking about in the jungle.

When Paul spoke next, he used the powers of command that his father had taught him as Duke and his mother had shown him through Bene Gesserit exercises. "Duncan, we will return to Castle Caladan. Hiding hasn't kept me any safer than if I'd remained with my father. I am the heir of House Atreides, and we need to be part of this. I will not turn my back in a fight . . . or a war."

Duncan was alarmed. "I cannot guarantee your safety yet, young Master, and these repeated attacks prove there is continuing danger."

"There is danger everywhere, Duncan." Though he was not a large or muscular boy, Paul felt like a full-grown Duke. The last week had fundamentally changed him. "You saw it yourself—I am *not* protected or sheltered by staying here on Caladan. Even with our best efforts to hide in the most isolated of places, the assassins keep coming after me. And think of all those who have died because of us—these tribesmen, the Sisters in Isolation, Swain Goire. What is the point in further hiding? I would rather stand with my father."

Paul saw Duncan wrestling with this decision. He could tell what the man *wanted* to do; he just had to convince him it was an acceptable decision. "Duncan, look always to the course of honor. House Atreides must fight together. Can you think of a better way to prepare me for what lies ahead?"

Finally, the Swordmaster wiped a hand through his curly black hair. "I would rather be on the battlefield at Grumman, no doubt about it. Our armies can protect you almost as well as I can."

Paul smiled and nodded toward the notched and bent blade that had once belonged to the Old Duke. "Besides, Duncan, you need a new sword."

PART V

EMPEROR MUAD'DIB

10,198 AG

⤳

*Some leaders create great works in order to be re-
membered; others need to destroy so that they can
make their mark on history. But I—I will do both.*

—from *Conversations with Muad'Dib*
by the PRINCESS IRULAN

Whitmore Bludd—architect and Swordmaster—
stood admiring the detailed projection model,
as if he himself couldn't believe what he had accomplished. He smiled at Paul. "Your magnificent citadel
will never be completed, my Lord, and that is by design.
Your followers will see the palace as a symbol that *your*
work will never be finished." With a limber movement
of his arms, he cracked his knuckles. "Nevertheless, I
proudly announce that I am satisfied with the portion I
call Phase One."

On the solido hologram that covered a conference-
room table, the main part of the immense fortress, already
as large as a small city and centered on the old Arrakeen
Residency, looked solid and tangible; semitransparent ex-
tensions marked new structures that Bludd still wished to
build. He had proposed additions that would be the size of
districts, towers so high that they would experience their
own weather patterns, and labyrinthine corridors that
(some quipped) would require a Guild Navigator to explore.

Paul frowned skeptically. "Master Bludd, the cost of
constructing such a thing would bankrupt CHOAM.

Do you think the financial resources of my Empire are infinite?"

The Swordmaster smiled at him again. "Why yes, my Lord, I do. I present this model not to ask for more money or workers, but to suggest a spectacular celebration, a . . . grand opening of sorts." He activated the holo-controls, and all of his proposed additions dissolved, leaving only the actual structure. "Think of it as a gala celebration. Representatives from every world conquered in your Jihad will come here to demonstrate their obedience."

Chani and Korba were both in the room; their brows furrowed as they tried to digest the foppish man's proposal and its implications. Alia sat at the end of the table, and the holographic image dwarfed her small body. "I think you merely wish to show off your work, Swordmaster," she said.

Bludd seemed embarrassed. "As always, child, you have a talent for cutting to the heart of the matter." He spread his hands in a deprecating gesture. "Naturally, I am proud of my work. Can you think of a better way to cement my place in history? Long after I am gone, I would like to be remembered in the company not just of my old friends Rivvy Dinari and Duncan Idaho, but also my famous ancestor, Porce Bludd, maybe even Jool Noret, the founder of the Ginaz School."

Korba said in a low voice, "Security will be extremely difficult with all those planetary governors and Landsraad representatives here. Many of them despise you, Usul."

Paul wished Stilgar could have been here, but the naib was leading a force of Fremen, chasing down another group of Thorvald's persistent followers. Paul frowned at Korba. "Do you say that protecting me is not possible in such a situation?"

Now Korba seemed offended. "Of course not, Usul."

Bludd asked, "With your prescience, could you not identify and eliminate any danger?"

Paul sighed. With every battle, every crisis, every failure (that his faithful viewed as "tests" rather than mistakes), he could not help but be reminded of how uncertain his knowledge was. Year by year, as the Jihad worsened and he saw no end in sight, he doggedly stuck to the path that had once seemed terrible but clear.

In recent days he'd experienced a recurring dream that baffled him, a vivid image of a leaping fish carved of wood over thick brown waves, also of wood. A symbol of his childhood on Caladan, now turned false? Was he the fish? He had no idea what the dream meant.

"My visions are imperfect and incomplete, Whitmore. I can see the great swell of dunes in the desert, but I do not always know the movement of individual grains of sand."

Even so, as soon as Bludd had suggested the festival, Paul had sensed a tumultuous and chaotic clash of futures, many of which held grave danger for him. Some possibilities even offered a path to martyrdom. But he knew that, whatever the cost, humanity must survive for an even more incredible battle to come in the far future. While looking so far ahead, though, he had to beware that he did not fall into a pit at his feet.

The very fact that so many people believed in him and prayed to him, that they believed Muad'Dib saw all and knew all, paradoxically muddled his ability to perceive the workings of the future. But the future was always there in front of him, alternately veiled or exposed in fine detail. Wherever his destiny led him, he could not escape it. The path he would take was, and would be, determined by both Fate and his own actions.

He made his decision. "Yes, it is time to announce my victories and give the weary people something to celebrate. Send for Irulan. Tell her I need her."

~

BECAUSE THE PRINCESS sequestered herself in her private chambers and offices, a few wagging tongues suggested that she had taken a secret lover since she did not share Muad'Dib's bed. The more faithful believed that Irulan simply meditated in private on her awe for Muad'Dib.

But Paul knew that Irulan spent most of her days occupied with the next volume of her massive biographical project. He had read some of her draft passages, noting occasional errors and fabrications designed to build his image as a messiah. Because her alterations almost always coincided with his purposes, he rarely asked her to change what she had written. He smiled, thinking of this.

She takes grains of truth and builds them into vast deserts.

He had asked his spies to watch for any seditious treatises or manifestos that she might attempt to circulate among the populace. Thus far they had found no cause for concern. He didn't think Irulan would try to foment a revolution, simply because it did not make sense for her to do so. Though he didn't trust her entirely, he could rely on her for certain things. Such as now.

Pursuant to his summons, Irulan arrived at the conference room where Bludd's citadel model still shimmered, although the wiry Swordmaster had already gone away to begin his preparations. An army of workers would complete the finishing touches, cleaning and polishing every corner, slab, and engraving, though Bludd insisted on doing the final ornate work in the Celestial Audience Chamber with his own hands, claiming his personal standards of perfectionism were far more rigorous than any other man's (though Korba disagreed).

Irulan's long blonde hair was tied back in a serviceable, yet not extravagant, style. Paul liked her better this way than with her formal hauteur. Her blue eyes studied the others who were present. "You summoned me, Husband?"

"I have a new task for you, Irulan—one for which you are well suited. It will require that you re-establish connections with the once-prominent families of the Landsraad." He explained about the proposed ceremony. "Help me to summon them here. Bring forth one representative from every world in my Empire to celebrate the completion of the first part of my palatial fortress."

When Korba spoke, he found a way to impart vehemence into every word. "This festival will also force every leader to prove his loyalty to Muad'Dib. My Qizarate will help administer the details. We will call this the *Great Surrender*. All must comply. Attendance is mandatory."

Irulan was surprised. "Even my father, from Salusa Secundus?"

Paul tapped his fingers on the table. "Shaddam IV is one of my subjects as well. He is not exempt."

Irulan's face took on a calculating expression. "I can help you write the invitations, send summonses that will not be ignored, but are you aware of how much such an extravagance will cost you? Plus the commotion, the security issues, the traffic flow through the spaceports? Can the Guild handle the transport details?"

"The Guild *will* handle it," Paul said. "And the lords themselves will help defray the expense. Each representative shall come to Dune with his frigate's cargo hold filled with water."

Irulan's eyes showed surprise, then admiration. "A neat trick. Such a thing will not unduly strain the coffers of any planetary lord, and the Fremen will delight in it. A perfect symbolic gesture."

"Symbolic and practical. We will distribute the water

to all the people in Arrakeen," Chani said. "It will show the benevolence of Muad'Dib."

Irulan bowed slightly to him. "I will write my father immediately and compose missives for Guild couriers to deliver to the Landsraad nobles and other dignitaries."

Paul had no doubt that she would sign each one "Princess Irulan, Daughter of Shaddam IV, Wife of Emperor Paul-Muad'Dib Atreides." And that was her due.

It was from Count Hasimir Fenring that my father learned to use people as bargaining chips.

—from *In My Father's House*
by the PRINCESS IRULAN

S ire, I bring a message from your daughter, the Princess Irulan."

Dressed in his gray Sardaukar uniform, Bashar Zum Garon held his officer's cap in one hand and with the other he extended a message cylinder to Shaddam, who had just finished breakfast with Wensicia and her husband in the austere drawing room of his private residence. An attendant had taken the baby away for now; Shaddam couldn't abide eating with all the fuss surrounding the infant.

"And what makes you think I want to hear from her?" Shaddam motioned for Wensicia to accept the transmittal. "I would rather hear from Count Fenring."

Sitting too close to Wensicia, Dalak brightened. "Sire, would you like me to write my cousin? Perhaps this time I can convince him to come back to us. I am happy to continue trying."

Wensicia frowned at her husband. "Stop overestimating your own importance and influence. It has become tedious. Count Fenring barely even remembers who you are." Dalak had left Salusa twice in the previous six months, brightly insisting that he could find and talk to his cousin. Each time, however, he had "encountered travel difficulties" and was unable to reach the Tleilaxu, much less find Fenring, though Bashar Garon never seemed to have such troubles. Both times Dalak had returned looking childishly abashed, shrugging in embarrassment at his incompetence.

Shaddam, however, had discovered exactly what Dalak was up to on these extracurricular expeditions. Wensicia's simpering husband was less of a fool than he appeared to be—and more of a Fenring. Shaddam intended to deal with the man's indiscretions in his own way. . . .

Wensicia studied the message cylinder suspiciously. "This bears both Irulan's personal seal and the royal seal of the Emperor."

"Official business," Garon said, still standing at attention. "And, no, Sire, I have not been able to make Count Fenring reconsider. He sends his regards along with a thousand apologies, but circumstances will not permit his return to Salusa."

"And did he give you any response to his dear cousin's pleas?" Shaddam looked pointedly at Dalak, who cringed.

"He made no mention whatsoever of having any contact with Wensicia's husband, Sire. But I will continue to press him with each visit to the Tleilaxu homeworlds. They have begun to develop your private army, as requested."

"Whether or not his cousin can convince him, as our plans build toward fruition, Hasimir won't be able to resist getting involved. I know it."

Dalak seemed eager to change the subject of the conversation. "I thought Irulan wasn't allowed to participate in official business?" He peered over his wife's shoulder to study the sealed message cylinder. "Is Paul Atreides finally going to send troops and work crews here to begin the terraforming? I would love for our little Farad'n to grow up in a more hospitable place."

Wensicia broke open the seals and read the missive.

"Muad'Dib means to show off his new citadel, which he claims surpasses the old Imperial Palace on Kaitain in both size and opulence."

His mouth curling downward bitterly, Shaddam looked out the reinforced window onto the devastated landscape. "Anything surpasses what I have now."

"He requests a representative from every world and every noble family, including the Corrinos on Salusa Secundus. He will even generously ease the travel restrictions that keep you bottled up here." Wensicia looked up. "It is more than an invitation, Father: It is a summons. You, or your representative, are *required* to attend a Great Surrender ceremony on Arrakis—bringing a cargo hold full of water as a gift for the Emperor."

"I am the Emperor." Shaddam made the comment out of habit, without much conviction.

"It is to be a gift for Muad'Dib. There are other specifics here, concerning the minimum amount of water."

"I was given to understand that similar messages have gone out to all planetary leaders. I do not advise ignoring the summons," Bashar Garon said. "His fanatics would seize upon any excuse to kill you and end the Corrino bloodline forever."

Shaddam knew the commander was right. "Does it specify exactly who must attend? Or will any representative do?" His gaze fell on Wensicia's milquetoast husband. The thin little man always dressed in silk and lace, and swooped around like a prince at a costume ball, oblivious to his stark surroundings or the plight of his father-in-law. "Maybe it's time for you to make yourself useful, Dalak. Give me the sort of advice and counsel that Count Fenring once provided for me. Kill some of my enemies, as he did. Go there as my representative and find a way to assassinate Muad'Dib."

"Sire?" Dalak's face turned the color of pale cheese. "Don't you have other people to do that for you?"

"No one as expendable." Shaddam was pleased to see the shocked expression on the man's face, as if he had never been so blatantly insulted before. "What good are you, Dalak? Hasimir could have done it easily. My daughter says that the first thing you do after you awaken is look at yourself in a mirror at the foot of your bed. Is this the best sort of ally I have now? No wonder House Corrino is in such disgrace."

Dalak stiffened, gathering a thin and fragile shell of pride. "I groom meticulously to present myself well in your royal court. I do it all for you, Majesty. And I would do anything you command. It is my duty. My life revolves around restoring glory to House Corrino."

"Ah, restoring glory to House Corrino. Perhaps I can help." Shaddam sent a signal, and four of his servants entered from a side door, nudging along several large crates that were lightened by suspensors. "These crates contain some of the greatest and most valuable Corrino family treasures. They are *restored* to us now. Somehow, they vanished from our private vaults and secret hiding places. These treasures found their way onto the black market."

From the panicked look on Dalak's face, Shaddam could tell that the man knew precisely what the crates contained. "I . . . I am glad to see them returned to their rightful owners."

Shaddam got up from the dining table and walked over to the man. "It was rather difficult, and expensive. I am sure, however, that those costs can be retrieved from your own private accounts."

Wensicia looked at her husband as if he had become a putrefying mass of flesh. "You stole and liquidated Corrino heirlooms?"

"Certainly not!" Dalak's indignant demeanor was not quite convincing. "I had nothing whatsoever to do with anything like that."

Shaddam continued, "We now know why he had such

difficulty reaching the Tleilaxu worlds and speaking with Count Fenring. He was much too preoccupied by other business."

"No—I deny it completely. Where is your proof?"

"An Emperor's word is all the proof any loyal subject should need." Indeed, he had sufficient documentation, hidden receipts, secret images of the transactions occurring. There could be no question at all. Shaddam glanced at Bashar Garon. "Do you have an extra weapon on your person that you might loan to this young man? One of the daggers or handguns you keep in your boots and sleeves? Or perhaps that little poison dart pistol in your inside jacket pocket. That seems an adequate weapon for my effeminate son-in-law."

Dutifully, Garon reached into his coat and brought out the tiny weapon, not certain what Shaddam intended. The dart pistol was flat and half the size of his hand.

Dalak was deeply frightened. Count Fenring would never have acted so, even in the direst of circumstances. "Sire, there has been a misunderstanding. I can prove my worth to you. Let me speak to my cousin. I can convince him to return to Salusa. I know I can! I will do anything you ask."

"Since Dalak is such a loyal subject," Shaddam said to the Bashar, "you'd best give him the weapon. I may need him to use it in my service."

Without questioning, Garon handed the deadly device to Dalak, who accepted it reluctantly. Shaddam saw Garon rest his hand on the hilt of his sword so that the weapon could be drawn quickly if necessary. Shaddam thought, *A Sardaukar is always dependable.*

In an icy tone, the fallen Emperor gave patient instructions to his son-in-law. "First, some basic information. To fire the weapon, lift that panel with one of your nice long fingernails and press the button beneath. Now, do you see where the darts come out?"

Dalak scowled at the device. "Uh . . . yes. Y-you want me to kill someone with this, Majesty? Who displeases you?"

"Don't point it in the wrong direction." He spoke as he would to a child. "Do you have the courage to use it?"

The man swallowed hard, looked at his wife, and then said with false bravado, "If you command me to do so, my Emperor." He seemed to think he could get out of this.

"Good." Shaddam gave his daughter a pitying glance, but she seemed intrigued rather than frightened. Although he hadn't told Wensicia about the thefts before today, the two of them had already discussed Dalak in detail and decided he was not the complete sycophantic fool he appeared to be. "Now, access the button, point the weapon at your own head, and fire."

"Sire!" He scowled like a stubborn little boy. "Is this some sort of test?"

"Yes, a test. You have already proved your flaws and your guilt. Can you prove your loyalty?" Shaddam turned to the Sardaukar commander. "Bashar Garon, are you willing to give your life if House Corrino requires it?"

"Always, Sire."

"So, a mere soldier is more loyal than my own son-in-law. Wensicia, you have made a bad choice of husbands."

"He was supposed to be more than that," Wensicia said.

"Marrying him should have been a peace offering to Count Fenring, but apparently Hasimir is no more impressed with this man than I am. Therefore, I see little point in keeping him around. Dalak has done his duty, gotten you pregnant so that you bore me a male heir, at last." He looked over at the crates of recovered family treasures. "But I shall not abide treachery against me, and I despise thieves."

The young man was both angry and terrified. "If this

is how the Imperial family sees me, then I will gladly leave Salusa Secundus."

"You'll leave, but not in the manner you'd prefer." Shaddam nodded to the stoic Sardaukar commander, feigning terror. "Oh dear, Bashar! Look, this man is pointing a deadly weapon in my presence! Protect us from this fanatic and his dart pistol. Kill him."

Dalak dropped the weapon as if it had stung him, and he raised his hands, backing away. "I am not armed. I am no threat."

Hesitantly, Bashar Garon slid his Sardaukar sword from its scabbard. The well-honed blade gleamed in the light of the room. "Are you certain, Sire? I would rather blood this in battle, than against an unarmed fool."

"But you will do it if I command you?"

Garon did not look pleased. "Of course."

"Oh, enough of this!" Wensicia snatched the dart pistol from the floor and without flinching fired an array of tiny darts into her husband's chest. Little flowers of red bloomed on his shirt, and he dropped to his knees, crying and whining. She leaned close to his ashen face, as if she meant to give him a last kiss on the cheek. "When he grows older, I'll tell Farad'n what a gallant, strong man his father was, and how you died defending us. History sometimes requires little fictions like that. We'll say that one of those renegade prisoners broke through security, and you saved us all."

Dalak wasn't listening anymore. He slumped to the floor and died.

"So much easier than a divorce." Wensicia tossed the dart pistol at the body. Watching her, both surprised and impressed, Shaddam thought this daughter was better suited to ruling than her older sister Irulan was.

As Garon resheathed his still-clean sword, Shaddam noticed that the soldier looked troubled by what he had just witnessed. "I apologize for this unpleasantry,

Bashar, but it was unavoidable. A matter of cleaning house."

The craggy-faced commander bowed his head in acknowledgement. "There is still the matter of sending a representative to Muad'Dib's Great Surrender ceremony, Sire."

Briefly, Shaddam considered sending the dead body of Dalak—now that would be an insult! "Does the summons require my ambassador to be alive?"

"I will go," Wensicia said, a little too eagerly. "As the daughter of Shaddam Corrino IV, I will speak on your behalf."

Rugi burst into the room carrying the baby, even though she had not been summoned. The teether in Farad'n's mouth had once been used by Rugi herself, and bore a golden lion crest. Seeing the dead body on the floor, she almost dropped the child. "Oh! What happened to poor Dalak?"

"A terrible accident," Wensicia said. "Lock the door behind you, please."

Rugi did so. Nervously, the young woman with light brown hair stepped around the corpse and passed the child to Wensicia. "Your poor husband! Shouldn't we call someone?"

"There's nothing to be done." Wensicia brushed the baby's dark hair out of his eyes. "You are not to discuss this with anyone until I have given you instructions. But first we are deciding who will go to a party."

Rugi's face showed her confusion. "We're having a party?"

Shaddam smiled at the baby and said, "Perhaps we should send little Farad'n. No mistaking that message."

Wensicia vehemently shook her head. "Farad'n is your only male heir, Father! He would be too vulnerable on Arrakis. Irulan might even kill the baby out of jealousy, since she hasn't been able to bear an heir of her own."

Shaddam paced in front of the window, then focused his gaze on Rugi. The youngest and most worthless of the brood he'd had with Anirul, Rugi was meek and empty-headed. Before his downfall on Arrakis he had expected to marry her into an important Landsraad house, but since the exile of the Corrino leader, suitors were likely to be men as dismal as Dalak Zor-Fenring.

The former Padishah Emperor smiled to himself. Perhaps Rugi might be useful to him after all. Sending his youngest and least valued daughter to the Great Surrender would also convey a clear message to Muad'Dib.

It is a delusion to believe that anyone can be controlled completely.

—the PRINCESS IRULAN, *private observation*

In the weeks after they met Dr. Ereboam's Kwisatz Haderach candidate, Count Fenring was interested to learn more about how the Tleilaxu had applied Twisting procedures to Thallo in an attempt to control him. With little Marie in tow, the Count and Lady Margot followed the albino researcher into an organic-looking, eight-story building filled with exotic testing machinery.

There, in a laboratory chamber, a large machine whirled an experimental subject around and around inside an oval capsule attached to a long metal arm. The capsule went up and down, in and out and around, subjecting the occupant to very high accelerations and gravitational stresses.

Marie stared at the contraption. "I would like to try that."

Lady Margot felt immediately protective. "Not now, dear child. It isn't safe."

"We would never subject our Kwisatz Haderach to anything unsafe." Dr. Ereboam's pinkish eyes followed the spinning, swooping pod. "It is primarily a centrifuge procedure, combined with precise bursts of finely calibrated energy that penetrate certain areas in the endorphin-infused brain. Think of it as a sorting and filing process. This technique isolates specific portions of the mind, closing off unproductive neural pathways and synapses, while opening others. We have empirical data to prove that such exposure improves both mental and physical performance. Our techniques have proved effective for centuries."

Fenring, though, had his doubts. Thallo might have followed a carefully prescribed genetic blueprint, but he was not as impressive as Lady Margot's own perfect little daughter. Smiling, the Count tousled the golden hair of the girl whose intelligent eyes continued to study everything around her.

When Ereboam turned off the machine, the lithe and muscular Thallo emerged, his body still covered by a beige filmsuit. He didn't look the slightest bit disoriented from the stressful experiment. When he fixed his gaze on Marie's, she met it with her pale blue eyes, unwaveringly. A strange spark seemed to pass between them.

As Thallo approached, the two continued to stare at each other. Much taller, the Tleilaxu candidate carried himself with a casual, almost derisive demeanor.

"We could be taught together," she suggested. Considering the intense training he and his wife were already giving the girl, Fenring was not averse to adding another advantage to Marie's personal arsenal. In order to succeed—with or without the Tleilaxu Kwisatz Haderach candidate—she would have to be the most precisely trained individual in the Imperium.

Ereboam found the idea intriguing. "In the years you have lived among us, Count, your Marie is one of the most interesting subjects I have ever seen. She could be an effective catalyst for Thallo's training."

"And vice versa," Fenring suggested.

↜

"THEY WATCH EVERYTHING we do." Thallo covered his own mouth and was careful not to gesture toward the poorly disguised observation plate mounted high on the wall of their enclosed exercise chamber. "They conceal themselves up there, several men at a time. Thus, the observers themselves affect their experiment. Appallingly poor science."

Marie looked, not caring if she was noticed by the ubiquitous Tleilaxu. During the six years of her life, she'd grown accustomed to having someone monitor her constantly, whether it was her parents, Tonia Obregah-Xo, or unseen spies. Usually, she didn't even think about it. The blank observation plate made no response.

Keeping his hand partially in place, Thallo smiled at her. "They don't see everything they believe they see. I have disrupted their viewing images, added special induction subsonics."

Marie was intrigued. "You can manipulate their technology?"

"They think they have taught me everything, though I have learned much more on my own." He looked at the observation window with a hint of scorn. "By manipulating their technology, I can manipulate *them.*" He seemed troubled. "They consider me to be perfect, yet they always underestimate what I can do. They don't even see the contradiction in their own actions."

"And are you perfect?"

He lowered his voice, revealing a secret. "Nothing can be perfect. It is an insult to the universe." He turned his back to the observation window, then slowly rolled up the stretching, flexible beige fabric of his sleeves to reveal vivid red cuts that marred the pale skin of his arms, interlaced with the scars of older injuries that had healed over.

She leaned closer, her eyes wide. "Was it an accident?"

"I've got more underneath." He stroked his leotard-covered chest and legs. "Flaws disguise the myth of perfection." He chuckled. "Dr. Ereboam knows, but he has kept it secret from his fellow Masters. He tries to hide sharp objects from me, but I always find alternatives. Your fingernails, for example. They've trimmed mine, but I could use yours."

"You want me to help cut you?" She was curious, intrigued.

"Not now." Moving with an eerie speed and grace, he led her toward a set of metal stairs up to the walkway circling the chamber. He stopped directly in front of the opaque observation film and stared at it, as if he could see inside.

Pressing her face against the barrier, Marie tried to discern even a shadow of the watchers on the other side, but could see only murky darkness. Thallo pressed his palm against the window, bulging his muscles until the barrier flexed inward, but he did not break it. The girl wondered what the observers thought they were seeing.

Quickly bored with that amusement, the two playmates crawled across pipe conduits in the ceiling and dangled high above the floor. Though a fall from such a height would surely be harmful, if not fatal, no panicked guards or researchers rushed in to stop them.

"Don't be afraid," Thallo said. "The Masters will not allow me to come to harm."

To Marie's alarm, he leaped away from the ceiling pipe and into the open air, dropping heedlessly toward the floor ten meters below. But before he could crash onto the hard surface, an emergency suspensor field cushioned him and lowered him gently to the floor. She wondered when and how he had discovered the unexpected safety net, and whether he had fallen by accident just now . . . or if he had tried to kill himself.

Without a moment's hesitation, Marie jumped as well, throwing herself into what would have been a suicidal fall, had it not been thwarted by the safety system. As she got to her feet, delighted, she saw Thallo sitting on the floor, looking as if all the elation had drained out of him. "I am only a candidate. They hope to perfect me, but if I fail, they will try again. And again."

"Fail at what?" She sat beside him. "What do they plan to do with you?"

"I am supposed to be their Kwisatz Haderach." His brown eyes glittered. "When they give me large doses of melange, I sometimes see multiple futures for mankind. One of them always clears up, like sunlight cutting through fog, and I see myself as the Emperor of the Known Universe. That is what they want—for me to be their puppet, after I overthrow Muad'Dib."

"Very ambitious." She did not doubt him for a moment. Her parents had said they wanted *her* to eventually sit on Muad'Dib's throne, so why were they cooperating with the Tleilaxu now? Did they expect Marie to be Thallo's consort someday?

"But because I can see the future, I *know* that I will not succeed. Therefore, I am not perfect." Thallo's voice trailed off and his shoulders sagged, as if the immensity pressed down upon him.

On impulse, Marie reached out and slashed a fingernail across his cheek, a wound that his filmsuit could not cover. Thallo recoiled. Then, seeing the blood flow, he grinned at her. "Friends," he said.

Moments later, Dr. Ereboam hurried into the chamber alongside Marie's parents. "Why did you do that to him?" the albino researcher demanded, grabbing Thallo's head and studying the deep scratch on his cheek. He wiped away the small amount of blood and sprayed a substance on the wound.

"We were just playing," Marie said sweetly. "It was an

accident." She exchanged glances with her mother, who frowned disapprovingly. Lady Margot had taught her daughter in the use of fingernails as a Bene Gesserit fighting skill.

Thallo agreed. "Just an accident."

"Have the girl's nails trimmed," Dr. Ereboam demanded.

"I will *not*," her mother said.

"She cannot really harm Thallo, hmmm?" Fenring said. "If he is to be your Kwisatz Haderach, he shouldn't be afraid of a little girl."

Marie put on the most innocent, cherubic expression she could manage.

~~~

IN ENSUING DAYS, Marie and Thallo were permitted to spend time with each other regularly. The Tleilaxu researchers established what they called "interactive scenarios" that sometimes put them together in formal laboratory chambers, while at other times their interactions were more casual and unchoreographed.

They played games, running through common rooms and corridors. The pair even ate meals together, during which Marie once started throwing food just to shock the observers, pretending to be a child having a tantrum. Noodles, stew, fruit, drinks, and plastic table settings flew back and forth. Finally, laughing, she and Thallo sat together in a mess on the floor . . . and she surreptitiously pressed a small item into his hand.

"Here. My mother gave it to me for self-protection," Marie whispered, keeping a hand over her mouth to cover her moving lips. "Use it to do little things to yourself. Keep the Masters from controlling you."

It was a multitool containing a tiny knife, an igniter to inflict minor burns, and a long thread that could be discharged and extended as an electronic whip. In the supposed privacy of his room, he could cut, burn, and flagellate himself to his heart's content—until someone forcibly stopped him. Nodding thankfully, he slipped it into a pocket.

Thallo whispered to her, "Someday I'm going to make an extravagant gesture that will really upset the Masters. I want them to be sorry they ever created me. As my friend—my *best* friend—you should help me."

With his wealth and power on Kaitain, my father could dispatch great armies to make entire worlds tremble, and he could command the execution of any ambassador who offended him. He preferred to be feared rather than loved, even by his own family. Sequestered with my sisters in the Imperial Palace, I saw Shaddam IV as a distant figure who would have much preferred to have sons.

—from *In My Father's House*
by the PRINCESS IRULAN

The lack of fanfare that greeted the embarrassingly small ship from Salusa Secundus was a snub to House Corrino. Even so, Irulan went on her own initiative to greet the vessel and whichever representative Shaddam IV had sent for the Great Surrender ceremony. She was convinced that her father would not have come himself.

When she left the citadel for the spaceport, Irulan considered doing so without any extravagant ceremony, dressing in common clothing. After all, Paul apparently liked to walk among the people, letting himself be swallowed up in the populace and pretending to be one of them, as when he went off on his foolish stunt, posing as a soldier on the battlefield of Ehknot. He thought it brought him close to his subjects.

But Irulan did not want to navigate her way through the press of people unguarded, where the dust and the stench of unwashed bodies would fill her every breath. She was the daughter of one Emperor and the wife of another, and insisted on maintaining appearances for her family, even if no one else did. Sometimes she felt that appearances were all she had left.

The Princess chose to dress in a dark blue gown rather than Atreides green or white, then swept her hair up in a simple twist. As she left her private wing of the palace, Irulan summoned a full escort of soldiers and asked several members of the household staff to carry the colorful and impressive banners from the doorway and precede her through the streets, as was her due. Though these were Muad'Dib's soldiers and his banners, they could serve her as well.

It was not the grand spectacle that the Corrinos truly deserved, but it would have to suffice, since too much ostentation could well be interpreted as an insult. She did not feel comfortable unduly flaunting the grandeur and wealth of Muad'Dib while the rest of her family was exiled to a devastated planet. Irulan already knew that her family considered her a traitor simply because she had accepted her situation; she did not wish to antagonize them further.

At the bustling spaceport out on the plains of Arrakeen, the latest Guild Heighliner had disgorged numerous diplomatic frigates that had come in response to Muad'Dib's summons. The clamor, movement, and confusion were incredible. Her father, who had spent much of his reign dabbling with regimented Sardaukar maneuvers, would have been offended by the inefficient chaos.

Frigate after frigate awaited their turns in the disembarkation zones while security troops scanned the exteriors, then boarded and inspected the passengers and their belongings. Each flight crew endured a lengthy interrogation before being released to go about its business.

The Mother Superior on Wallach IX had offered to send dozens of Truthsayers to assist with the interrogations, supposedly as a token of Bene Gesserit loyalty. Such Sisters could detect falsehood among anyone who would try to hide their motives from the Qizarate guards. But Paul had spurned the offer, claiming he did not trust witches any more than he trusted would-be assassins.

The diplomatic frigates were lined up in no particular order on the paved expanse. In the first year of his reign, Paul had increased the spaceport's landing area tenfold, and again as he acquired more ships for his Jihad. Now, each of these vessels carried at least one representative from a surrendered Landsraad family.

Paul had formally demanded a tribute of water from every ship. Qizarate priests were everywhere, guiding groundcar tankers that pumped the water from the holds to fill large decorated cisterns, whose spigots would be opened up for the people during the festival.

At last Irulan tracked down the Corrino frigate by identifying the faded, barely discernible lion symbol of her family painted on the hull, a design that had graced incredible structures and inspirational flags for thousands of years. Now the emblem was but a pitiable, stained reminder of the past, and the ship attracted no particular notice. Paul had decreed that the Corrino representative was to be viewed not as a member of the Imperial family, but as a spokesman for a minor House based on Salusa Secundus.

Security guards had already boarded the frigate, and Irulan could see that they had nearly completed their inspection scans of the interior. The ship's cargo holds were being emptied of water. Though Salusa was a harsh planet, devastated by the old holocaust, water was not particularly scarce there. Certainly not like Arrakis.

Irulan called for a fanfare, asked her welcoming party to raise the banners and clear a path for her while her guards stood at arms. Then she stepped forward as the passenger hatch opened and the ramp extended. Onlookers were all around Irulan, watching the constantly changing show of strangers coming from distant planets. By now, they had seen so many hundreds of arrivals that they all looked bored, although the escort party's flags of Muad'Dib gave them something else to consider.

Accompanied by ten disarmed Sardaukar guards, the Salusan representative finally appeared. She looked like a waif, her skin pale, her eyes large and round, her hair a mousy brown rather than Irulan's rich gold or the lush auburn of her sister Wensicia. The girl looked completely overwhelmed.

"Rugi!" Irulan startled the escort guards. Amidst all the background noise, the Arrakeen security troops gave Irulan only a cursory glance, then allowed her forward.

When her sister took dainty steps down the ramp, Rugi was breathing heavily, fighting to control a disturbed expression on her face. She had chosen to wear one of her finest court gowns, which she had taken into exile with her from Kaitain. A stiff, gem-encrusted collar rose higher than the top of her head. Her billowing skirts dripped prismatic lace; a choker of Hagal emeralds encircled her tiny neck, while Mallabor pearls looked like a lather of sea foam across her bodice. Rugi looked as if she wanted to dart back into the safety of her frigate.

Irulan kissed her little sister on the cheek. Though the young woman was about the same age as Paul Atreides, she appeared vastly younger and more innocent. Because of her low ranking even among the daughters of Shaddam, Rugi had received only cursory training from the Sisterhood. She had lived a sheltered life, first on Kaitain and afterward on Salusa Secundus. Irulan understood immediately the message the fallen Emperor was sending: *I could not be bothered to send anyone more important. Thus, I sneer at your summons, Muad'Dib.*

A dangerous game to play, Irulan thought, worried for her father's safety and concerned that he might be planning something even more foolish.

She took her sister's dainty hand—too dainty. Obviously out of her depth, this was a girl who had been bred for court life in the old Imperium, nothing more. "I'll take care of you, little sister. Muad'Dib has guaranteed you his protection." Irulan half expected her sister to pull away and reject her as a "traitor to House Corrino." Instead, Rugi clasped Irulan's hand tightly. With a smile, Irulan said, "We have an apartment for you in the new citadel, in my private wing."

"And rooms for my Sardaukar?" Rugi asked, her voice quavering. "Father told me not to stray from them."

"Yes, we have quarters for them as well." The magnificent Citadel of Muad'Dib could house the entire population of Salusa and still have rooms left over, she thought.

"Father is not happy with you, Irulan."

"I know. We'll have time to talk about that."

Rugi summoned what bravery she possessed. She released Irulan's hand, taking her arm instead, and the two of them strolled together away from the spaceport, followed by the Sardaukar retinue. "I thought Salusa Secundus was bad." Rugi stared at the dusty streets, and winced at the noise and stench. "But this place is much, much worse."

You can have all your paradise worlds; I see Eden in the desert, and that is enough for me.

—*The Stilgar Commentaries*

Jericha had impressive mountains—gray, craggy peaks thatched with glistening snow that provided too many hiding places for Thorvald's rebels. In the five years since the start of the Jihad, Stilgar had seen many things that went beyond the wildest things he'd ever thought of as a Fremen naib. In Sietch Tabr he had considered himself a wise and powerful man, yet he had never seen beyond the horizon of his own planet. Dune had been enough for him then.

But when Muad'Dib asked him to do more, he could not refuse.

In preliminary reports, Stilgar had heard about the harsh conditions that awaited his troops once they got high above the tree line to the windswept fastnesses where Memnon Thorvald's guerrilla troops had concealed a weapons stockpile. He had laughed at the warnings about weather. Cold, snow, blizzards—such weather could not possibly be more dangerous than the sandstorms he had endured for most of his life.

As the date of the Great Surrender ceremony approached, more than a thousand representatives had already traveled to Arrakeen to pledge themselves and show their humility. Stilgar longed to be back in Arrakeen where he could stand at Muad'Dib's side and be the first to embrace him. But the press of the Jihad did not slow for festivals or celebrations. The fighting would not stop, no matter what Muad'Dib decreed. For now Stilgar had another job to do.

The nine surviving rebel nobles in Thorvald's persistent insurrection had sent a defiant announcement to a number of fringe worlds. Thorvald had proclaimed his own gathering of opposition leaders and provided cryptic instructions on where to meet.

Paul had looked genuinely sad as he dispatched Stilgar and a special group of crack soldiers to Jericha. "Everyone else in my Empire needs to prove their loyalty to me, Stil, but not you, and not Gurney Halleck."

For the important assignment Stilgar had selected a few of his best Fremen warriors, including Elias, one of the bravest of Muad'Dib's death commandos. Most of this army, though, was composed of Caladan troops, trained and dispatched by Halleck as he did his part to continue the fight. Jericha was a water-rich world, and after his unsettling debacle in the marshes on Bela Tegeuse, Stilgar had requested soldiers with more proficiency in the type of environment they were likely to encounter.

Their path to the rebel stockpile in the Jerichan mountains was slow and tedious. In a brilliant tactical move, Thorvald's followers had obtained and deployed powerful suspensor-field jammers, dangerous and expensive Ixian technology available only on the black market. The jammers were capable of shutting down the engines of scout fliers and airborne assault ships. Stilgar had discovered this to his dismay when he'd sent his first assault team to investigate and destroy the enclave. Every ship in the first wave crashed, plummeting into the rugged mountains before they could manage to get off a single shot.

So, Stilgar had been forced to plan another approach. Since standard flying vehicles and even 'thopters were not reliable against the jammers, he decided to use a more conventional means of locomotion. From small tundra villages—whose men and women enthusiastically swore their loyalty to Muad'Dib as soon as they saw the overwhelming military force—they obtained ruh-yaks: sturdy, shaggy, and smelly beasts of burden. The creatures could carry men and equipment, and their plodding footsteps did not slow (or hasten) regardless of the load they carried. Invoking the name of Muad'Dib, Stilgar had commandeered the entire herd and all the necessary saddles, harnesses, straps, and goads.

With the ruh-yaks, his team could pass through a green stream valley and up into the barren rock to a high pass, following trails that the rebels in Thorvald's stronghold were not likely to suspect. Based on intelligence reports, Stilgar had no doubt that his fighters would overwhelm and crush the enemy. The only question in his mind was how many lives it would cost him.

Leaving the tundra village nearly empty after the people helped Muad'Dib's fighters, Stilgar's men set off to find the weapons stockpile. The ruh-yaks were offensive beasts, stupid, flatulent animals whose thick, matted fur was a haven for biting insects that seemed to prefer the taste of human blood over that of the animals. Some were ornery and stubborn and often made such loud noises of complaint that Stilgar despaired of approaching his target quietly.

Proceeding up steep slopes, plodding relentlessly for more than a day, they finally reached a second river valley that led even higher into the crags. Drawing tributaries from several adjacent drainages, the mountain stream itself was wide and deep, greatly swollen by spring runoff.

"I am not certain we can ford this," said Burbage, the highest-ranking man of Stilgar's Caladan troops, a non-com. "Normally, I wouldn't recommend a crossing for another month or two, until the waters go down. It's the wrong season."

"Muad'Dib cannot keep track of every season on every planet in his Empire," Stilgar said. "He sent us here to wipe out a nest of vipers. Would you like to go tell him he will have to wait?"

Burbage seemed more dismayed than intimidated. He touched a long, thin mark on his cheek. "I got this scar fighting in Duke Leto's War of Assassins, facing the charging stallions of Viscount Moritani. I have been following Atreides orders since long before Master Paul became the man you call Muad'Dib. I'll find a way."

The Caladan man urged his beast to the edge of the river. The current looked deceptively motionless, showing only a few feathery ripples across the surface. Nevertheless, Stilgar could hear the hollow chuckling of water that stirred past rocks on the bank.

"Deep and cold." Burbage raised his voice to the Caladan troops. "But I can swim, and cold doesn't bother me. Shall we go?" His men cheered, and Stilgar was caught up in their confidence.

Burbage's ruh-yak lurched into the water with a great splash, and the other Caladan riders charged forward, cheering as if it were a game. Within moments dozens of the beasts had plunged into the deep, wide stream, striking out into the current and pushing downstream. Quickly the water became too deep for the beasts to find footing, and they began to swim.

Stilgar, Elias, and his Fremen were caught up in the charge, driven into the river, which carried them farther down the valley. When they were in the middle of the channel, algae-slick rocks just beneath the surface began to churn the current into rougher water.

Some of the Caladan troops had already made it across, while several men had fallen off of their mounts and were soaked. They splashed to the bank, laughing, pulling some of their friends back into the water to engage in horseplay. These soldiers had been born and raised around water; they had learned to swim as easily as they walked.

But Stilgar was awed by the swift and powerful current. Elias slipped off of his ruh-yak and flailed in the river, rushing downstream to where he was caught up against jutting boulders. He clung to them, bellowing for help and not willing to let go to swim for the far bank.

Burbage shouted for ropes and swimmers to retrieve the Fremen. Stilgar tried to get close enough to help Elias, but his own thrashing ruh-yak slipped beneath the water. Stilgar went under and instead of letting out a yell, he swallowed and inhaled a mouthful of the river. He began to cough and gasp uncontrollably. The weight of his heavy pack pulled him down.

The struggling ruh-yak tried to throw off its rider and the packs. The equipment fell off first, whisked along in the current. Stilgar couldn't catch any of it, couldn't even keep his hold on the saddle and reins. He found himself drifting free, in clothing that was soaked and heavy. The coldness of the water settled into his chest, squeezing his lungs like an icy fist. He kept going under, choking and coughing; he hadn't been able to draw a decent breath since his accidental gulp of water. The stream seemed so deep, so cold.

He saw a light above and struck out for it, but something grabbed his shoulder, sharp and powerful, like a monster's claw under the water. A tree branch. Tangled in it, he couldn't stroke upward. As his need for air became more and more desperate, he forgot everything Gurney Halleck had taught him about swimming. He felt something tear at his skin. The strap of his pack was snagged on the waterlogged branch.

He had to breathe. His lungs were being crushed. His vision was growing dark. *He had to breathe.* No longer able to bear it, Stilgar stretched his arms toward the sunlight above, pulled, tried to free himself, but finally had no choice but to inhale.

The only breath he could draw, though, was filled with cold, liquid blackness.

⤚⤙

HE AWOKE SPEWING bile-tasting water from his mouth and nostrils. Burbage had pressed hard on Stilgar's upper stomach, making him retch and forcing the water out of his lungs.

A battered and bedraggled Elias stood over him, looking deeply worried, as the naib drew several shuddering breaths. "He will be like Enno, a Fremen dead from too much water and come back to life."

"No fighters will be drowning today," Burbage said with a nod.

Stilgar tried to say that he would be fine, but he vomited again, rolled over, coughed, and spat up more water. His knees and arms trembled. He had no words to explain what he had seen within the light and the water. In the darkness of death he remembered something, but it was fading quickly. A warm, tingling amazement began to spread through him.

Burbage had already sent his soldiers up and down the riverbank to retrieve as many packs as possible. Seventeen ruh-yaks had gone under, while others wandered, wet and dazed, on both sides of the river. Some had vanished completely.

"We're going to miss our weapons and supplies. Now we'll have to move faster to get up to the mountain stockpile," Burbage said. "Otherwise we'll run out of food and fuel before we get there. We'd better hope the rebel larders are well supplied."

Stilgar got to his feet. The sunlight seemed brighter, the drying water on his skin and the foul taste in his mouth were undeniable signals that he was alive. A part of him knew that he had surrendered to death, and would have stayed there if these men hadn't brought him back. It was God's will that he was still alive. He had more work to do for Muad'Dib.

Still slightly disoriented, he recalled when he had first sworn fealty to the young man who would eventually become the leader of the Fremen and the whole Imperium. A huge chamber filled with Fremen, shouting, cheering . . . and he had drawn his crysknife, pointing it over the heads of the throng. The cavern filled with a roar of voices, an echoing chant. "*Ya hya chouhada! Muad'Dib! Muad'Dib! Muad'Dib! Ya hya chouhada!*"

Long live the fighters of Muad'Dib!

Paul had made him kneel, taken the naib's crysknife, and made him repeat, "I, Stilgar, take this knife from the hands of my Duke. I dedicate this blade to the cause of my Duke and the death of his enemies for as long as our blood shall flow."

And much blood had flowed.

But now, through his near-drowning, Stilgar had also come to a deep realization, perhaps even an epiphany. With his own eyes, he had looked upon green forests and swamps. He had seen the sea and fast-flowing rivers. Soon, he would be up in the mountain snows. But Muad'Dib had nearly lost his services because of a clumsy accident. He was certain of where he belonged.

A Fremen was out of place when he was not in the desert. Stilgar needed to serve Muad'Dib back on Dune.

He had been named planetary governor of Arrakis, and Muad'Dib had offered him a position as his Minister of State. He did not belong on the battlefield anymore. He knew that now, as clearly as he knew anything. Others could do this fighting. He would be far more valuable on Arrakeen, fighting political battles.

After he accomplished this mission, he would return to Muad'Dib—and find a way to remain with him on Arrakis.

❧

Weapons come in an infinite variety of shapes and designs. Some look exactly like people.

—*The Assassin's Handbook*

A s little as I am, I can still defeat you." Marie grinned at Thallo. "You may have fooled them into thinking you are perfect, but I know you have weaknesses." The girl crouched in a fighting stance, which made her look even smaller than she really was. Less threatening and deceptively benign. Like her rival on the grassy playfield, she wore a full-body filmsuit and remained barefoot.

"You look just like a harmless child," he countered mildly. "But I no longer make the mistake of underestimating you."

It was early afternoon, a cool day in Thalidei, with trees swaying in a breeze blowing across the polluted lake. Tleilaxu men held onto their weather-hats. Despite the illusion of freedom, Thallo's trainers and observers were always close by. Two lab technicians watched from opposite sides of the field, dictating notes into lapel imagers that sparkled in sunlight.

In the guarded park, Thallo towered statuesque and confident over Marie. He moved only enough to watch the little girl as she circled him. "You bruised me yesterday," he said, "but it will not happen again."

"You enjoyed the bruises." That time, after Marie had struck his lower legs with hard kicks, Thallo had limped back to the laboratory building, unable to hide the pain. Technicians had rushed to apply fast-healing medical packs on him, but Dr. Ereboam insisted on tending the injuries himself, shooing everyone else out of sight—including Marie—before peeling away the beige filmsuit.

Marie realized the truth: Because the albino researcher knew about Thallo's propensity for cutting himself and had carefully hidden the fact from his peers, Ereboam couldn't let anyone see the fresh scabs and old scars. The girl wondered how often the mysterious and insular Tleilaxu lied to each other.

Today, Thallo's limited range of movement suggested that his legs still hurt. Nevertheless, he lunged unexpectedly, striking out at her with a stiff-fingered hand, but she slipped to one side so that he missed her by centimeters. His blow brushed past her, and she didn't even feel the breeze.

With her varied and intense training, Marie considered herself more than a match for this maladjusted Tleilaxu creation. Still, she played—and fought—with him, observing carefully, continually learning, and Thallo was learning from her as well. They would be a formidable fighting team.

Using perceptive techniques her mother had taught, Marie had come to understand Thallo. He had exceptional fighting skills and a wealth of encyclopedic knowledge, but the Tleilaxu treated him as a specimen, a valuable experiment, a child. Sometimes he acted the role of child for his own amusement. Spurts of action and game playing were only distractions for him, after which he would often wallow in depression, as if slipping into a dark chasm. He was falling now; she could see it.

She kicked at his shins with her hardened feet. He dodged, moving back defensively. She pursued, kicking again and again, but narrowly missed each time. Despite her best efforts, even when she was certain the blows had landed perfectly, she never managed to touch him.

Thallo taunted her. "You have to do better than that!" His voice didn't sound quite right; it seemed to come from all directions, as if the breeze scattered it all around her. Was he throwing his voice to distract her?

Marie executed a series of speed-somersaults, spinning past him and then coming around from behind. Finally, just as he turned to face her, she landed with her hands on the grass and launched her tiny body toward him in a proven Bene Gesserit bullet maneuver. She hit the middle of his abdomen—and passed completely through his body, landing in tumbling disarray on the rough lawn.

Thallo laughed at her astonishment "I'm too fast for you!" His lips moved as he spoke, but once more the voice did not seem to come from the right direction. "I am the Kwisatz Haderach. I can do anything."

Marie brushed herself off, glanced over at the observers, whose expressions showed consternation. "How did you *really* do that?" she asked in a low voice.

His face remained cool, like a porcelain mask. "Does a magician reveal the secret of his tricks?"

"To his best friend, he would."

"Friends." He had a perplexed, troubled expression. Then he whispered, "I can't tell you here."

Thallo stood like a statue, exploring his own internal realms. What was he thinking? Was he performing Mentat calculations? His face had gone uncharacteristically blank, and though he stared back toward Marie, he didn't seem to see her. His expression shifted, as if currents were ebbing and flowing in his psyche. She noticed how quiet the training field had grown. On the other side of the bluish grass, the observers seemed to be holding their breath.

"Follow me." Abruptly adopting a childlike personality, Thallo shouted, "Hide and seek!" With that, he darted off. As she ran after him, Marie heard the lab technicians trying to keep up, and calling ahead for assistance. She saw a guard spring into action, running toward them from the right.

With his long, muscular legs and athletic ability, Thallo easily outdistanced the guard and the technicians. Marie kept up with him as she ran down a short slope and entered a moss-overgrown tunnel that passed beneath a walking bridge. In the shadows, Thallo ducked to his right and disappeared from view. She hurried after him into another tunnel, but to her surprise she heard him call from behind, "Not that way. Over here—now!"

Confused, she turned and saw him in low light, just inside the entrance of another tunnel. Thalidei was riddled with them, but he couldn't possibly have moved so swiftly. "How did you get here?"

"More magic." Then, whispering in her ear, Thallo added, "That was just an enhanced solido holo-image out there. I adapted their technology beyond what even the Tleilaxu think they can do. That's why you couldn't touch me. I have been waiting down here all the time."

A light flickered out in the opposite tunnel as the guards pushed inside, angrily trying find them. They did not guess what Thallo had done to their own systems.

Thallo continued in an excited rush, "I can defeat any security and surveillance system they have. This time I will let them catch me, but only because I'm not ready yet."

"Not ready for what?"

"We don't have much time." He whispered his confession to her. "By being so close to perfection, I can plainly see how far I fall short of the mark. Dr. Ereboam knows I am not the flawless Kwisatz Haderach. As soon as the other Masters realize it, they will terminate the experiment—and Ereboam as well. Then they will try again."

Their pursuers came at them from different directions in the shadowy tunnels, shouting, shining lights. Looking meek and immature again, Thallo stepped forward and raised his hands in mock surrender.

≈

THAT EVENING, THALLO disabled the security systems around him and used the same trick for Marie, leaving full-spectrum holos of them in their respective beds. Though the girl was uneasy about slipping past her unsuspecting parents, she calculated that it was a wise investment to see what her purported friend had in mind. *Information is the best defensive weapon.* Before she could confide in her mother and father, she needed to understand Thallo's game.

On a moonless night, the pair of playmates slipped away into silent and brooding Thalidei. They found a place to sit in the middle of a skeletal, abandoned construction site near the shore of the fetid-smelling lake, and they talked for much of the night. As they gazed back toward the flickering lights of the city, Marie continued her own work of understanding, and perhaps even shaping, the young man's psyche as her parents had taught her, hoping to shift Thallo's loyalty to *her* instead of to the Tleilaxu.

This Kwisatz Haderach candidate had more potential than she'd realized at first. Maybe he really could peer into the murky future as he claimed, and maybe he did know with absolute certainty that he was doomed to failure. But if so, he had a blind spot when it came to Marie, and a glaring weakness that she intended to exploit. Thallo was desperate to escape the clutches of the Tleilaxu, and Marie would help him do exactly that.

Danger is the background noise of my life. I cannot separate out a particular threat any more than you could hear a single pop of static in the midst of a lost signal.

—*The Life of Muad'Dib, Volume 1,*
by the PRINCESS IRULAN

The Great Surrender ceremony was planned with even more care and precision than any military strike in Paul's Jihad. When she was not spending time with Rugi, Irulan kept an eye on the preparations, making suggestions from time to time. Armies of devoted volunteer servants, all cleaned up and given new household uniforms, had decorated the enormous citadel in its entirety. Immense banners hung from the cliff faces to the north.

The people of Arrakeen, from beggars to merchants to city guards, had pleaded for a chance to perform even the most menial activities, just so they could say they had been a part of the event. Several deadly knife fights had occurred as people fought over limited slots on the expanded staff.

Security around Paul had been further tightened. Before being allowed to attend the ceremony, every Landsraad representative was interrogated a second time to weed out possible threats. Paul's Fedaykin security did indeed uncover two admittedly inept schemes to smuggle weapons into the Celestial Audience Hall. The would-be assassins' planning had not factored in the sheer size of the chamber in which Muad'Dib would receive them all. None of their little weapons even had the range to reach the Emperor, unless they happened to be seated in the front few rows, and neither of the suspicious nobles had the social standing to be anywhere but the rear of the room. Now, instead of attending the ceremony, the two awaited further interrogation sessions in deep, stone-walled cells.

Irulan saw to it that her sister Rugi had one of the most prominent seats in the hall, right in the first row near the inlaid stone dais. Emperor Muad'Dib would sit in a newly carved elaccawood throne designed and built especially for the occasion. He said the elaccawood from Ecaz reminded him of the War of Assassins from so long ago.

Paul had installed two lower chairs on either side of the new ceremonial chair, one for Irulan, the wife in name only, and the other for Chani, the more significant wife of his heart. One step lower and in the front rested a child-sized but equally ornate chair for Alia. Thus, Muad'Dib was surrounded by three uniquely powerful women.

In an apparent contradiction, Paul had issued orders that—for safety—no one was to use a personal shield in the huge audience chamber. For centuries, the fear of the devastating pseudo-atomic consequences of a lasgun-shield interaction had been a cornerstone of the rules for all forms of warfare. No man would have overstepped those bounds, knowing that the blast would kill not only a target but himself, as well as cause inconceivable collateral damage.

But the emotions, fanaticism, and hatred spurred by his Jihad had lifted many such restraints. One person firing a cleverly concealed lasgun—even a tiny one—upon a shielded person could vaporize the huge palace, Muad'Dib and his entire family, and much of Arrakeen.

An act of once-inconceivable brutality was now a very real possibility. There would be no active shields for the ceremony.

The Celestial Hall was a cavernous, vaulted chamber displaying the pinnacle of architectural finesse and ostentation. Familiar with the Imperial Palace on Kaitain, Irulan had not thought she could be impressed with grandeur, but this was beyond even her ability to absorb. Everyone from the lowest handler of the dead to the wealthiest monarch of a conquered world would feel cowed by this immensity. Yes, Whitmore Bludd had surpassed all expectations.

As part of the upcoming ceremony, Paul intended to commend the Swordmaster-turned-architect in front of all these people, though Bludd had abashedly insisted that his work spoke more eloquently for him than any words he could possibly say. "How could I require adulation from the audience, when I have your respect, and I have this magnificent citadel to show for all history?" Nevertheless, it was plain to see that Bludd would bask in the recognition.

Around the elaccawood throne, the ornately patterned walls were comprised of kaleidoscopically repeating keyhole arches, each the size of a pigeonhole, alternating with small windows of stained glass cut into various geometric shapes. Irulan knew that the intricate pattern had been designed to conceal any number of the Emperor's spy-eyes and sensors. Bludd had been very secretive and dedicated about all his work, like an enthusiastic child working on a special project. Now, the Swordmaster sat in a seat of honor in the front row just below her, resplendent in such fine clothes that he reminded her of one of the peacocks that had once strutted around the palace grounds on Kaitain. He wore his thin rapier and a broad smile.

Nearby, Korba seemed to be praying; he had emphatically refused to be recognized for his part in the work,

wanting no name associated with the palace other than
Muad'Dib's.

When the ceremony finally began, Irulan felt small and
overwhelmed to be facing the hundreds of noble representatives who had answered Paul's direct summons, as
well as the uncounted thousands who had crowded into
the opulent fortress. After Muad'Dib's bureaucratic corps
tallied all those ambassadors who answered the summons
from other planets, comparing names against a chart of
expected visitors, the Emperor would know who had
spurned his command. Then punitive operations would
begin.

As the crowd fell into a hush, Irulan looked at Rugi
waiting among the sea of faces near the front. During
the course of her stay with Irulan here on Arrakis, Rugi
had begun to blossom. Day by day, her confidence had
grown. Even so, Irulan was surprised that today, for the
first time in her memory, Rugi was beautiful. Dressed in
Corrino finery, she wore her family pride like a garment.
Gone were the shyness and insecurity she had shown at
first. Rugi's demeanor made it clear that she was an Emperor's daughter.

Irulan glanced at Chani, noticing how serene and
beautiful the Fremen woman looked. Since she'd been
raised in a political arena, Irulan was willing to accept
political realities. She knew Paul had chosen her merely
to secure his rule, while he kept his desert concubine as
mate. Of course, Muad'Dib could take whatever he
wanted. No one would challenge him if he chose two
wives or took a dozen lovers. Irulan didn't care if he be-
stowed all his *love* on his Fremen woman, but Chani,
like a she-wolf, was not inclined to share her man.

Because of the design of the chamber, the background
sounds were muted. The walls that surrounded the great
throne and its platform, as well as the huge hall, were tex-
tured so as to drown out the murmurous crowd noises.

When Paul stood, the onlookers fell into silence as if they had all been struck dumb. "At the end of war, there is peace." His voice was repeated and amplified cleverly by hundreds of speakers throughout the Celestial Hall. "Over eight hundred representatives and their entourages have come to bow in my name and carry the banner of Muad'Dib. My victory is inevitable—and I would much prefer to do the rest without bloodshed." He paused, and the spectators remained quiet, hanging on his words.

In the ensuing moments of silence, Irulan heard an unnatural, sinister humming sound. Chani noticed it too and spun, trying to pinpoint the source. Irulan saw movement and realized that dozens of the tiny cubbyholes had begun to open up. Small black mouths emitted a faint buzzing noise. Swordmaster Bludd was already on his feet, yelling a warning.

A swarm of hunter-seekers flew out into the room like angry wasps.

I see the monster growing around me, and within.

—from *Muad'Dib and the Jihad*
by the PRINCESS IRULAN

Humming on their small suspensor fields, the hunter-seekers drifted out like predatory eels, accelerating as they acquired targets. Cylindrical shafts as long as a hand, each sporting a poisoned needle at its nose, they rode forward noisily on suspensor fields.

With a flash of icy dread, Paul realized that he had seen this before in a dream—many little attackers, countless stinging needles, a thousand painful deaths. His prescient visions were often confusing and rarely literal. And now another recent dream clicked into place, like a tumbler in a complex locking mechanism: a vivid image of the detailed design carvings on the audience chamber walls blurred together with the wooden fish carving leaping over the wooden waves . . . and the image sharpened enough so that he knew where he had seen it before: on the old headboard of his bed in the Arrakeen Residency.

The headboard that had folded down so that the first hunter-seeker could emerge. That was what the dream had been trying to tell him, but he had not been able to interpret it properly. Not soon enough.

Now he counted at least a dozen of the weapons, then saw at a glance that they had a modified design based on bootlegged Ixian models: self-guiding tracker systems and kill-programming driven by rudimentary impulses. Though based on the same general principles, these looked different from the one that had emerged from his headboard, which had been a mere sliver of metal. These hunter-seekers were more complex, though their primitive programming could target only general victims, not specific individuals. Nevertheless, a Caladan dragon shark was primitive as well, and extremely deadly.

The faint sound of ominous movement, the gaudily dressed audience members, the grand celebration—every instant echoed in Paul's mind in a horrible flash of déjà vu: His father's wedding day, the flying razor-edged disks, Swordmaster Dinari and his heroic death, Archduke Armand mangled. Ilesa so lovely in her nuptial gown . . . then covered in blood.

Chani!

He could not let it happen again.

In a cluster, four hunter-seekers shot toward the throne. With a swift and desperate push, he forced Chani to the floor even as she stood to fight. "Stay down!" In a blur, he then knocked Irulan sideways, sending her to scrabble for shelter under her overturned chair, while Alia bounded down the steps and out of the way.

The first hunter-seeker slammed its needle prow into the center of the throne where Paul had been sitting only seconds earlier.

Reacting without hesitation, Fedaykin guards sprang from the aisles and the sides of the chamber and dove forward to protect Muad'Dib with their own bodies. Bludd bounded onto the stage, his rapier drawn to slash at the whirring projectiles.

But Paul was moving to stop the hunter-seekers himself. The floating needle weapons came so fast that he could avoid them only one at a time. One buzzed beneath his arm, and he twisted violently to the left to avoid its sting. Two Fedaykin threw themselves in the hunter-seekers' paths to intercept the deadly devices with their chests. The men lay writhing and spasming from the discharged poison; they would be dead within moments.

So much panicked movement, and so many people swarming around the throne area, confused the devices' targeting. At least twenty hunter-seekers had been launched, maybe more, and many had already found victims.

With a sharp thrum of metal like a struck tuning fork, Bludd's rapier knocked one of the flying devices out of the air. He stood his ground in front of Irulan, who took advantage of whatever protection her overturned chair might offer. Another hunter-seeker came close, and Bludd battered at it with a flurry of his thin blade.

Without understanding the nature of the threat, the terrified audience began to flee the Celestial Audience Chamber. Those in the front rows turned to run, pushing up against the crush of bodies packed into the immense hall.

Another volley of hunter-seekers emerged from the ornamented openings, and the second wave came streaking toward Paul. Chani lay rigid on the floor, knowing that any movement would draw the attention of the questing devices. But when one of the nearby Fedaykin was struck and collapsed thrashing beside her, she rolled over, instinctively trying to help him.

Paul saw a hunter-seeker change its trajectory and flash toward Chani, but he had become preternaturally aware of each movement around him. With furious speed, he jumped to grab the thing out of the air. Knowing the suspensor field would make a firm grip difficult, he squeezed hard as he clamped down.

He felt a painful, burning sting.

A Mentat assessment flashed the immediate answer to him. The middle of the hunter-seeker's cylindrical shaft was girdled with *another* ring of short, fine needles, also dripping poison. Though the lethal points bit into his hand, he squeezed tighter, seized control, and smashed its nose onto the polished stone of the platform.

He could already feel the poison working its way into his blood, but he had the ability to neutralize it. With the Bene Gesserit cellular powers he had learned, Paul identified the chemicals, unlocked their modes of toxicity, and altered the molecules to neutralize the poison. It took only a moment, but it was a moment he did not have. More hunter-seekers sped toward him.

But now he was immune to that particular toxin, and his body's biochemistry manufactured the antidote. Lunging back to his feet, he grabbed another hunter-seeker that buzzed directly in front of his face. He felt the sting of the needles again as he smashed it to the floor.

Turning to find another target, however, Paul realized that the second device had contained a different poison from the first—equally deadly, but one that required a new, independent effort for him to alter its chemistry and make himself immune. Either of the toxins would have been fatal to a normal human, and Paul had to expend the extra effort to counteract two toxins instead of just one. It was nonsensically redundant.

He suddenly understood that in planning this attack, someone had tailored it precisely, taking Paul's abilities into account—someone who had intimate knowledge of the Emperor's particular skills.

The mysterious opponent had not underestimated Paul-Muad'Dib Atreides. The assassination attempt had come when he was with those he loved, which forced him not only to protect himself but to protect all of them—which meant he was facing a threat as convoluted and extravagant as the most tortuous training sessions that Duncan Idaho and Thufir Hawat had concocted for him when he was a boy. If not for Bludd's assistance, Irulan would probably already be dead.

Paul became like a whirling dervish, grabbing hunter-seekers, smashing them into each other, slamming them to the floor, leaping for others with hands outstretched before they could strike Chani, Irulan, Alia, or even Bludd. His chair was studded with stray hunter-seekers, and each projectile he grabbed was armed with a different poison. More and more complexities!

He was exhausted, his body clamoring from the effort of his accelerated fight as well as from driving back the toxins.

By now the air was abuzz with more hunter-seekers than he could stop, perhaps a hundred. His hands, arms, chest, and back had been stung repeatedly. He could barely concentrate now, forced to devote most of his effort to counteracting the dangerous chemicals building up in his bloodstream. Bodies lay in heaps on the dais and out in the audience. The crowd was a cacophony of screams.

From out in the audience, Korba bellowed orders, finally acting like a Fedaykin again rather than a priest. He commanded the soldiers to shoot out the cubbyholes, preventing more weapons from being launched. Someone— Bludd?—thrust a body shield at Paul and activated it; the field would slow the hunter-seekers, making it easier to intercept them. Bludd activated a shield of his own, apparently having brought the protective devices despite Paul's orders that they were not to be used. Rather than insubordination, the act now appeared to be remarkable foresight.

Korba's men, also wearing full shields, waded through the bodies, using clubs, stretches of fabric, and gloved hands to eliminate more of the hunter-seekers. Over half of the men perished in the effort, but their companions continued, regardless.

Despite his difficulty focusing, Paul at last saw the threat diminishing and he concentrated more of his personal energy on stopping the waves of poison within him. When he finally returned to awareness and found himself collapsed near the base of the throne, breathing heavily, he realized the attack was over.

Or was it? He sensed something more, a brooding danger like a subsonic pulse throbbing at the back of his mind.

Chani came toward him, looking exhausted, but her eyes were bright and her skin flushed pink. She was intact, though her clothes were torn and her hair in disarray. "Usul, you are hurt!"

"I will live." Feeling uneasy, he looked around at the horrific aftermath. Most of the crowd had been evacuated from the Celestial Hall, while more guards and medical personnel were trying to push their way in. All in the audience who had been touched by a hunter-seeker's poison were either dying or dead, and many other hapless celebrants had been injured in the panic.

Paul tried to calm himself, but a threat still clamored inside his skull. As far as he could see, all the devices had been neutralized, and the cubbyholes had been destroyed. Then why did he still feel such imminent danger? It pulsed in his mind, refused to go away.

His head rang, and he found it difficult to think clearly. Though he had counteracted the poisons in his body, their aftereffects left him physically drained.

Still, the sense of supreme danger roared around him like a wind.

Chani sat at his side and put her arms around him, imparting strength to him as she held him close. Suddenly, the silent warning blared in his mind, like an unexpected spike on a power grid. He couldn't understand it, but couldn't ignore it, either. Paul did not question what he felt.

Using the last of his strength, he grabbed Chani and began to move. In the same instant, Swordmaster Bludd surprised them. "My Lord! Down!" Like a juggernaut, Bludd pushed them both so that all three tumbled away from the throne and off the edge of the dais. They fell onto the grisly cushion of dead bodies strewn on the floor about them.

A fraction of a second later, a small, hidden bomb exploded from beneath the elaccawood throne, hurling a rippling fireball over the entire dais.

There is an arrogance to perfection. When one insists on perfection and receives only flawed humanity, the resulting disappointment breeds unrealistic anger and proves only that those in charge are human as well—and deficient.

—*The Dunebuk of Muad'Dib*

W e shall provide a new entertainment today." Thallo's low voice simmered with excitement as he met Marie in one of their designated training areas. The Tleilaxu observers seemed to consider their time together as constructive "play," but Dr. Ereboam had been growing increasingly nervous as he watched the mounting strain on his Kwisatz Haderach candidate. To a great extent Thallo was like a void in human shape, revealing few answers to the questions he sparked about himself.

"What sort of entertainment?" Marie looked around, but saw nothing unusual in the small laboratory chamber. The walls were lined with interactive game simulations and exotic exercise machines. Behind one of the dark, mirrored surfaces she knew the ever-present monitors were watching them. Though she maintained a bright, childish expression, Marie was alert, wary of what Thallo might do next.

Ignoring the observers behind the mirrors, he took her small arm and led her out into the corridor. "I want you by my side. It is a special day, and I have been waiting a long time for this." He marched her toward a security check station where two alert-looking Tleilaxu guards sat, but the lavender scanner lights dimmed and switched off as Thallo and Marie approached. The Kwisatz Haderach candidate and the little girl walked right past the apparently attentive middle-caste guards, who didn't seem to see them at all.

Thallo's ability to manipulate Tleilaxu technology and perceptions seemed almost supernatural. "The Masters have such high hopes for me, but apparently low expectations. They cannot guess the half of my capabilities." His perfect lips quirked into a smile. "Why create a Kwisatz Haderach and then assume he will fit into narrowly defined parameters?"

They passed a second security station, but as before, the pair proceeded without being noticed. At a doorway, Thallo touched an identity pad on the wall, and a heavy door slid upward to allow them access. He flexed his hand. "I know much, much more about Thalidei than they can ever guess."

Marie's wariness increased as they slipped into a high-ceilinged chamber—clearly a heavy-security zone. Her companion sealed the door behind them and reinforced it with a second, heavier plate. "There, now we are barricaded in. We're safe."

"Safe from what?" All of her senses anticipated danger—but from Thallo.

"Safe to do our work." His usually guarded expression had a manic, edgy quality. "Through the prescience the Tleilaxu gave me, I know I am doomed to fail. The mode of my failure, however, is under *my* primary control. And if I am to be a failure, I may as well make it a spectacular one." He touched his forearm where a wet line of red from a particularly deep cut had begun to seep through the filmsuit. "Painful lessons are the ones best remembered."

Inside the chamber, Marie was startled to see nine electronic containment cells, each holding an apparently identical version of Thallo, all muscular, perfectly formed young men. "Meet my brothers," he said. "Replacements prepared by the Masters."

The identical Thallos stood caged in their containment chambers, looking out imploringly. They all appeared awake, hyperaware, and completely trapped, each awaiting his turn. "See, they hope for me to be discarded so that they can be next. Despite what Dr. Ereboam says, the Tleilaxu are a long way from achieving their superhuman."

"Are you going to free them?" Seeing the nine remaining clones, Marie wondered how many previous versions of Thallo had been tried, and discarded. Had he been inside one of those confinement chambers, himself looking out, counting endless days, waiting? How many previous Kwisatz Haderach candidates had been labeled unacceptable and then killed?

Moving with a lithe grace, Thallo bounded up to a mezzanine walkway above the containment chambers. Marie followed him, not showing her uneasiness, looking down at the caged clones that stared out at them, following Thallo's every movement. The Kwisatz Haderach candidate stood motionless in front of an intricate control panel, his gaze far away, as if the complexities had placed him in a trance.

Marie stood at his side, silent and intent. Thallo spoke to her in a low, wistful voice. "Throughout my life the Masters have slapped scanners on my brain, performed chemical tests, twisted my thoughts, recorded my movements and words. But I fixed it so they can do that no more. I fooled them." He looked down at her, his face a mask of pain. "I fooled you, too, Marie."

She said carefully, "I think you're playing another trick on me."

"The extreme knowledge and prescience is too much for me to endure. The impossible expectations placed upon me are more than overwhelming." His face was locked in a grimace, but she'd seen Thallo's swift mood swings before. His outstretched hands hovered over the controls, as if feeling the heat rising from the circuits themselves.

Marie tensed, ready to take necessary action.

"I am more than a clone, more than a ghola," he said, "and much more than a person. Dr. Ereboam fused specific molecular memories into me, from the cells of historical figures that he thinks will aid me in becoming their superpowerful puppet. I sense that I am Gilbertus Albans, who founded the Order of Mentats. I am Jool-Noret, the greatest Swordmaster in the history of Ginaz. I am Crown Prince Raphael Corrino, too—as well as thousands of others."

"I prefer *Thallo* for my playmate," Marie said, sounding intentionally immature. "Let's call Dr. Ereboam. He can make you feel better. Or let my mother try her Bene Gesserit techniques."

"I don't *want* to feel better. I want to make a *statement*. How else to make the Tleilaxu see what they have created, their hubris in believing that such a flawed race could create perfection, and then control it?"

She tried to distract him. "We can escape from here. We can get away from Thalidei, from this planet—see the whole galaxy, just the two of us."

"No matter where I go, I am still a prisoner in here." He tapped his forehead with a finger. "Escaping physically doesn't help the part that's inside me. Or what will be inside *them*." He pointed down to the confinement chambers.

Marie tried to lure him away from the controls. "I don't like this game."

"Game? Call it that if you wish. Now see how I win." When his fingers danced over the controls, the caged duplicate Thallos all screamed in eerie unison, a piercing noise that hurt Marie's ears. "The Tleilaxu are very efficient at killing. They conduct many experiments. Have you seen their catalog of poisons?" The high tone modulated, and blood began to stream from the eyes and nostrils of the numerous copies. Thallo showed no outward pleasure or distress from causing them so much agony. "The nerve agent should be fast acting. I have seen this happen before."

The duplicate Thallos twitched, clawed at the curved but impenetrable plaz walls of their chamber, and then slumped dead, folding their bodies into small volumes like poorly stored marionettes.

"Why did you have to kill them?" Marie was more curious than anguished.

Thallo's porcelain face was flushed with excitement. "I freed them. Now, I shall free myself—and you, too, Marie. I know the impossible expectations your parents have placed on you, too. You and I are the same."

"No!" She put a hand on his arm. "I don't want that."

But his fingers again became a blur over the controls, activating a deep subroutine, awakening a rumble and purr of machinery. The floor and walkway vibrated. "The Tleilaxu Kwisatz Haderach program can never be perfect."

"I'm not perfect either," Marie said, "but I can still do what I need to. My parents trained me. You are highly trained yourself. Think of what we could do together." She lowered her voice as she repeated, "Think of what we can do. . . ."

"I have already done it—I powered up the biogenerators for all of the labs in Thalidei and the underground ducts, the atmosphere-distribution system that runs under the streets and buildings. A most effective nerve toxin, instantly fatal, prepared for a man named Thorvald to be used in his rebellion against Muad'Dib. Thorvald will never receive his poison, though. The entire shipment will be dispersed in a rush throughout the city. The Tleilaxu have good reason to be proud of their poisons— this one is so toxic that the merest whiff will fell the largest man." He smiled, touching the console in front of him and thrilling to the vibrations he felt. "The large containers are currently being pressurized for widespread release." Thallo patted her stiff shoulder. "It will erase everything, clean everything. Air currents might even carry the gas as far away as Bandalong before it loses its potency."

Marie looked at the controls herself. "Shut it down!" Struggling with what she knew, the girl altered her tone to place all the emphasis she could summon, attempting to use Voice. "*Shut it down!*"

Thallo paused for a second, then looked at her, unaffected. He sighed tenderly as he continued to explain, like a teacher. "We still have a little time left together, but no one can stop what I intend to do. I have been working on this for months. Even before I met you."

Marie heard alarm sirens and horns sounding outside. She used her most sympathetic tone. "And what will happen to *me*? You don't want to hurt me, do you, Thallo? I'm your friend!"

"That is why I brought you in here with me. We have a pact, you and I. We can thwart the Masters and erase their Kwisatz Haderach program." He stroked her golden hair. "Never again will either of us be controlled by others."

"Who says I let myself be controlled?" Marie's voice was cold and calculating. "Don't you see? I manipulated *them*."

He didn't want to hear any more. He sounded far away. "The nerve agent is filling the sealed pipes throughout Thalidei."

Marie heard men pounding on the doors and shouting in

strained voices over the intercom system. She also heard whirring, screeching sounds outside—drilling and cutting tools.

"They won't get to us in time." Thallo's face became beatific. "Finally I've found my inner peace, and my closest, dearest friend is with me."

Trust is a luxury I no longer have. I have experienced too much betrayal.

—from *Conversations with Muad'Dib*
by the PRINCESS IRULAN

In the immediate aftermath of the attack in the Celestial Audience Hall, Irulan longed for silence, but she heard only terrible screams and moans. Irulan realized she was turning slowly around, barely able to absorb everything with her eyes. It looked as if a Coriolis storm had passed through the enormous vaulted chamber.

From a very young age, as an Imperial Princess, she had been prepared for sudden attacks; her father had thwarted frequent assassination attempts, and Count Hasimir Fenring had probably foiled many more that she had never learned about. With his Jihad, Paul-Muad'Dib attracted more violence than Shaddam IV ever had.

She watched Paul pick himself and Chani up after the explosion of the new throne. Bludd had saved them. His ceremonial uniform and his grayish skin were flecked with red spots and tiny slashes. Facing Chani, Paul held her shoulders and gave her a quick but thorough inspection. "Are you hurt? Are you poisoned?"

Chani hardened her gaze. "Only bruises and scratches, Usul."

He touched her skin, as if by simply looking at the fresh wounds he could tell whether or not they were contaminated. She brushed him aside. "Not now. We have much to attend to here."

"Alia!" Paul shouted, looking around. "Are you safe?"

The girl appeared, looking unruffled. "I got out of the way, but the Fedaykin protecting me didn't fare so well."

Bludd also got to his feet, brushing himself off and looking drained. The wiry Swordmaster's fine clothes had been shredded by flying debris, and his left arm showed a deep gash. He swayed on his feet, glanced over at Irulan. "At least . . . I saved the princess this time." He touched the bleeding cut, then dropped to his knees again. "But I'm afraid one of the hunter-seekers must have scratched me. I feel very . . . strange."

Paul shouted for a medic, and the nearest doctor hurried to him, climbing over bodies in order to do so. "This man's been poisoned—save him!"

"But, Sire, without knowing the poison, I cannot possibly derive an antidote!"

In a brisk voice, Paul listed the eleven poisons he had identified in the hunter-seekers, so the doctors knew where to begin in treating Bludd. His team hurried the limp Swordmaster to a triage area outside the chamber.

Once the cavernous hall had been evacuated, it became clear that more of the victims scattered on the floor had been trampled than killed by the hunter-seekers. With a glance, Irulan counted dozens of bodies, mainly concentrated near the stage.

Paul stood with narrowed eyes and a countenance that was terrible to behold. She had never seen him so murderously furious. He came to her. "Irulan, are you injured?"

She had already assessed herself with Bene Gesserit intensity, finding only small scratches and tiny cuts. "I was not the target. Your Swordmaster protected me."

Irulan's mind was already racing through the consequences. At this Great Surrender ceremony, all the powerful families had been gathered. How many heads of noble

Houses had been killed here, merely as collateral damage? The shock waves this would send through the Landsraad! Even though Muad'Dib had not been killed, the assassin had struck a severe blow by proving that the Emperor's much vaunted security was inadequate. Had that been the real message here? So much for Muad'Dib's vow to impose peace and calm upon the galaxy. He couldn't even protect his immediate surroundings.

As she scanned the bodies strewn in front of the stage, Irulan saw bent arms and legs, gruesome, twisted forms, a flash of fine blue fabric. Rugi! Her heart froze. She scrambled down from the dais, picked her way through the dead, and rushed to where her little sister had been seated. The young woman had been so proud of her prominent position close to the Emperor's throne, formally representing Salusa Secundus.

"Rugi!" In the background noise, Irulan strained to hear a response, even a moan of pain. The silence now was more horrific than the screams had been.

Determined, unwilling to admit to herself what she *knew* she would find, Irulan began searching for the young girl, the smallest of her four sisters. She had never really been close to Rugi—the thirteen-year disparity in their ages had been too great. By the time Rugi was born, Irulan had already finished much of her basic instruction and managed to embroil herself in court politics on Kaitain. She had watched her father's manipulations, his games of alliances, the assassination attempts, and his palpable scorn for his "useless" daughters. And since Rugi was the youngest, Shaddam had made no secret that he considered her to be the most useless of all.

Irulan called her name again. Continuing her search, she stumbled on a slack-jawed, glassy-eyed man—a dead nobleman with bright handkerchiefs stuffed into his pockets like some kind of rank insignia. She rolled him away, angry at the corpse, as if it had intentionally tried to hinder her.

Beneath him lay Rugi's thin-limbed and childlike body. Irulan grabbed her sister by the shoulders, pulled her up, and touched her neck, desperately feeling for a pulse. "Oh, Rugi! Dear Rugi!"

She shook the girl. A dribble of blood trailed from Rugi's lifeless mouth, and her heart did not beat. Her eyes were half open but did not blink. Moaning, Irulan cradled her sister's body, letting the girl's head roll limply against her. Rugi had never understood what a pawn she'd been.

Paul walked to the main aisle, flanked by a dozen surviving Fedaykin, including Korba. The investigation had already begun, and Korba's men were combing through the bodies, searching for survivors and a perpetrator. Inspectors used tweezers to pick up evidence from the shattered remains of the elaccawood throne and from the smashed hunter-seekers.

"Find out who did this!" Paul's voice cut the air like an arctic wind. "I don't care how long it takes or how many people you must interrogate, but bring me answers. Learn who was responsible . . . and I will deal with them."

"Muad'Dib, we can be sure it has something to do with Memnon Thorvald," suggested Korba.

But Paul was not convinced. "We can be sure of nothing."

Filled with grief, Irulan looked up at him, feeling her own accusation rippling from her in waves. "You gave my sister a promise of safety! You swore to protect her, granted her Imperial security." She cradled the young woman's body, as if to prove his lies. She had blocked away any expression of feelings toward Paul for the past several years, but she did not want to control the flood of emotions she felt now.

Paul had no answer for her. So many people hated the Emperor Muad'Dib.

Each morning when I open my eyes, my first thoughts are of violence.

> —Tleilaxu lab recording of the
> Kwisatz Haderach candidate

Count Fenring had never seen the Tleilaxu men so frantic in all the years he had lived among them. Eerie alarm horns hooted through the city and echoed across the turgid lake water. Lady Margot looked at him, and he mirrored her sudden concern. "Marie—we *must* find Marie!"

Moments later, a uniformed security officer pounded on the sealed door of their quarters and demanded that they go with him to Ereboam's main laboratory complex. Without explanation, he rushed them into the backseat of a groundcar. Fenring could detect the man's urgency, but knew this mid-caste underling would have no answers for him.

The vehicle raced through the narrow streets of the city, and Fenring feared the emergency had something to do with their little daughter. From all directions, alarms sounded, and multicolored emergency lights flashed on buildings. He suspected that either Marie had caused the crisis, or Thallo had.

A harried Ereboam met them at the entrance to the central lab. "Your child and Thallo have barricaded themselves inside one of the chambers!" With his snow-white hair in disarray, the albino researcher looked even paler than ever. His spoiled-milk skin showed splotches of angry pink, and he shouted to be heard over the alarms and clamor. "They disabled the security systems, and have accessed and completely drained our stockpile of a new nerve poison, enough to kill every living creature in Thalidei. They will wipe out our programs, our research—our very lives! Why would your daughter do this? What plot have you Fenrings hatched?"

Lady Margot shouted back as they followed him into the building at a run. "Marie knows nothing of your security systems or machinery. Your Thallo is the mastermind here." Ereboam did not seem to want to believe it.

They reached the chamber door, where sluggish lower-caste Tleilaxu workers operated drilling equipment. Nearby, another group unleashed controlled, silent explosives in an attempt to knock down the wall itself, but their own security systems thwarted them. So far, Fenring saw only a small dent in the outer hatch. More equipment was on the way, but he doubted there would be enough time.

"Talk to your daughter through the intercom. Tell her to stop this!" Ereboam activated the communication system. "Find out what she has done to corrupt our Kwisatz Haderach candidate."

"Ahh, I believe your Thallo was thoroughly unstable without any help from Marie."

"Impossible. He is faultless!"

"So perfect that he is about to kill us all with poison gas—*including* our daughter." Lady Margot hurried to the intercom. "But I'll try."

Frantic Tleilaxu men scuttled out of her way, some of them glaring at her, apparently for no other reason than that she was a female. When his wife spoke into the intercom, Count Fenring recognized the command inflection of Bene Gesserit Voice. She knew precisely how to manipulate her daughter. "Marie! If you are in there, open this door at once."

The girl did not—or could not—respond.

Fenring had deep concerns for Marie's safety. Even though she was not his biological daughter, he had been her father from the moment of her birth. And he had pinned so many hopes and plans on her special abilities. *We need her!*

~&~

ON THE OTHER side of the sealed blast doors, Marie heard the call on the intercom and noted the compelling intonation, but her mother had taught her how to identify and resist Voice. Not even her nanny Tonia could command the little girl, and now Marie resisted Lady Margot's orders. She had to. By remaining here close to Thallo, at least she had a chance of averting the disaster.

But defeating a highly advanced Kwisatz Haderach candidate would require her utmost skills. This, she knew, would be more difficult than all of her previous vigorous exercises. This was what she had been born and trained for.

Obviously, Thallo was convinced she could do nothing to stop him. His classically handsome face appeared on the verge of rapture, hypnotized by the colored patterns in the control panel. His fingers danced efficiently over the pressure pads, making adjustments, shutting down safety systems and interlocks, ensuring that the pressurized nerve gas built up continuously and spread to all simultaneous release points around the entire city.

Over the intercom, both her mother and Fenring continued to shout and plead, desperate for some response.

Slowly and silently, Marie melted out of the aberration's peripheral vision, so that she could get a good running start against him. She considered removing her shoes, since her bare feet were hard and deadly, easier to inflict a precise killing blow. Bene Gesserit training. But with the bioreactors reaching overload, every second mattered. The gush of nerve toxin would kill everyone. She did not dare risk Thallo noticing her.

He doesn't have eyes in the back of his head, and his prescience—if he has it—doesn't seem to see me, either. Nevertheless, Thallo's hearing was acute, his reactions amazingly swift . . . and he was determined to die in a huge incident.

Marie, however, was just as determined to live.

She had become his friend, showed this awkwardly "perfect" Kwisatz Haderach that he was not alone in his alienation. Marie had also trained with Thallo, fought against him in mock battles, and she was proficient in the best Bene Gesserit killing techniques along with Count Fenring's assassination skills. She was not a child; she was a weapon. Killing even a Kwisatz Haderach was not beyond her abilities.

Coiling all of her energy, summoning every skill she had been taught, Marie launched herself toward Thallo, a guided human projectile. She saw a muscle flicker on the back of his neck. He began to turn, blindingly fast. She had anticipated his reaction, though—had planned for it, in fact. His hand blurred up, but he hesitated for the merest fraction of a second, either reluctant to release the controls . . . or afraid to hurt her.

With the rigid tips of both feet, Marie slammed into his neck. She heard the cracking sound of breaking bone.

Thallo's head bent forward at a sharp, unnatural angle. His face slammed into the panel, and he slumped to the floor. As his fingers slid away from the controls, she pushed aside the heavy body of the would-be Kwisatz Haderach. No longer concerned about him, Marie concentrated on the complex banks of controls. She would have only moments to throttle back the pressure release.

❧

OUT IN THE CORRIDOR, Count Fenring heard the explosions rippling beneath the city. A deep thump came, and then another, much closer. Ereboam wailed, "It is too late!"

But the rumbling seemed distant, the angry thrumming of energy discharges fading away. Fenring looked at his wife, saw her eyes filled with love and fear. The Count cocked his eyebrow at the researcher, speaking harshly, "Perhaps you should find out exactly what is happening, hmmm?"

Tleilaxu researchers scurried to their update panels and control systems, speaking on comlines and chattering as they received results. Dr. Ereboam glanced around in amazement, his shock of white hair mussed. Presently he said, "You heard the explosions, but the discharge was . . . focused. The nerve gas was released into the lake, and the water reaction will render it inert." He spun to the Count and his Lady. "Thallo has averted the disaster!"

"Even so, I wouldn't suggest going outside without a mask for some time," Fenring said, still struggling with his deep concern. "Are you certain the lake water can neutralize the chemical?"

"Poisons, by their very nature, are quite reactive. Some are activated by water, others are made safe."

Before he could continue his lecture, the heavy vault door opened, and Marie emerged, looking small and strong. Behind her, in transparent containment cells, nine Thallo clones lay dead, and on the mezzanine control deck above, the failed Kwisatz Haderach lay sprawled with his head lolling on a limp stalk of broken neck. Oddly, he wore a serene smile on his face.

Marie hugged her parents, then gave them the most innocent of expressions. "My friend was broken, and I couldn't fix him. He wasn't right."

*That one says he is my friend. The other one de-
clares himself my enemy. With all my prescience,
why is it so hard to tell the difference?*

—from *Conversations with Muad'Dib*
by the PRINCESS IRULAN

Korba began the investigation of the assassination
attempt with high fervor, exactly as Paul expected
him to do.

Swordmaster Bludd, clearly a hero for his bravery in
shielding Princess Irulan and for knocking Paul and
Chani clear of the bomb blast, had nearly died from his
poisoned wound. Once he gathered sufficient strength,
Bludd left the medics and retired to his quarters to recover.

Meanwhile, Paul shut himself inside the enormous
citadel, not out of fear or paranoia, but because he was
so overwhelmed with fury that he did not trust himself
to be seen among the populace. Though he'd had murky
dreams, his prescience had been unable to prevent this.
Such a reckless, hateful attack against him, with no regard for all the innocents who had been slain in the
attempt.

Duke Leto must have felt like this after the wedding-
day massacre sucked him into the bloody War of Assassins; it was why his father became such a hardened man,
a protective psychological response that anchored him
against the tragedies. At the time, Paul had not under-

stood the depths of his father's difficulties, but he did now.

Investigators stripped the Celestial Audience Hall down to its structural components. Chemical signatures were analyzed. Work logs were inspected to discover who might have had an opportunity to set up such a plot. The conspiracy had to be large and widespread; too many pieces had fit together perfectly. Unfortunately, by ordering his soldiers to blast the panels from which the hunter-seekers had emerged, Korba had also destroyed some of the evidence.

The modified assassination devices were traced to an exiled Ixian merchant who had provided many technological toys and amusements for Muad'Dib. But the man's ship had recently—and conveniently—been destroyed in a small Jihad skirmish on Crell.

Many of the new servants hired for the Great Surrender ceremony were interrogated, and an unfortunately high percentage of them died during the aggressive questioning. Korba was certain they must be hiding something from him, even though no one divulged any useful information.

Despite the nagging objections of his conscience, Paul allowed the merciless inquisition to continue. Innocent deaths? There had already been plenty, and there would be more. He even considered recruiting Bene Gesserit Truthsayers, but decided against the idea, because he could not entirely convince himself that the Sisterhood was not involved.

But whom could he trust? Paul had only a few faithful confidantes—Chani, Stilgar, Alia. He could also trust his mother, and Gurney Halleck, but they were both far away on Caladan. Perhaps Korba, too, and Bludd. What about Irulan, though? He neither trusted nor distrusted her. She had lost her sister in the attack, and his truthsense picked up no deception on her part. Could it have been a botched Corrino scheme, with Shaddam's youngest daughter as a sacrificial lamb? Or some hitherto unknown Harkonnen heir?

Other names and questions surfaced in Paul's mind, but he set them aside. He didn't want to go too far along that line of thinking, because paranoia could drive him mad. *I must be more alert than ever. New security measures must be established to keep my enemies off balance.*

Not surprisingly, amidst the uproar, Memnon Thorvald dispatched a pompous-sounding message through disguised intermediaries, taking credit for the massacre. Expressing satisfaction from his hidden planetary base, he crowed about how he had infiltrated the Emperor's security and struck close to Muad'Dib's loved ones. But too many of the details in his claims were wrong, his narrative rife with contradictions about what had actually occurred. It appeared that in this instance, at least, Thorvald was merely being an opportunist, attempting to use the tragedy to his advantage. But the rebel leader did not seem knowledgeable enough to have put such an extravagant scheme into place.

In addition to invoking echoes of the Elaccan flying disks from the wedding-day attack, whoever had assembled this plot knew Paul well enough to choose *hunter-seekers*, a weapon once used in an attempt to kill him in the Arrakeen residency after he first arrived on Dune. This time, where one hunter-seeker might fail, more could succeed—especially given the variety of poisons. The plotter, or plotters, understood Muad'Dib's abilities quite well.

But not well enough to kill him.

The sheer mechanics of installing so many hunter-seekers and the bomb beneath the elaccawood throne required extended, unfettered access to that section of the citadel construction site. Looking into this, Korba's Qizarate seized all workers involved in the project and questioned them with more fanaticism than finesse. Oddly, many of the suspect workers had recently been killed on the streets, the victims of random robberies or assaults. The ones who remained alive passed the closest questioning.

When the spotlight of suspicion shone on Korba himself, he protested vehemently. Documents and testimony proved that *he* had imposed many alterations to the citadel's detailed plans, some of them at the last minute. Throughout the construction, Korba had demanded architectural changes that seemed capricious and dictatorial; viewed in the current light, they looked doubly suspicious, opportunities to install booby traps.

Hearing these questions raised, Paul recalled a time during the Harkonnen occupation, when he and his Fremen band had captured Gurney Halleck and a group of smugglers out on the open desert. After Gurney had revealed to Paul that some of the men were not to be trusted, *Korba* had been given the task of searching the men carefully. Several of those smugglers had indeed been disguised Sardaukar, but somehow Korba had failed to find the false toenail weapons, the shigawire garrotes in their hair strands, the daggers hidden in their stillsuits. An outrageous lapse in security. Had it been intentional even then?

Listening to Korba take umbrage at the accusations, Paul thought he protested too much. Was it possible that Korba sought to make Muad'Dib into a martyr, using that as a springboard to seize greater religious power for himself? Yes, Paul decided. Korba might very well be capable of that.

And yet, in the end, Paul's truthsense convinced him that the man was not lying.

When Swordmaster Bludd himself became a target of the investigation, Paul knew that Korba was just being thorough. Bludd had thrown himself into the fight without regard to his own safety, had saved Irulan and shielded Paul from the explosion, and nearly died from a poisoned wound.

Even so, Bludd had brought a body shield, despite Paul's orders against it. And he had sensed that there was a bomb hidden under the throne. Or had he *known*?

Paul felt a cold tingle on his skin.

Astoundingly, the recovering Swordmaster did not bother to deny his involvement when Korba confronted him in his quarters. "I had expected you to talk with me sooner. You could have saved yourself a great deal of difficulty." He sniffed. "And you could have saved the lives of all those poor innocents you interrogated. Before I say more, I demand to speak with Paul Atreides."

Bludd wore his finest, most outrageously formal outfit. Though Korba himself had begun to dress in the finery of offworld clothiers, unconsciously following the Swordmaster's lead in fashion, he snapped orders for the foppish man to be stripped, searched, and scanned as thoroughly as they would have done to any captive Sardaukar.

Korba took great delight in yanking the sleeves and collars, ripping the fabric, and slicing open Bludd's breeches until he stood naked, his well-toned body a patchwork of bandages from his various cuts. Handling him roughly, guards scanned his hair for shigawire garrotes, analyzed his teeth for hidden suicide weapons, tested the sweat from his pores for specifically targeted neurotoxins. They even peeled off his fingernails and toenails to make sure they contained no hidden wafer weapons.

The Swordmaster endured the excruciating pain without so much as a whimper; rather, he looked impatient and offended. "You have nothing to fear from me." Not believing this, they probed him again.

Finally, bruised and bloody yet still walking with a somewhat graceful limp, Bludd was brought before Emperor Muad'Dib. Instead of his finery, the traitor wore only a plain loincloth. His bandages showed bright spots of fresh blood from wounds that had reopened. He smiled ruefully up at Paul. "I am sorry I could not be more presentable, my Lord. My garments were damaged by your zealots. But no matter." He shrugged his shoulders. "These rags take me back to my roots. I feel like a young Swordmaster in training on Ginaz, somewhat like Duncan Idaho."

Paul rose to his feet. He felt weary and furious; wanted to understand Bludd's motivations as much as he wanted revenge. "You don't deny what you did?"

"To what purpose? You could detect a lie the moment I spoke it. Ah, I wish it had not come to this. It wasn't what I intended."

Korba stepped forward and shouted at the prisoner. "Tell us all of the members of your conspiracy. How far does it spread? How many others are traitors in Muad'Dib's court?"

Bludd gave the Fremen leader a withering frown. "I needed no one else. This was my plot, and mine alone. I wanted to be a hero—and I succeeded. Everyone saw me save you, Chani, and the Princess."

Korba confronted the near-naked man in his bindings. "You could not have done this by yourself. No man could."

"Maybe not one ordinary man, but one *Swordmaster* could. I planned it all in every detail, without help." Then Bludd began to regale them with the entire scheme, rattling off specific details of every phase of the operation that had taken him many months to put into place—step by step, one part of the plan after another.

Korba snorted in disbelief at the preposterous claims, but Paul realized that Bludd was not exaggerating. As the Swordmaster talked, he seemed impressed with his own cleverness, though a bit sheepish to reveal it. "I have been caught with my hand in the proverbial cookie jar, and now you have me. I presume that my service to you is at an end, Sire? You must admit, I did excellent work on your citadel."

Paul was genuinely baffled. "But *why* did you turn on me?" He couldn't remember the last time he had felt so confused. His words came out in a rush. "What did you have to gain? How did I offend you? What could possibly have sparked such absolute hatred?"

"Hatred? Why, I do not hate you, Sire. You have been exceedingly fair and kind to me, and I never sought to harm you." He sighed, and Paul finally detected a deep-seated wound that the man had carried inside for many years, a scar that had never faded. "But history has been less kind to me. I wanted to add my own flourish to the record."

"Explain yourself, man!" Korba growled.

"I lived my life as a great Swordmaster and accomplished many deeds of valor. Can you name them?" He raised his eyebrows, looked wearily at Korba, then at the guards, and back at Paul. "Come, you must remember some of them? Any of them? *You* certainly do, my Lord. Or do you only remember Rivvy Dinari, who died protecting Archduke Armand during the wedding-day attack? Not poor Swordmaster Bludd, who failed to save Ilesa." He lowered his head. "I missed my chance then. I failed and was brushed aside, but Rivvy went out in a final flash of glory, a true hero. In fact, he was the star of all the historical accounts. Have you read them, my Lord Paul?"

"I was there. I don't need to read them."

"I fought with the Ecazi and Atreides soldiers on Grumman. I helped in the final showdown with Viscount Moritani—does anyone remember? As Archduke Armand clung to life all these years, I served as steward of House Ecaz and apparently accomplished nothing! For you, I oversaw the construction here of the greatest work of architecture in human history, but it will always be known as the Citadel of *Muad'Dib*. Korba is right about that. I am just another footnote."

Defiant tears sparkled in his eyes, but he drew no shred of sympathy from Paul. "I demand a grand ending for the history books, not a fading-away. No matter what I've done before, this should have been seen as my last great act as a Swordmaster." Bludd looked around, as if expecting cheers.

"Your secret police can relax, my Lord. I had no political motivations in doing this, I assure you. All your security, your protective measures, your tests . . . kept looking outward for enemies, imagining motives and eliminating any threats you could perceive. But my motive? I just wanted the attention, the recognition, the *respect*." He smiled and lowered his voice. "Despite all, I must confess that I am glad to see you are still alive. And I suppose I will not be remembered as a hero after all. Ah well, it is better to be famous than infamous, but it is better to be infamous than forgotten altogether."

Anger honed Paul's voice to a dangerous edge. "What makes you think I will not have your name stricken from the historical record—like House Tantor after they unleashed their holocaust on Salusa Secundus?"

Bludd crossed his sinewy arms over his chest. "Because, Paul Atreides, you have too much respect for history, no matter what Princess Irulan writes." He brushed at his bare chest, as if imagining wrinkles in a ruffled shirt he no longer wore. "You will sentence me to death, of course. There is nothing I can do about that."

"Yes, you are sentenced to death," Paul said, as if in an afterthought.

"Muad'Dib, I refuse to believe he acted alone! Such a complex conspiracy?" Korba said. "The people will never believe it. If you execute this one man, they will see him as a token, perhaps even a scapegoat. They will believe we are unable to find the true perpetrators."

Bludd laughed sarcastically. "So you will punish random people because you are too narrow-minded to believe that a man with talent and imagination could accomplish what I did? How appropriate."

Paul was too tired and sickened to deal further with the matter. "Continue your investigations, Korba. See if what he says is true. But do not take too long. There's enough turmoil on Arrakeen, and I want to end this."

Bludd was taken away in chains, looking oddly satisfied, even relieved.

Individuals can be honorable and selfless. But in a mob, people will always demand more—more food, more wealth, more justice, and more blood.

— Bene Gesserit analysis of human behavior,
Wallach IX Archives

The open square in front of the Citadel of Muad'Dib was spacious enough to hold the population of a small city, but it could not encompass all those who clamored to witness the execution of Whitmore Bludd.

From just inside his high balcony—designed by Bludd himself, so that the Emperor could stand above all his people and address the multitudes—Paul watched the throng shift like waves of sand on endless dunes. He heard their grumbles and shouts, felt their charged anger ready to ignite.

It concerned him, but he could not deny them this spectacle. His Empire was based on passion and devotion. These people had sworn their lives to him, had overthrown planets in his name. While pretending to be a brave hero, the traitor Bludd had tried to harm their beloved Muad'Dib, and they felt a desperate need for revenge. Paul had little choice but to grant it to them. Even with his prescience, he could not foresee all the harm that would arise if he dared to forgive Bludd. *If he dared!* He was the ruler of the Imperium, and yet he was not free to make his own decisions.

Out in the square, guards cleared a central area so that

the group of condemned prisoners could be brought out. Guards wearing personal shields used clubs to drive the people back, but it was like trying to deflect the winds in a raging sandstorm. In the mob's frenzy, some of them turned upon each other, overreacting to an unintentional shove or the jab of an elbow.

It is a tinderbox down there. Paul saw now that he had addicted them to violence as much as they were addicted to spice. How could he expect them simply to accept peace? The crowd below was a microcosm of his entire Empire.

Fedaykin guards brought Bludd and ten other men forward from the citadel's prison levels. The men plodded along in heavy chains.

Seeing them, the crowd responded with a roar that rolled through the square like a physical wave. At the forefront of the captives, Whitmore Bludd tried to stride along with a spring in his step, though he had been severely beaten, his feet were bruised and swollen, and he was so sore he could barely walk. The men behind him were allegedly fellow conspirators who'd had some part in the terrible massacre.

Two of the ten were the pair of inept assassins who had also plotted to kill Muad'Dib but had been caught in the early stages of their plan. Korba had offered up the other eight as sacrificial lambs, but it was clear to Paul that the evidence against them had been doctored, their confessions forced. Paul was sadly unsurprised to note that all eight were known to be Korba's rivals, men who had challenged his authority. Paul felt sick inside. *And so it begins. . . .*

In the square beneath the balcony, a stone speaking platform had become a gathering place for priests, newscriers, and orators proclaiming the glory of Muad'Dib. Now the platform had been reconfigured as an execution stand.

Though limping, Bludd maintained some semblance of grace and courage, but three of the men behind him stumbled or resisted and had to be dragged along. Those men protested their innocence (correctly, perhaps) by their gestures, their expressions, their wails of anguish. But the thunderous roar of the crowd drowned out their words.

As soon as the foppish Swordmaster was hauled up to the speaking platform, the crowd let out another roar that soon began to coalesce into words, a chanted, mocking, hate-filled chorus of "Bad Bludd, Bad Bludd!"

Half of the doomed men fell to their knees trembling, but not the Swordmaster, who stood with his chin high. The others turned their heads down in dismay and terror.

Defiant, Bludd squared his shoulders and gazed at the crowd. His long ringlets of silver-and-gold hair blew in the hot breeze. Even now the Swordmaster seemed to consider this to be part of a performance, determined not to be remembered by history as a gibbering coward. He smiled boldly, swelling his chest. If he was going to be infamous, then Bludd would be truly extravagant in his infamy.

Paul allowed the crowd's emotions to rise. Finally, passing smoothly through the moisture seals, he emerged onto the balcony and stood under the warm yellow sunlight. Many faces in the crowd turned rapturously toward him. For a long moment, he said nothing—just absorbed the throbbing wash of emotions, and let the onlookers absorb *him*. The shouts rose to a cacophony, and Paul raised his hands for silence.

He could have spoken in a normal voice, not even requiring the amplifiers that were spaced around the vast square. But he shouted, "Justice is mine."

Even Bludd turned to face him. It seemed as if the Swordmaster wanted to give him a salute, but his hands were bound.

Paul had decided against a long and ponderous speech. The crowds already knew the crime, and knew who had been found guilty. "I am Muad'Dib, and I give you this gift." He gestured down toward Bludd and the other men. "Justice is yours."

The guards removed the shackles from Bludd and the other prisoners, and let the chains tumble heavily onto the speaking platform. Knowing what was to come, the guards vanished quickly into the crowd. With a dismissive gesture, Paul stepped back into the shadows, out of sight, as if he had washed his hands of the matter. But he continued to watch.

The mob hesitated for a minute, not sure what they were supposed to do, unable to believe what Muad'Dib had just said. Two of the prisoners tried to bolt. Bludd stood on the execution platform with his arms crossed over his chest, waiting.

The crowd surged forward like a crashing wave. They howled and clawed at each other to get closer. Paul watched, sickened, as they tore Bludd limb from limb, along with the ten hapless scapegoats.

Chani slipped into the shadows beside him, her face dusky, her eyes large and hard. She had a Fremen's bloodthirstiness, wanted to see pain inflicted upon those who had tried to harm her and her beloved. Even so, at the sight of such violence and fanaticism, revulsion showed on her face.

Paul knew exactly what he had created here. For so long, he had been forced by prescience to use violence as a tool in order to achieve what needed to be done. And violence was an effective and powerful tool. But now it seemed that the slippery instrument had turned, and the violence itself was using *him* as its tool. A dark part of him wasn't sure if he would be able to control what he had unleashed. Or if he even wanted to.

They are reasonably good fighters," Bashar Zum
Garon admitted as he looked at the trained group
of gholas that the Tleilaxu presented in an enclosed
arena in Thalidei. "No match for my Sardaukar or
Muad'Dib's Fedaykin, but I do see considerable skills
out there. Emperor Shaddam may find them acceptable
for his secret army."

"Ah, hm-m-m-m," Count Fenring said, sitting next to
Margot in the spectator seats of the combat area. "That
was a nice parry from the tall, bearded one." They
watched a hundred uniformed soldiers engage in practice
matches with an array of simulated weapons that left
marks on their opponents to show "kills" and "wounds."
They were using swords, stunners, knives, darts, and projectile simulators.

"And the man in red just made a decent thrust against
his opponent, but they're half a step slow," Lady Margot
pointed out.

Dr. Ereboam nodded knowingly. "When we have
finished honing them, they will successfully compete
against Sardaukar and Fedaykin, because they begin with
the same raw material. Their minds remember nothing of

their past lives, but their bodies remember their training. Our battlefield harvesters take cells from fallen warriors, even intact bodies if they are reparable. These gholas have the same muscle reflexes and superior potential as the most celebrated fighters. They *are* the most celebrated fighters."

"Hmmm, I would submit that any soldier who does not *survive* a battle is not, ahh, by definition, the best fighter."

The albino researcher scowled. "These are the best of the best, those who not only possessed superior skills, but who died bravely. These resurrected fighters can become a spectacular army for Emperor Shaddam—an army that Muad'Dib knows nothing about. They appear on no census rolls, their names no longer exist. Provided we can smuggle them to Salusa Secundus, they will seem to have appeared out of thin air."

Garon nodded seriously. "I will inform the Emperor of what you offer. As gholas, none of them fear death. Yes, they can be fierce, indeed."

Though Fenring was loathe to participate in any more of Shaddam's schemes that were bound to fail, he had to admit that this one showed a certain measure of promise. He feared, however, that the fallen Emperor would never truly understand how different and formidable a foe Muad'Dib was, with his fanatical armies that felt no sense of self-preservation.

Count Fenring and Lady Margot knew their own plans for Marie were much more likely to succeed than Shaddam's tiresome schemes to restore himself to power. Even at her young age, Marie had outwitted and outfought the deranged Thallo. The Tleilaxu were quite dismayed after the disaster, but Fenring did not need their flawed Kwisatz Haderach candidate for his own success.

Yes, the little girl's skills were developing nicely.

Fenring watched as a mock town appeared at the center of the enclosed arena; building facades emerged from places of concealment in the floor. The ghola soldiers divided into two squadrons designated by red or blue waist sashes, then faced off on the faux town streets and alleys, firing marker darts at one another. None of them spoke a word.

"My Marie could defeat the whole pack of them down there," Count Fenring mused. "You'll have to do better than that, Doctor."

Ereboam let out a shrill, scoffing sound. "Against so many trained opponents she would not stand a chance!"

"Oh, she would stand a chance all right," Lady Margot agreed. "But perhaps saying she could kill a hundred warrior gholas is a bit too boastful. I am confident she could eliminate a dozen of them, however."

"Yes," Fenring said, correcting himself. "Make it fifteen."

Bashar Garon seemed deeply disturbed by the suggestion. "That little girl? Against hardened warriors? She can't be more than seven years old."

"Ahh-hm-mm, she is six," Fenring said. "And her age is not the question here, only her skill level." He lowered his voice, adding a dangerous undertone. "Perhaps I should send *her* to Shaddam's court. Our dear Emperor would find her far more difficult to kill than my dear cousin Dalak."

He had not loved Wensicia's husband, or even known him well, but the fool had indeed been a member of Fenring's family. When Garon reported the "unfortunate incident" of Dalak's death—first telling Shaddam's lie, then admitting to the dishonorable truth—the Count had been extremely annoyed. He could not ignore the insult, even for the sake of his supposed childhood friend. For his own part, the Bashar remained offended by many of Shaddam's recent actions, and Dalak's murder was only one of them.

One more reason not to assist Shaddam, one more reason to despise the man's ineptitude. Fenring had half a mind to expand his plot and exterminate the Corrinos as well as Muad'Dib. Kill them to the last man, woman, and child. Burn their planets. Wipe them off the map of the universe.

Maybe later. With Marie on the throne, it would be done. *Everything in its time.* Muad'Dib was the true enemy. Shaddam was just . . . irrelevant.

"Why don't we let the child demonstrate her abilities against Dr. Ereboam's ghola soldiers?" Fenring said, intentionally taunting the albino researcher. Right now, he needed an outlet for his rage. Marie waited nearby, alone in a game room. Since killing Thallo, she no longer had a playmate.

"Do you seriously wish to pit your girl against a dozen trained ghola soldiers?" Garon asked, in disbelief.

"Fifteen," Fenring said. He knew that in private training sessions she had already proved herself more than capable of handling such a challenge. "Mmm, yes, that should be fair enough."

⁓

MARIE'S EYES FLASHED dangerously as she was led into a small indoor combat arena. She had been told it was time to play. Fenring felt a rush of adrenaline as he smiled at her, feeling complete confidence in the sweet little girl.

Lady Margot seemed just as eager. "Now you shall see what a Bene Gesserit child can do when seasoned with my husband's advice, and a dash of Tleilaxu Twisting techniques. She has a far broader skill set than any previous assassin."

Fifteen uniformed ghola fighters chosen by Ereboam

had already been sent into the combat room and armed with real weapons, at the insistence of the Fenrings. The Count patted Marie on her blonde head and handed the girl a dagger. "This is all you should need, hmmm?" He bent down to kiss her forehead.

"It's all I need."

Margot kissed her daughter's cheek before sending her into the enclosed arena. The muscular, fully grown soldiers faced Marie, looking at the girl in uneasy confusion as the door sealed, leaving the observers outside.

"Now," Margot said, using the implacable command of Voice, "extinguish all the lights. She will fight in complete darkness."

"Hmm-ah, yes," Fenring agreed, his eyes sparkling. "That should make it more of a challenge."

THE COUNT COULD see that Bashar Garon was alarmed to hear a flurry of commotion on the combat floor—darts flying and weapons clashing, cries of surprise and pain from the ghola fighters. Several screamed as they died. The darkness remained absolute.

He smiled to himself and gripped Lady Margot's hand on her lap. He felt her pulse quicken. "Just a little controlled violence," Fenring said to the Sardaukar commander, as if to ease Garon's concerns.

"But they are so many and she is so small," the Bashar said.

Men continued to cry out, and then everything fell eerily silent. Thirty seconds later, the lights went back on.

On the floor, Marie stood looking up at the viewing area. Motionless bodies lay at her feet—the best fighters that the Tleilaxu had to offer. At some point she had discarded her dagger; the girl was speckled with blood on her hands, feet, and face. Count Fenring was still struck by how small and innocent she looked. He couldn't have been prouder.

"Amazing," Garon said.

"A waste of our best gholas," Dr. Ereboam added bitterly.

"Perhaps you need to start with better genetic material," Lady Margot said with an edge of sarcasm.

Fenring watched the other Tleilaxu Masters conferring among themselves in their rude, secret tongue. He didn't care what they were saying. Their body language revealed enough.

Marie had functioned with deadly precision, synthesizing the wealth of teachings she had been given. With a thrill of fear, he wondered if the girl might be able to best even him. Fenring turned to his wife and saw that her eyes held a sheen of unshed tears. Joyful tears, he thought.

He said tersely, "She is ready."

A written "fact" is considered innately more true than spoken gossip or hearsay, but physical documents have no greater claim to accuracy than an anecdote from an actual eyewitness.

—GILBERTUS ALBANS,
Mentat Discourses on History

The Imperium reeled from the impact of the violence in the Celestial Audience Chamber, and the people's reactionary anger displayed itself in increasingly deadly raids on new planets. The jihadis demanded retribution on Muad'Dib's behalf, and many innocent populations paid the price.

Worse, Irulan watched Paul turn a blind eye to the unjust bloodshed.

No one of importance paid any attention to the death of her sister. Rugi was merely a name on a list of casualties, and few people remarked on the fact that she was the youngest daughter of the Padishah Emperor, a man once described as "the Ruler of a Million Planets." The spotlight of history focused only upon Muad'Dib and the ever-mounting violence around him. House Corrino had become no more than a footnote in history . . . just as Swordmaster Bludd had vowed not to be.

But Irulan could not drive away the memory of holding her sister's body in her arms, and she allowed herself a flash of hatred for Paul, because he had not cared about her grief. Had not even *noticed* it.

Preoccupied with his new crackdowns and increased

security after the threat, Paul did not acknowledge *her* universe of pain. How hardened he had become! How brutal, steely, and inflexible. Perhaps those were valid traits for the revered godlike leader of a galaxy . . . but not for a human being. She could not help but feel bitter.

According to reports, her father had wailed with grief when he learned the news. He had fooled few people with his crocodile tears, but he had certainly gained some sympathy. Poor Shaddam had dutifully sent his youngest and "most beloved" daughter to attend the Great Surrender ceremony, and Muad'Dib had allowed her to be killed! Her father was certainly shrewd to use the tragedy to build momentum, possibly as a lever in another bid for power.

The Corrino Princess suspected that he had already sent emissaries to find Earl Thorvald, calling upon familial connections, asking the brother of her father's "dear but regrettably lost" fifth wife, Firenza. Irulan thought he might even succeed, for a while at least.

Irulan once again took control over her emotions, using her Sisterhood training to discover a resolve that allowed her to balance her conflicting roles. She was not permitted direct influence in the government. She was not a true wife. She was not Paul's lover.

But she was still his wife, and the daughter of an Emperor.

Paul knew her worth, from her writing ability to her knowledge of politics. She had nearly finished writing his early-life ordeals during the War of Assassins, and, like Scheherazade, Irulan would continue to make herself indispensable. His followers devoured any glimpse into his life, his philosophy, his vision for them, for Dune, and for all inhabited planets. His mother, after all, had been a Bene Gesserit. He knew full well the value of mythmaking.

Irulan's quarters, with the adjacent offices, solarium, and enclosed dry-climate garden, had been specifically designed to be conducive to her writing. She had plenty of light, meditation areas, uninterrupted concentration, secretaries if she needed them. By Muad'Dib's command, historical documents were surrendered to her; friends of House Atreides, eyewitnesses to events, even former rivals were strongly encouraged to grant the Princess any interviews she desired.

Irulan promised herself that one day she would also tell the story of her own upbringing in the Imperial household and find a way to make the death of poor Rugi meaningful. With each passing day the next manuscript neared completion. . . .

Three Fedaykin guards marched into the enclosed garden where she sat at a small table surrounded by shigawire spools and a reader, filmbooks, and clean spice paper on which to take notes. She looked up, surprised to see Paul himself coming toward her.

Other than the silent guards, they had no audience, so she felt no need to be overly formal. "Husband, it is quite an unexpected event when you decide to visit me in my private wing."

"I have paid too little attention to your writings," he said in a voice as flat as the blade of a Sardaukar's dagger. "There is great unrest, and I am anxious for you to release the next chapter of my story. Nevertheless, I must be careful about what you publish. This time, I will read it more closely."

"To censor it?" She feigned indignation, but she had never expected to complete the work without interference.

"To read it. You know well enough what you should and should not say. I trust you that much."

Paul stood before her waiting, not at all relaxed, while Irulan remained seated at her table surrounded by the paraphernalia of the project. The three guards seemed decidedly uncomfortable that she did not throw herself to the ground and abase herself before him. She smiled at this. "I think you should appoint me your official Minister of Propaganda."

"You already serve the role—and you do it well." His eyes narrowed. "Though I am not entirely certain why you do it. You are a *ghanima,* a prize I won in battle. You cannot revere me as a husband, and I don't think you lust after power for its own sake. What is your real motive?"

"I am a scribe of history, my Husband."

"No historian is without an agenda. That is why no genuine truth is ever recorded. Is it your wish that I believe you are loyal to me—to the exclusion of your family and the Sisterhood—that you wholeheartedly accept your role? You have no hidden agenda, no scheme?"

Irulan looked down at her notes, giving herself a chance to marshal her thoughts. "Ask yourself that question, Paul Atreides. Function as a Mentat. Why would I remain secretly loyal to House Corrino, to my father? He failed. Why would I follow the secret instructions of the Bene Gesserit? They failed, too. Where do I have the most to gain? *As your loyal wife.* Look at me, ask the question, and decide for yourself where I should invest my efforts." She watched him follow the logic.

He bent over the table, picked up a few pages from the stack of papers on which she had been writing, and skimmed them, his eyes darting with the speed of static electricity. Then he picked up the entire manuscript.

"Before long, I will depart. I feel the need to . . . go on a meditative retreat after the recent terrible events. In the meantime, Korba will read this."

Irulan gave him a mirthless smile. "Korba sees what he wants to see."

Paul handed the manuscript to one of the guards, who took it as if the pages contained either holy scripture or incriminating evidence. "Yes, he is predictable. But useful because of that."

And so am I, Irulan thought.

PART VI

Young Paul Atreides

10,187 AG

In the jungles of Caladan, Paul Atreides learned the value of ferocity, of going after his enemies instead of letting them pursue him. From our current perspective, this must be seen as one of the factors that made him the most aggressive Emperor in the long history of the Imperium. He accepted the necessity of pursuing his enemies and killing them without a modicum of compassion or regret.

In his first experience of actual war, joining his father on the battlefields of Grumman, Paul saw how violence could infect men with irrationality, how hatred could extinguish reason. And he came to understand that the most dangerous enemy is not the man with the most weapons, but the man with the least to lose.

—*A Child's History of Muad'Dib*
by the PRINCESS IRULAN

A sharp edge does not automatically make a sword a good weapon. Only the wielder can do that.

—Swordmaster credo

When he and Duncan rejoined the Atreides troops on Ecaz before the combined force departed for Grumman, Paul proudly wore a new Atreides uniform. After surviving in the wilds of Caladan, the young man took care to present himself properly to his father, without looking like a popinjay or a cadet who had never felt dirt under his fingernails. Paul had noticed that none of the veterans, such as Duncan and Gurney, looked *overly* polished. They had a hardened, professional appearance, and their weapons were worn from use and frequent cleaning. Not gaudy, but perfectly serviceable.

He and Duncan went to the landing field outside the Ecazi Palace, where the Atreides and Ecazi armies prepared for their primary strike against Hundro Moritani. This combined fighting force would be more than enough to crush the Grumman leader and avenge those who had been killed by the Viscount's ruthless schemes.

Paul and Duncan found Duke Leto standing in the shadow of the Atreides private frigate. The young man couldn't wait to tell him what he had been through. He wondered if the Duke would shed a tear upon learning of his mother's death. . . .

Leto surveyed his troops from the base of the embarkation ramp. In an instant, Paul noted the extra shadows around his father's eyes. The scars on the nobleman's heart had never healed from the deaths of Victor and Kailea, and the tragedy of his friend Rhombur. The murder of Ilesa had opened fresh wounds and, studying his father now, Paul saw a new haunted look. Duke Leto had been through his own ordeal here on Ecaz.

He embraced Paul, but seemed hesitant to show his relief and joy. He smiled at the Swordmaster. "Duncan, you've kept my son safe."

"As you commanded, my Lord."

As the clamor of activity continued around them, with soldiers checking weapons and hustling aboard frigates, following their subcommanders, Paul and Duncan told their stories. In turn Leto told them how he had killed Prad Vidal by his own hand. He seemed to take no pride in it. "That is what a War of Assassins is all about, Paul. Only the correct combatants face death, not innocents."

Armand Ecaz came to them, accompanied by two gray-suited Guild legates, a male and a female, though both looked remarkably sexless. "Leto, we have formalities to attend to." The Archduke kept his empty sleeve pinned to his side, like a badge of honor; by now he had recovered enough that he could complete his duties without being slowed by the handicap. "Forms and agreements."

"Yes, we follow all the rules," Leto said bitterly. "The prescribed niceties of civilization."

The Guild legates peered through droopy eyelids, and when they spoke they were entirely passionless, as if only husks of their bodies remained. "The forms must be obeyed," the female legate said with emphasis.

"And we have obeyed the forms," Leto replied, somewhat curtly. Paul knew he was anxious to dispatch the frigates to the Heighliner and head off to Grumman. He looked up at Gurney Halleck, who scowled at the bureaucrats from the entry hatchway. When Paul caught his friend's gaze, the lumpy face transformed to a smile.

"All necessary documents have been filed with the Landsraad, and copies sent to Spacing Guild headquarters on Junction," said Archduke Armand. "This is a proper, legally sanctioned military action."

Leto added, "Thufir Hawat presented our case before the Emperor, and an Ecazi ambassador has done the same. Shaddam IV publicly censured Viscount Moritani, so he has implicitly accepted our grievance."

Gurney spoke up, " 'Once God casts His game piece, it is best to stay out of the way.' " Paul had never heard the quote before, and wondered if Gurney had made it up. "And now, by the grace of God and under the shield of vendetta, we intend to hit the Grummans hard." Gurney's words carried an unspoken dare, as if provoking the Guild legates to try and stop them.

The strangely identical representatives simply bowed and took a step backward. "It is so. You may bring this battle to House Moritani, though the Emperor himself reserves the right to intervene, if he so chooses."

"Intervene?" Leto asked. "Or *interfere*?"

Neither legate answered the question. "You have permission to load your military forces aboard the Heighliner." They departed swiftly.

Archduke Armand snapped orders for his troops to board the frigates in an orderly fashion. Gurney hustled about, keeping the operation in order, shouting even louder than the warming spacecraft engines.

Duncan, though, remained beside the Duke, looking saddened, even shamed. He unwrapped a bundle he carried under his arm and presented the worn hilt and discolored, damaged blade of the Old Duke's sword. "My Lord, this was your father's weapon. You told me to carry it with honor and use it to defend House Atreides. I have done so, but I am afraid that—" He could not speak further.

Paul said, "Duncan used it to save me, many times over."

Leto looked at the famous sword that Paulus Atreides had used for his popular spectacles on Caladan and his legendary battles during the Ecazi Revolt fighting alongside Rhombur's father. Duncan had carried the proud blade for years, fought with it, trained Paul against it.

Duke Leto's chuckle was a startling contrast to Duncan's glum demeanor. "That weapon has more than served its purpose, Duncan. It shall be retired with honor when we get back to Castle Caladan. For now, I need your fighting arm and a sharp blade in your hand. You are a Swordmaster of Ginaz, in service to House Atreides. It is high time you had a sword of your own."

Duncan looked at Paul, smiling uncertainly, then back at Leto. "A fresh new blade before going into battle on Grumman. Yes, my Lord, that would be a fine christening."

❧

AN ODDLY QUIET Swordmaster Bludd meticulously searched the armory and museum wing of the Archduke's palace until he found a sword he considered appropriate for Duncan Idaho. He insisted it had to be a masterpiece of metallurgy and craftsmanship that had never been used in battle.

The foppish man carried the gleaming weapon solemnly. As he stepped forward, he flexed the blade and made quick, expert thrusts to each side. "A fitting piece," Bludd said. "I tested it myself." He looked teary eyed as he presented it to the Duke, who then turned to Duncan.

"When we return victorious to Caladan, our best met-alsmiths will add a hawk sigil to the hilt. But this blade is yours, Duncan. Use it well, and in defense of House Atreides."

Duncan bowed, then accepted the sword. "My own sweat will be enough to mark it until that time, my Lord. I will use this with honor."

Leto's voice took on a stern tone. "And you still have the charge of protecting my son's life. We are going into a larger battle, and I can't have you joining the fight with an inferior sword."

All around, Paul saw military aircraft lifting off from the field—frigates, cargo vessels, fighter craft heading for orbital rendezvous with the Heighliner. Gurney Hal-leck, who had appeared to watch the brief ceremony, nodded when he saw the new sword.

"I think Gurney should write the ballad of Duncan Idaho someday," Paul said.

"Duncan's got to distinguish himself first, young pup. I can't be writing songs about every average warrior." Gurney smiled.

"Duncan is not, and will never be, average," Leto answered.

⁓

*Those who seek fame and glory are least qualified
to possess it.*

—RHEINVAR THE MAGNIFICENT, Jongleur artiste
(rumored to be a Face Dancer)

E ven though the Baron despised being put over a bar-
rel by Viscount Moritani—outright blackmail!—he
struggled to find a solution that would still be advantageous to House Harkonnen. As Hundro Moritani had
amply demonstrated, he was volatile, violent, unpredictable, and untrustworthy—conditions with which the
Baron was familiar, yet now they were turned against
him. He hated to waste a division of his own soldiers to
fight in this ill-advised engagement on Grumman, a
hopeless battle that could not possibly turn out well. Soldiers were expendable, of course, but they weren't cheap.

The Viscount's strategy was foolish, heavy-handed,
and provocative, and Baron Harkonnen had been happy
to grant the man as much rope as he wished, so long as
he hung *himself* with it. Now, though, Moritani was
forcing *the Baron* to participate in this folly, and to send
his heir apparent into the jaws of the conflict.

Glossu Rabban was the eldest son of the Baron's soft-
hearted brother Abulurd. Since Rabban was older than
Feyd, and since those two were the only direct heirs to
House Harkonnen, the Baron had no choice but to name
one of them his successor. Rabban fully expected to be

the na-Baron, but Feyd seemed far more competent and intelligent, more worthy of the responsibility the role required.

The two brothers had a rivalry, potentially a murderous one, and Rabban was certainly capable of killing Feyd in order to assure his title. The Baron had warned him against taking such rash action, but Rabban was often deaf to warnings or common sense.

Perhaps Viscount Moritani's ultimatum provided a neat solution to the problem. After all, House Harkonnen didn't really have a choice.

He delayed as long as possible, then summoned Rabban into his private chambers. The Baron had removed his suspensor belt and reclined in a reinforced, overstuffed chair. Rabban marched into the room, looking as though he expected to be reprimanded for making another poor decision.

"I have good news for you, my dear nephew." Smiling, the Baron lifted a decanter of Kirana brandy and poured a glass for himself and one for the burly, younger man. "Here, a toast. Come now, it's not poisoned."

Rabban looked confused, suspicious. Nevertheless he sipped the brandy, then gulped more.

"I'm making you commander of a full division of Harkonnen troops. You will be going to Grumman where you'll help fight beside our ally, Viscount Moritani."

Rabban grinned like a fool. "A full division on the battlefields of Grumman, Uncle? Against the Atreides?"

"Yes, you will fight the Atreides." The Baron relished the idea almost as much as he relished the taste of his own brandy. "House Harkonnen's involvement must be kept entirely secret, or there will be major repercussions. I saw the Emperor during the censure hearing in the Landsraad Hall. He would not be pleased to learn we are secretly aiding House Moritani. You will wear a Grumman uniform, as will all of our soldiers."

"I will not disappoint you, Uncle."

The Baron struggled to keep his expression unreadable. *I have no expectations of you whatsoever, so I cannot be disappointed.*

He sipped his brandy and smiled. For insurance, he was putting subordinate officers in place to watch his nephew and make sure he didn't make a big mistake. Rabban, who had already drained his glass, seemed disheartened when the Baron didn't refill it for him.

"Now, go. The troops already have their orders. You must depart immediately so that you reach Grumman before our enemies arrive. If you get there too late, there will be no one left for you to fight."

ON THE DRY hills outside Ritka, Beast Rabban lifted his chin, drew a deep breath of the bitter-smelling air, and watched with pride as his Harkonnen soldiers marched in formation to the edge of the dry seabed. All of the troops wore the yellow uniforms of House Moritani, with padded shoulders and metallic armbands. Observing them, Rabban thought that his disguised division moved with great precision, while the Grumman counterparts seemed more like an unruly band of barbarians. But at least they were muscular, hardened by their squalid lives, and determined to fight.

Once the enemies arrived, the local terrain would determine the initial layout of the battle. Nestled into the crook of rugged foothills, the city of Ritka was defensible from the rear and sides. Shields around the fortress would protect it from aerial bombardment and projectile fire, but infantry could still pass through the shields. The dry seabed stretched out in front of Ritka, where centuries ago ships had come to port. Now it was an open expanse, the only way that opposing armies could approach en masse. Atreides and Ecazi war frigates could land on the far side of the rocky pan, out of range of Ritka's guns. From there, the armies would emerge and make a frontal attack.

The Grumman leader, with his shaggy hair and overly bright eyes, sat astride his huge black stallion, caparisoned in spiny armor. His redheaded Swordmaster Resser rode another mount beside him. Moritani grunted appreciatively as the massed Harkonnen troops flowed into the ranks of his own soldiers. "Baron Harkonnen has met the obligations of our alliance. Our enemies will soon come, and this clash will be remembered for centuries." He gazed wistfully out on the open plain, as if imagining the glorious battle to come. "I have no doubt the Emperor will arrive to intervene as well. Shaddam cannot resist a chance to prove his manhood."

"I have no need to prove my own," Rabban said, with a sneer.

"Boasting of your bravery and demonstrating it are two different things," Resser chided coolly. "We are counting on you to lead your Harkonnen troops and hold back the invasion as long as you can. We expect to face overwhelming numbers."

"I won't merely hold them back, I intend to defeat them utterly," Rabban said.

"You may try," the Viscount said wryly. He reached out a hand as a soldier handed him a thick helmet topped with a brush of black feathers. The Moritani leader placed the helmet upon Rabban's head and moved his steed back a step. "You are my Warlord now."

The helmet felt heavy, and Rabban was sure he must look magnificent.

"Brom, come here!" Moritani shouted. A bearded, broad-shouldered warrior nearly as tall as the Viscount's towering mount came forward. "Brom is your lieutenant, Rabban. He and his troops will follow your commands in battle. You are responsible for them. You are the heart that beats red blood into their veins."

The Grumman officer looked disturbed and resentful at the choice of Rabban as commander, but when the Viscount glared at him, Brom stepped back, his expression unreadable.

"I have great plans, Rabban, and you are a key part of them. I give you a horse and a command," Moritani said. "My Swordmaster will stay with me inside the fortress, protected by house shields. You will have the honor of being out front, but you must lead according to my orders."

"As long as I can be in the thick of the fighting against the Atreides." Rabban could hardly wait for the opposing armies to appear.

What is the point of being the Emperor of the Known Universe if people don't do as I say, when I say it? That is very troubling to me, Hasimir.

—PADISHAH EMPEROR SHADDAM IV, letter to Count Hasimir Fenring

This has gone on quite long enough," Shaddam said, looking at the latest reports. "I have been generous, benevolent, and forgiving. I don't care what kind of bribes Viscount Moritani has paid to the Lion Throne—I will not continue to be insulted."

At his side on the spacious private terrace, regarding the lavish expanse of the capital city on Kaitain, Hasimir Fenring bobbed his head. "Hmmm, Sire, I was wondering when you would reach your limit. And what, aahh, will you do about it? How do you propose to respond to this flagrant defiance by the Grummans?"

Shaddam had shooed away his concubines and spent many hours in his private quarters. Lately, he was also beginning to lose interest in his new wife, Firenza, which was a decidedly bad sign, certainly for her. Instead, the Emperor preferred to survey the metropolis from this balcony. While the city itself was only the tiniest fraction of all the worlds and peoples he ruled, the impressive view helped remind him of his importance. It was good for an Emperor to shore up his confidence when he was about to take drastic but necessary action.

"The Imperium operates within a safety net of rules

and laws. Any person who tries to sever the strands of our safety net endangers us all." Shaddam smiled to himself. He liked that. The words had been spontaneous, but eloquent; he would have to use them in a proclamation someday. "Years ago, we stationed Sardaukar on Grumman to keep that Moritani madman in line, but as soon as the troops left, he returned to his old antics. Obviously the Viscount does not fear my military as much as he should."

"More importantly, Sire, he does not fear *you* as much as he should."

Shaddam turned abruptly to his friend. Fenring's assessment was entirely correct. He scowled. "Then we must do something about him, Hasimir. I will take as many Sardaukar as I can load aboard our frigates and go personally to Grumman. This time I will bring my camp and my supporters, and we will occupy the Viscount's planet. I will strip him of his titles and find someone else to take over the siridar fief of House Moritani."

Fenring pursed his lips, tapped his fingers on the burnished gold balustrade. "Hmmm, it may be difficult to find someone who even *wants* Grumman. The planet is all used up. Even the Moritanis have been trying to unencumber themselves for some time."

"Then we shall assign it to someone we *don't* like! Either way, I want House Moritani out of there—and I mean to do it personally. I must show the Landsraad that the Emperor pays attention to any slight against his good name."

Fenring did not seem quite as overjoyed or enthusiastic as Shaddam thought he should be. The sounds and smells of the nighttime city wafted about the men in a rich and heady stew. "Have you considered, aaahh, Sire, that this may be exactly what the Viscount wants? He has been baiting you, pushing you, as though hoping you would go there in person, rather than let someone else dirty their hands on your behalf."

Shaddam sniffed. "For something so important, I would not delegate the responsibility—even to you, my trusted friend. Once we land with all the might of my Imperium, Viscount Moritani will abase himself before me to beg my forgiveness."

Fenring suddenly showed interest in sparkling holographic flames that erupted as an illusionary torch from a tower, so that Shaddam couldn't see the expression on his face when he said, "Aaahh, perhaps you expect a little too much."

"That is not possible. I am Emperor."

Despite the Count's lackluster reaction, Shaddam felt good about what he had decided to do. This would not be a mere military campaign, but an awe-inspiring event, a genuine spectacle with all the pomp and glory that House Corrino could provide. This would teach Viscount Hundro Moritani—and all the Houses of the Landsraad—a valuable lesson in obedience.

Just as Leto Atreides was shaped by his father, so it was with young Paul. A strong sense of honor and justice passed from generation to generation. This made what eventually happened to Paul an even greater tragedy. He should have known better.

—BRONSO OF IX, *The True History of Muad'Dib*

Leading the military forces against House Moritani reminded Duke Leto of words his father had spoken when Leto was barely seven. *The law is not a ball of twine, to be picked at and unraveled until there is nothing left of it.*

At the time, he had not understood what Paulus meant, but the imagery had remained with him. Gradually, Leto learned the distinction between truly noble houses and those that relied on situational ethics and conditional morality. For House Atreides, the law of the Imperium truly meant something. For others, it did not. House Moritani fell into the latter category.

Now, from where he stood beside his son on the command bridge of the flagship, Leto gazed out on a morning sky thick with dropships crowded with Atreides and Ecazi soldiers, ground cannons, and other long-range armaments, while small hawkships darted through the air on surveillance assignments for the joint strike force.

Ritka was an unadorned, fortified city on the edge of a long-dry sea, butted up against rugged foothills. "Not much worth fighting for here," Duncan observed.

"We are not here to conquer for profit, but to avenge," Leto said.

"Look, he cowers behind house shields!" Archduke Ecaz transmitted from his command craft. "I expected no better from him."

Leto could see that Ritka was covered by massive protective barriers, shimmering force fields that made the fortress keep impervious to projectile fire and aerial bombardment. "He is forcing us to make a conventional ground assault, with our soldiers using personal shields. Hand-to-hand combat, on a big scale."

"Good old-fashioned bloodshed," Gurney said. "If that's what he wants, then we'll give it to him."

Paul studied the terrain, thinking of his tactical studies with Thufir Hawat. "The dry seabed gives us a huge staging area to land all our ships, deploy our vehicles and equipment, and organize our troops in ranks."

Several divisions of Grumman warriors had formed a line on the shore of the seabed near Ritka, where they intended to face off against their enemies. Most were on foot but others sat astride muscular warhorses—House Moritani's famed stallions. "They've selected the battlefield," Leto said. "It appears they want plenty of elbow room. Good—that works better for us, too."

"This is too easy," Duncan warned. He and Gurney sat at illuminated instrument consoles, poring over preliminary scout surveys. "Too obvious."

"It could be a trick to lure us closer, but Viscount Moritani is not a subtle man," Leto said. "Get on a secure line and remind the officers and pilots to be extremely cautious." He turned to where Paul was eagerly studying details on the projection screen. "Your first war, Paul. Many lessons for you to learn here, no matter what happens. I hope you can pick up something vital. There are rules of conduct, conventions of war."

As if he had heard his father's previous thoughts, Paul murmured, "The law is not a ball of twine."

Leto smiled, always amazed at the boy's intuitive mind, especially now, under pressure. Despite the dangers they were likely to face, the Duke knew he had done the right thing in permitting his son to accompany him into battle. Sometimes it was best to learn under fire. He knew he might not always be there to guide Paul, just as his own father's death had thrust Leto into a position of responsibility long before he was ready. Grumman would be a proving ground, and the boy would become a fine and honorable Duke himself someday.

Once it was formally declared, a War of Assassins placed distinct legal limitations on the materiel and methods that the combatants could employ. Ultimately, the battle would boil down to hand-to-hand combat, supposedly among champions—with few casualties among innocent noncombatants. But House Moritani had already broken so many rules that Leto could not rely on the Viscount to abide by any accepted conventions in the impending combat. Even the Padishah Emperor would not be able to turn a blind eye to such flouting of Imperial law.

Duke Leto watched another flight of dropships setting down on the ground at the far shore of the dry seabed, disgorging soldiers and armaments. He placed a hand on the young man's shoulder. "Watch closely, Paul. We could have an unfair advantage here, but we will use no tactics that our honorable ancestors would not have condoned."

"Even if the Viscount uses them first?" Paul asked.

"We follow our own standards—not anyone else's."

Paul continued to stare at the preparations and disembarkation. "In that case, although the Atreides and Ecazi forces appear to have military superiority, we'll effectively be fighting under a handicap."

"A code of ethics is never a handicap," Leto said. He

turned to Duncan. "Put me on the main channel. It's time to start this."

A shimmering bubble appeared in front of Leto, and he spoke into it, transmitting directly to the Ritka fortress. "Viscount Hundro Moritani, by the rules of kanly and the laws of the Imperium, we demand that you stand down and surrender immediately. We will guarantee you a fair legal forum to insure that true justice is served. Otherwise, your defeat will be swift and sure."

Static sounded over the open channel, and the image of the Viscount's Swordmaster, Hiih Resser, appeared, looking pale but determined. Duncan was clearly startled to see Resser, his former friend from the Ginaz School, but he did not interrupt as the other man spoke. "Viscount Moritani rejects your demand and charges you with violating the War of Assassins. You are making an illegal military incursion on a sovereign planet, an action that is expressly prohibited under the Great Convention."

"You quote such rules to *us?*" Archduke Ecaz shouted, transmitted from his command craft. "This is no longer a War of Assassins—you have turned it into open warfare."

As if to emphasize the fact, a volley of Grumman missiles streaked out of launchers embedded just outside the shimmering shields of the Viscount's fortress city. Because the landed Atreides and Ecazi war frigates were also shielded, the heavy projectiles skipped harmlessly off the barriers, but a cry of outrage rose from the soldiers lining up in ranks on the battlefield.

Resser's image had vanished as soon as the missiles were launched. It was more a gesture of defiance than an intent to cause any real damage to the opposing army, but it demonstrated the lengths to which the Grummans would go.

Bristling with anger and indignation, Leto ordered his forces to advance on the fortress city.

Trying to plan every detail of a large and complex battle is like mapping the winds—expect chaos, unpredictability, and surprises. That is all you need to know.

—JOOL-NORET, the first Swordmaster

From his position of safety in the foothills, Rabban watched the impressive and well-coordinated landing of the enemy armies. The sheer number of war frigates astonished him. What an expense! He knew how much it had cost his uncle to send just one division of Harkonnen soldiers to Grumman. House Atreides and House Ecaz must have each spent at least ten times that.

To Rabban, it indicated how outraged Duke Leto and Archduke Armand must be over the wedding-day attack. He couldn't help but smile. It was too bad that House Harkonnen couldn't take public credit alongside Viscount Moritani, but he saw his uncle's wisdom in letting the Grummans accept the blame.

The provocation had certainly worked . . . though he wished he had a better understanding of Moritani's plans. Rabban assumed that his uncle understood what the Viscount was truly up to.

Wearing the black-plumed helmet that designated him the Warlord in charge of the defending armies, Rabban sat straight in the saddle, gazing over the battlefield. He flexed his muscles, restless to get into the fight. But he would let the Grumman warriors take the brunt of the first impact. Then he could get down to business himself.

The Ecazi army moved first, leaving the swarms of landed frigates and shielded soldiers to embark on a ground assault across the dry and dusty expanse. The flat plain would define the parameters of the battlefield. Atreides soldiers followed them in a second wave.

Rabban had stationed half of his mounted troops on the rocky shore to stand guard. Behind him and up the slopes, impenetrable house shields enveloped the Viscount's armed fortress. They were under strict orders to wait, to remain visible as defenders of Ritka, but not to move against the enemy army.

His horse was powerful and restless and continued to shift nervously. He touched the controls on the pommel, sending a jolt to the proper nerve center of the horse's conditioned brain, forcing it to stand still. He had neither the time nor patience to become accustomed to his mount, so he needed to keep it under control. Nearby, Brom and the other lieutenants sat astride their own trained stallions.

Marching forward in ranks across the seabed, the Ecazi and Atreides soldiers wore body shields. Rabban pressed his thick lips together, contemplating tactics. A single soldier firing a lasgun into one of those shields would create a pseudo-atomic explosion powerful enough to vaporize the entire military force. But Rabban wouldn't go that far, even if he could find a way to escape the detonation himself. Such tactics would invite far too many questions in the aftermath.

Since the shields on both sides made projectile weapons and explosives useless, as well as aerial attacks, this battle would seem almost medieval: sword against sword, personal combat won by skill and strength. Rabban could already imagine the resounding clamor.

As the front lines of Ecazi troops marched slowly toward Ritka, he grew impatient and clenched his fists. The Viscount had ordered him to wait, specifically forbidding him to send his troops into battle. Until when? No one had told him. Rabban made a disgusted noise. It seemed foolish to ignore such a prime opportunity. Why waste so much time and let them grow closer, unchallenged? "Our troops could engage them out there right now! Is this a battle, or isn't it?"

Before a command could leave Rabban's mouth, though, Brom said in a deep warning voice, "Wait for the right moment. Not yet."

"But this is insanity. What is the right moment? Look at them!"

"The Viscount knows his plan. It is not a warrior's business to understand his master, but simply to obey and wait for the signal."

Rabban ground his teeth together, remembering quite clearly that this unpredictable Moritani lord was not his master.

He heard loud horns, shrill whistles, and a startling clamor of metal on metal, even the sharp reports of small explosions. Brom gestured toward the expansive canvas-roofed corrals and stables that held Moritani's prized Genga stallions. Driven ahead by screaming warriors, the monster horses flowed out of their corrals, hundreds upon hundreds of angry wild beasts armed with spikes and sharp razors. The unleashed stallions swept around the low hills, then surged in a wild, unstoppable mass across the dry plain directly toward the oncoming enemy army. The whooping, goading warriors wheeled away and retreated to the stables, letting the stallions continue their stampede.

Rabban had not expected that at all. He chuckled and looked over at Brom. "Yes, now I'm glad that we waited."

❧

WHEN THE ATREIDES troops followed the Ecazi army in the forward march, Paul carried his own sword as well as a dagger. He walked between Duncan and Gurney, both of whom seemed to be overprotective. After fighting off the assassin-trackers on Caladan, the young man had insisted upon participating on the battlefield, despite his father's clear uneasiness.

Leto had said, "If you are to be a Duke someday, Paul, you must learn how to *command*. Keep your perspective on the whole battle and know your place. You are not a common soldier."

"But I am not a Duke yet, Father," Paul had replied. "As you've always said, before I have the right to make decisions involving the lives of the men, I must understand what they go through. This fight is more about honor than glory or conquest. Isn't that what House Atreides is all about?"

Leto had been forced to concede with a thin smile. "If I didn't believe that, I would never have considered letting you come to Grumman in the first place. All right, but Duncan and Gurney are not to let you out of their sight."

Paul knew he was as good a fighter as almost any soldier in the House Atreides forces, and the other two men vouched for him. He did not doubt, though, that his father would be monitoring him closely from the command ship.

Now they marched across the virgin battlefield, following in many trampled footsteps and so far to the rear of the shielded troops that Paul doubted he would ever see any direct combat.

Nevertheless, when the raging wall of riderless horses hurtled into the armies like an unexpected sea squall, the resulting confusion and turmoil made it seem as if the battle had turned into a rout.

Waving his sword, Gurney bellowed, "Stand firm!"

Duncan pressed closer to Paul, ready to use his new

sword. "This is lunacy—running horses can't penetrate our shields!"

Paul quickly realized the true objective. "No, but they're confusing our ranks, breaking our momentum."

The neatly organized battle lines were suddenly scrambled. Hundreds of stallions, their hooves knifing down, careened into soldiers, knocking them over inside their protective shields. The dust thrown into the air by the thunderous stampede made it impossible to see. Static sparkles outlined the coverage area of Paul's shield.

"Paul, stay close!" Gurney called over the tumult.

A wild-eyed horse, mottled brown-and-white, reared up before Paul. The boy ducked sideways as the sharp hooves came down and skittered harmlessly off the shield. One of the metal spines of the war horse's armor managed to slide partly through the barrier, so that Paul had to twist away to avoid being impaled. Next to him, Duncan was trying to hold fast.

More horses crashed against shields, and many soldiers panicked at the sight of the monsters coming at them. They struck out with their blades, slashing at the horses, killing some, wounding others. Maddened by the cuts, the stallions went wild, crashing into each other, inflicting further injuries with their war spikes.

Paul remained crouched, not certain how to fight against such a force. A number of the warhorses actually broke through shields, penetrating the soldiers' defenses and killing them. Some of the troops shouted for their commanders and tried to stand together, but the well-trained units had been disrupted into a disorganized mass. Few could hear the orders of the commanders over the uproar.

The stampede seemed to last forever, though the maddened horses were not guided; they'd simply been turned loose on the armies of Ecaz and Atreides. Dozens of the stallions were killed before the wall of wild horses passed.

Gurney began yelling at the top of his lungs, trying to impose order. "Atreides, Atreides to me! Form ranks!"

Paul could barely see through the billowing dust the stallions had stirred up on the dry plain. He felt certain that this was not the only trick Viscount Moritani would unleash upon them.

~

FROM HIS VANTAGE point, Rabban watched the mayhem with smug pleasure plain on his face. The enemy forces were in complete disarray from the hundreds of armored horses that had plowed through their ranks. He knew what to do next. This must be why the Viscount had told him to wait.

Now it was his turn to take charge. "I'm sending forth our armies to attack before they can re-form ranks."

Brom glared at him. "The Viscount ordered us to wait for his signal."

"As your Warlord I am in command of this battlefield, and I see an opportunity that the Viscount didn't plan for." Snarling, Rabban activated his transmitter and sent his command to the soldiers. "All troops, push forward and strike the enemy. We will never have a better chance."

"This is not wise, Rabban!" Brom insisted, raising a gloved fist. "We follow the orders of the Viscount."

"Your Viscount made *me* Warlord. Obey my instructions, or die at the point of my sword." He gestured to the chaotic enemy army below. "Isn't it obvious? Look!"

Reluctantly, the Grumman soldier placed a hand over his own chest armor, and turned his gaze aside.

Barking another command, Rabban ordered two of his Harkonnen officers to join the troops, which they did, galloping off on their stallions. Moments later, the disguised Harkonnen division, as well as the Grumman warriors, raised a howling battle cry and plunged forward onto the dry plain that had once been a shallow inland sea.

The Ecazi troops saw the charge and required no orders to know how to respond. With an answering howl, they raised their weapons to meet the enemy, and rushed forward.

Rabban glanced up at the shielded fortress keep, knowing that Moritani must be watching with interest, most likely applauding Rabban's snap decision. He guided his uneasy horse down out of the hills toward the edge of the battlefield.

Brom followed. "If you insist on this fight, Warlord, we should participate ourselves—as true commanders."

"I agree." The two men, with fifty of the elite Moritani warriors who had been stationed with them, rode toward the edge of the seabed, ready to join the main forces immediately after the initial clash. The bulk of their troops rushed across the plain toward the enemy at full gallop.

Explosions rumbled from beneath the ground. The surface of the seabed began to collapse inward, dropping away like countless trapdoors beneath not only the Ecazi army, but the mounted Grumman soldiers riding toward them. Rabban couldn't believe what he was seeing. "What the hell is happening?"

An entire section of the plain collapsed, revealing hundreds of underground tunnels and shafts. Rabban knew that House Moritani mined and extracted chemicals and minerals from beneath the ground, but now it seemed that someone had detonated the support walls of the fragile honeycombed shell, causing these particular tunnels to collapse.

In an instant, more than half of the Moritani and Harkonnen soldiers had plunged to their deaths, along with an equal number of the enemy Ecazi, swallowed up by the battlefield itself.

Stunned, Rabban wondered about the explosions. Who could have done that? His mind went blank. Had this entire scenario been a trap, intentionally set by the Viscount to lure the enemy across the battlefield? Suddenly, he saw the logic of it.

Furious that Moritani would keep such vital information from him, he turned to look at Brom, but saw only murderous, accusing hatred on the other warrior's face. Brom drew his sword.

"What?" Rabban said, pointing out at the collapsed battlefield. "Your own Viscount must have done that! To our troops as well as the enemy! He should have warned—"

"The Viscount knew his plan," Brom said. "He gave you instructions. You disobeyed."

Rabban backed up his stallion, but Grumman soldiers began closing in around him.

I want no allies but myself. Friends can be as dangerous as enemies.

—GLOSSU RABBAN

The rumble of explosions and the billowing dust took a long time to subside. The screams continued much longer. Making certain that Paul was unharmed, Duncan Idaho struggled to grasp the disaster that had just swallowed the front ranks of the Ecazi-Atreides army. Hundreds of tunnels had collapsed beneath the advancing forces—a primitive trap, but an effective one. Moans and shouts echoed from the rubble, along with whinnies and clatters as the last frenzied stallions crashed about and stampeded away, some of them falling into the yawning pits.

Gurney stood beside Duncan, his face twisted in anger and shock. "That was intentional—like a hunter's covered pit, with explosives planted so deep our mine sweepers could not detect them."

"But his own cavalry charged right into the middle of it, too," Paul said. "I don't understand—why would the Grummans do that? By rushing out to meet us, they lost as many forces as we did. All those men . . . all those men . . ." He stared ashen at the disaster before him. "It's as though the Viscount's own commanders didn't know what was going to happen."

Out on the field, Ecazi and Atreides officers shouted orders, trying to regroup their surviving fighters into ranks. The allied soldiers gathered their weapons once more and picked their way across the hazardous ground. They were angry now, and their murmur rapidly built to an uproar.

Duke Leto's hovering command vehicle rushed to the edge of the battlefield, and Duncan went to meet him, keeping Paul close by his side. "Your son is safe, my Lord," he shouted over the roar of the engines. "He is here with us."

Leto opened the hatch of the suspensor-hovering craft. The tone of his voice allowed no argument. "Paul, come aboard with me. Now."

The young man let himself be pulled up into the hovering command vehicle. Obviously, he'd had enough of the battlefield.

As the dusty air cleared, Gurney stared transfixed at the far side of the dry seabed, where the commander of the Grumman forces, wearing a gaudy black-plumed helmet, sat astride a tall stallion not far from the shielded fortress city. The warlord had been giving the orders earlier, rushing along at the rear of the abortive charge that had been swallowed up in the collapsing seabed.

Gurney saw him up on the hillside now, with other soldiers around him. "My Lord, if Duncan and I were to take a pair of fast scout cycles, we could intercept their commander and take him prisoner. That might break the Grumman resistance."

Duncan added, "He seems to have lost half of his troops already."

With a firm and protective hand on his son's shoulder, Duke Leto frowned. "Even if you succeed, I don't think the Viscount places any value on hostages."

But Gurney grinned fiercely. "After what just happened, it'll be good for *our* morale, and it might well finish this ground assault in one bold step. Then Viscount Moritani will have to come out and command the troops himself instead of hiding in his fortress."

Duncan raised his new sword. "I agree with Gurney."

"You two are my best fighters." Leto drew a deep breath. "Go and show that Grumman commander the meaning of Atreides vengeance." The Duke summoned two fast scout cycles for the race across the plain.

Duncan nodded appreciatively at the sleek vehicles. "That warlord is only on horseback. We'll catch up to him in no time." He smiled at Gurney. "My new sword is thirsty for blood."

❦

THE ANGRY GRUMMAN warriors closed in around Rabban. Five of the unmounted, well-muscled men held sharpened blades. Brom, astride his stallion, glowered at Rabban. "It is the way of the warrior. The blood of an army is the blood of its commander."

Rabban neither understood nor cared about Grumman philosophy, despite his personal interest in violence. "Find out how many of our soldiers survived," he shouted, trying to salvage his command. "Brom, rally the remaining fighters, and we will make a stand! The Viscount has other weapons he can use, if he ever decides to support us."

The Grummans moved closer, appeared to be on the verge of pouncing. "This battle is already lost," Brom said. "We *will* make a stand, but your head will be on a pike to watch us. Maybe your ugly face will frighten the enemy."

Rabban's stallion shifted again, backing away.

"The blood of an army is the blood of its commander," repeated another Grumman warrior, advancing with his blade.

"You can't kill me! I am the heir to House Harkonnen!"

"You are a failure." Brom raised his sword. "And you have led *us* to failure."

Rabban activated his body shield just in time to deflect the slashing blow. As the other warriors plunged toward him, he wheeled his stallion about, desperately slapping at the behavioral controls. The animal bolted. Brom pursued hotly, while the other Grumman warriors ran howling after them.

Rabban fled, knowing he was out of his element. With the attached controls, he commanded the armored stallion to take him up the steep hillside and around the fortified city, along a trail that wound through stunted evergreen trees that offered little cover.

He had intended to prove himself to his uncle in this War of Assassins, had hoped to return to Giedi Prime as a conquering general. Now he'd be lucky to make it back at all. He didn't know if he would rather face the wrath of the Baron, or death on this faraway world.

The stallion galloped up the rugged slope with surprising grace and smoothness. Rabban felt the animal's powerful muscles pulling beneath him, and despite the incline, the horse didn't seem to tire. At a fork in the trail, the Genga darted to the right into a grove of taller trees that offered slightly better shelter. The horse forded a narrow stream and kept climbing.

Rabban headed up into the rocks, following a narrow valley in the parched hills, through which a stream ran. He found a game trail and followed it; other wild horses must have come down to this water to drink. He was panting hard himself, though the horse did all the work, gaining higher ground where more tangled trees covered the hilltops. The farther up he went toward the headwaters, other streams converged, making a rough white torrent that cut a deep gorge.

Rabban's body ached so much he could barely sit in the saddle, and the rough terrain wasn't helping. Brom was behind him somewhere and had surely summoned other Grummans to continue the pursuit. The stallion struggled past trails that branched off into side canyons. Rabban looked back, expecting angry Grumman warriors to be on his heels.

By the time he heard the humming of the enemy scout cycles, it was too late to hide.

Two men in Atreides uniforms streaked up from the valley, chasing him with cycles that skimmed over the ground, barely touching it. Rabban spun and lurched back, grabbing onto the saddle's pommel. His fingers fumbled for the neural control buttons, but the horse was already planning its escape. The stallion reared. Unable to maintain his hold, Rabban tumbled from the horse's back, landed hard on the rocky path and rolled partway down the hill. The animal bolted, and within seconds Rabban found himself alone.

With jet-bursts the Atreides scout cycles went airborne over the widening canyon, then headed toward him.

∼

"BY THE SEVEN Hells, that looks like Beast Rabban!" Gurney shouted. In the slave pits, Rabban had humiliated Gurney, scarred him for life, killed his sister. "Can it possibly be him?"

Hunched over his cycle controls, Duncan had seen the same thing. As a little boy, he'd had his own experience with the man, surviving Rabban's staged hunts through the catacombs of Barony and in the dangerous wilderness of Forest Guard Station. "It *is* Rabban." Duncan shunted aside the myriad questions that sprang to mind, such as why the Baron's nephew would be here, how much the Harkonnens were involved in this War of Assassins. His only interest right now was in capturing the man. "And now the tables are turned—we're hunting him!"

After his tumble from the horse, Rabban had regained his feet, and was running as fast as his burly legs could carry him up the long hillside. He was heading toward the shelter of rock outcroppings that stood above the fast-flowing cascade. No doubt, Rabban intended to hide like a rat.

Side by side, Duncan and Gurney raced their scout vehicles up the slope, skimming over the land. On a flat, rough patch of stone, they set down their cycles and proceeded on foot, running. Duncan drew his sword when he saw Rabban's black-tufted helmet wedged into a crack between the boulders where the man had discarded it. Not far ahead, they could hear him plunging forward, knocking rocks loose, blundering along a ledge.

The pursuers took different paths around the lichen-covered stones, which thrust upward and created many barriers, like a labyrinth. Duncan thought he smelled fear in the air. He licked his dry lips, tasting the faintly alkaline dust of Grumman. Earlier, he had been engrossed in the main battle, shocked by the sudden turnabout with the Viscount's appalling tactics on the dry seabed. Now he could only concentrate upon the memories of his childhood: the terror and rage he had felt at being chased by Rabban and his fellow hunters. He had barely survived by outsmarting Rabban and escaping . . . but in the intervening years, how many other victims had this man killed?

Too many.

Duncan put on a burst of speed, knowing that Gurney Halleck hated the Harkonnen brute as much as he did. Though they were friends, Duncan did not want to surrender the satisfaction of the kill, even to his bosom friend.

The outcroppings of stone channeled Rabban's flight into particular directions, and as he ran, he would have chosen the easiest route. Every time Duncan rounded a towering pinnacle, he expected to see his enemy there, waiting to ambush him.

Finally, the path petered out among towering talus boulders. Duncan passed a dead tree, rounded a tall rock, and found an open ledge—a cliff, forty feet above the rushing cascade that raced down the gorge toward the dry plains. Rabban stood at the dead end in dismay, looking over the precipice. He turned toward his pursuer, desperately clutching a fighting knife that seemed to have more jewels than blade, a clumsy ornament rather than a deadly weapon.

Duncan lifted his sword and stepped closer to him, feeling a deadly calm inside. "I would rather run you through, Rabban. But if you choose to stumble and fall off the cliff, that would be satisfactory as well."

Rabban spat forcefully at him, but the wad of spittle struck to the inside of his personal shield and went no farther, dripping and sparkling against the invisible barrier.

"You don't even recognize me, do you?" Duncan said, thinking Gurney might have made more of an impression on the so-called Beast. "He's over here!" Duncan glanced quickly aside as his comrade approached.

While Duncan's attention was diverted for an instant, Rabban plunged at him with the dagger. "Don't need to remember you," the other man grunted. "I can kill you." Duncan easily parried, and Rabban did not compensate enough for the presence of the shield, so that his dagger was deflected. Duncan was much more proficient at close-in fighting, and his new razor-edged sword slashed along the meat of his opponent's upper arm, drawing a bright scarlet line of blood.

Rabban growled and swung the dagger again, but it slid ineffectually off Duncan's blade. Duncan pushed, shield against shield. "Second time I've beaten you— and this time I'm not just a child."

Rabban's heel slipped off the edge of the cliff, and the close-set eyes flew wide open as he lost his balance. Duncan instinctively reached out to grab the man, but Rabban fell, dropping into the foamy white torrent below.

Gurney shouted, more in disappointment than concern. The two men stood watching as Rabban flailed helplessly in the sweeping water, narrowly missing one of the wet dark boulders, and was swept tumbling down the cold stream. His shield continued to shimmer, protecting him from rocks, but he could still drown.

"Now how are we going to fetch him?" Duncan said in disgust.

"Maybe there's a big waterfall ahead," Gurney added. "We can hope."

They heard angry shouts, more horses coming. Duncan spotted other Grumman warriors approaching up the hillside and converging from a side canyon. "We have to go," he said.

Gurney nodded. "The Duke needs to know that the Harkonnens are involved here as well."

"I would rather have Rabban's head for proof, but our word will be good enough for the Duke." Duncan looked at the fresh stain on his new sword. "At least I've blooded my blade."

"Wipe the blood on your sleeve. Maybe it can be tested."

As the Moritani forces came closer, he and Gurney made it back to their scout vehicles and used jet-bursts to fly out over the canyon. As they raced away, they looked for any sign of Rabban's battered body in the rocks. But to their disappointment, they did not see him.

There is no rationality in vengeance.

—ARCHDUKE ARMAND ECAZ

At the edge of the collapsed plain, Duke Leto and Archduke Armand demanded a swift battlefield assessment from suspensor-borne scoutcraft. Because the Ecazi troops had been in the forefront of the armies marching across the open seabed, they had suffered the largest losses to the cave-ins, with whole divisions falling into the yawning pits. Forming the rear guard, the Atreides ranks remained mostly intact, and now the Caladan army pushed forward to reinforce the Ecazis, moving onward to Ritka.

The Archduke looked devastated by this additional tragedy, but seemed to take grim satisfaction in realizing that the Moritani losses appeared to be as great as his own. Shouldn't the Viscount's cavalry have known better?

Even more astonishing, scout probes showed that the remaining Grumman cavalry and foot soldiers had turned upon their own, slaughtering fighters who wore similar uniforms, yellow against yellow, as if they represented two rival clans or military groups. "I don't understand it," Leto said, "but it makes our fight easier."

From his adjacent command vehicle, Armand sent an

angry transmission. "We must move into the chaos, my friend. Both sides have been decimated, but that merely diminishes the *scale* of the battle, not the reasons. The Viscount has given our soldiers all the more incentive to fight."

Beside his father, Paul pored over the constantly changing tactical projections and weaponry assessments. Something about the pieces here did not add up. He could not comprehend the true strategy or goal of House Moritani. Something major seemed to be missing. *We do not have a vital part of the data. The Viscount is relying on that.*

"Something must be hiding in that fortress keep behind the house shields," Paul said. "There's got to be more to his plan. It's the only way Moritani's actions make sense."

"I agree, Paul. I don't believe he has played his entire hand yet." Duke Leto looked alternately at the instruments and out through a magnification port. "We must be cautious."

As the combined forces continued to press toward the boundary of Ritka, they followed the more stable shore to avoid the collapsed pits. Scanner scouts mapped the ground ahead, dismantling landmines and other booby traps that slowed their progress. Leto was less surprised to see the desperate measures Hundro Moritani had laid down, than he was troubled that so much of the Viscount's strategy seemed to be a *delaying* tactic, not a plan for victory. He knew Paul saw it, too. Did Moritani intend to engage in a war of attrition, rather than a War of Assassins?

Just then, Archduke Armand relayed a report he had received from his front-line squads. "The Grumman forces are retreating to new positions around Ritka, reinforced by troops that were holed up in bunkers there. Their commanders are vowing to fight to the death."

"It'll be a bloodbath before we can get through the shields and enter the city." Leto shook his head in frustration.

Duncan and Gurney returned from their pursuit of the black-helmeted warlord, breathless, dusty, armed with startling news. Leto's stomach knotted in anger as they described their discovery of Rabban's involvement. "It's Harkonnens, my Lord," Duncan said. "If they did not declare their participation in the War of Assassins, they will face extreme sanctions once this is brought before the Emperor."

"That's Rabban's blood on Duncan's sleeve," Gurney said. "Can you have it tested for DNA?"

"Not here, not now," Leto said. "Later, maybe, but that won't prove where we got the blood. They can say we faked it, got it somewhere else. But we'll know."

Gurney shook his head. "Without proof, the Baron will deny everything. But we saw what we saw."

As his father's expression darkened, Paul came to a quick conclusion. "That may be why the Grumman troops are attacking each other—they aren't *all* from House Moritani. Some may be Harkonnen soldiers disguised in Moritani uniforms, and for some reason they've turned on each other."

"I have no doubt the lad is right," Gurney said. "They're doing our work for us."

Still apprehensive, Leto watched the Atreides and Ecazi troops rush into their first encounter with the entrenched Moritani survivors outside the Ritka shields. "Victory first. Once we're done, we'll have ample time to look for additional evidence of Harkonnens."

"You sound confident, Father."

Leto looked at Paul. "I try never to enter a battle unless I am confident of victory."

SEVEN HOURS HAD passed, and the sun was dropping behind the mountains, painting a palette of color across the dry, rocky hills. Though the entrenched Moritani forces continued to hold their positions around the fortress city, Atreides and Ecazi commando teams on the ground sought weak spots and entrances to Ritka, trying to reach the shield controls and shut the system down.

Then a Heighliner arrived and changed everything.

The gigantic Guildship in orbit over Grumman disgorged a force of hundreds of military frigates, which flew down in full battle formation. The new influx of weaponry and troops would alter the balance of the opposing forces so significantly that the war would be over swiftly.

With a sinking heart, Leto thought he understood why Viscount Moritani had been stalling: He must have known these reinforcements would arrive, and he needed only to hold out until they came. "It's possible the Harkonnens have decided to show their hand. This may be a full army from Giedi Prime."

After several urgent transmissions requesting explanations, the Atreides command vehicle finally received a response. When the comline opened, Leto was astonished to see a familiar image in the holo: Prince Rhombur of Ix.

"I thought you might like a little help, Leto, so I brought the full military of House Vernius. Those bastards tried to kill Bronso, too."

"Rhombur, you are a sight for sore eyes!"

"That's what Tessia always says. I'm afraid I had to make plenty of concessions to the damned technocrats, but I'm here. I couldn't afford not to help after what you did for me. . . ."

The Grumman troops reeled when the battle turned entirely against them. Rhombur brought his military frigates down to join the armies of House Atreides and House Ecaz. Archduke Armand had joined Leto by the time the cyborg Prince boarded the hovering Atreides command vehicle. At the entry hatch of the large craft, the two men clasped hands, then strode side by side to the bridge, Rhombur droning in his synthesized voice about new Ixian military technologies that could breach the Moritani house shields. His scarred face formed a grin. "We'll be in the Viscount's throne room by breakfast."

Suddenly a powerful transmission blared out, pre-empting the chatter on all command frequencies, and a face filled the screens on every command bridge. "This is the Padishah Emperor Shaddam IV. By Imperial decree, I command that all hostilities hereby cease. I am required to take extraordinary action to prevent this War of Assassins from escalating into a full-scale Landsraad conflict."

The Emperor's image radiated smug confidence. "I have come personally to accept the surrender of House Moritani. The Viscount has already transmitted his request to present himself to me in person to face my Imperial judgment. It is the only way to avoid further bloodshed."

Looking through the forward viewing window of his command ship, Leto saw another craft settle down next to Rhombur's vessels, having trailed the others to the ground. This one bore the scarlet-and-gold markings of House Corrino.

The human race is bound not only by common ge-
netics but also by universal standards of behavior.
Those who do not willingly follow the guidelines
of civilization can no longer be considered truly
human.

—Bene Gesserit axiom

When the next morning dawned upon the enforced peace on Grumman, an armada of Corrino warships hung in the gray sky. Guarded by Sardaukar soldiers in imposing dress uniforms, the Padishah Emperor and a delegation of noblemen and Landsraad officials gathered outside the grand entrance of the Ritka stronghold, garbed in their own importance. The huge fortress lay exposed and vulnerable, like a supplicant. Viscount Hundro Moritani had been forced into submission.

During the night, the Grumman defenders had retreated into the fortress city, and the Viscount had willingly shut down his house shields to allow the Corrino dignitaries and the leaders of the opposing armies to enter. Now, the formal group stood before tall wooden doors engraved with the spiny horsehead crests of House Moritani. The forward walls of the ancient fortification, with turrets, ramparts, and bastions, towered high overhead. Yellow banners snapped in a cold breeze.

In the delegation from the offworld armies, Paul stood with his father, along with the one-armed Ecazi Archduke and the cyborg Ixian Prince, waiting for the ornate doors to open. Overnight, they had cleaned themselves

and changed out of their battle clothes into dress uniforms that proudly displayed their House crests on the
lapels and collars. Armand's empty sleeve was pinned up
by a medal bearing the symbol of House Ecaz.

Paul noted how old and scarred the Ritka fortress
looked; over the centuries, it had obviously survived numerous battles. Beneath the crest on each door, carved
panels depicted military exploits from the long and
checkered history of House Moritani, some of which
Paul already knew from his studies. Conspicuously absent, however, were depictions of the modern atrocities
the Viscount had committed against Ginaz and Ecaz.

As they waited to enter, Paul realized he had never
stood so close to Shaddam IV before. And he had to admit to himself that the Padishah Emperor looked quite
majestic and powerful, surrounded by the trappings of
his office. Did the man really rule a million worlds, or
was that just hyperbole? The Emperor seemed satisfied
and eager to wrap up the Moritani "unpleasantness" and
make his way back to Kaitain. He and his retainers were
obviously vested in the idea that disputes could be resolved through the force of law, but that assumption
remained valid only so long as all parties abided by the
same rules.

"I don't think this will end as neat and clean as the
Emperor expects," Gurney said in a low tone. "The Viscount doesn't finish conflicts by signing a piece of paper."
From what he'd seen so far, Paul could only agree. He
had a queasy feeling in his stomach, and saw tension on
his father's face.

Looking around at the waiting party, however, Paul
sensed an eagerness on the part of many of the Imperial
retainers, minor Landsraad observers, and officials of
various committees. They appeared filled with admiration that Shaddam could solve the problem simply

through the force of his presence. The Sardaukar remained alert, their puissant rifles at the ready.

With a grating fanfare of strange Grumman horns, the heavy doors swung inward, and men in yellow livery somberly led the visitors into the nobleman's reception hall. There, Viscount Hundro Moritani stood alone in the middle of the chamber wearing thick layers of furs and fine, colorful cloth. At the far end of the room, his blocky throne remained pointedly empty. His brow was moist with perspiration, and he looked red-eyed, haggard, and edgy.

Shaddam IV strode in, followed by his entourage. He surveyed the room with disdain, frowning at the brutish throne and faded tapestries on the walls. "This place will be adequate for the surrender ceremony and my decrees, but I do not intend to remain here long afterward."

The Atreides party followed the Emperor into the room, but Duncan's step faltered when he noticed the redheaded young man who stood at attention beside the defeated Viscount. "Hello, Duncan Idaho," said Hiih Resser. "Old friend."

Paul had heard stories of Duncan's comrade, who had remained on Ginaz even when the other Grumman students were expelled from the Swordmaster school. Because of the lessons his father had taught him so many times, Paul understood the intricacies of honor that could force a man to abide by an oath even when it bound him to a bad man.

"I wish you had joined me at House Atreides," Duncan said to him. "I'd rather be fighting at your side than against you."

"It was not a choice I could make," Resser answered.

"There will be no more fighting," Shaddam interrupted them peremptorily and seated himself on the Grumman throne to preside over the ceremony. "I have already had the standard documents drawn up." He motioned for a retainer to hurry forward and hand him a gilt-edged proclamation.

The Viscount seated himself on a chair not far from the throne, beside a squat writing desk. The station seemed designed for a chamberlain or scribe to record documents for Hundro Moritani. Now, the Grumman leader accepted his subordinate place without argument. Resser stood stiffly behind his master.

"I will need to study your terms in detail before agreeing to them," Moritani said, with a lilting sneer in his voice.

"That will not be necessary." Shaddam leaned forward. "The terms are non-negotiable."

Rhombur seemed pleased by the defeated leader's discomfiture. Standing with the Ixian, Armand Ecaz looked brittle, as if his anger had been the only glue keeping him together; Duke Leto remained carefully wary, absorbing details.

One of the Sardaukar guards presented the Imperial parchment to the Viscount, who placed it on the desk. Paul could sense a strange excitement emanating from the man, a tension that made his movements jerky and frenetic. Behind him, Resser looked nauseated.

The Grumman leader perused the document, then said, "Shall I sign using the name Moritani? Or—since this constitutes yet another instance of Corrinos stripping everything from my family—perhaps I should sign as *House Tantor*."

Instead of the dramatic reaction the Viscount appeared to have expected, the Emperor and the rest of the audience responded only with puzzled muttering. "Tantor?" Shaddam asked. "Whatever do you mean?"

The Viscount exposed a concealed control panel in the surface of the small desk and instantly placed his fingers on the illuminated touchpads.

Suspecting treachery, the Sardaukar guards rushed toward him, ready to defend the Emperor. Resser drew his sword and placed himself in front of the Viscount, while Duncan drew his, in return.

"Stop!" the Viscount roared. "Or you will all die in an atomic flash—even before I wish it to happen."

Shaddam rose from the crude throne. "Atomics? You would not dare."

Moritani's eyes flashed. "A *Tantor* would dare. The Tantors *did* dare, many centuries ago. When my ancestors were betrayed by Corrinos, backed into a corner and given no choice or chance for survival, they deployed all the atomics of their House and destroyed nearly all life on Salusa Secundus."

"Tantor?" Shaddam still sounded confused. "Was that their name? No matter. They were hunted down and killed, their bloodline ended and all traces expunged from Imperial history."

"Not all. Our survivors planted new seeds, and we reemerged, built ourselves up again, and became House Moritani. But now, our world is used up and my son Wolfram is dead—the end of our hopes for the future. We have nothing left, and neither will you, Shaddam Corrino. I knew you would come personally to intervene here." His hand was frozen over the controls, his fingers touching the activation contacts. "All my family atomics are here in Ritka, most of them placed by my Swordmaster in the catacombs beneath our feet. My fortress keep and all of Ritka will be turned into radioactive dust." He let out a long sigh that sounded like an exhalation of ecstasy. "I just wanted you to know before the final flash of glory. I have already dispersed records to Landsraad members. From this day forward, history will never forget the name of the House that brought down the Corrinos. Once and for all, it will be done."

All in the same instant, Shaddam shouted a command, and Sardaukar guards charged forward. But Paul saw that no one could intervene in time.

With his eyes closed and a serene smile on his face, the Viscount activated the touchpads.

Paul shouted to his father, trying to make contact one
last time, but the incinerating flash did not come.
Startled, Moritani stared down at the control panel that
had just gone dim.

Duncan did not slow as he charged toward the writing
desk, his sword upraised, but Hiih Resser interposed
himself between Duncan and the Viscount. Instead of attacking Duncan, however, his former comrade held up
his own blade in a gesture of surrender. "No need, Duncan. It's over."

Sardaukar collided with the Viscount, throwing him
bodily to the floor and roughly dragging him away from
the chair and the console. He thrashed and fought, but he
was no match for the Emperor's elite soldiers.

Resser gave up his sword, extending it hilt-first to
Duncan, speaking with sadness. "Honor does not know
politics, only obedience. He was my noble master, and I
swore my loyalty to him. But in this I could see no way
to condone his action, so I took matters into my own
hands."

"What did you do?" Duncan asked.

"I placed the atomics around the city, just as the

Viscount ordered. I knew what he intended to do. But I could not allow him to trigger the warheads in the spectacular holocaust he planned. It would have been an unforgivable crime against the Emperor, the people of Grumman, and all of you, whom he has already wronged so greatly." He took a long breath, and his agitated expression relaxed slightly. "So I disabled the linkages."

Moritani screamed at him. "You betrayed me! You broke your blood oath!"

Resser turned to the Viscount. "No, my Lord. I swore to follow your commands, and more importantly I swore to protect you. I planted the atomics, just as you ordered. Then, by preventing you from killing yourself, all of these nobles, and the Emperor himself, I saved your life and many more. My honor is intact."

⋙

"HEAR YE ALL," announced the Padishah Emperor Shaddam IV in a ponderous voice. "Heed our decision and our Imperial command."

Having moved his court back to his flagship, he sat now in his decadent jeweled robes on a portable simulacrum of the Lion Throne. His somber gaze swept the gathered nobles, the prisoners, and the observers inside the metal-walled chamber. Shaddam sounded greatly important, as though the Grumman victory was solely his doing.

Feeling out of place, Paul stood beside his father, along with Duncan, Gurney, Archduke Armand, and Prince Rhombur, still in their formal attire.

Viscount Moritani, on the other hand, wore rumpled fur-lined robes, his hair disheveled, his eyes bloodshot, looking both wild and cunning. The man made Paul uneasy simply to look at him. Though he was a nobleman,

Hundro Moritani was carried into the Emperor's presence by Sardaukar, restrained in a stiff-backed metal chair that contrasted sharply with the flamboyant throne on which the Emperor sat. Moritani's arms were bound at the wrists by shigawire and his legs fastened to the chair. Putting a nobleman in restraints was unheard of, but the Sardaukar chief of security had insisted on it.

House Atreides had a legitimate blood-grudge against the Viscount, as did Archduke Ecaz, but Paul was sure that Shaddam would give his own vengeance precedence. The remnants of the renegade House Tantor? How many people had suffered from this madman's hatred over an event that had occurred thousands of years earlier? How could anyone seek revenge after so long? Then again, the Atreides and the Harkonnens had hated each other for so many millennia that the reasons for their breach were almost lost in the distant blur of history.

Finally, looking weary yet oddly at peace, Hiih Resser stood by himself, like an island in the crowd. Shortly before the Emperor's meeting here, in a poignant gesture Resser had asked Duncan to give him his fighting knife; Duncan had offered it to him reluctantly. "You aren't going to do anything foolish, are you?"

The redheaded Swordmaster had hesitated for a long moment, then shook his head. "Not what you think, Duncan." Using the sharp point, he sliced the threads of the horsehead insignia patch on his collar, cut it free, and threw it to the floor. He then excised the rank marks from his shoulders and sleeves.

Now, seeing what his Swordmaster had done, the bound Viscount Moritani spat on the floor.

Commanding the attention of all inside the royal chamber of his flagship, the Emperor extended his jeweled staff of office and struck it on the deck with a great echoing report.

"Viscount Hundro Moritani, for your crimes there can be any number of punishments. Because you have explicitly acted against House Corrino and conspired to harm Our Imperial Person, I should order your immediate execution. However, considering the cumulative consequences you must face, execution need not be the first of them." Shaddam's eyes glinted with anger and cruel humor. Moritani had been ordered not to speak, and threatened with a gag if he refused to obey.

"As a first and vital step, I hereby revoke all of your lands, titles, and possessions: your Grumman resources, buildings, subjects, CHOAM holdings, wealth, investments, and even your wardrobe." He smiled. "We will provide suitable clothing for you in the Imperial Prison on Kaitain. Fifty percent of your liquidated assets shall be given to the Throne.

"The remaining half"—Shaddam spread his empty hand in a benevolent gesture—"will be split among the other wronged Houses—Ecaz, Atreides, and Vernius, in proportion to the losses they suffered at your hands." He nodded to himself, satisfied with his munificence. But Paul noticed that his father had stiffened. Rhombur didn't look entirely pleased either, as if he considered it an insult to reap a monetary reward for aiding his friend.

Shaddam leaned back on his throne. "As for the planet Grumman and the siridar governorship, we present it as a new holding of House Ecaz. All of its planetary wealth and natural resources are now in your control. Archduke, you may exploit this world and profit from it."

Armand stood silent and stony. His response conveyed no joy. "Thank you, Sire." The mined-out planet—its lands barely fertile, its population poor, unhealthy, and exhausted—was no prize. It would be more of an albatross around Armand's neck than an asset.

"Viscount Moritani, I reserve the right to order your execution at any time. However, in the spirit of harmony

PAUL OF DUNE 505

in the Imperium, I propose that you be delivered forth-with to Kaitain in a prison frigate, for trial in Landsraad court. Your fellow nobles will decide your specific fate."

The Viscount snarled bitterly, unable to restrain himself further. "I look forward to speaking in my own defense. I am sure that you and the Landsraad nobles will be most interested in what I have to say . . . given the proper forum. Never assume that even an Emperor knows everything that goes on in the Imperium."

Paul studied the defiant Grumman nobleman—his mannerisms, expression, and tone of voice. He wore a cloak of madness, which made him difficult to read, but Paul detected neither bravado nor a bluff. Moritani did, indeed, have something more to say. Wheels within wheels, and another set within those.

Shaddam's eyes narrowed, a calculating expression. "We look forward to your testimony, although perhaps certain other Great Houses might not."

Paul looked at Duncan, recalling the encounter with Beast Rabban here on Grumman. At long last, Duke Leto actually gave a weary smile. No member of House Atreides would be disappointed if the Baron was found culpable in these heinous acts. Not only would House Moritani fall, but House Harkonnen could also be stripped. With luck, Baron Harkonnen would find himself in a cell next to Viscount Moritani.

The Emperor nodded in satisfaction. "My work here is done." He gestured dismissively toward the furious Viscount, clapped his hands, and announced a feast to celebrate the end of the War of Assassins and the prevention of a much larger, interplanetary war.

Men who are fundamentally weak look upon threats as the ultimate expressions of power. Men who are truly powerful, however, view threats as yet another vulnerability.

—BARON VLADIMIR HARKONNEN,
Advice for Assassins

The Baron was furious and went out of his way to let Rabban see it. He also felt strangely unsettled, but he carefully hid any sign of that from his blundering nephew.

Only two days earlier, he had received a terse, cryptic note signed by Duke Leto Atreides. "We trust your nephew Rabban is recovering from his sword wound. A pity we could not spend more time with him on Grumman."

The message offered no further explanation, and the Baron felt an ominous heaviness in his chest. So, Rabban had been identified. The Atreides Duke *knew* the Harkonnens were somehow involved in the conflict . . . though apparently he possessed no proof: otherwise the message would have been accompanied by a summons to the Landsraad Court. So, Leto simply wanted House Harkonnen to know that *he* knew.

Infuriating, yes, but no harm done. Let the Atreides stew over their inability to take action. If they dared declare kanly on such flimsy innuendo, then the Baron would play the wronged party.

This afternoon the Beast had finally made his way back to Giedi Prime, pushed past the household guards and presented himself to his uncle without delay. For all his considerable flaws, the man did have some good points. As one example, Rabban realized how much trouble he was in, and that his fate rested solely in the Baron's hands. That demonstrated at least minimal intelligence. Apparently, the rest of the disguised Harkonnen troops had been killed.

Looking breathless and disheveled, Rabban stood in the Baron's study. A bloodstained healing pad was secured to the side of his head, where a medic had also shaved some of his reddish hair short to treat the injury; it gave him a battered, off-balance appearance. A wound on his arm was tightly bound with healing tape. The sword cut Leto had alluded to?

"I tremble with anticipation to learn of your adventures." The Baron's basso voice dripped sarcasm as he sat at his dark, richly carved desk. Feyd sauntered in, eager to hear of his older brother's escapades as well. The rangy young man glanced disdainfully at his muscular, thick-headed brother, who shifted his weight nervously from foot to foot. Feyd lounged on a divan where he could watch.

In abrupt sentences with occasional contradictions, Rabban explained that he had been stranded with murderous Grumman soldiers, all of whom wanted his head due to their own military failures, and how the entire division of disguised Harkonnen soldiers had either fallen into the battlefield pits or been slain by vengeful Moritani barbarians. He told how he had been chased by Atreides soldiers but escaped with only a minor wound. Then, after the Vernius ships had arrived followed by the Imperial delegation, how he'd hidden in a warehouse and barely eluded capture.

His nephew wasn't entirely without resources or imagination. Nonetheless, the Baron's face darkened. "You were *seen* by Atreides soldiers. They recognized you."

"How do you—"

The Baron slammed a beefy fist on his desk, then showed him the message from Duke Leto. "Do you understand that if you had been caught, or if you left behind any evidence of Harkonnen involvement, we would find ourselves mired in an impossible crisis?"

Rabban stood his ground. "I left no evidence, Uncle. If the Atreides Duke had any proof, he would have sent more than that message."

The Baron smiled slightly, surprised at his nephew's perceptive response. Feyd let out a rude noise, but made no other comment.

Rabban continued, "Fortunately, the Emperor brought such an army of retainers and servants with him that I was able to kill one and take his uniform and identification. In the confusion of his crackdown in the Ritka fortress, I slipped in among them, flew back with the Imperial entourage, then got passage back here."

Feyd said in his most annoying tone, "So, you can be clever after all!"

The quaver had left Rabban's voice and was replaced by confidence. "I thought I did rather well."

"You did well *getting away*. You did not do well at the task I assigned you. Have you heard the Emperor's recent announcement?"

"I heard that House Moritani has been stripped of its title and planet."

"That isn't the important part," Feyd said, looking a little too knowledgeable. "Viscount Moritani was placed on a prison frigate bound for Kaitain so that he could be charged before a Landsraad Court. He vowed to testify and expose all his little secrets."

Rabban flushed red. "You mean he'll reveal his involvement with us?"

"Oh no, of *course* not," the Baron said with treacly sarcasm. "Once he lost everything, his life on the line, and in total disgrace, we should expect the Viscount to keep our secrets because, after all, we're such good friends." He glowered at his nephew, and Rabban looked away.

Rabban was a first-order thinker: To him, actions were concrete, standing by themselves. If he threw a rock into a pond, he didn't expect to see ripples. Rabban had his strengths, though the Baron rarely complimented him for them. He had various advantageous qualities. There were times when brute force was necessary, and Rabban had few peers in that arena. More important, he truly did not have any lofty ambitions. He wasn't devious enough to seize more responsibility. The Baron didn't have to fear a dagger in the back or poison in his drink from that nephew.

Feyd, on the other hand, had a sharp and nimble mind. It often darted from topic to topic, yet like a careful juggler, he never lost his grip on any one concept. Devious? Yes, perhaps. And for all his youth, he was already showing signs of impatience to be named the successor to House Harkonnen. The Baron didn't need to announce his decision yet, but Feyd . . . lovely Feyd was the future of House Harkonnen. The Baron could see that by watching the earnest expression on the young man's face, the shrewd eyes, the obvious eagerness to learn.

But could the young man be trusted?

"Moritani has no incentive to protect us," Feyd pointed out. "In fact, there is every reason for him to exaggerate our participation."

Looking at Rabban, the Baron let his older nephew stew for a few moments, then eased the man's mind.

"Fortunately, this is not a problem so great that it cannot be repaired. In fact, while you were taking your leisurely path back home, I set an alternative solution in motion."

Rabban looked almost childishly relieved that his uncle had a plan. He didn't even need to hear the Baron's explanation of what he had done, only the simple comment that things would be all right.

The Baron withdrew a document from his private desk, a slender filmpaper scroll. "This came from an official news courier, telling of a tragic and mysterious incident. The prison frigate transporting Viscount Moritani was in transit aboard a Guild Heighliner, berthed alongside other passenger ships—even some leftover Imperial vessels withdrawing from Grumman. As you know, Heighliners do not pressurize their cargo holds. Alas, a freak accident depressurized several airlocks in the prison frigate and the Viscount was exposed to vacuum. I'm afraid he didn't survive long, and his body was found bloated and frozen. The expression on his face must have been quite hideous."

"And you arranged for this, Uncle?" Rabban said enthusiastically.

The Baron scowled at him.

Feyd snickered. "It was an *accident*."

"You admire me, Feyd, I can tell," the Baron nodded. "Someday—though not anytime soon—you will be just like me."

Feyd's retort was quick and surprising. "But not so fat, I trust."

The greatest personality change in a young man's maturity occurs when he discovers that his own father is mortal, human, and fallible.

—*The Life of Muad'Dib*, Volume 2,
by the PRINCESS IRULAN

Over the nightside of Caladan, the Heighliner disgorged troop carriers and fighter craft, followed by the Atreides family frigate. Ever respectful of those who had fought so valiantly for him in the War of Assassins, Duke Leto insisted on sending all of his soldiers home first.

With Paul sitting beside him near a wide observation window, Leto mused, "I look forward to seeing your mother again, especially after what we have just been through. She . . . she can make me feel alive again. Right now, I am too numb." Restless, the Duke stood, motioned for his son to follow, and strode down a corridor on the starboard side of the craft as the frigate descended into the atmosphere. They passed a bank of portholes that showed the running lights of the Duke's escort ships disappearing below.

"I understand how you feel, Father. I learned a great deal from what I experienced. Most of all, I hope I never have to see battle again."

"You may hope for that, but I fear it isn't likely. You are the son of a Duke. Even if you don't seek out conflict, it will find you."

The Atreides frigate broke through the last layers of cloud cover, enabling Paul to see the twinkling lights of coastal villages below and the bright target of the Cala City Spaceport. A capricious wind buffeted the descending ship, and Leto braced himself against the unexpected movement. The frigate bounced down through the edge of the storm. Peering through wind-driven rain, Paul caught glimpses of Castle Caladan and the first group of ships already landing at the spaceport, taking indicated positions like pieces on a large game board.

A large monitor screen on the bulkhead showed a tally of ships, and each time one of the vessels set down safely, an amber blip turned green. The Duke fired instructions to his officers over the comline and received reports back from them. He was satisfied and relieved to see them all come safely home.

Their family frigate circled over the spaceport, then swooped toward the main landing field. Through a starboard window Paul saw the windblown sea crashing against the cliffs. Before sunset, the fishing fleet had come back to harbor ahead of the storm, and even though the boats were lashed to their docks, they rocked heavily against the pilings. Paul knew the good people of Caladan could easily survive storms. There would always be rough weather, but that did not diminish their love for their planet.

The frigate made a bumpy landing and taxied into a large hangar, where other landed ships had already taken shelter. As Paul and his father disembarked and stepped onto a floor wet from rain running off the smooth hull, they found Lady Jessica already there waiting for them. Damp streaks in her bronze hair and speckles of water on her cloak showed that she had been caught in the downpour on her way to the hangar.

Eschewing formality, Leto pulled her close and kissed her gently. "I'm sorry you were caught in the storm."

"Just a little rain. Not so bad." They held each other, speaking little although Paul knew they had much to say to each other. During Leto's betrothal to Ilesa Ecaz, Jessica had been like a rudderless boat on the open sea. The wedding-day massacre and the War of Assassins had swept over their relationship like a rogue wave. Now, they both had decisions to make and damage to repair. Neither of them was the same as before.

Wrestling with his thoughts, Leto stared at her with his steely-gray eyes, while Jessica simply waited. Paul watched his parents until finally his father said, "There is no better time to say this, Jessica, and our son should hear it, too. I am weary of politics and feuds, and I will no longer entertain further proposals of marriage alliances from other noble Houses." He took her hands in his. "You are my one and only lady, my one and only love for all time. Though I cannot marry you, I will never agree to marry anyone else."

She seemed flustered. "You can't give me such a promise, Leto. You have to keep the other nobles guessing. You must at least keep the option available, for I am only a bound concubine."

"My love, you are much more than that to me." Reaching over to Paul, he gathered the boy into his embrace. "And you are the mother of our son, the next Duke."

PART VII

EMPEROR MUAD'DIB

10,198 AG

Is there anything more deadly than innocence, anything more disarming?

—*The Stilgar Commentaries*

Leaving the scarred Celestial Audience Chamber empty, Emperor Paul-Muad'Dib sat on the great Hagal quartz chair and held court in his original throne room. Every day, he heard the clear, heart-wrenching misery expressed by so many faithful people, but he could not allow himself to be swayed. Yes, some of them had been crushed under the wheels of Paul's own government, but he could not allow himself to care for all of them, to feel the million little cuts of their individual pain. In a sense, their suffering was essential to humanity's continued existence. Paul's prescience had forced him to look at the larger picture, and hold a steady course. It was the greater, terrible purpose within him, the only way he could lead humankind to the end result. He had to be Muad'Dib, even if that meant he must appear harsh and cold.

Duke Leto Atreides, and before him Old Duke Paulus, had loved to meet the people face to face. They considered direct interaction with their subjects a vital aspect of remaining in touch, ruler to ruled. After Bludd's shocking actions, though, and the subsequent discoveries of one embryonic conspiracy after another, Paul found the process of holding court to be exhausting, frustrating, and dangerous. The previous Caladan dukes had managed a single group of people, a single planet—but Paul had to shoulder the burden of so many planets that he could not name them all without calling upon his Mentat training.

Henceforth, he decided that he would delegate more of these responsibilities to Alia. She seemed to have a different relationship with her conscience, a way to compartmentalize what must be done. His sister, with all her past lives and remembered experiences, could govern with a firm, stern hand. And because the people were frightened of the girl's strangeness, they would see her more as a priestess than a ruler. Alia could use that to her advantage.

One morning, before the first group of supplicants was allowed into the heavily guarded chamber, Princess Irulan appeared before Paul, asking permission to speak with him. Beside the throne, Stilgar and Alia looked at Irulan with their usual suspicions, but Paul understood her motives better and trusted her to behave according to established patterns.

She wore a look of concern and puzzlement on her face. "My Husband, I have received a message from a Guild courier. It was addressed to me, asking for my intercession." Frowning, she extended the cylinder to Paul.

Intrigued, he took the document, noted the intricate seals that Irulan had already broken open. As Paul read, Irulan explained to Stilgar and Alia, "Lady Margot Fenring requests a favor."

"Lady Margot?" Alia asked, drawing upon her mother's memories as well as her own. "We have heard nothing from her in years."

The Count and his Lady, after initially joining Shaddam IV in exile on Salusa Secundus following the Battle of Arrakeen, had remained only a brief time before embarking on their own and disappearing from view— apparently with no love lost between them and the fallen Emperor. Paul knew the Count was quite a dangerous character, a schemer to rival the most Machiavellian of the Bene Gesserits or the Harkonnens.

Paul read the message, feeling a flicker of warning in his prescient senses, though nothing distinct. Much about Hasimir Fenring—another failed Bene Gesserit attempt to breed a Kwisatz Haderach—had always been murky to him. "It is odd that they took sanctuary among the Tleilaxu," he said. "I did not foresee this request. I had forgotten that Lady Margot has a daughter."

"And what does this woman want from you, Usul?" Stilgar asked. After nearly drowning on Jericha, the faithful naib had returned to Arrakis and now chose to serve directly at the side of Muad'Dib, as Minister of State. Stilgar had decided his true worth was in leadership, rather than fighting on distant planets, and Paul had to agree.

The Emperor set the message cylinder aside. "She asks permission to send her daughter Marie here, wants her to be raised and trained in our Imperial court."

Irulan was clearly unsettled by the idea. "I do not understand why."

"A better question is, why would you be suspicious of her, rather than advocating it?" Alia countered. "Count Fenring was a close friend of your father's, while Lady Margot is a prominent Bene Gesserit. Wasn't Margot a boon companion to your own mother, Lady Anirul?"

"And to your mother as well," the Princess replied. "But I am always troubled by things I do not understand."

"Is Count Fenring the natural father of the child?" Paul asked.

"Lady Margot does not suggest otherwise. I cannot tell either way."

"And if Count Fenring is no longer with Shaddam, was there truly a falling-out between them, or is this part of an overall scheme?" Alia added. "Our spies have suggested that the Count has a great deal of antipathy toward Shaddam. Is the rift real, or merely an act?"

Paul remembered the dire insult and the obvious coolness that Fenring had exhibited toward the Emperor in the immediate aftermath of the Battle of Arrakeen, while Paul himself had felt an odd sort of kinship with Fenring. Though they were entirely dissimilar men, he and the Count had certain exceptional qualities in common.

"Salusa Secundus is not a pleasant place," Stilgar said. "Or so I have heard."

"Comforts mean little to Count Fenring," Paul said. "For years, he served on Arrakis as the Imperial Spice Minister. I suspect that he left Salusa, not because he wanted a finer palace, but because he could no longer stand being with Shaddam."

Irulan's demeanor hardened. "My father often took action before he possessed all the facts. He simply expected the rest of the Imperium to bow to his will, whether or not his decisions were wise or rational. He often acted without consulting Count Fenring, and as a result got himself into terrible debacles. The Count grew tired of cleaning up after my father's messes."

With a sigh, Paul leaned forward, rested his elbows on his knees. "The question remains—how shall we respond to this request? Lady Margot wishes to send her little daughter here for schooling, and no doubt to make connections. The girl is only six years old. Could their motives be as straightforward as wanting to get into my good graces, since they abandoned Shaddam IV?"

"Occam's Razor suggests that may be the real answer," Irulan said. "The simplest answer does make perfect sense."

"Occam's Razor is dull where the Bene Gesserit are concerned," Alia said. "I know from the clatter in my head that they have always schemed and plotted."

Paul lifted the filmy sheets again and read the words Margot had imprinted there: " 'Emperor Paul-Muad'Dib Atreides, I humbly and respectfully request a favor. Though my husband has chosen to take refuge among the Tleilaxu, I am convinced that this is not the environment in which our daughter should be raised. The misogynist Tleilaxu culture is reprehensible in my eyes. I ask leave for Marie to come to your court in Arrakeen and spend the remainder of her formative years there, if her company should prove acceptable to you.' "

Paul set down the sheets. "Then Lady Margot also reminds me—unnecessarily—that she was the one who left a message in the conservatory of the Arrakeen Residency to warn my mother of a hidden Harkonnen threat. There is no disputing that, or the accuracy of her information."

"She has placed a water-debt on you," Stilgar said. The old naib's brow furrowed, and he ran his fingers along the dark beard on his chin. "And yet, I cannot understand why she would offer us such an important hostage."

"That works both ways," Paul said. "We may have the little girl as a hostage, but we are also allowing a potential spy into the royal court."

Irulan was surprised. "She's only a child, my Lord. Just six years old."

"*I* am just a little girl too," Alia said, letting the rest of them draw their own comparisons and conclusions. Then she crossed her legs and sat down on the step in front of the Lion Throne, adjusting her child-sized black aba robe. "I think I would like to have a playmate, Brother."

*Increasingly, I am only able to see myself through
the eyes of the monster.*

—from *Muad'Dib and the Jihad*
by the PRINCESS IRULAN

Paul hadn't slept well for seven nights in a row, and
he couldn't hide the fact from Chani. She got up in
the still darkness and came to stand by him on the balcony. Paul had passed through the moisture seal and
wore only a loose, lightweight tunic in the dry air, wasting water. No stillsuit. Chani did the same.

When did I forget the basic lessons of Arrakis? he
thought. *Just because I am Emperor, does that mean water costs me nothing?*

Listening to the humming restlessness of the vast city,
he absorbed the vibrations in the air, the mixture of scents
that filled every breath, unfiltered by stillsuit nose plugs.
Arrakeen reminded him of an insect hive, filled with
countless skittering subjects, all needing someone else to
think for them, to decide for them, to command them.

He looked up into the night sky, saw the stars and
imagined all the worlds out there, all the battles still taking place. With a faint smile, he recalled something
Irulan had added to one of her stories, an obvious yet
mythic fabrication—that at the moment of Duke Leto's
death, a meteor had streaked across the skies above his
ancestral palace on Caladan. . . .

"It pains me to see you so troubled every night, Beloved."

He turned to Chani, let out a long sigh. "My Sihaya, the *people* trouble me. I have known since childhood that this must come to pass, and I wanted them to trust me, to join me in this journey, to cooperate instead of forcing me to become a tyrant. Now they obey not because it is the right thing to do for the ultimate good of humanity, but because Muad'Dib commands it. If I walked out in the streets during any hour of the day, crowds would form and demand incessantly 'Guide us, my Lord! Guide us!' Is that what humanity needs, the danger of relying on a charismatic leader?"

"Perhaps you need guidance yourself, Usul," Chani said quietly, stroking his dark hair away from his ear. "The guidance of Shai-Hulud. Perhaps you need to remember what it means to be a Fremen. Go out in the desert, summon a worm, and make your own hajj."

He turned to kiss her on the mouth. "As always, you make me see clearly. Only in the desert can a man's thoughts be still enough for him to think." This was exactly what both Paul Atreides and the Emperor Muad'Dib needed.

~

LEAVING ALIA BEHIND as his delegate, he granted her the authority to make the appropriate decisions and perform necessary court functions, with Stilgar positioned as the girl's adviser and protector (not that she needed one). Paul had offered to take Chani along on his journey, but after studying his face for a long moment, she declined. "You require solitude and stillness, Usul. You and the desert have much to say to each other."

Sometimes she thought in ways that did not occur to him, as if her mind filled an essential portion of the container of his life. Their relationship was far more than that of a man and a woman, or of kindred spirits, or of any of the usual clichés. The feelings they held for each other stretched across the eons of human existence.

As the sun rose, he took a 'thopter beyond the broken Shield Wall, past the water trenches that kept the deep-desert worms at bay, and landed at the edge of the vast, open desert. Unfortunately, though he had intended to depart alone, without ceremony, an entourage of assistants, advisers, and gawking observers soon followed. Korba transmitted that he had summoned them to provide Muad'Dib with the fanfare he deserved.

Ignoring them, dwelling on his own concerns, he turned his back on the unwelcome crowd and walked away from his landed 'thopter, trudging out onto the dunes where he could summon a worm. He glanced over his shoulder and was dismayed to see eight 'thopters and perhaps a hundred people, some dressed in desert fashion, some wearing the robes of the Qizara priesthood. At least a third of them did not even wear stillsuits.

Korba should know better. When had it changed that people would venture out to the desert as if attending a parade? Paul felt that the purity of the sands had already been lost. The Fremen were so enamored with their continual string of Jihad victories that they failed to recognize the loss of their heritage, the loss of their very souls.

Paul planted a thumper, winding the clockwork mechanism and setting the pendulum to make the rhythmic *lump-lump-lump*. Although he had done this many times, he still felt awe at the experience. He was an offworlder, yet he was also a wormrider who had proved himself among the Fremen. He had raided the Harkonnens many times. Back then, unlike now, the enemy had been clearly defined, as had victory.

In his Jihad he had offered larger and larger rewards for bringing down Earl Memnon Thorvald, whose rebellion continued to flare up, employing more desperate measures and unexpectedly violent tactics that reminded Paul of the defeated Viscount Hundro Moritani. But the Fedaykin seemed to relish having a persistent enemy to fight. Their outward-looking hatred bound them as a unit.

Behind him by the 'thopters, some of the observers actually applauded his rote actions in calling a worm, as if he were giving a performance just for them. The thumper continued its droning rhythm. Paul waited, listening for the hiss of sand made by a behemoth worm, scanning for the faint ripple of dunes stirred by underground movement.

The thumper continued to pulse.

The distant audience began to mutter, surprised at what they saw. Finally the clockwork spring ran out, and the thumper fell silent. No sandworm had come. They would call it an inauspicious omen.

Paul lifted the counterweight, rewound the device, and jammed it deeper into the sand before he activated the syncopating mechanism again. He felt awkward. So many people read meanings into everything he did. Muad'Dib didn't want this.

And now he heard the people continuing to murmur, wondering if Shai-Hulud had abandoned Muad'Dib. Paul began to grow angry, not just at them but at himself. Shai-Hulud did not perform for audiences!

Then, just before the thumper fell silent for a second time, he noticed a stirring of the dunes. A shallow trough ran toward him as a sandworm raced toward the sonic disturbance. His pulse quickened.

Korba saw it next, and the people emitted a loud cheer. The fools! Their noise would distract the creature, and the small barrier of rocks on which they had gathered would never stop a large sandworm.

Paul grabbed his ropes, his Maker hooks, his spreaders. When the sand parted and a huge rounded head exploded upward, he stepped back and clanged his worm hooks to-gether to make a loud reverberating sound, seeking to tug the creature's attention away from the observers who had finally fallen silent in terror and awe.

"Shai-Hulud! To me!" Paul planted his feet properly, gauging the worm's approach, and at just the right mo-ment, hooked one of the ring segments. He clasped the rope and scrambled up the worm's pebbly side.

This was only a medium-sized sandworm. It would serve him well enough, without being impressive, though he was sure the observers would describe it as the greatest ever seen on Dune. Without a backward glance, paying no heed to the cheers and praise, Paul scrambled onto the beast's back. He inserted the spreaders in a practiced manner, opened the worm segments to the sensitive flesh beneath, and struck the worm's head with his goad. An-choring himself with his ropes, he turned the beast and raced out onto the open dunes, spraying sand and dust.

He was comforted by the solitude and heat, and the odors of sulfur and cinnamon that clung to the creature. As the worm raced off, Paul's conscience came clamor-ing after him, even into the deepest desert. Kilometers rushed past, but Paul Atreides could not leave his demons behind.

People fear me. I never wanted to be feared.

—ST. ALIA OF THE KNIFE

After her brother went into the deep desert, Alia sat on a throne that was much too large for her. Because of her small size and innocent appearance, she embodied a dramatic contradiction—generations of wisdom and a stern hand of justice wrapped up in an unprepossessing form.

The people viewed Muad'Dib as a godlike figure, but they spared some of their religious awe for Alia, too. Supplicants came before her without knowing which of her many moods they might face, aware that they were taking a risk.

Two legates from the recently surrendered world of Alahir arrived in stiff and formal uniforms that looked impossibly hot and monstrously uncomfortable, designed for the airy coolness of their planet rather than the dry heat of Dune. They brought gifts and pleaded for an audience with the Holy Emperor Muad'Dib. After being told he was unavailable, they walked uncertainly to present themselves to his sister Alia instead. When the two men glimpsed the little girl on the throne they grew indignant, assuming this was some insult to their world and their leader. "We have traveled on a Guild

Heighliner across many star systems to see the *Emperor*."

Alia did not move from her throne. "I speak for my brother. You will see me, or you will see no one."

The lead Alahir ambassador had a long slender neck and a high piping voice. "But we have sworn our loyalty. We are faithful subjects of His Holiness. It is our right to see him."

With a gesture and few terse words, Alia sent the men away under heavy Fremen guard. Despite their protestations, they were escorted back to their frigate and taken up to the Heighliner. By her command, they would make the long journey back to their planet before they would be allowed to turn around and make the journey all over again, this time with more humility. She dispatched a dour Fremen guard to accompany them and make certain the two actually returned home and set foot on Alahir.

Some observers in the crowded audience chuckled at her heavy-handed treatment of the men. Others, seeing her stern and uncompromising mood, slinked away without airing their grievances. At one time, Alia might have had guards follow those men to determine what they had been about, but now she presumed they had simply realized that their cases were weak or frivolous. She wished many more of them would melt away like that and solve their own problems—exactly as her brother wished.

The next supplicant was a tired-looking man whose face showed the deep, sunburned creases of a hard life. His entire body seemed to be a callus, yet he wore pride and self-esteem like armor. Though not neatly barbered, he kept his hair combed and tied back. His garments were poor, but had been meticulously mended; only Alia's sharp eye noted the signs of wear. This was not a careless man.

He was the accuser, and the two defendants in his case

looked much more careless and sloppy, though they wore finer clothes and scented their bodies with oils and colognes. The weathered-looking man stepped forward and gave a salute from the Jihad, as if Alia were actually Paul. She liked that.

"I fought faithfully in Muad'Dib's Jihad," he said. "I stood on the battlefields of five planets, including Ehknot. My commander discharged me with honors and provided me with a pension. That should have been enough for a home in Carthag, enough to support my wives until I could establish myself as a stonemason." He glared at the pair of defendants. "But these men took all of my money."

"He lost his money, yes, Mistress Alia—but he lost it fairly," cried the pudgier of the two men.

Alia turned to the accuser for more information, and he said, "I gambled with them. We played the game of tarot dice, and they took everything from me."

Now Alia frowned. "When one gambles, one risks losing. That is the way of it."

"When one *gambles,* Mistress Alia, one knows the rules and expects fair play. But these men cheated."

"We did no such thing!" the second defendant said.

"Just because you lost a game does not mean they cheated," Alia pointed out.

"They cheated. I swear it on my honor, on my life . . . on my water!"

Alia sat back. "You say these men cheated you. They say they did not. How am I to determine who is correct?" In fact, Alia *could* tell. Even without truthsense she would have known that the two exceedingly nervous defendants were hiding something, while the accuser did not waver in his conviction and righteous indignation.

She sprang from her throne and trotted down the stone steps, jaunting like a little girl, intentionally, to disorient them. "I will play a game with these men.

Show me the tarot dice that were used." Reluctantly, they withdrew the cubes, and Alia squatted on the floor. "Come beside me, and we will play." The two defendants looked extremely nervous, but they could not refuse her request.

She held the five dice in her small hand. Each face bore a different coded image that had symbolic meanings far beyond the game itself. These dice would not be noticeably weighted one way or the other, but she realized they had been altered somehow to give the owners a distinct advantage. The rules of even the basic game of tarot dice were complicated, but Alia knew them in detail. She rolled first before the men could complain: leaving face up two wands, a scythe, a star, and a water pitcher.

"An auspicious omen!" one of the men declared, as if out of habit. "Now let us place our wagers."

Alia harbored no doubt that the first roll was designed to be positive, to lure a player into more extravagant betting. Hustlers. The two defendants shuddered, looking gray. They placed their wagers—modest ones—and then rolled, building upon the prophecy, lining up their omens. They didn't know whether they should try to win or lose, but because Alia demanded larger and larger bets from them in front of the eager audience, they could not simply surrender. She refused to let them withdraw.

During this, their accuser stood with his arms crossed over his chest, glowering down at the play, while other audience members cheered her on, offering their advice.

Though Alia could not control the mechanics of the dice rolls, she gradually began to realize how these men were interpreting—and manipulating—the results. As for herself, she had a far more interesting means of cheating. With glimpses of prescience, Alia could determine how most of the rolls would come out. Even with the dice subtly weighted to give unexpected results, she could frequently see which dice to hold back and which ones to play, then place bold wagers accordingly. "Luck" was with her in a more concrete way than any other gambler could imagine.

The two terrified defendants could not stop the game. The audience murmured with appreciation, but not surprise, as Alia won again and again, defying the rolls that would be expected from untainted dice. Over the course of the game, the perceptive members of the crowd recognized that these men had somehow altered the pieces to their advantage, and that even so Alia was thwarting them. Her gradual swell of winnings forced them to raise their bets and put more of their personal fortunes on the line. Guards stood around the room to ensure that no one left.

Finally, both men raised their hands, sobbing. "We are ruined, Mistress Alia. You have taken all of our wealth. We have nothing more to gamble."

"You have your lives," she pointed out. "Now, would you care to wager them?"

"Please, no! We beg you!"

She let them squirm for a few moments, then stood up. "All right, we'll end this game. The guards will accompany you to ensure that you pay what you owe me. Since I won so many times, I cannot claim you were cheating." Some members of the audience chuckled at her clearly facetious statement, for the evidence of the dice had been quite plain. She turned to the accuser, meeting his troubled expression. "From my winnings, I will repay half of what you have lost—but only half. The rest goes into the Imperial treasury." She raised her voice. "All of life is a gamble, and opponents will not always play by neat and tidy rules. If you would participate in the game, you must be prepared to lose."

The old veteran seemed more than satisfied with her unique form of justice. The three left by separate doors, and Alia returned to her high throne. . . .

～

A SHORT WHILE later, Alia received word that Lady Margot Fenring and her daughter had arrived at the Arrakeen Spaceport and were being escorted to the Citadel of Muad'Dib. Stilgar and Irulan had already discussed with her how best to receive their visitors.

Lady Margot did not bring a large entourage, arriving as a traveler of no particular importance on a Heighliner bound from the Bene Tleilax worlds via Richese, Junction, and a number of unremarkable planets, until reaching Dune. Stilgar guided her into the throne room, and the supplicants parted for them.

Margot Fenring was beautiful, trained to use every bit of her appearance and personal magnetism to achieve the Sisterhood's aims. In this visit, though, Alia wondered whose aims were at play. Her own mother had made different choices. Was Lady Margot content to be a pawn for the Bene Gesserit? And how did little Marie fit into the game plan? Something to do with breeding, no doubt.

Alia looked down with a bright smile, and her eyes met the other girl's. Marie appeared so young, though Alia knew that this was how she herself looked to strangers.

"We present ourselves to the Emperor's throne," Count Fenring's wife said, bowing slightly.

Stilgar stepped up to the dais, acting as a chamberlain. He spoke to Alia out of the side of his mouth in Chakobsa, the ancient tongue of the desert, though Margot Fenring could understand him as easily as Alia could. "I don't like this witch or her daughter."

"You have already made your feelings plain, Stilgar."

Alia raised her voice to make sure the audience could hear her. "It will be good for me to have someone my own age at court. Princess Irulan laments that I should act as a child more often." She stepped down to meet Marie, who stood facing her with bright and exceedingly intelligent eyes, exquisite features, and perfect manners.

"My brother is unavailable right now," Alia said to Lady Margot. "We do not know when he will return, but I am happy to welcome you to our court. I grant our protection to you and your daughter."

"Thank you, your Royal Eminence," Margot said. A rather startling title to use, but Alia did not dispute it.

Alia then turned her attention back to the little girl. "I'm very pleased to have you here, Marie. We'll have so much fun together." She indicated the uppermost step of the dais, just below her throne. "Come, sit next to me and watch as I continue to dispense a mixture of Fremen and Atreides justice."

Arrakis: Men saw great danger there, and great opportunity.

—the PRINCESS IRULAN, entry in *Paul of Dune*

Of all deaths, one is the most difficult. This was the death of his name, of his family honor, of everything that mattered to him as a man and a leader. The desert had made him see that.

With the face mask of his stillsuit thrown back, Paul sat alone, gazing out across the sea of dunes with the blue-blue eyes of a Fremen. The night's coolness still clung to the shadowed pocket, but it would vanish rapidly with the awakening day. He had spent the night sitting motionless on a large flat stone, absorbing the rich aroma of windblown, powdery spice. Al-Lat, the golden sun, was just rising over an escarpment, but he did not yet feel its warmth. A deep desert chill had settled into his bones, and into his thoughts.

Though his body had hardly moved, his mind had ranged far.

The course he had chosen for mankind was difficult. Billions of people had already been killed in his name—some justifiably, many not. Wave after wave of violence came as his warrior legions surged out into space, hunting any enemy of Muad'Dib, whether real or imagined. Allowing such horrendous damage to be done in his name had left an indelible mark on his soul. But it was his terrible purpose.

He remembered the joy of returning home from Grumman when he was a boy, the smell of the Caladan seas and the drifting cries of seabirds. Not so long ago, Paul had been the proud son of a nobleman, heir to the Atreides tradition, destined to be a Duke.

How could I have forgotten Caladan so easily? he wondered. *Dismissing those people my father loved so well? No one should consider himself that important.* Duncan Idaho and Thufir Hawat would have given him a powerful dose of humility. Had Gurney himself given up on Paul, retiring from the uncontrollable Jihad to find a bit of peace on Caladan?

Paul felt like a man tumbling off a cliff, taking everyone he loved and all of his followers with him. He heard the harsh, unsettling cry of a bird. Looking up into the brightening sky, he watched two vultures drifting overhead, as if examining him with interest. Presently, they flapped their wings and moved on. Paul was not dead, but he was dying inside.

A distant and mechanical sound intruded, and he saw an ornithopter circling to the east. With the sun behind it, the operator was trying to avoid being noticed. Undoubtedly, Muad'Dib's Fedaykin had picked up his location and were monitoring him, making certain he was safe.

No one leaves me alone.

Korba's motives were transparent and refreshingly understandable. The Fedaykin leader had used Paul to broker his own power, his own religion . . . but the reverse was true as well, and Paul had exploited others like him, those who sought personal power through the new order. By fanning the flames of his holy war, the divine Emperor had intended to purge the old ways of the Imperium and set up a future in which there would be no more wars. Throughout history, however, many others had used the same excuse. . . .

In embarking upon that terrible but necessary course, he had known from the outset that it would not be possible for him to remain a purely heroic figure. Never had any one person held such absolute power. It was inevitable that he would become hated, especially when he did what prescience demanded.

He had already seen a turning point in the wildfires of rebellion around the Imperium, blazes that kept flaring up no matter how hard his soldiers tried to extinguish them. Opposition was to be expected, and Memnon Thorvald wasn't particularly competent or effective, yet he provided a constant reminder that not everyone worshipped the sand on which Paul-Muad'Dib walked. Assassination attempts and conspiracies would spring up for as long as Muad'Dib ruled, and one day there would be a point at which the fires of rebellion would rise higher than his own light. A funeral pyre would burn for House Atreides.

Ultimately, out of the ashes, history would be written by the survivors, and no matter how many volumes Irulan left behind about the Emperor Paul-Muad'Dib, he would be reviled as a monster . . . until someone worse came along. Was that his true legacy? He heaved a great sigh of resignation. Chani knew of his pain over this. So long as some people realized why Muad'Dib had done what he did, all was not lost.

Now alone, Paul considered wandering off into the desert and vanishing. His skills were sufficient that he could avoid the Fedaykin indefinitely. But he could not bear the thought of leaving Chani, of never seeing her again. It was not a path he could take.

Sunlight warmed the spice sands around him, causing their rich cinnamon odor to seep into his mind, enhancing his consciousness. Multiple futures shifted in and

out of his view. Prescience was always with him, sometimes as a whisper, sometimes as a shout. Paul saw
countless circuitous paths, any one of which could be
triggered by the tiniest act.

In his mind's eye, he saw marching armies in every
color and cut of uniform, their varied weapons dripping
with blood, surging across vast sectors of space. He could
barely discern his own legions in their midst, so dwarfed
were they by the shadowy shapes of mankind's future.

Across Paul's melange-saturated mind, myriad possibilities spun and clashed and tangled, then fused into one
path of certainty. *Memnon Thorvald.* Paul saw Guild
Heighliners traveling clandestinely between planets, loading the secret battle fleets of Landsraad nobles and delivering them to a staging area in orbital space over the
rebellious earl's planet. He recognized the indigo-and-
yellow colors of House Thorvald, along with the banners
of CHOAM, the Spacing Guild, and even golden lion
crests and blue griffins on a handful of ships. Though
both House Corrino and House Harkonnen had been devastated at the beginning of Muad'Dib's Jihad, their stubborn, ragtag remnants still resisted him.

In his vision Paul watched Thorvald receive sanctuary
and shielding from the Guild, aided by CHOAM—both of
which saw the turmoil of the Jihad as bad for commerce.
Normal warfare provided numerous economic advantages
for the trading conglomerate, but Paul's fanatics did not
follow predictable lines. They caused damage without the
compensation of increased profits.

Paul suddenly *knew* what was different. These families allied against him had been emboldened by Bludd's
spectacular hunter-seeker attack in the Celestial Audience Chamber. Thorvald had continued to take credit for
the act, though he'd had nothing to do with it.

No longer content to be seen as mere gadflies and
annoyances, these rebels had gathered their resources to

make a concerted strike. They had carefully selected a target that would hurt Muad'Dib deeply.

They intended to destroy Caladan.

He saw that all of the ships carried aboard two Guild Heighliners would be disgorged over the ocean world. Thorvald would unleash his most devastating weaponry, specifically targeting Castle Caladan, the Lady Jessica, Gurney Halleck, and Cala City. Everything Paul remembered and loved from his childhood, and all that Duke Leto had held so dear, would be sterilized.

They're going to destroy Caladan!

Paul tried to shake himself free of the vision, the nightmare. With sand dropping through the hourglass of the future, he could not afford to sit and watch the remaining details. He had to return. He had to stop this.

For several long moments, his eyes would not open, and he could not hear or feel anything. Finally, in bright sunlight, he gazed out on the sands and saw the ornithopter flying in the sky, searching for him. Paul rose to his feet and signaled it. Time to stop hiding.

He shook with fury.

Children play with toys and games. My brother Muad'Dib plays with Empires and entire populations.

—ST. ALIA OF THE KNIFE

Because of her unique background, Alia could immediately see how peculiar a child Marie was. She had the demeanor of something *else* about her.

After Lady Margot had departed to rejoin her husband, leaving her daughter behind in the care of Muad'Dib, Alia delved within her Other Memories as they became accessible to her. She reviewed Bene Gesserit training scattered throughout her mother's past, as well as some of the interconnected Fremen lives Jessica had obtained from the ancient Sayyadina Ramallo. Alia knew the Sisterhood's tricks in honing and shaping a young girl's personality, and Lady Margot Fenring was herself an adept. No doubt she had shared that wisdom with her daughter. In addition, Marie had been raised under strange Tleilaxu oppression, and Alia, even with all of her inborn pasts, still knew nothing about those closed worlds or the cloaked society of the Tleilaxu.

Months ago, Princess Irulan had admonished Alia to find a childhood of her own, so she had decided to try. Now that she had a playmate, she attempted to wall off the inner voices in order to ignore those myriad other lives and their incessant, often contradictory, advice. Sometimes it worked, and sometimes it didn't. Usually, the voices grew quiet.

Alia had discovered how to create youthful experiences for herself, and Marie did the same. "I have never had playmates my own age, either," the other girl said. "We were kept isolated among the Tleilaxu, and they do not have children . . . in the normal way."

Alia could remember uncounted births, even her very own. But she was intrigued to learn that the Tleilaxu reproduced differently, somehow. "How do they do it, then?"

Marie just shrugged. "They wouldn't tell us." That, Alia decided, was a mystery she might have to look into.

The two spent much of their days exploring the citadel, occupying themselves with games such as hide-and-seek. With so vast a complex in which to conceal themselves, the diversion quickly grew untenable, until they agreed to restrict the areas in which they could hide to certain reception wings and banquet rooms. They also enjoyed playing tricks on the ever-increasing number of amazon guards, Fremen-trained women among the palace staff who were assigned to watch over Alia. The female guards responded with great awkwardness to the games, not sure how to treat the girls.

As the two became more comfortable with each other, Marie pressed her companion about what her childhood had been like in the Fremen sietch, living in caves, wearing a stillsuit every day. With a gleam in her eye, Alia replied, "I shall show you a game Fremen children often play. You'll find it amusing."

Marie lowered her voice to a conspiratorial whisper. "Let's give it a try."

ONCE THE WIFE of Jamis, Harah had been a battle prize won by young Paul Atreides, and then willingly taken by Stilgar. She was a consummate Fremen woman, elevated by Stilgar to be first among his wives. Despite her traditions and her own superstitions, Harah had been one of the few in sietch who was not terrified by the strange child Alia. Harah had given the girl her love and attention, rather than calling her Abomination and muttering that she be put to death.

When Stilgar returned from the Jihad battlefields, glad to be back in the pure desert, Harah was his source of strength, his anchor. She was not a meek woman; in fact, Harah frightened Stilgar's other wives and any Fremen, male or female, who dared to get in her way. Now she came to him with a facial expression as dangerous as a Coriolis storm. "Alia is gone. She and the Fenring child have disappeared. I suspect treachery."

"You always suspect treachery, Harah. You know Alia better than anyone, and you know she can take care of herself."

Harah stamped her foot. "But I do not know that other girl. She could be a weapon programmed by the Tleilaxu or Count Fenring or any of Muad'Dib's enemies."

Stilgar looked into her eyes and saw the genuine concern. Harah was not an alarmist.

"I have already searched the likely places," she said. "I have dispatched the household staff to search as well, and told them to forsake their other duties until the children are found." Stilgar felt a cold hand grip his heart, as Harah added in a low, warning voice, "When Muad'Dib returns from the desert, I would not like to be the one to tell him his sister has been lost."

"I will summon the guards and the Fedaykin. Chani will lead them, I am sure."

FOR NEARLY A full day, swarms of desperate searchers pushed through every corridor, every wing, and every chamber in the huge Citadel of Muad'Dib. In their scrutiny they discovered crimes and indiscretions, numerous hidden vaults, and a great deal of material that could be used as blackmail, all of which Korba promptly seized and locked away in private Qizarate files.

But they found no sign of Alia or Marie, not a trail or a clue. The two had vanished.

Search parties combed the outlying districts of Arrakeen, forcing their way into dwellings, ransacking merchants' warehouses and marching through places of worship built by the countless sects that had sprung up to honor and revere Muad'Dib. They found many things, but no sign of the missing children.

Stilgar was sickened, expecting at any moment to receive a ransom demand or, worse, Alia's severed head sent in a package to the citadel. Stilgar authorized the Emperor's treasury to offer a breathtaking reward for information about Alia's whereabouts, and word spread around the city of Arrakeen. Orinthopters flew overhead and out into the desert in tightly arranged search patterns, craft that were fitted with the most advanced scanning technology. But the daily winds would quickly erase any footprints the children might have left.

Finally Stilgar received a message from a poor desert family that lived in one of the squalid villages at the fringe of the Shield Wall, where breezes blew sand into the sheltered basin and radiation from Muad'Dib's atomics still lingered at barely tolerable levels. Children were often seen playing at the edge of the desert. This family had reported noticing two girls that they did not recognize.

Stilgar barked a command that the family be taken as guests to the citadel, so they could receive their reward if the information proved accurate. He climbed into a small 'thopter himself and seized the controls. When the articulated wings began to shudder, he did not wait for the other troopers to scramble into their own aircraft. He took off from the citadel landing pad before the others even started their engines. The rest of the vessels swooped after him, then concentrated their search in the appropriate area. The 'thopters swarmed out over the dunes, looking for any sign of figures.

Stilgar went out several kilometers, though he was certain that Alia had sense enough not to go too far into the deep desert. On the other hand, the child was exceedingly unpredictable. Though he had no evidence, he would not have been surprised if Alia knew how to summon a worm and ride out into the open bled. She could have taken Marie with her, perhaps to find Paul on his long pilgrimage. The girls might have thought it would be fun.

At last, he spotted two small figures huddled in the sand. The winds had died down, and their tiny footprints left a centipede-like path along the crest of a dune, then down into a shallow valley. The 'thopters landed like a full-scale invasion force, and the two girls stood up, shielding their eyes and ears from the blowing sand and the noise of engines. Stilgar sprang out of the 'thopter even before the articulated wings had slowed. He strode forward, his face a mixture of anger and relief.

The children had sticks, a literjon of water, Fremkits, a stilltent, and the basic essentials for surviving for days out in the desert. Marie held up her stick, at the end of which dangled a squirming, gelatinous mass.

"Hello, Stilgar," Alia said in a carefree voice, as if he and all the 'thopters had simply come to bring the children a platter of honeyed spice cakes. "We're catching sandtrout, just like Fremen children do."

Marie played with the primitive creature she had caught, stretching its body membrane. Stilgar came forward, looking furious enough to strike Alia, and swept her up in an awkward bear hug. "Never do that again, child!"

Now that he was no longer worried, Stilgar felt a strange sense of satisfaction about the incident that at first he could not articulate. Finally, he was startled to realize that this bad decision, this foolish activity, was something a *normal* child might do. Perhaps some small part of Alia was learning to be an ordinary little girl after all, and that wasn't entirely a bad thing.

But a normal child she was not. And neither was her new playmate.

*Our secrets are not as safe as before. The old
security measures are no longer adequate.
Muad'Dib has an advantage better than any network of spies: He has prescience.*

—Spacing Guild report to CHOAM

On the way home from his desert pilgrimage, Paul
walked through the streets of Arrakeen, unrecog-
nized in his dusty traditional garb. He had felt the murmur of crowds and the anonymous press of people all
around him. The solitude and stillness of the desert rapidly slipped away from him. As soon as he returned, people would demand to speak with him about all those
supposedly crucial matters that had been held in abeyance
during his sojourn.

But he had more important matters to take care of: He
had to stop Memnon Thorvald before the rebel leader
launched his attack on Caladan. Those were Paul's people. Duke Leto's people—*Atreides people.* They might
imagine that he had forgotten about them, but he would
prove otherwise.

Paul-Muad'Dib entered the citadel unannounced and
weary, his face, hands, and stillsuit covered with fine dust
and sand. Although he was angered by what the spice vision had shown him and burning with the knowledge that
he had to stop Thorvald's hateful plan, he went first to see
Chani. He had to impose at least a moment of sanity on
his thoughts before he plunged into violence again.

She welcomed him in their quarters, delighted to see him back. Irulan came to the chamber door a short while later, and Paul realized that her network of informants must be quite impressive. No one else had been told of his return.

"Irulan," he said, since she was the nearest one available who could make things happen, "summon Chatt the Leaper. Tell him I demand to see a Guild representative immediately, someone who can take me up to whatever Heighliner is above us so that I may address the Navigator directly." He let his simmering anger show in his voice. "If no one with sufficient authority is here within the hour, I shall decrease the Guild's spice allotment by five percent for the next Standard Year, and dock them another five percent for every further hour of delay."

Irulan was shocked. "But Husband, you are not presentable . . . your dirty clothes, your stillsuit. You cannot meet with an ambassador dressed like that."

"Muad'Dib can do as he wishes," Chani said, her voice icy as a polar wind. She had stiffened as soon as Irulan entered. "Unpresentable to whom? All come to him. All bow before him."

Paul said, "I concentrate more easily with dust on my hands and while wearing my stillsuit. Send for the Guild representative, and get Stilgar to the throne room if he isn't already on his way."

By the time Muad'Dib and Chani reached the audience chamber, word of the Emperor's wrath had spread through the fortress's halls. Administrators rushed to see how they could serve him, while others (either more fearful or more sensible) made themselves scarce.

Alia was already there with Marie Fenring; the two girls had secretive smiles on their faces. "My brother is very angry at someone," she whispered to her companion.

With only two minutes to spare in the deadline, a lanky,

lantern-jawed man in a gray Spacing Guild robe stumbled breathless into the audience chamber. He was accompanied by the quiet, almost sullen Chatt the Leaper, Paul's liaison with the Guild. The gray-robed man introduced himself as Olar and made an exaggerated bow before the enormous emerald throne. "Emperor Muad'Dib demands my presence?"

"Emperor Muad'Dib requires much more than that. I must speak with you, with your Guild—and with that Navigator up there." Paul jerked a forefinger toward the ceiling. "Get me a shuttle. I have no time for middlemen or diplomats."

The Guild representative looked at him, aghast. Chatt remained stony, as did Stilgar. In the prolonged silence, little Marie began to giggle. Olar swallowed once, twice. "As you command, Sire."

The Guild usually made excuses that their Navigators were never to be seen, that the security of their Heighliners was paramount, and that only certain spokesmen could respond on the Guild's behalf. But not now. Though many Navigators were so advanced that they had difficulty communicating with primitive human minds, Paul knew they would certainly understand what *he* had to say. Olar would get him aboard.

Without further delay, Paul marched out of his throne room and gestured for the Guild representative to go with him. "Stilgar, you will accompany me as well. This is a military matter. I may require your knowledge and advice."

Olar was the type of ambassador Paul preferred: Even though the man was filled with questions and his expression exhibited a great deal of alarm, he was smart enough not to voice every thought that sprang to his mind. Other more garrulous diplomats would have begged for clarification, and made excuses or apologies regardless of what the problem was.

But these Guildsmen knew damned well what they had done: how they had knowingly aided bloodthirsty rebels and were about to assist in an appalling attack on the world Paul had called home for much of his life. Seeing Muad'Dib's mood, Olar had concluded correctly that he would get no answers, and that questions would only make matters worse.

When the shuttle was finally aboard the Heighliner and had settled into a docking clamp, a walkway extended so that Paul could disembark onto the shell decks. At the end of the walkway stood Guild security men wearing sidearms and blocking his way.

Stilgar barked, "Stand aside and remove your weapons in the presence of Muad'Dib!"

Another Guild representative, also in a gray robe, stood behind the security men like a shadow. "Apologies, Sire. For reasons of safety and security, it is Spacing Guild policy that no outsider can disturb a Navigator aboard a Heighliner. All matters must be brought before the appropriate officials. As the highest-ranking representative aboard this ship, I will be happy to deal with the Emperor's concerns."

"You may come with us, then, but I *will* speak with the Navigator."

"Sire, perhaps I was not clear—" the man began. The security men still did not move.

Paul said, "This is my ship, as are all Guildships. Instruct your guards to stand aside immediately and tell your Navigator to anticipate my arrival, unless he would like to spend the rest of his life breathing whatever spice vapors remain in his tank, for if you defy me I will allow no further melange to leave Arrakis."

Olar interceded. "This is an extraordinary request, but *Emperor* Muad'Dib so rarely makes demands upon us. I suggest we listen to what he has to say."

The Guild official, who probably outranked Olar,

scowled but gestured for the security men to stand aside. Paul strode between them, with Stilgar half a step behind. The Guildsmen led the way to the Navigator's deck.

The Navigator was an exotic creature, enclosed in a tank of thick orange gas that reeked of melange, even through its seals. The dense cloud disguised some of the creature's deformities—which were somehow linked to his mental enhancements—but through the thick plaz Paul could discern the bobbing, overlarge head on a wattled stalk of a neck. He had never seen a Steersman personally, but he could not waste time staring now.

"Beric," said Olar. "Our Emperor Muad'Dib wishes to—"

Paul interjected loudly, without preamble. "I know of the plot Memnon Thorvald intends to launch against my homeworld of Caladan, and I know of the Guild's collusion with him."

"Sire, we have no knowledge of this whatsoever," Olar said.

"The Spacing Guild is loyal to Muad'Dib," stated the other official, whose name was insignificant to Paul. "We know that you control the spice, and thus control all space travel. Why would we support any rebellion?"

Beric the Guild Navigator, interestingly, said nothing.

Paul said, "With my prescience, I have seen Thorvald's warships being taken aboard two Guild Heighliners. I have also seen that this very ship in which I stand has carried the troops and weaponry of twelve other rebel noblemen who are allied with him. Thus, I know the Guild is not only aware, but is willingly cooperating."

"Perhaps . . . prescient vision . . . imperfect," Beric finally said, a distorted voice through the speakers of his tank.

"And is your prescient vision imperfect, when you choose safe paths for a ship to travel?" Paul countered.

"Not . . . *mine*," Beric said. "But prescience is . . ." His eerie voice trailed off, as he apparently decided not to pursue a particular line of reasoning.

Paul looked around the thick-walled chamber. The smell of recycled spice was dizzying. Indeed, in the Navigator's presence with its folds of tangled timelines, the acuity of Paul's predictive vision was greatly diminished. Admittedly his own prescience did not always function perfectly. In this case, however, his melange dream had shown him all of the ships and all of Thorvald's soldiers. Without any doubt, he had seen the attack they meant to lead.

He *knew.*

"Would you like me to describe every one of their ships?" Paul said. "Shall I name every one of the planets where they were picked up? The Guild has willingly provided transport to those who are leading an insurrection against me. All of Thorvald's allies will be aboard two specific Heighliners. They intend to launch an assault against Caladan—against *Caladan*! They want to take my mother and Gurney Halleck hostage, or kill them . . . and you have cooperated in this."

Listening to the accusations, Stilgar seemed to tense, like a tightly wound spring; he clearly did not like this Navigator. The naib's blue-within-blue gaze flicked back and forth, and he wrapped his hand around the crysknife at his waist, ready to kill if necessary.

Both Olar and the unnamed official vehemently denied the charges, but Paul would hear none of it. "These are the commands of your Emperor. The Heighliners containing Memnon Thorvald and the ships in his rebel fleet will be taken out into deep space. There, the Navigators will empty their holds. Completely. Every enemy war vessel, with all soldiers aboard, are to be stranded there. Leave them surrounded by emptiness, with no hope of finding their way home, with no extra supplies and no additional air."

Olar bit back a yelp. "Sire, that will kill them all!"

"Yes, that will kill them all—for a start. Stil, I want you to arrange for a military assault on Lord Thorvald's home planet. Bring as many weapons as you require—enough to *sterilize* that whole world. Everyone dead."

"Sterilize?" Stilgar opened and closed his mouth, not sure what to say. Then: "Is that really necessary?"

Paul saw in the desert man's eyes the thought of how long his people had struggled to nurture life on Dune, following the long-term vision of Pardot Kynes and his son Liet. How could Muad'Dib possibly suggest annihilating all plant and animal life on an entire planet? Now, when so much work was being done to breathe a renewed ecosystem onto Arrakis?

But Thorvald was willing to attack Caladan. And Paul's mother. Duncan Idaho had once told him, while they were fleeing the assassin-trackers in the wilds of Caladan, "There is no room for compassion toward people who are trying to kill us."

Worse, if the appalling Caladan attack succeeded, then other enemies might grow bolder and target additional victims the Emperor cared about, all of whom were easier to get to than he was: Chani, Alia, Stilgar, and even Irulan.

He could not allow it. The lesson must be taught—a lesson that would stop further violence. *Let the perpetrators feel the pain they would have inflicted upon me.*

"*Sterilized*, Stil. The Guild will provide transportation for whatever ships you choose to send. And when it is done"—he turned back to the Navigator in his tank—"only then will I consider forgiving you for your indiscretions."

Olar swallowed twice more. "You cannot mean this, Sire. Ejecting those ships into deep space, sterilizing a planet—"

"Five years ago when the Emperor's troops were here, I threatened to destroy all spice on Arrakis in order to make my point. Why should I make any lesser threat now? You have seen the ferocity of my followers. If it is meant to be, my Fremen will have no objection to staying on Dune, without space travel, completely cut off. They can survive, *will* survive. They don't care if anyone else does."

Finally, from inside his tank, Beric conceded. "What you command, my Lord, shall be done."

Paul was gratified to note that this Navigator had the good sense to be afraid of Muad'Dib.

Once, I struggled in my small body, knowing that others saw something innocent and harmless. They underestimated me. My Harkonnen grandfather underestimated me, and I killed him with the gom jabbar. Now that people view me with awe, I have the opposite problem. They are beginning to believe I am perfect, infallible, and omnipotent.

—ALIA, letter to Lady Jessica on Caladan

In her private rooms, Alia kept the poisonous scorpions inside their tank, mainly to protect others. Occasionally, with her door closed and the moisture seals in place, she opened the tank and let the creatures run loose, skittering into corners and under her bed. Some of them even liked to climb the stone blocks of the walls, as if trying to escape into the freedom of the desert.

Since their adventure out on the open dunes catching sandtrout, Alia and Marie had been watched much more closely. Fortunately, they had plenty of other activities with which to occupy themselves. For the past several days, they had gone back to hiding in particular sections of the vast citadel complex, each girl using logic and detective work to discover where the other might conceal herself. The amazon guards allowed them a certain freedom of movement, and they seemed to accept this childish version of Alia more easily than the frighteningly intelligent one.

Today, the two girls remained locked in Alia's chambers, where they could talk and play in private. Having loosed her scorpions again, Alia sat on her pallet and let the creatures crawl over the blankets and climb up her arms and legs; some were in her hair.

Alia lay back and relaxed, letting the scorpions skitter over her body. "Even if they sting me, the poison will have no effect. I am a Reverend Mother. I can control my body chemistry." She cupped one of the arachnids in the palm of her hand. It twitched its long tail, threatening to sting, but did not harm her.

Marie sat down on the bed beside her. The scorpions scuttled away, then turned about and approached cautiously. Alia warned, "I let them out only for myself. Their poison will be fatal to you if you are stung. You must be careful."

"I am being careful, and I'm not worried." Marie plucked one of the creatures from the blanket on Alia's pallet. Gently, she folded its angular legs together, then set it on her forearm. Agitated, the scorpion twitched its tail back and forth, then raised its claws in a combat position. "They won't sting me either."

Not moving, Alia watched with curious intensity, not wanting to startle the scorpion. The one in her hair moved about as if searching for a place to nest, then came forward to peer over her bangs.

Marie picked up a second scorpion and set it on her leg, while Alia breathed evenly, fascinated. "They won't sting me," Marie said again, with complete confidence.

And they didn't.

All blessings be upon Muad'Dib, just as His blessings flow like cool water upon the faithful. His Holiness cherishes beauty and purity. In Him, we shall all be safe. Muad'Dib the Protector.

—Fremen hymn

The face of Guild Representative Olar was somber and unreadable as he offered a cylinder to Paul— a solido holographic recording encased in ornate and costly trappings. "Muad'Dib issued his command and did not require proof from the Spacing Guild. We accept that as a measure of your trust."

"I had no doubt you would follow my instructions," Paul replied from a heavy chair of polished windstone. When the Emperor made no move, Stilgar accepted the gift from the Guild and regarded it curiously.

With Irulan and Chani, they were in a small, thick-walled war council room. Though Paul sensed the import of Olar's message, he chose to meet him here in this austere, windowless place, rather than in the cavernous audience chamber with all the trouble of having security teams sweep and resweep, scanning visitors and crowds of onlookers for hidden weapons. Rumors were already rushing through the citadel and the streets of Arrakeen that the Guildsman had returned.

Olar took two respectful steps backward. "Then consider this recording neither evidence nor proof, but merely an item of interest. An Emperor should witness firsthand the absolute defeat of his enemies."

Stilgar inserted the cylinder into a display mechanism. Images recorded by the Navigator in a distant Guild Heighliner began to unfold in the air before them. The viewfield showed the starry void of space, and the Guild-ship's curved doors open to expose an immense hold. Then hundreds of warships were dropped pell-mell from docking cradles and ejected into the emptiness, as if the Heighliner had spewed them from its belly. Afterward, like a great metal whale, the craft moved on, leaving the smaller craft scattered and disoriented.

The audio was filled with comline chatter from the stranded crews and passengers: demands, curses, pleas. One of the embedded images showed Thorvald himself, with his pale skin and large silver-shot beard shaking with fury. "We paid you! We demand our passage."

The Heighliner did not respond.

"Where are we?" Thorvald shouted. But the Heighliner merely drifted away until the cluster of rebel warships was merely a spray of sparkling lights in its wake, not unlike the stars from which the stranded people had emanated.

Left alone, in the absolute emptiness.

The projection faded, and the viewfield vanished.

In the chamber, Olar spoke. "They are in a great desert of space, and the nearest star system is eighteen parsecs distant. No one but the original Navigator can find them, Sire."

"How long will their life-support systems last?" Irulan asked.

"A few days, at most. They were expecting only a brief passage."

Paul's brow furrowed as he completed his mental arithmetic. "Wait twelve days and have your Navigator retrieve the ships. When you return with the bodies—*all* of them—I will grant the Guild a generous reward of melange."

Olar bowed, but not before a faint smile touched his lips.

Paul could see from the hard expression on Chani's face that she would have inflicted a more heinous Fremen torture upon this man who had caused so much harm to the Jihad and to her beloved. But he had seen enough excesses and would not add to them unnecessarily.

Paul turned to his Minister of State. "Stilgar, see to it that this recording is widely distributed amongst my subjects. Many of them have had a taste for Thorvald's blood for a long time."

Next he regarded Irulan. "Prepare a message cylinder for Caladan as well. I fear I have trampled the feelings of those people. There are things I want them to know."

~

WHEN THE COURIER arrived with the sealed message cylinder and its accompanying copy of the Heighliner holo recording, Jessica stood in a high tower of Castle Caladan. For a long moment, she avoided breaking the seal. It disturbed her to think that she did not really know her own son, that she could not guess what demands Paul—or perhaps it was safer to think of him as the Emperor *Muad'Dib*—would make of her. What Imperial plans did he have for Caladan? What if he summoned her back to Arrakis and insisted that she sit at his side?

And what would happen if she refused?

Out of habit, she murmured the Litany Against Fear, then opened the cylinder. She ignored the brief formal message from Irulan and sank into a window seat to read the words Paul had written in Atreides battle language on a sheet of spice paper.

"Mother, I have not forgotten Caladan. Its people, its land and oceans are dear to me. I have done, and will continue to do, everything in my power to preserve them."

She felt a knot form in her stomach as Paul described Thorvald's plot to devastate Caladan. The knot tightened as she watched the recording of what he had done . . . and then read of his further intention.

Finally she pressed her lips together and nodded to herself. Yes, her son had asked without asking, wanting her to let the people know. She would show this message to Gurney first, and then they would do as her son wished.

❧

AT STILGAR'S SUGGESTION, the punitive assault on Ipyr—the home planet of Memnon Thorvald—was conducted by House Atreides battleships. Thorvald's intent to harm Caladan was a blow aimed toward Paul himself, and House Atreides would respond with indomitable force. The punishment inflicted upon Ipyr would resonate across the worlds of the Imperium.

A Heighliner carried one hundred of the largest and most powerful Atreides vessels, each loaded to capacity with weapons, explosives, highly toxic chemical bombs, defoliants, and wide-dispersal incendiaries. Paul had never given such a frightening command before: *Sterilize the world.* Memnon Thorvald's people had to be more than defeated, more than exterminated. They must be . . . *gone.*

The Atreides ships gave no warning, engaged in no negotiations, gave no quarter to the people of Ipyr. They switched off all but their battle communications systems, so no one would hear the wails of terror, the cries for mercy or, afterward, the resounding silence. The heavily armed vessels circled down, calling up charts of every single planetary settlement, and the annihilation began.

~

BY THE TONE of the cheering outside the Cala City stadium, Jessica knew that her announcement was exactly what the people needed to hear. In the now rarely used amphitheater that Old Duke Paulus had constructed for his gala bullfighting spectacles, Jessica spoke in a clear voice. Gurney Halleck stood beside her, wearing his best black Atreides uniform.

"Let no one believe that my son has forgotten his beloved Caladan," Jessica said. "The galaxy knows him as its Emperor, while Fremen praise him as their Muad'Dib. He is the military leader of the most expansive Jihad the human race has experienced in more than ten thousand years . . . but he is also my son. And the son of your revered Duke Leto."

Cheering, the people waved their green pennants.

Gurney gave a gruff rumble of agreement, then stepped forward to describe how Thorvald had intended to bring his rebel ships to Caladan, to burn the villages and slaughter the people, inflicting great harm on the homeworld of House Atreides.

"But my Paul has saved you," Jessica continued. "He has protected Caladan. He will let no harm befall you."

Inside the large arena, giant projectors had been rigged to display the images of the stranded and doomed rebel warships, left to drift in space, their air failing, food and water gone. By now, everyone aboard would be dead, their bodies retrieved by Guild vessels.

"Paul will never forget Caladan." Jessica's voice was soft now. "The Emperor will never forget the people he knew as a boy, the people who helped shape him into a man. He cannot be simply your Duke, but this does not mean he has turned his back on you. Paul will preserve you. He cherishes what is beautiful about Caladan, and he will guard you with his gentle touch."

She smiled almost beatifically. The people seemed relieved, content. Yes, they had always known how devoted House Atreides was to them and to Caladan, how benevolent a Duke could be. They would remember.

～

THE BOMBARDMENT OF Ipyr lasted thirty-three standard hours. Battleships crossed and recrossed the terrain, expending all of their stored weaponry, and when they were done, no building was left standing, no city or village unburned, no field able to produce a crop. The forests were gone, leaving only charred sticks and ash. The sky was a soup of caustic smoke and acidic vapors. The oceans were brown frothing sinks, poisonous to all life, land- and sea-based alike. Some of the larger weapons had set the atmosphere itself on fire.

Afterward the battleships circled in low orbit for two more days, scanning for any transmissions from survivors, any signs of life, mercilessly targeting those few remaining spots that were not completely dead. The log archives and image libraries of the one hundred ships were filled with records of the absolute devastation.

Ipyr might never again support life. It was a new scar upon the galaxy that could neither be ignored nor forgotten.

It was a message from Muad'Dib.

Though Reverend Mothers project unanimity to out-siders, their organization is anything but cohesive, especially since the failure of our long-awaited Kwisatz Haderach. Therefore, the Sisterhood has made allowances and contingency plans for inter-nal strife and tension. Strict controls can go only so far.

—Wallach IX Archives

Through her private sources of information, Princess Irulan learned of the imminent arrival of a Bene Gesserit delegation from Wallach IX, but she could not as-certain the nature of their mission, only that the women intended to call upon her personally, without warning. She prepared herself. In order to maintain her hidden sources of information on Wallach IX, she would need to show just the right amount of surprise when they appeared.

The three high-level Reverend Mothers came boldly to the huge citadel, as if their foundations of power re-mained as firm as before the overthrow of Shaddam IV. Paul had specifically banned his nemesis Gaius Helen Mohiam from setting foot on Dune, but he allowed other members of the Sisterhood to move about with some freedom, though their political clout was substantially diminished. Unlike the Padishah Emperor, he did not need his own personal Truthsayer, nor did he call upon Reverend Mothers for advice, except for Alia and possi-bly his mother.

Irulan knew that the Bene Gesserit must be starving from the drastic reduction in their influence. Would they demand her cooperation in restoring them to Imperial good graces? With a terse smile, she acknowledged that would never happen. Muad'Dib already understood the Sisterhood too well.

No doubt they would whisper to her and use coded finger-language, trying to snare her into some scheme or other. Though Irulan had been raised and trained by the Bene Gesserit, she had concluded that despite their millennia of studying human nature, even they did not fully grasp who Muad'Dib was and what he could do. It was not her place to instruct them.

Perhaps she would give the Sisters a copy of her first volume in *The Life of Muad'Dib*. . . .

Wearing a formal day dress, she went about her regular duties in her private portion of the citadel, inspecting a small white gazebo that was being added inside the immense conservatory, at the center of a maze of hedges and pathways. It was a perfect place for writing and contemplation. Sunlight slanted through plaz window panels high above, and she saw the glint of an ever-present surveillance device high in the branches of a tree.

At Paul's insistence, Korba had already read every page of her current draft, marking numerous complaints and objections, but in truth he had found nothing to cause a particular uproar. She hadn't expected him to. Irulan was adept enough to use layers upon layers of subtlety. On the whole, in fact, Korba seemed pleased with the book and impatient for the next volume to be published.

A craftsman was putting the finishing touches on the little garden structure, attaching the last of the decorative trim pieces that she had specified. In her younger years on Kaitain she'd had a private area like this, all the way back to when she was a young girl. Here on this alien world where people had to be sealed away from the elements, she hoped to recapture some connection with less troubled times.

The craftsman was quite aged, with a deeply creased

face, snowy hair, and overhanging brows. His coveralls were worn and frayed, but relatively clean. He completed his task and began organizing his tools, taking great care to put each item where it belonged. Straightening, he looked at her inquisitively, seeking approval.

"I have never seen better workmanship. Muad'Dib will be pleased." She doubted Paul would ever notice this area; the contents of her gardens remained at her own discretion, a small hint of power. A faint, respectful smile formed on the man's face as he bowed, then departed.

She waited. It wouldn't be long now.

Beyond the central hedge, Irulan heard the rustle of robes as her visitors negotiated the spiral maze, coming unannounced. So, they had managed to get past the guards, although the labyrinth itself had slowed their approach. Turning to the three Reverend Mothers as they arrived, she could tell they were trying not to look flustered.

"Why, Sisters! I did not expect you."

"And we did not expect to face such a gauntlet in order to gain an audience with one of our own," said the one in the center, an oval-faced woman who appeared to be in her early twenties.

Irulan already knew the woman's identity—Reverend Mother Genino—and her younger companions were Naliki and Osted. All three looked too young to have undergone the Agony, but already they were successful and powerful, and counted themselves among the select personal advisers to the Mother Superior herself.

Irulan offered no sympathy. "I am the wife of Emperor Muad'Dib. Security measures are unavoidable, as you well know. If you had informed me you were coming, I could have made your passage more seamless."

"We wished to be . . . discreet," said Naliki. She was a large-boned woman whose face was florid from the exertion of the walk through the complex maze.

"Ah, then a few complications are to be expected,"

Irulan said. "Come, let us go where we can talk. I am interested to learn your business here." She led the way up three steps into the small open-walled gazebo, where they all took seats on benches.

Genino shifted to pleasantries. "You are even more beautiful in person than I had heard. Fine breeding from the Corrinos, grace acquired from the Sisterhood, and confidence from being wed to an Emperor." The small, dark eyes of this woman concealed much, but not all.

Irulan smoothed a fold on her elegant dress, then rested her hands on her lap. "I so rarely receive Bene Gesserit visitors. What brings you to Arrakis?"

"Surely, you must have guessed," Osted said. She was the shortest of the delegation, with close-cropped auburn hair and an overlarge nose that detracted from her beauty.

Irulan allowed a bit of impatience to seep into her voice. "I am quite busy with my duties here. State the purpose of your visit, please."

"Time is not a good thing to waste," said Genino. "The Mother School has dispatched the three of us to help train Alia Atreides and Marie Fenring. Given the inherent potential in their bloodlines, their youthful interaction should not be left to chance. You will see that we have the appropriate access to them."

The Princess bristled. Paul would not like this at all. "Their instruction is well in hand. I have taken a personal interest in Alia, and in Marie as well. Your assistance is not required."

"You do not understand the importance of Margot Fenring's daughter," Osted warned.

"Lady Margot herself told me when she delivered the child here. I am aware that the Sisterhood closely monitored her upbringing among the Tleilaxu. And as for Alia . . . she could teach the three of you some things."

With her hand sheltered in the folds of her robe, Genino used her fingers to transmit a message, assuming Irulan could not speak freely because their words were being monitored. But Irulan looked away, refusing to accept that form of communication. With a frustrated scowl, Genino spoke aloud. "Monitoring of important persons is only standard practice."

"The Atreides daughter is an Abomination," Naliki said. "We cannot have a pre-born contaminate the delicate balance of Marie's education. We must intervene."

Irulan smiled at the comment. "I see very little that is delicate about Marie Fenring." She had her own suspicions that the child's purpose here wasn't entirely innocent. She suspected it had something to do with spying for the Sisterhood, with their craving for information.

Genino said, "Nevertheless, the interaction between Marie and Alia must be managed properly."

"Managed by you?" Irulan said. "And does Lady Margot approve? Before she departed, she did not express a need or desire for any further Bene Gesserit teachers."

"The birth mother's wishes are not relevant in this matter," Naliki said.

Irulan struggled to keep her expression neutral. Typical Bene Gesserit arrogance. "Muad'Dib will not permit anyone to interfere with his sister, or with the daughter of Lady Margot, who has been entrusted to our care."

Osted's expression became sly. "But you can influence him. It is a small request to provide the girls with a Bene Gesserit education. How could he refuse?"

"How little you know Muad'Dib! Any attempt to manipulate him would be fruitless."

"Do not forget your allegiance is to the Sisterhood!" Genino exclaimed, rising from her bench. "Out of respect for your royal station, we have been polite, but don't make the mistake of thinking that this is a matter open to discussion. We command you to do as we say."

Irulan also stood, making no further pretense of welcome. "Indeed, it is not a matter open to discussion, so

I shall debate with you no more. Did you disembark with luggage? If so, I will arrange to have it sent back to the spaceport. I advise you to depart on this evening's shuttle, to avoid incurring the Emperor's displeasure. Reverend Mother Mohiam has already been banned from traveling here. Would you like that stricture to be extended to all members of the Sisterhood?"

"We will not be herded around!" Genino's anger and surprise were so great that she allowed hints of it to slip past her control. Irulan was astonished, marking the reaction with great interest. Obviously, Marie Fenring was even more important to the Sisterhood than Lady Margot had revealed.

Irulan heard footsteps from the pathway on the other side of the hedge. Familiar footsteps. "Ah, the Emperor approaches—he must have been informed of your arrival. You may ask him yourselves, if you like."

Paul emerged from the labyrinth, attired in an elegant green-and-gold robe of state. He looked as if he had just interrupted his duties, and his expression showed palpable annoyance. He strode directly to the gazebo. "Why was I not informed immediately that Reverend Mothers had arrived in Arrakeen?"

Irulan formally curtsied. Half a beat later, the other three women did the same. Genino found her voice quickly. "We came to visit Princess Irulan, noble Sire."

Irulan said in a soft voice, "They did not come at my invitation, and they are departing immediately." She shot a cool smile at the three women. "They demanded influence over the education of Alia and Marie."

"Absolutely not." Paul didn't take even a moment to decide. "I forbid it."

Irulan added, "Apparently, Lady Margot Fenring was not aware of their intentions, either."

The three Reverend Mothers looked startled at Irulan's

detached behavior. But their priorities were no longer hers. In the process of compiling the story of Paul-Muad'Dib Atreides, she had begun to learn other threads of cause and effect—and serious missteps—that made her wonder about the Sisterhood's wisdom. She discovered that the Bene Gesserit had shaped portions of the historical record as they saw fit, concealing their mistakes and embellishing their successes. Certain facts were like clay in their hands. So it was with Irulan as well, in the telling of her famous husband's story.

"We make no attempt to interfere, Sire," Genino said. "We are merely here to offer—"

Paul cut her off, his expression dangerous. "You would be wise to consider your words before you speak further. With my truthsense, I hear your lies as if they are shouts."

The robed trio departed hastily, with awkward motions. Irulan realized that she was surprisingly amused, though her heart pounded at the thought of what she had dared to do. The repercussions here, and on Wallach IX! She listened until they were well into the hedge maze, then said to Paul, "How they will talk when they return to the Mother School."

"I do not fear their talk." Paul looked at her with unusual candor. "I was something of a disappointment to their breeding plans myself, like Count Fenring. Presumably, his daughter Marie is quite precious to them because of her genetics."

Irulan nodded. "With your permission, I would like to inform Lady Margot Fenring of this incident. Perhaps it will make her more of an ally. This was, after all, as much of an affront to Marie as it was to Alia."

He studied her momentarily. "You surprise me with your dimensions of complexity, Irulan."

"Thank you, my Lord."

"Yes, send your message to the Fenrings and tell them what the Bene Gesserit attempted to do here. I am curious to see how they will react." Paul whirled and left.

Alone at the center of the maze, Irulan performed a prana-bindu breathing exercise to calm herself.

Even the best plans can come unraveled if a frayed end is left untended.

—Bene Gesserit axiom

In their many years of marriage, Margot Fenring had seen her husband in bad moods, but never quite like this. Learning from Irulan of the Reverend Mothers' attempt to interfere with Marie's training had set him off on a private tirade. "Bene Gesserit blundering could jeopardize our delicate plans. What could they have been thinking? Now that Paul Atreides is aware of the Sisterhood's interest in Marie, he may start asking inconvenient questions. We must accelerate our timetable."

Margot bitterly resented the Sisterhood's interference. Had she and her husband not been clear enough with Reverend Mother Mohiam when they went to Wallach IX? Now they would have to act even more blatantly to bypass the Sisterhood. "Our plan must adapt to circumstances, my love, and we have a sudden opportunity. This provides a convenient catalyst. Now that Irulan has informed us of this outrage, we simply *must* visit Arrakeen to assure ourselves that Marie is all right."

His overlarge eyes glittered. "Hmm-ahh. Yes, the Emperor would not deny us that privilege. Our poor, dear daughter, threatened by the meddling witches." Fenring kissed her on the cheek. "We shall arrange for immediate passage to Arrakis."

⋘

THE COUNT NEEDED no reminders about their plan as he and Lady Margot disembarked at the spaceport outside Muad'Dib's stupendous, sprawling capital. The journey had given them ample time to discuss nuances, contingencies, and shadings of behavior that they would follow. Their goal remained paramount, the key intersection point of all the lines of possibility.

Even so, Fenring could not deny the fact that he was eager to see their daughter again. By now she must be ready.

He and his Lady looked up at the battlements and ramparts of the huge citadel complex that sprawled across the northern suburbs of Arrakeen, centered on the old Residency, and extended all the way to the Shield Wall cliffs—so different from when the Fenrings had lived here! Gigantic suspensor cranes loomed over portions of the vast compound as work continued.

Margot must have noted a slight quivering in the muscles of his primary weapon hand—tension, preparation. When his wife touched that forearm and made eye contact with him, he felt his pulse slow, just a little. He said, "Mmm, I will let you do the talking for both of us."

Yes, they had woven a deadly tapestry of plans, but the Imperium was full of plans and unseen linkages. They had both been surprised to learn of the assassination attempt during the Great Surrender ceremony—not by any of Muad'Dib's numerous sworn enemies, but by a purportedly faithful Swordmaster. The Count found it amusing. With many attempts brewing, sooner or later some plot was bound to succeed against Paul Atreides.

He was like the pretentious, widely despised master of a carnival sideshow, but on a galactic scale.

Apart from the inconvenience to himself and to his beloved wife, Fenring had not been sad to see Shaddam dislodged from power; by the same token, he would be glad to see an end to the brief, terrible reign of Muad'Dib. In its place, after the turmoil, he would make sure he was in a position to establish something far more efficient and . . . *majestic*. Ultimately, whoever sat on the throne would need popular support, as well as a network of fail-safes to maintain power.

Paul Atreides should have come to him for advice in the first place.

One of the Spaceport soldiers marched toward them, a statue in motion. Blocking their way, he raised one hand in a stiff, halting gesture, while keeping the other near a sheathed dagger. No emotion showed on his chiseled, weathered face, like something sculpted by sandstorm winds. "State your business in the city of Muad'Dib."

"There is no need to be impertinent," Lady Margot said. "We were cleared on the shuttle. Our daughter is a guest in the Emperor's household, and we have come in response to an urgent message sent by the Princess Irulan."

"Hmm-m-mm, you will treat us with the respect we are due," Fenring said, his eyes dangerous. "I am a Count of the Landsraad and this is my Lady."

Too late to do anything about it, Margot saw that her husband was provoking the self-important brute. When the soldier began to draw the dagger at his waist, it was like touching a trip wire. Fenring hurled himself upon the larger man and struck his wrist a sharp blow, causing the fingers to release the knife just as it came free of the sheath, and the blade clattered to the ground. A second blow to the elbow numbed the soldier's entire arm, followed by a blurring kick that snapped his ankle sideways, causing

572   Brian Herbert and Kevin J. Anderson

the man to topple to the ground. With the side of his hand, Fenring then delivered a precise blow to his opponent's temple, after which he slammed an elbow into the man's face. The soldier moaned and went limp, bleeding from one of his eyes.

Fenring stepped back, looking amused. "Ahh, one of Muad'Dib's finest, I see."

Margot spoke over the sound of running boots and the shouts of other soldiers. "Well, my dear, at least we have their attention now."

In a fluid motion, Count Fenring crouched with the recovered knife in his hands, ready to face the men running toward them. Margot went into her own fighting stance with her back to his. This had been one of their projected scenarios, and she hoped it would play out as she anticipated. They could act greatly affronted, insulted by the treatment Muad'Dib gave to his invited guests, and they might experience the slightest relaxation in security around them, later.

And even if that didn't happen, she was confident they would survive this minor confrontation.

The special guards circled them warily, a score of men with drawn weapons—long guns, pistols, dart throwers, swords. Without personal shields, the two of them could easily be cut down, regardless of their fighting skills. But these guards would need instructions from higher up before doing that to a nobleman and his lady. "Hmm-ah-hmm, my apologies," Count Fenring said, raising his hands in surrender. "That man insulted my Lady, and I, ahh, tend to be overprotective. Entirely my fault."

The soldier behind them—who had cleared the Fenrings before they left the shuttle—conferred in low tones with a superior officer. The gruff officer nodded, which seemed to reduce the level of tension by a fraction. He looked in disgust at the wounded soldier trying to recover himself on the ground.

Then the ranking officer ran his gaze up and down Fenring. "Any soldier who can be so easily bested by a mere . . . visitor has no business serving among Muad'Dib's guards. He is relieved of further duty." He motioned, and the tense Fedaykin put their weapons away. The officer said, "Allow me to show you into the citadel. You can state your business to Princess Irulan herself."

Fenring grinned as Margot took his arm, and the two strolled after their escort.

❧

WHILE SERVANTS STOOD nearby, Irulan greeted the Fenrings at the arched door of her private citadel wing. Tall and elegant, the eldest daughter of Shaddam IV wore a long gown of black parasilk, cut low at the front and sparkling with tiny Hagal emeralds on the bodice and half sleeves. Her blonde hair was tightly coiffed with a brilliant fire-diamond tiara. She had obviously donned one of her finest court dresses, as if she were back in the Imperial Palace on Kaitain.

After greeting her guests, Irulan escorted them past a writing desk piled with notes. Fenring glanced curiously at one of the pages, but Irulan quickly directed him toward a dining table where a sumptuous luncheon had been set out. "Won't you join me for a light repast? I have already summoned Marie, but as you can see this royal fortress is very large."

"We are, hmm, quite anxious to see our dear daughter." Fenring leaned forward to sniff at a sealed tureen, but no odors escaped. He glanced back at the desk, still interested in what Irulan had been doing. Was she writing another one of those damnable propaganda tracts?

Margot continued, "We were most disturbed to hear about the Sisterhood's attempt to take over her training.

We chose to send Marie here because we did not want her to be entirely indoctrinated in Bene Gesserit ways. But it seems even in the Imperial Court she could not entirely escape them. Is she safe here on Arrakis?"

The Princess slipped gracefully into a chair at the head of a long table covered in white linen and laid out with silver. "Although you and I are Bene Gesserits, Lady Margot, even we can admit that occasionally the Sisterhood oversteps its bounds. There is no longer a problem as far as your daughter's schooling is concerned, because Muad'Dib has spoken." At the memory, her lips quirked in a tight smile. "The Mother School made a grave error in offending him, and he is not likely to forget anytime soon."

A servant unsealed the tureen to reveal a thick, dark potage. "Caladanian boar soup," the Princess said. "My husband's favorite."

Though the visitors tasted their soup and made appropriate sounds of appreciation, Irulan did not sample hers. She said, "Even without Bene Gesserit supervision, questions remain about your daughter and the instruction she has already received. The child is showing certain unusual signs. How has she been trained?"

Fenring exchanged a quick glance with his wife and said, "Only . . . ahh, as required, as we saw fit. Her upbringing in Thalidei has not been especially pampered. She has received a broad foundation in numerous disciplines." The Count ran a finger around the lip of an empty glass. "In our zeal to protect the child, I taught her what I know, as did my wife. And the Tleilaxu had some interesting . . . ahhh, seasoning for us to consider."

Worried that some detail might have slipped, Margot looked at Irulan and asked, "What sort of unusual signs have you seen? Has Marie done anything wrong?"

"Not at all. She and Alia have become quite close in only a few short months. And Alia, as you are well aware, was born under extremely strange circumstances."

"An Abomination," Margot said, then quirked her lips in a smile. "Another overzealous Bene Gesserit label. Do you suggest Marie is also pre-born?"

Irulan shook her head. "No, but she seems every bit Alia's match and equally as cunning. You have not been entirely candid with us from the beginning."

"Our daughter is a special child," Margot said.

The Count smiled. "Ah, um-m-m. It sounds to me like the two girls are quite suited to each other as playmates. We couldn't have asked for better."

Moments later, little Marie came running into Irulan's private apartments. She wore a pink-and-white party dress with a lacy frill on the hem and white shoes that clicked on the floor as she ran. Her parents rose to their feet, and she went to the Count first and hugged him.

"Thank you for sending me to Arrakeen. I love it here," Marie said to him. "Everyone treats me well, and I've been a good girl."

"We're pleased to hear that, darling."

Paul Atreides, like his father the Red Duke, al-
lowed dangerous people into his inner circle. A
risk-taker, he claimed it was the best way to keep
his senses honed.

—from *The Life of Muad'Dib, Volume 1*, by the
PRINCESS IRULAN

Y our daughter is an interesting child, Count Fenring," Paul said, as he led his visitor down an underground stairway.

"She has remarkable genes," Fenring answered, without elaborating further. "I am pleased you find the girl as
exceptional as we do."

Workers had found this old passage when they were
excavating the citadel, deeper than the original foundation of the Arrakeen Residency, so well hidden that it
had not been detected during the initial scan for Harkonnen traps long ago. Paul doubted Fenring knew of its existence, though the tunnel was incomparably older than
the building above, and its existence led him to believe
there might be other passages tangled beneath the ancient
structure. The air here was clean and cool, the steps heavily worn from the passage of many feet in ancient times.
Thousands and thousands of years ago.

Fenring followed several steps back, descending carefully in the dim light, looking around with his overlarge
eyes. In the low yellow illumination from glowstrips recently applied to the sides of the steps, the narrow-faced
man looked nocturnal, ever alert and wary.

On short notice that morning, Paul had summoned the Count, taking him beneath the eastern wing of the citadel—away from guards and eavesdroppers. "Do you doubt my ability to defend myself—even from someone like him?" Paul had asked the anxious Fedaykin, and they had withdrawn their objections. Nevertheless, where this man was concerned, Paul's prescience was hopelessly unreliable.

Count Hasimir Fenring. Such a notorious, dangerous reputation he had, but Paul had always felt a faint echo of compassion for this person who had served Shaddam IV, sensing that perhaps he had more in common with Fenring than either of them realized.

"I know what you are, Count—what the Bene Gesserit wanted you to be. I sensed things about you from the moment I laid eyes on you in the Padishah Emperor's presence. You are much like me."

"Hm-m-m-m. And how is that?"

"Each of us is a failed Kwisatz Haderach—failed in the eyes of the Sisterhood, at least. They didn't get what they wanted from you, and they cannot control me. I am not surprised they would be so fascinated with your daughter."

"Ahh, who can understand the myriad breeding schemes of witches?"

"Who can understand the many things we must do?" Paul added.

After ending the Thorvald rebellion with emphatic violence, Paul had been forced to sterilize two more planets, completely eradicating their populations. Sterilization . . . worse even than what had happened on Salusa Secundus, worse than what Viscount Moritani had threatened to do on Grumman. Paul realized that he barely felt any guilt over what he had done.

Have I become so accustomed to causing death and destruction? At the thought, a cold wave passed through his chest.

He remembered killing Jamis in combat, the first life he had ever taken. He had been shaken but proud of his accomplishment, until his mother brought down a hammer of guilt on him. *Well, now—how does it feel to be a killer?*

He had grown too comfortable with the feeling. Muad'Dib could order the annihilation of worlds without a second thought, and no one would question him. Paul, the human, could never allow himself to forget that.

Because Count Fenring had also been groomed as a Kwisatz Haderach, also intended to be a pawn . . . maybe the two of them had a common basis for understanding that Paul could not experience with anyone else, not even with Chani.

Reaching the bottom of the stairway, Paul stood at the opening of a rock-lined tunnel. "I am not a god, Count Fenring, despite the mythology that has arisen around me." He motioned to the left, where a side passageway was illuminated by glowglobes that bobbed with the slight disturbance in the air.

"We, hmmm, have much to learn from one another. And perhaps through that understanding we can better learn about ourselves. You would like us to be, ahh-hmm-mm, friends? Do you forget that Shaddam told me to fight you after the Battle of Arrakeen?"

"I remember that you refused. It is the difference between pragmatism and loyalty, Count. You saw who was the victor and who was the vanquished, and you made your choice."

"Yes, hmm, but I did voluntarily accept exile with Shaddam, until I felt the need to move on. We did not want our daughter raised on Salusa Secundus."

They rounded a bend, where the passageway narrowed. "All relationships change, Count Fenring, and as humans we must adapt to them or die."

"Adapt or die?" Warily, the Count peered down the tunnel in one direction and another. "Um-m-m-ah, do you have interrogation chambers down here?"

"All Empires require such things," Paul answered. "The Corrinos certainly did."

"Hmm-ahh, of course. I am sure that the intrigues in your citadel are not so very different from what they once were on Kaitain." He cleared his throat, as if something dry had lodged there.

"Actually there is a difference, Count, because I am as much Fremen as Atreides. The desert determines my actions as much as my noble blood, and I have more than mere politics—I have religion. As much as I don't want to be, I *am* a religion. Similarly, my warriors are more than simple fighters. They also see themselves as my missionaries."

Paul paused at a small, dark opening, where he activated controls to seal a metal door behind them, removing all light. In the darkness, he heard Fenring breathing, and smelled his fear-saturated perspiration. *Involuntary moisture loss.* After only a brief pause, he opened a second door and entered a larger chamber where dim, awakening illumination responded to their arrival.

"In a sense, we're going back in time." He waited for Fenring to notice the paintings and writings all around them, strange designs on every possible surface of walls, floor, and ceiling. "This is an ancient Muadru site, long buried. Probably older than the Fremen presence on Dune."

"Fabulous. How fortunate you are to find such a site. In all my years in the Residency, it seems I was unaware of the treasures beneath my feet."

Hearing this, Paul felt his truthsense twinge, like an alarm beginning to go off but not quite sounding. Did it have something to do with Paul's inability to see Fenring with his own prescience, some clashing of the auras of two failed Kwisatz Haderachs? Or was it a bit of a lie from the Count about the Muadru site? But if so, why would he hide such knowledge?

The Count was careful not to disturb any of the markings. "Ahh, I was far too interested in the more obvious treasures of melange, I suppose."

Paul did not try to conceal the awe in his voice. "This chamber is the smallest hint of the race that settled numerous planets, long before the Zensunni Wanderers. Apparently they arrived on Dune before it became such a desert. Some legends suggest they even brought the sandworms from elsewhere, but I cannot say. We know very little about them."

"Your name comes from the Muadru?"

"There appears to be a linguistic connection between the Fremen and the Muadru, but the latter race vanished at independent sites all over the galaxy—suggesting a terrible cataclysm that took them all at once."

The unlikely pair walked around the chamber, looking closely at the drawings, numerals, letters, and other artwork; there were color paintings using unknown pigments, and etchings in the cool stone. "Hmm-ah, perhaps you missed your calling, Sire—you might have been an archaeologist instead of an Emperor." Fenring chuckled at his own suggestion.

"People know me for my Jihad, but I like to think I am excavating the truth of humanity, digging up what must be found and purging what must be eliminated. Always seeking the truth, always pointing toward it." Paul sealed the chamber again and led Fenring back the way they had come. "So many legends and stories surround me, but how many of them are really true? Who can know what really happens in history, even when you live through it yourself?"

Fenring fidgeted. "I happened to observe, ahh-hmm, that Princess Irulan is writing yet another volume in her ever-growing biography. Revisionist history?"

"Just more of my story. The people demand it. Billions speak of me in heroic terms, but the stories about me are incomplete. Just as they are about you, I suspect. We're alike, aren't we, Count Fenring? We are much more than what people say about us."

"We have our loyalties," he said enigmatically.

Paul had no illusions about his guest. If it suited his needs, Fenring could very well turn against him. On the other hand, an Emperor could use a man with Fenring's clandestine skills and subtlety. The Count certainly knew his way around in elite circles. Paul guided him down a new corridor rather than returning to the stone steps that would lead them back up into the light.

"Where, hmm, are we, ahhh, going now?"

Paul opened another door. "One of my private cellars. I'd like to share a bottle of Caladanian wine with you."

"Much better than a torture chamber," Fenring said.

The human body and the human soul require different types of nourishment. Let us partake of a feast in all things.

—CROWN PRINCE RAPHAEL CORRINO,
Call to the Jongleurs

It was supposed to be an intimate banquet for Paul and the Fenrings, with Chani, Irulan, and the two girls, but for the Emperor Muad'Dib nothing was permitted to be informal.

Alia knew that the places had been chosen with care. Paul and Chani would sit beside one another at the head of the table, with Alia next to her brother on his right side, then little Marie, and farther down the table would be Count Fenring and his Lady, far enough away from Paul, should the Fenrings make any attempt against him. On the left side, Irulan would sit closest to the head of the table, across from Alia and Marie; then Stilgar, and finally Korba where the two Fremen could watch the Count and Lady.

The room had been swept for chemical explosives such as the bomb that had detonated beneath Muad'Dib's throne, metal objects, weapons of any kind, automated tools of assassination. Grim Fremen stood guard in the kitchen, monitoring the preparation of every dish. Poison-sniffers hovered over the banquet table. All utensils were smooth and dull, minimizing their potential use as weapons.

Ever since Bludd's hunter-seeker attack, Stilgar had insisted that Paul and his party wear shields when in the presence of visitors, even at meals, though it always made the process of dining somewhat awkward.

Korba felt that Paul's own prescient skills, though erratic, could enhance even the most extravagant security preparations. During the planning stages he had insisted, "Muad'Dib, if there is danger, your predictive powers could give us warning."

Paul had cut the man off. "Where Count Fenring is concerned, Korba, little is clear to me, ever."

Although Fedaykin guards were stationed in the hall, Stilgar could not allow himself to merely be a fellow dinner guest; instead, he vowed to serve as Paul's personal bodyguard. Ever suspicious of the Count, Stilgar had personally scanned Marie's clothes and paid close attention to every item Fenring and his Bene Gesserit wife brought into the banquet chamber, but he found no weapons, no poisons, nothing unusual.

The dinner party met in the former dining hall of the old Arrakeen Residency. This was a historically significant room, where Alia's brother and parents had broken bread when they first arrived on Arrakis—before Harkonnen treachery had changed everything. There had been no straight-line progression in her brother's life from then to now, nor in Alia's. As servants put the finishing touches on the table and the chefs were hard at work, Alia stood near her chair, waiting for her eminent brother to enter.

After Marie's parents had arrived on Arrakis, the girl's style of play had altered subtly as they improvised more games, making Alia wonder if her friend was somehow subdued or intimidated by them. "Are you afraid they'll take you back to Tleilax?" Alia had asked in a whisper.

"I will never go back to the Tleilaxu." Marie sounded as if she was stating a fact, rather than making a defiant pronouncement.

At the appointed time, Paul and Chani entered the dining hall and took their seats at the head of the table. Forsaking formality, they wore clean yet simple desert clothes. Visible under his cape Paul had also chosen to wear a black tunic emblazoned with the red Atreides hawk crest, no doubt for the Count's benefit. Paul's shield mechanism was apparent, as was Chani's, but not activated.

Hasimir and Margot Fenring strolled into the banquet hall arm in arm: the not-quite-misshapen man and the beautiful Bene Gesserit seductress who clearly adored him. Alia wondered how far the Sisterhood's breeding program had missed its mark in Hasimir Fenring, how close a counterpart he was to her brother's abilities. She sensed great danger in the man. On the other hand, she had to agree with Paul: he could be a formidable ally.

Lady Margot looked like perfection in a gown made of gray and black elfsilk; at her pale, smooth throat she wore a long strand of large muted-lavender diamonds whose color seemed enhanced by the sleek dress. So thorough were the security precautions, Stilgar had scanned the strand itself to make sure it was made of breakable thread, rather than shigawire or some other cord that could be used as a garrote.

Little Marie walked slightly ahead of her parents, excruciatingly well-mannered but barely able to contain her energy. An impish grin touched her lips.

For the occasion Alia had decided to wear her favored black aba robe, which gave her the paradoxical appearance of both child and Fremen matron. In stark contrast, Margot Fenring had taken great care to dress Marie as a perfect daughter in a fine little gown made of expensive fabrics, whale-fur, and lace. Her golden hair was bound up in a mist of tiny jewels. Alia hardly recognized her companion.

Fenring placed his elbows on the table and leaned forward, his chin on his interlocked hands, as he looked past the two girls to where Paul sat. "Hmm, Sire, I have a gift for you before we begin. I could have presented it earlier, but I was waiting for . . . aahh . . . the correct time." He stroked his clean-shaven chin, looked awkwardly across the table. "Your man Korba has it."

Korba was taken aback because he had not expected this. When Paul looked at him, the Fedaykin clapped his hands and gave hushed orders to one of the guards, who dashed out of the room.

Alia leaned over to Marie. "What is it? What did they bring?"

The girl glanced at her. "Something interesting."

Finally, two men bustled in from the hall carrying a wrapped package. "I hope you've kept it safe," Lady Margot said.

Korba seemed insulted. "It was placed in my care." He set the object in front of Paul and unwrapped folds of black cloth to reveal a jewel-handled knife. The edge seemed to radiate light.

Paul scowled. "You brought me a dagger? What sort of message is this?"

"It is a historically significant weapon, Sire. You may recall that this is the same blade carried by Emperor Shaddam, which he gave to your father Duke Leto after the success of his Trial by Forfeiture, but Leto eventually returned it to him." After a pause, he added, "It is also the knife Shaddam offered to Feyd-Rautha for his duel with you."

Paul frowned down at the offering. "Is there a deeper message I should read into this?"

Fenring wrinkled his forehead. "You are well aware of a certain, aahh, friction in my relationship with Shaddam. In an attempt to lure me back to his side, he sent me this blade as a gift, hoping I would return to Salusa Secundus and be his companion."

"And you are giving it to me instead?"

Count Fenring smiled. "That is my answer to His Fallen Majesty, Shaddam Corrino IV."

Paul passed the weapon to Chani. She examined it, placed it on the table between them.

Marie fidgeted in her place, and Lady Margot caught her eye, gave her a sharp look. Alia searched for any hidden code in the gesture, but it seemed to be no more than the scolding of an impatient mother.

The first course was brought in, accompanied by an intriguing savory aroma. "Hmmm, smells wonderful." Fenring picked up one of the cubes of meat. "What is it?"

"Broiled pit snake in a piquant sauce," Chani answered, letting the Count draw his own subtle meanings.

The guests each had a large goblet of water flavored with bits of cidrit rind. Imported olives were accompanied by a salad of chopped lettuce and portygul wedges in rosewater. Alia knew that the Fenrings fully recognized the largesse of moisture that Paul was showing, though Lady Margot hardly took a sip of her water.

"When House Atreides took possession of Arrakis," Paul mused, "my father hosted a banquet to present himself to important personages of the city, and—I am certain—to sniff out potential enemies." He glanced down at the jewel-handled knife beside his plate. "Are you my enemy, Count Fenring?"

"I don't believe so, Sire."

"You are aware that I have truthsense?"

"I am, aahh, aware of when *I* have told the truth and when I have not."

"Perhaps you shade the truth now?"

Fenring didn't answer, as Paul looked at him warily. Paul sensed something, but what?

Alia continued to eat, but watched the reactions around the table. For some reason, Marie giggled.

The chefs had chosen a main course of roasted butterfish, one of Paul's favorites from Caladan. Gurney Halleck had recently sent a shipment of the delicately flavored fish, which was now served in a traditional peasant style. With her small, nimble fingers, Marie peeled away the scales and skin, exposing the pale flesh and vertebrae as if she were an excellent dissectionist.

Fenring held up one of the curved sharp ribs of the butterfish. "One could easily choke on a fish bone. I hope I am not to construe this as a threat? No one but Shaddam would have ever served such an intrinsically dangerous meal."

It was poor joke, but nevertheless Lady Margot and Korba chuckled.

"My father had good reason to fear assassination attempts," Irulan said sourly. "He should have spent more effort strengthening his Empire, instead of conspiring with you, Count Fenring." Alia was surprised to hear the bitterness in the Princess's voice. "Many of his most troublesome ideas came directly from you."

"Hmmm? Your assessment is entirely unfair to me, Princess, as well as factually incorrect. If dear Shaddam had listened to my ideas more often, instead of acting on his own, he would have gotten into far less trouble."

Marie continued to toy with her fish. With her round-handled spoon, she tried to cut a hard-glazed vegetable, a dwarf Ecazi turnip—a slightly sweet, tasty morsel. The vegetable rolled suddenly off her plate and dropped to the floor beneath the table. As if hoping no one would notice her faux pas, the girl ducked down from her chair to retrieve it. Alia hid her amusement.

"Shaddam has been disarmed in every possible way," Paul said. "Most of his Sardaukar have transferred their allegiance to me. Only one legion, comprised mostly of older men ready for retirement, remains with him in exile as his police force."

"Hmm, I think you are too trusting, Sire. Sardaukar are blood soldiers. They are sworn to defend their Emperor."

Chani's voice was dangerous. "You forget, Count Fenring, that *Muad'Dib* is their Emperor now."

Lady Margot glanced under the table to see what her daughter was doing.

Paul continued, "The fact that my Fremen defeated them so resoundingly was a mortal blow to their confidence. It is the law of the vanquished: I have proven myself the leader of the human pack, and they must bare their throats in submission."

When she thought no one was looking, Alia slipped beneath the table as well. "Marie, what are you doing?"

The girl darted a glance back at her like a snake. Marie had peeled something long and thin from the table leg, barely thicker than a thread but as long as her forearm. A flexible band was wrapped around her knuckles. It had been hidden among the cracks and ornate carvings beneath the banquet table's trim. Seeing Alia, Marie activated a minute power source, causing the object to extend and became rigid.

Alia recognized it for what it was—*needlewhip dagger*—a contraband Ixian assassination tool made from sharp, braided krimskell fibers. Because it was organic, it gave off no chemical signatures that would have tripped either a poison or explosive snooper. Marie could have placed it there during one of their games.

Alia's thoughts tumbled into place, spelling out the details of a long-planned murder. The little girl had been planted like a cuckoo's egg in the nest of the Arrakeen citadel. "Paul! Stilgar!"

She lunged toward Marie under the table, but the other girl slapped a hidden switch in one of the curlicue knobs on the table's trim, activating another booby trap. From the stone block walls near the main door came a popping *crack,* densely packed powders released by a tightly wound spring-dispersal mechanism. When the two inert dusts mixed, a chemical reaction caused the fumes to spread out in a noxious cloud of foul-smelling yellow smoke that billowed blindingly into the room.

Someone screamed, repeatedly. At first it sounded like a woman, but Alia realized quickly it was Korba.

The explosion of smoke, cleverly planted without energetic chemicals or any kind of detectable ignition device, sent the door guards running to the wrong place. The delay and diversion needed to last only a few seconds. Marie was already there under the table, and with her small but deadly body she rose up between the table and Paul, even as he pushed back to get into a defensive position.

Marie pressed forward, far stronger than she looked, and drove herself into Paul's now-activated shield, inserting the deadly needlewhip through the barrier. She slowed, using the resistance to her advantage. The weapon's fine tip slid through the barrier like the needle of a medic administering a euthanasia injection.

Moving smoothly at the first instant of turmoil, Lady Margot Fenring snapped the thread of her necklace and spilled her strand of lavender diamonds into the goblet in front of her. Immediately upon contact with the water, the Tleilaxu gems released their impregnated chemicals, a potent but short-term paralytic not detectable by the banquet room's poison snoopers. She and Count Fenring had already consumed a prophylactic antidote. She hurled the goblet's contents away from her, splashing it across the table at Korba and Stilgar even as the men lunged to their feet. Some of the fumes even reached Irulan.

Alia saw Paul grab Marie's small wrist and hold her off, preventing the needlewhip from extending more and plunging its fine, sharp point through his forehead. By now, the power source would have built up a substantial electrostatic charge, and a single burst could quickly and effectively short-circuit her brother's brain.

At the far side of the room, yellow smoke continued to spread out. People were choking. The guards nearly tripped over each other. Stilgar and Korba had collapsed, stunned by the paralytic; Irulan could barely move.

Count Fenring had already acted, moving through the blinding smoke to reach the thick stone wall of the banquet room, where blocks fitted together perfectly to form a corner that, to even the most detailed inspection, appeared to be perfectly aligned. He knew the precise crack to push, the slight sliding to the left and then upward to reveal another mechanism—all the components of which were made of exactly the same kind of stone. Then a release, and the passage opened: access to the ancient tunnels underneath the Residency.

Many years before the Atreides occupation, Count Fenring had discovered the network of incalculably old passages beneath the foundations, and he had installed several access points in key areas. Because the system was his own clever design, Fenring knew these hidden entrances would have remained undetected in all the subsequent time.

Now, it would provide a perfect way for them to get away after the murder of Muad'Dib, leaving Arrakeen in an uproar. According to the plan he and Lady Margot had developed so carefully, an armed escape craft was already waiting outside, and from there they would reach the Heighliner and fold space to freedom.

The right people had been bribed, the entire process made easier by the fact that the Emperor Muad'Dib was so widely hated, even by many of those closest to him. The assistance of the Spacing Guild didn't hurt, either. In all likelihood, the Count, Margot, and Marie would fill the power vacuum after Paul's death, or find someone compatible who could do so. Even if not, without such a charismatic, prescient leader, the Jihad and this fanatical government would consume itself from within.

But first, Muad'Dib had to die.

When Marie threw herself upon Paul, however, surprise and treachery had been her main advantages. As Paul stalled the initial attack for a moment, Alia burst out from beneath the table and sprang at the other girl like a mongoose.

Breaking free of Paul, Marie lashed out at Alia with the needlewhip, and Paul's sister danced back. Alia was more than a match for the other girl's fighting ability, but she had no weapon of her own. Marie jabbed, and the hair-fine rapier made a whistling sigh through the air. "Let's play, Alia."

Though her muscles could barely respond from her exposure to the paralytic, Irulan crawled to one side, out of the way. Stilgar lay sprawled with his head, shoulders, and arms on the table, where he had collapsed. He twitched and struggled, his eyes fully aware, as he tried to pull himself up. Chani held her drawn crysknife, looking as formidable a fighter as any Fedaykin.

Alia sprang onto the dining table, trying to get out of reach of the needlewhip. Marie lashed and spun as she followed her up there, knocking settings aside while Alia dodged. It was clear the little Fenring assassin meant to dispatch her quickly. So much had happened in only a few seconds. "Now who is the scorpion?" Marie laughed.

Alia took another step across the tabletop and kicked a plate with a half-eaten fish carcass at Marie. The girl ducked to one side, her hard gaze never wavering. Alia spotted the Emperor's ornate knife near her brother's plate. In a blur of motion, she grabbed the blade and jumped toward her opponent, slashing beneath the needlewhip, catching the girl on the wrist, severing tendons. "I can sting, too."

Marie's hand instantly became useless, and the deadly weapon dangled from the loops wrapped about her knuckles. With no more than a hiss of pain, Marie jumped off the table and pounced on the half-paralyzed Irulan, choosing any victim she could find.

But Alia was unleashed now. The voices in Other Memory howled at her like a bloodthirsty mob. She raised the jewel-handled knife and slammed it into the back of the little girl. The blow was true, and the Emperor's sharp blade pierced Marie's heart.

"Marie!" Fenring cried, turning away from his exit tunnel and bounding forward. "No, not my daughter!"

Alia stood up, leaving the Emperor's blade firmly planted within the twitching body of the treacherous girl. "You were never my friend."

Korba looked on in awe, still seated where he had slumped helplessly back into his chair, and just starting to recover from the paralytic gas. As far as Alia could tell, the Fremen had not lifted a finger during the brief but intense battle. "The knife," he said in a slurred voice, his lips moving slightly. "St. Alia of the Knife."

Caught in the swirl of events around her, Alia realized that she stood at the threshold of her own legend.

*Who can love a monster? It is an easy thing when
one allows love to interfere with reason.*

—Bene Gesserit report on Abomination

Paul switched off his shield and strode over to the
fallen body of Marie Fenring. Alia stared at the
jewel-hilted knife protruding from her former playmate's back, as if she could not believe what she had just
done.

Chani stood with crysknife in hand, coiled for further
violence and ready to protect Paul. "Stilgar, do you
live!" she called.

Though he moved like a man half asleep, the naib
said, "I live . . . The poison was temporary."

Count Fenring had fallen to the floor on his knees and
looked absolutely shattered. "Marie! Marie, my sweet
little girl!" His shoulders hunched and shuddered as he
lifted the dead child and cradled her. Behind him, an
opening in the wall led down a sloped ramp and worn
stairs into the dark tunnels of a secret labyrinth underground. His wife knelt next to him, also stricken. Both
of them seemed to have abandoned their dream of escape.

A backwash of danger clamored in Paul's mind, but
in his prescient blind spot he could sense no details.
Though he had always known the Count was devious, he

had wanted to believe that he shared a bond with the other potential Kwisatz Haderach.

All along, though, Fenring's deadly plot had been ticking like clockwork. He must have known it was a risky attempt, yet he had been willing to send his own daughter behind enemy lines and unleash her as a weapon, seeking to destroy not only Paul, but the Jihad. Had this man raised Marie from infancy with that sole purpose in mind? What kind of father could do that? He realized how Duke Leto might have reacted if the Harkonnens had actually killed Paul.

Lady Margot was white and rigid, as if she had discarded any attempt to maintain Bene Gesserit control over her emotions. Paul saw the agonized sorrow of a mother, but most of all he felt the sheer misery of Count Fenring. Raw, authentic emotion boiled up from him like a hot cloud.

Paul said, "You used a child as a pawn in an assassination plot. Your own child!"

"Oh, Hasimir is not her father, Paul Atreides." Lady Margot's voice dripped with scorn. "You knew her father. *Feyd-Rautha Harkonnen.*"

Paul snapped his gaze to her in surprise.

In that instant, Count Fenring moved like a coiled viper, his muscles trained and retrained with years of practice as the Emperor's most reliable assassin. Fenring yanked the Emperor's dagger out of Marie's body and drove the blade deep into Paul's chest.

"One of my backup plans," he said.

Reeling backward, Paul experienced every moment splintered into a million shards of nanoseconds. Each event had been as carefully laid out as the puzzle pieces in a Chusuk mosaic. Either the plan had originally been designed in extravagant and impossible detail, or Fenring had enhanced the scheme with so many branch points and alternatives that all possibilities had intersected in this single crux point.

The knife wound created a yawning gulf of pain in Paul's chest. He heard a shrill wail from Chani. "Uuuussssuuuullll!"

She cried out again, but this time it was barely audible, a galaxy away.

Bleeding, Paul-Muad'Dib fell, as if tumbling into a vast chasm.

My Sihaya is the water of my life and the reason my heart beats. My love for her anchors me against the storms of history.

—PAUL-MUAD'DIB, private love poem to Chani

In the uproar that ensued, the room reverberated with shouts and barked orders. Count Fenring sprang away from Paul even as he fell. Still holding the Emperor's knife, the assassin activated his shield and retreated to a corner, trying to reach the open passageway, but Fedaykin had already blocked it. Thwarted, he stood with his back to the stone blocks, prepared to defend himself. Margot Fenring joined her husband, also ready to die. Though she had no obvious weapon, she was a Bene Gesserit, and skilled in killing as well.

The horrified and enraged guards pressed close, a barely recovered Stilgar beside them, while Korba still struggled to pick himself up.

"Take him alive!" Irulan cried, her voice quavering as she tried to assert authority. She inhaled deeply, forcing control on her stunned muscles. "If you kill him, we will never know what other schemes he may have put in place! Do not make the mistake of believing this is the only plan afoot."

Stilgar did not need to be given orders by the Princess. "We will not kill him—at least not now, and not swiftly." Then his voice became a growl. "After the execution of Whitmore Bludd, the mob has a taste for it. I would not deprive them of their satisfaction."

"I look forward to your interrogation games, hmmm?" Fenring mocked. "Perhaps we shall share advice on techniques?" Inside his body shield, he passed the bloody dagger from hand to hand.

Chani felt numb. Noisome smoke still drifted through the room, and Paul lay on the floor, bleeding to death. Desperate to save him, she pressed her hands against the wound; blood seeped through her fingers, red and slick.

Paul Atreides may have been Fremen in many ways, but he did not have the genetic desert adaptations that thickened blood for rapid coagulation. "Send for medics! A battlefield surgeon! A Suk doctor! Quickly!"

Two guards rushed out into the hall. Stilgar and the other Fedaykin would not let the Count escape. With a sneer, Fenring said, "Perhaps you should tend to your Muad'Dib, hmmm? He may have final words for you."

Chani needed to stop the hemorrhage. "Usul, Beloved, how can I help you? How can I give you strength?"

She clasped his hands and felt a faint flicker, a twitch of the fingers, as if he were trying to signal her. Maybe the doctors could heal him, if only they arrived in time. But if Paul died before they could get him into surgery . . .

He was fighting, struggling within himself. Chani knew he had learned many things about his body after discovering his true nature as the Kwisatz Haderach, but she doubted if he had the skill to deal with such a severe, obviously mortal wound.

Alia was beside her, but even with all of her Other Memories and unusual knowledge, the girl could not help. "My brother is on the brink of death," she said in a peculiar tone of awe. "I should have saved him."

"We could still save him if only we could slow the bleeding, if only we could stop time—" Suddenly Chani straightened. "Alia! Run to my quarters, in the sealed jar by the table at the window. As a Sayyadina of the Rite, I keep some sacred Water of Life. Bring it for Muad'Dib."

Though surprised, Alia was already on her feet. "The trance—my brother's trance. Yes, we must induce it now!" The girl ran off, as swiftly as the wind.

Chani remembered when Paul had foolishly tried to prove himself, not just to the Fremen men by becoming a wormrider, but also by doing what only the most powerful women had achieved. Believing himself to be the Kwisatz Haderach, Paul had taken the unaltered poison, the exhalation of a drowned worm. Only the tiniest amount.

"One drop of it," Paul had said. "So small . . . just one drop."

Even so, it had been enough to plunge him into a coma so deep that he'd lain like a corpse for weeks, in suspended animation. Finally, with the help of both Chani and Jessica he had broken through that impasse, and had emerged able to detect and convert poisons. But that sort of manipulation required great effort and conscious volition.

Alia came rushing back in. Clutching a plaz container, she squirmed past the two medics who were only now entering with emergency-response kits. Alia arrived first, dropping to her knees and extending the jar to Chani. When the Fremen woman unsealed the lid, the bitter alkaloid stench rose up, so powerful it stung her eyes. The Water of Life was perhaps the most potent of toxins known to humankind. But right now, it was what Muad'Dib needed.

Chani touched her finger to the liquid, withdrew a single drop, and gently brushed Paul's pale lips in a loving gesture, a faint caress. She knew that if she gave him too much, his body would not be able to counteract the chemical; he would go into a deep coma and his valiant heart would stop beating.

After the kiss of the poison, she sensed a new rigidity in his body. The blood finally stopped flowing, but she couldn't sense him breathing anymore. His eyelids no longer fluttered.

One of the Suk doctors nudged her aside. "Lady Chani, you must let us tend him. We are his only chance."

The other smelled the poison. "What is that? Take it away! We have no use for Fremen folk medicines."

The first doctor shook his head. "So much blood. He can't possibly survive this." They knelt, felt for a pulse, applied monitors and talked quietly between themselves. "We are too late. He no longer lives."

There were moans from the guards, while Stilgar looked ready to explode. Irulan actually wept, causing Chani to wonder if the tears were false or real.

Seeking calmness within, Chani simply said to the doctors, "You are mistaken. Muad'Dib survives, but his life is below the threshold of your detection." When he had undergone the same thing before, many Fremen had also believed him dead. "With the Water of Life, I bought you time. Work your medicine, patch the wound."

"Lady Chani, there is no point—"

"Do as I command! His body already knows how to fight off the effects of the coma. Act quickly, before the window of opportunity closes."

∽

ON THE FLOOR of the dining hall the doctors set to work, calling for assistants, more surgical tools, even blood transfusions that would do little if Paul's heart refused to pump.

Feeling helpless, angry, and vengeful, Irulan watched, an outsider as the pivotal events transpired around her. Chani, Alia, and Stilgar formed a cordon around the wounded Emperor, keeping her away. Irulan did not understand the mystic Fremen ritual Chani had applied, saving Paul by giving him poison, but she did not protest. It certainly could do no harm.

Irulan could not venture close to the Count and Lady Margot either, who by now faced a dozen murderous guards waiting for any excuse to attack. She doubted the couple would survive the next hour if Paul died, and if he died, she would not bother to protect them.

Using a delicate cellular sealant and tissue grafting applied with probes and surgical instruments that were far more precise than an Ixian needlewhip, they attempted to repair the grievous damage caused by the sharp blade.

Irulan did not know how long the silence and tension would last.

One of the Suk doctors mumbled, as though expecting no one would hear him, "This is work more suited for a mortician than a surgeon." In nearly an hour they had seen not the faintest signs of life. Nevertheless, the doctors worked feverishly until it was clear they had done all they knew how to do.

It was up to Paul now.

At the sight of her husband suffering, Irulan felt stunned and despondent. Princess Irulan's mother and all her Bene Gesserit instructors would have been surprised at her automatic reaction. She wondered where the cool and politically savvy schemer within her had gone.

For a frightened moment, she considered whether or not she actually felt a flicker of love for him. But that was not a sentiment she could share with anyone— probably not even with him, if he survived. Her devotion to him was less appreciated than that of a pet. But *love*? She wasn't sure.

Beyond her personal concerns, Irulan was shaken by the realization of the horrendous political turmoil that was sure to follow the death of Muad'Dib. With so many factions struggling for the throne—including, surely, her own father trying to reclaim his place—the galaxy would be ripped apart in yet another horrific civil war. When added to the damages of the continuing Jihad, could humanity survive?

Her husband's first heartbeat came so suddenly and unexpectedly that it startled the two doctors. Then a few seconds of silence, followed by another heartbeat.

And a third. The gaps between beats grew shorter and shorter, and finally the monitors showed a slow but steady pulse.

The Emperor Paul-Muad'Dib came back to life, still weak and barely holding on. Irulan felt fragile herself after the ordeal; her own heart thumped rapidly. This was Muad'Dib—of course he lived!

His eyes flickered open, and that was all Irulan needed to see. She wiped away her tears, and then they flowed anew. Tears of joy? Yes, she decided, and of anger that anyone had attempted this against her husband.

❧

WHEN PAUL FINALLY sat up, his black tunic torn open and soaked with blood, Count Fenring switched off his personal shield and surrendered. His shoulders sagged, and he extended the bloodstained dagger, hilt first. "It appears I have nothing to gain by continued resistance, hmmm?"

Korba, now braver, grabbed the dagger out of Fenring's hand. The guards rushed forward and seized both the Count and his Lady, binding them in shigawire and removing them from the banquet room. During the distraction of the arrest, Korba surreptitiously slipped the ornate Imperial knife up his own sleeve.

Irulan saw him do it, and knew there was no danger in it. She wondered where the well-traveled weapon would eventually wind up, if it would be stored as a holy relic somewhere or sold to a particularly devout (and wealthy) patron.

Paul insisted on getting to his feet. The doctors helped him, but he preferred to lean on Chani, placing his other hand on Alia's shoulder. Irulan stood stiff-backed and gazed at him, content in the knowledge that he lived.

After pausing to catch his breath, Paul spoke in a surprisingly strong voice. "Find substitute . . . quarters for the Count and his Lady. They do not need to be comfortable, but ensure that they are not harmed—until I give specific instructions."

The most important battles are always waged inside a leader's mind. This is the true proving ground of command.

—from *The Wisdom of Muad'Dib*
by the PRINCESS IRULAN

Wearing shackles and flanked by four burly guards, Count Fenring stood at the foot of the Lion Throne. His once-fine trousers and coat were wrinkled and soiled, while his white silk shirt was torn and still bloody from the attack on Paul.

Paul had recovered miraculously—at least he had made it appear so. Already Irulan was working on the story that would add to the mythology of his life, and the people would believe it wholeheartedly, expecting nothing less from Muad'Dib. It would all be part of the growing legend. Princess Irulan now sat beside Paul's throne with a writing tablet on her lap, but eyewitness accounts of the events had already gotten out.

Consuming great quantities of melange, he had found the energy to appear in court the following morning, where he sat on his throne and made pronouncements—all to prove that Muad'Dib still had the strength to guide his holy empire. Through prescience and plain common sense, Paul knew the havoc that would result if his followers decided to seek unbridled vengeance on anyone they could think of.

Paul knew he had to remain alive, not just for his own

sake, but for the future of humanity. Paul remembered who he had been when he killed Feyd-Rautha here in a much different version of this room—a determined young man with victory in his hand and an empire at his feet. He had accepted his mantle of supreme command then, despite knowing the dark and dangerous slope that lay ahead of him. No one else could have guessed the full extent of what Paul-Muad'Dib would become. No one, not his mother, nor Gurney, nor Shaddam. Not even Chani, who understood him best.

From the beginning of his rule, Paul could have given the Imperium a glorious but temporary prosperity. Or he could have chosen ultimately to be seen as a ruthless tyrant. He could have made certain decisions to eliminate turmoil for the immediate future, to foster peace, to administer the government in such a way that all his subjects would love him. Had he handled it differently, history would have painted a favorable portrait of him . . . for a few generations, maybe even for millennia.

But that way was a dead end.

In his heart, he would much rather have lived in peace with Chani. Given different choices, he could have been like Duke Leto Atreides, beloved by all, fair to all, wise and honored for who he truly was. Instead, obeying no one but himself and the guidance of his prescience, he had sacrificed his personal happiness and the present to save the future. Thus Paul became not what he wanted to be, but what he *needed* to be . . . and what humankind needed him to be.

As Muad'Dib, he had taken the guilt upon himself by allowing the sacrifice of billions in order to save trillions. And only he fully understood it. He could not place the blame for this on anyone else, and so he accepted the burden and steeled himself to continue doing what needed to be done.

Now he sat in judgment over Count Hasimir Fenring,

boon companion of the fallen Emperor Shaddam IV. This man had tried to kill him.

"Ah, hm-m-m-m, I suppose this means you will not be offering me your finest wine again?" Fenring infused his words with bravado and impertinent humor, but his demeanor betrayed uncertainty. His large eyes flicked from side to side, taking in the Fedaykin guards, Stilgar, and the bloodthirsty Chani. He seemed to be wondering which one of them would deal the death blow that was sure to come.

For a moment Fenring focused on Alia, who was seated on the edge of the dais in a black robe. She looked like a tiny executioner, awaiting the command from her brother. She casually kicked her dangling feet. It was a childlike pose like the one she had struck when Shaddam IV sat on this same throne, just before she surprised and killed the Baron Harkonnen.

In a way, she looked somewhat like dear Marie. . . .

"Here on Dune, water is more precious than wine," Paul said. At a small ornate table beside the Hagal quartz throne, he removed the stopper from a jewel-encrusted ewer. He poured himself a small goblet and another for Fenring. Chani took the cup to the prisoner.

Eyeing it suspiciously, Fenring lifted his heavily shackled hands and accepted the goblet with brave resignation. "So, you've decided on poison, hmm-m?" He sniffed the contents.

Paul sipped from his own cup. "It is pure water." He took another drink to demonstrate.

"It is well known that Muad'Dib can, ahh, convert poisons. This is a trick, isn't it?"

"No poison—on my honor. *Atreides* honor." Paul locked his gaze with Fenring's. "Drink with me."

Alia poured herself a goblet and quaffed it with obvious relish.

Fenring scowled down at the liquid in his cup. "I served

for many years here on Arrakis, so I know the value of water." He drank from the goblet, then rudely let it clatter to the floor.

Paul took another sip. "That was the water distilled from Marie's body. I wanted you to share it with me." He casually poured the rest of the liquid on the dais and set aside the goblet, upended.

Doubling over with sudden nausea, the Count shuddered, then jerked at his shackles as if reaching for a weapon he didn't have.

Now Lady Margot Fenring was brought into the chamber to stand beside her husband, with Korba and Stilgar behind her. The Count instantly showed worry, as if his wife's fate concerned him more than his own. In a traditional Bene Gesserit black robe, Lady Margot still projected the hauteur of a noblewoman, despite the lack of opportunity to groom herself.

At a gesture from Paul, Alia sprang off the dais and stood in front of Marie's mother, who gazed down at her with a stony expression. His sister held a long needle in her hand, the deadly gom jabbar. Margot Fenring stiffened, but Alia did not strike. Not yet.

Showing no weakness despite his injuries, remembering how the one-armed Archduke Armand Ecaz had insisted on going to war against Grumman after the wedding-day massacre, Paul rose from the throne and stepped down from the dais onto the polished floor. His motions were slow, deliberate, and charged with lethal intent. He stood directly in front of Fenring.

The Emperor drew his own crysknife and pointed its tip at the Count. The guards moved aside, and Fenring went rigid, every muscle in his body petrified. He stared beyond Paul, as if seeing the death that awaited him there.

"Please do not kill him," Lady Margot said.

"We die regardless," Count Fenring said, half to her and half to Paul. "The mob would tear us to pieces anyway, as they did to Swordmaster Bludd." Now, shaking slightly, he looked at Paul. "Would it help if I were to fall to my knees and plead for you to spare her? She did save your life years ago, by warning you and your mother of Harkonnen treachery."

"Your own treachery erased that water burden," Stilgar interjected sharply.

Fenring acted as if he did not hear the naib. "If pleading would help, I'd abase myself in any manner to save the life of my Lady."

Without answering, Paul circled the Count slowly, considering where to strike the mortal blow.

"You know I am more guilty than she is," Fenring continued, babbling uncharacteristically. "I did not act out of loyalty to Shaddam, nor was this any Bene Gesserit scheme that my wife encouraged. I speak truly when I say I despise Shaddam, because his foolishness shattered any obligations I once had toward him. He removed any chance for the Imperium to be strong and stable. Imagine the scope of his failure—Shaddam's rule was so hateful and corrupt that many people prefer even the fanaticism of your followers!"

Paul smiled savagely, but said nothing. He kept circling, pausing, and then continuing.

"It was not a personal thing, ahhh, I assure you. My hatred for you and your rule is purely logical. I needed to excise a particularly aggressive form of cancer for the sake of human civilization. With Muad'Dib removed from the equation, then Marie, myself, or a puppet might have had a chance to restore stability and grandeur."

Finally, Paul said, "You knew Marie had little or no chance of success, but sacrificed her with the knowledge that you might have a moment of opportunity while feigning grief over her death."

Fenring's eyes flashed with anger. "I feigned nothing!"

"He didn't!" Margot shouted.

Alia waved the gom jabbar in front of her.

Without taking his eyes from the Count, Paul said, "A trick within a trick, and at the precise moment of my weakness you almost succeeded."

"You are the monster here, not I," Fenring said. He maintained his resolve, his defiance. Then, turning, he fixed a long, lingering gaze on his wife. "I bid thee farewell."

"And to you, my darling," she said, looking at the poisoned needle in Alia's hand.

If the situation were reversed, Paul knew that the Fenrings would not have granted him or Alia a reprieve. The Fremen side of Paul's nature wanted to draw blood, and he knew that Alia had the same longing. Her upward gaze hungered for permission to strike with the gom jabbar.

Paul stopped, still holding his milky-white blade. He considered how his father would have dealt with such a situation. Duke Leto the Just. He remembered how the Atreides nobleman had been given that name. Thinking back, Paul recalled his father's words: "I sentence you to *live*," he had said before sending Swain Goire off to exile. "To live with what you have done."

A wave of sadness came over Paul as he considered how often he had made decisions that were different from those his father would have chosen. Paul did not expect Fenring to be wracked with guilt, not after his long history of violence. The Count was no Swain Goire. But execution was too easy, and Paul had had enough of barbarism.

Without warning, he slashed across the front of Fenring's throat. An exquisitely accurate cut, delivered with precise muscle control.

Lady Margot screamed, lunging against her own restraints. "No!"

The Count staggered, lifting his shackled hands, clutching heavily at his neck. But he came away with only a smear of crimson on his palms.

"By tradition, once drawn, a crysknife should always taste blood," Paul said. Calmly, he wiped both sides of the wormtooth blade across Fenring's jacket, and resheathed the weapon.

Still on his feet, Count Fenring gingerly touched fingertips to his throat in astonishment. The precise slash had penetrated only a hairsbreadth. Tiny droplets formed a red necklace on the skin.

"This is not your day to die," Paul said. "Every time you see that faint scar in the mirror, remember that I could have cut deeper."

Paul turned his attention to the nobleman's wife. "Lady Margot, you have lost a daughter, and that is already a terrible punishment for your crime, because I know you truly loved Marie. It is your misfortune to love this man who deserves only contempt."

His head held high, Paul strode back to his emerald green throne, then raised an arm and made a dismissive gesture. "In ages past, it was said there was a curse on the House of Atreus, my ancient predecessors. Now, *I* am the one who imposes a curse. Hear this! I exile both of you to Salusa Secundus, where you are to be bottled up with Shaddam Corrino. Permanently. May your loathing for him grow day by day."

How much of Muad'Dib's legend is actual fact and how much is superstitious myth? Since I have compiled the information and written the story, I know for certain. By any measure, the truth about Muad'Dib is surprising.

—the PRINCESS IRULAN,
mandatory report to Wallach IX

She sat inside her private chambers, comfortable at the writing desk and deep in thought. These fine rooms no longer felt like a prison to her, or merely a place to store forgotten objects. Though Paul refused to share her bed, Irulan had become more than a trophy won in the old Battle of Arakeen, more than a token wife. Despite the obstacles in her path, she had earned a genuine position in Muad'Dib's government, and perhaps in history itself. Even Chani could not fill this particular role.

"A story is shaped by the teller as much as by the events themselves." Irulan remembered the Bene Gesserit aphorism, similar to an old saying the Jongleurs often used. In her hands—and her writing stylus—she had the power to influence what future generations knew . . . or thought they knew.

Here inside the magnificent Citadel of Muad'Dib, the Princess felt herself pulled in many directions. Her father and the rest of exiled House Corrino, expecting her loyalty, had rejected her for choosing her husband over her own family. Similarly, the Sisterhood still could not believe she would forsake them—refusing their demand that she exert influence over the Emperor, desperately hoping that their long-awaited Kwisatz Haderach was not lost forever to their control.

Irulan was no longer sure where she owed her allegiance. Everyone wanted something from her. Everyone needed something from her. And, she was coming to believe, her husband needed her most of all . . . in his own way.

Paul-Muad'Dib had died of a grievous knife wound and come back from the other side. Irulan tried to imagine how she would describe this in the next volume of her ever-growing biographical treatment.

I will write that Muad'Dib cannot be killed. And the people will believe that. They will believe me.

How could they not?

Paul had never claimed to love Irulan, had never offered so much as a hint of affection for her, though he had come to respect her knowledge and experience. Seeing him dead and pale in a pool of his own blood had shaken her more than she could have imagined.

The appropriate words were forming in her mind. She would remain here and write, and she would let history decide.

By the holy grace of Muad'Dib.

Take an exclusive look at an
excerpt from the all-new Dune novel,
The Winds of Dune.

⪼

PART I

10,207 AG

Since overthrowing Shaddam IV, Paul-Muad'Dib
has reigned as Emperor for fourteen years, establishing his new capital in Arrakeen on the sacred
desert planet, Dune. Though his Jihad is over at
long last, conflicts continue to flare up.

With Paul on the throne, his mother, the Lady
Jessica, has withdrawn from the constant battles
and political schemes and returned to the Atreides
ancestral home of Caladan, to serve there as
Duchess.

In my private life on Caladan, I receive few reports of my son's Jihad, not because I choose to be ignorant, but because the news is rarely anything I wish to hear.

—LADY JESSICA, DUCHESS OF CALADAN

The unscheduled ship loomed in orbit over Caladan, a former Guild Heighliner pressed into service as a Jihad transport.

A young boy from the fishing village, apprenticed to the Castle as a page, rushed into the garden courtyard. Looking awkward in his formal clothing, he blurted, "It's a military-equipped vessel, my Lady. Fully armed!"

Kneeling beside a rosemary bush, Jessica snipped off fragrant twigs for the kitchens. Here in her private garden, she maintained flowers, herbs, and shrubs in a perfect combination of order and chaos, useful flora and pretty pleasantries. In the peace and stillness just after dawn, Jessica liked to work and meditate here, nourishing her plants and uprooting the persistent weeds that tried to ruin the careful balance.

Unruffled by the boy's panic, she inhaled deeply of the aromatic evergreen oils released by her touch. Jessica rose to her feet and brushed dirt off her knees. "Have they sent any messages?"

"Only that they are dispatching a group of Qizarate emissaries, my Lady. They demand to speak with you on an urgent matter."

"They *demand*?"

The young man quailed at her expression. "I'm sure they meant it as a request, my Lady. After all, would they dare to make *demands* of the Duchess of Caladan—and the mother of Muad'Dib? Still, it must be important news indeed, to warrant a vessel like that!" The young man fidgeted like an eel washed up on shore.

She straightened her garment. "Well, I'm sure the *emissary* considers it important. Probably just another request for me to increase the limits on the number of pilgrims allowed to come here."

Caladan, the seat of House Atreides for more than twenty generations, had escaped the ravages of the Jihad, primarily because of Jessica's refusal to let too many outsiders swarm in. Caladan's self-sufficient people preferred to be left alone. They would gladly have accepted their Duke Leto back, but he had been murdered through treachery at high levels; now the people had his son Paul-Muad'Dib instead, the Emperor of the Known Universe.

Despite Jessica's best efforts, Caladan could never be completely isolated from the outside storms in the galaxy. Though Paul paid little attention to his home planet anymore, he had been christened and raised here; the people could never escape the shadow cast by her son.

After all the years of Paul's Jihad, a weary and wounded peace had settled over the Imperium like a cold winter fog. Looking at the young messenger now, she realized that he had been born after Paul became Emperor. The boy had never known anything but the looming Jihad and the harsher side of her son's nature. . . .

She left the courtyard gardens, shouting to the boy. "Summon Gurney Halleck. He and I will meet the delegation in the main hall of Castle Caladan."

Jessica changed out of her gardening clothes into a sea-green gown of state. She lifted her ash-bronze hair and draped a pendant bearing a golden Atreides hawk crest around her neck. She refused to hurry. The more she thought about it, the more she wondered what news the ship might bring. Perhaps it wasn't a trivial matter after all. . . .

Gurney was waiting for her in the main hall. He had been out running his gaze hounds, and his face was still flushed from the exercise. "According to the spaceport, the emissary is a high-ranking member of the Qizarate, bringing an army of retainers and honor guards from Arrakis. Says he has a message of the utmost importance."

She pretended a disinterest she did not truly feel. "By my count, this is the ninth 'urgent message' they've delivered since the Jihad ended two years ago."

"Even so, my Lady, this one feels different."